Darling, You're Not Alone

Summer House Media LLC.
For rights, literary requests, or other inquiries, please contact Chris Varonos.
chris@summerhousemedia.co
www.summerhousepublishing.co
www.jdwritesbooks.com

Edited by Alison Rolf, Christine Nielson and Chris Varonos
Book design by Nuno Moreira, NM DESIGN.ORG
Copyright © 2022 JD Slajchert
All rights reserved.
1 2 3 4 5 6 7 8 9 10
ISBN: 978-1-7372920-3-6

Darling, You're Not Alone

THE SECOND NOVEL BY

JD Slajchert

For Janette Mallory.

I'll never forget being that teeny redhead reaching for your hand, walking out of our old sliding door, and stargazing.
Mom, this book is for you.

PRAISE FOR DARLING, YOU'RE NOT ALONE

"*Darling, You're Not Alone* is a heartening reminder that life is a battle, and it is up to us to decide the perspective with which we choose to live our lives. Since I've known JD Slajchert, I've always been impressed by his uncanny ability to use anything negative in the world as his fuel to do something good with, and this book is an example of just that. It's a novel that's as riveting as it is inspiring. I thought I was blown away by his first book, but Slajchert takes his second to a whole new level few writers can."

- Gabe Vincent, Miami Heat Guard and Olympic Athlete.

"No one is guaranteed a perfect life, but the reality is that it is not so much the events themselves but how we respond to them that create a life. *Darling, You're Not Alone* explores this truth in a profound and poignant way allowing the reader to not only change their perspective but to realize their own self-agency. A must read that will change your life."

- James R. Doty, MD, Founder & Director, The Stanford University Center for Compassion and Altruism Research and Education and the *New York Times* bestselling author of *Into the Magic Shop: A Neurosurgeon's Quest to Understand the Mysteries of the Brain and the Secrets of the Heart*

"JD Slajchert's YA novel *Darling, You're Not Alone*, among other themes, explores the devastating interpersonal impact of a community crisis. As someone who has spent her entire career on the frontline fighting the forces that threaten the physical and mental wellness of families, this story resonated with me deeply. It reminds us that the power of the human spirit is both resilient and transformational."
- Linda Small, Executive Director, George Lopez Foundation

"JD Slajchert emerges as a powerful new voice for young adults with his novel *Darling, You're Not Alone*. He doesn't shy away from topics we care about and neither does he try to Band-Aid them with superficial fixes. Instead, he offers us a chance to explore hard questions in the context of a great story and lets the reader evolve as a resilient, critical thinker. I loved this book!"
- Michael Campion, Star of Netflix's *Fuller House*

"JD Slajchert strikes again with *Darling, You're Not Alone*. A brilliant, emerging young voice is on full display through a story that both challenges your perspective and leaves you encouraged to take ownership over your responses to life's circumstances."
- Miles Burris, Star of Disney's *Safety*, and former Oakland Raiders NFL Linebacker.

"A powerful story written by a powerful kid. JD Slajchert really went for it with *Darling, You're Not Alone*. When I heard he was writing another book, I didn't know it was going to be so soon. In this business, focus needs to meet productivity, and JD prides himself on both. I can't wait to see what he does next!"

- Clifton Powell, Award-Winning Actor

"JD has the gift of storytelling and *Darling, You're Not* Alone is just another glowing example of it. The story brings many of our worlds most challenging issues directly to the forefront of the conversation. And as we learn throughout the story, it is these difficult and uncomfortable topics that ultimately spur the most growth. It's been a pleasure to watch JD's growth as a writer, particularly his ability to create characters with such relatable perspectives. It is a common theme in his work to take tragic moments and teach the necessary lessons of how you can always find a silver lining. These are life lessons that we all can and should learn from. I strongly recommend *Darling, You're Not Alone* to anyone who wants to go on a thought provoking journey that is both challenging and inspiring."

- Duncan Robinson, Miami Heat Forward

"Love is my religion — I could die for it."

- John Keats

Give them heaven.

1994

1

I won't look again. If I keep looking, I'll drive myself into a state of disappointment no matter what it says. I just need to wait a little bit longer. But how long is a little bit? Time always moves slower when your eyes are closed. I open them and look at the clock.

Five more minutes to six a.m.

I start to feel my toes dance up and down. I couldn't keep waiting, but I didn't want to be rude. I think time moves more slowly when you're young. Old people always move so slowly and are never excited. All they do is sit.

Three more minutes to six a.m.

I hate sitting. I hate sleeping.

Two more minutes.

Why would you ever *sleep* when you can *do*?

Six a.m.

I pushed myself out of bed as quickly as I could to poke out the window. The Ferry was parked in the driveway, which meant he was home. A smile slid over my face. Any bit of the tired feeling was then gone.

I burst through my door and leapt atop my parent's bed in one move. They were both still asleep.

"Good morning! Good morning! You said we could go to the

park before the party...and it's morning! Right now! Up! Up! We need to beat everyone there!"

I could see my dad sort of smile, but his eyes were still closed. My mom groaned.

"Come on, guys! It's my party! Logan Park! Remember?"

My mom sat up and did a vertical arm stretch before kissing me on the forehead. She then whispered, "Let's go downstairs, Noodle, and I'll make you something to eat. Dad needs a little more sleep. He got home late last night."

It was all my favorites: sideways French toast, diced strawberries, bacon, and fresh-squeezed orange juice.

I was eating fast because I didn't want to waste any time. When my dad got downstairs, he'd want to just have some coffee and go.

"Don't forget to breathe, Phoenix," my mom said as she stood over the sink, sipping a mug of her own.

Wiping a dribbling mixture of syrup and orange juice off my chin, I said, "What time will Shay be at the party?"

But my mom was still drinking her coffee and looking out the window.

I asked her again, this time with more fire.

My mom turned toward me in a calming smile. Her auburn hair was a tangled mess from sleeping, but she looked happy. "I'm not sure exactly, Noodle, but I spoke to her mom last night. It's seven in the morning and we didn't tell people to get there until ten. I don't think anyone else is awake right now in all of Darling."

My energy dropped. "I know, but Dad said he might have to leave early for work."

The window behind my mom shivered in the wind. A spray of leaves tapped the glass. She hovered to my side. Her hand landed on my cheek.

"You know your father's job is different."

"Yeah, I know."

"But I'll call Brianna again to make sure Shay's there early. As soon as the sun's up. Okay?"

"Please, Mom. Please. I want to tell her the elephant and giraffe story. Remember? The one you told me."

My mom smiled. "I'll call. Now stop your worrying, Phoenix. It's your birthday."

The second I heard the telltale creak of the top stair, I whipped my head around. My dad was head-to-toe in full uniform. His belt clicked as he made his way down, his gun hanging in its holster at his hip. His badge glistened under the kitchen light, his name plate fastened above it.

My mom handed me his mug of coffee she'd made, and I ran it over to him—cupping it with both hands—as fast as possible.

"Thank you, Phoenix. Happy birthday." He stopped and took a sip. "The big one zero. How does it feel to reach double digits?" He ran his other hand over the top of my head as I fell into his hip.

"Good," I said, smiling and looking up at him under his sharp chin. The red of his skin told me he'd just shaved.

A beam of light cut in through the kitchen window. The rest of the party would be arriving at the park in only a few hours.

"Should I bring the balloons straight to the park when I meet you to set up, or will you guys be able to pick them up?" my mom asked.

I waited as I continued to look up at my dad. He took another long sip of his coffee. "Can you grab them? Phoenix and I have a bit of an investigation to do at the park."

"An investigation!" I burst out. They both laughed.

My dad continued to drink coffee, so I began to pull on his leg with both hands. "So let's go! Come on. All you do is drink coffee!"

My dad laughed. "Okay, let's get on out of here then."

Inside the Ferry, I could already feel my heart beginning to race. The smell of his car I'd always associated with adventure. The car itself was a story, some famous Greek one he'd told me once, but I'd forgotten the details. He told me lots of stories. All the stories sometimes fell together into one long adventure that contained all different types of mysteries for us to solve. I was still hoping to find a way to put them all together.

"Is it a police investigation? Like, for work?" I asked as I turned toward him. I noticed again the shine of his name plate on his chest.

"Think of it more as a journey. A sort of adventure in that kind of way."

"Is it a puzzle? Or are we going to try and find someone? It's a puzzle, isn't it? I always knew it would be a puzzle."

The blinker clicked as my dad carried on driving. He turned down the radio that was playing Harry Chapin, as usual.

"Today, Phoenix," he began, with his voice progressively sounding more and more awake, "today, we're on a journey to discover, 'The Key of Courage.'"

I waited for my dad to continue, but he didn't say anything else. I squirmed in my seat, holding on to the cushions.

"And what's it do?" I finally blurted out. "Does it have special powers?"

"It does, in fact. Very special powers. Very, very special powers. This key…it unlocks in whoever has it in his or her possession the courage to do great things."

"And it's at Logan Park? How will we find it?"

"That's what we're trying to investigate, Phoenix. Plenty of people look for it, but I'm afraid it's been hidden, waiting for the right person to come along. But it was last seen in the possession of a king. And the king is somewhere in Logan Park."

As my dad continued to explain, I could hardly contain all my excitement. I wondered so much then about what this key might look like and what it could all mean, the possibilities ahead. I had so many more questions, but I knew I should wait to see what else might come up once we got there. I began to grow nervous, then, as I hoped I was worthy.

Logan Park was as magnificent as always. Adults walked around, people fed ducks at the foot of a small pond at the center of the park, picknickers sandwhiched, and kids yelled and played. It was my favorite place.

The smells of flowers and grass arrived with the sight of the tapping water. Different shrubs and trees accompanied stemming blue columbines.

Standing next to the orange slide, I saw that a bunch of kids were running around in the woodchips and sand. Behind them even further, it looked like there was a baseball game.

"So, what does the king look like?"

My dad bent down to my level and responded with his signature warmth. "Well, maybe he doesn't look like what a king would normally look like, because this isn't the place you would normally look for a king."

Looking out, I saw that there were strangers everywhere. To approach anybody was scarier to me than trying to fall asleep in the dark. I went for my dad's hand.

"Don't be afraid," he whispered.

I closed my eyes and took a few deep breaths, remembering how much I'd been looking forward to today. I thought about how important it would be to be strong, to show my dad I could be a hero like him.

When I opened my eyes, I started to look beyond the strangers. Not at what they were doing, but who they could have possibly been. Offering less judgment on their physical appearance and more thought about who they really could be.

It was strange really. Suddenly, they all looked different. My mind ran with each of their possible stories. I was looking out, and instead of seeing strangers, I saw good friends, brothers, sisters, moms, and dads. I saw that all of them were families too. All of them had a story to tell, and suddenly, I could hear them.

While scanning, I came across a small, pop-up store and read the word "Kings" plastered on a sign. There was a line of people outside, as if they were selling food and warm drinks.

We ran toward the line and waited until we eventually got to the front. A teenage girl who was working behind the counter looked at me, although despite her warmth, I couldn't help but instantly look down. I wanted to be brave, at least for today, but it was hard. All of it was sometimes just too hard.

"Can I help you gentleman?" she asked.

I continued to look down and hoped that my dad would start talking, but he didn't say anything.

I found another deep breath and eventually peered up. "I'm Phoenix."

I said it quick, trying as best I could to get it all out.

"Herman," my dad added while reaching out his hand.

"Nice to meet you both."

My nerves slowed. I was able to look back up and see her better this time. She seemed pleased to be speaking with us. I wasn't getting the feeling we were being judged either.

"And what can I help you with then, Phoenix?"

I looked up at her once more. "My dad and me are looking… looking for a king. We think he might be here."

I waited, as I watched her smile slightly once more.

"Oh…the king," she began. "I only know very little about him, but what I do know is that he is normally at the highest point in the park. Where he can best see everything. That's where I would look."

My dad looked down at me. I instantly knew where she was talking about. The lookout point. There was a perch at the top of the park where people would go to bird-watch all the time. From there, you could see a clear view of everything. My dad and I would count the stars there on the nights when he had the time.

We took off over the hill and up a long, wooden staircase, all the way to the top. We ran faster and faster.

From the top, we could see all of Darling winding through the little valley below. The sunlight kissed the rooftops, the surrounding mountain peaks still dusted in snow, even though it was the beginning of summer. The town was starting to wake, cars rolling through the streets and the murmur of voices joining the flutter of aspen trees.

But as we looked around, out and over the entire flat part of the overlook, there wasn't anyone there. A few birds lightly tapped the railing, looking out, but it was otherwise completely empty. There was no king.

I took off once more and searched everywhere I thought to look, hoping to at least find a clue, or anything at all, to let me know that I was on the right track, but I didn't find anything close. I found dirt, bushes, fallen leaves, and trash. Lots and lots of trash. As time went on, I knew that the party would be starting soon, and people would begin to show up. I started to grow disappointed, discovering that nothing magical was up here.

"I still don't get it," I said to him as we looked out. It suddenly felt colder.

My dad carried on admiring the changing sky. The moving clouds and the breeze that came and went.

"Sometimes in life, son, you can spend all of your time searching for something when that really wasn't even the most important thing all along. Say, look at this morning sky before us. Take a moment to really look at it, Phoenix. Try and really see."

I looked past him then but didn't notice anything other than a normal sky. The same sky that I'd been under for as long as I could remember.

"There was a very famous artist your grandma used to tell me about when I was a boy, just like you are now," my dad began, while still looking out. "The artist's name was Vincent van Gogh, and your grandma used to tell me about one of his most famous paintings. It was of a sky, just like this one, Phoenix. It was of a beautifully, simple sky. He called it *Starry Night*, and he described it as 'watching the sun rise in all its glory.' He painted the entire thing from his bedroom window, and now it's one of the most recognizable paintings in the whole world.

"Your grandma used to explain to me that the beauty is in the less complicated. The most magnificent painting in the whole world is not of somewhere famous or memorable, but it's, instead, of something everyone gets to see. Something that isn't for some people, but all people, everywhere. The clouds, the sky, the sun.

What a clear treasure those are. Sometimes it need not be more complicated than that. Almost always in life, it truly is the journey itself that's the reward."

I was suddenly so full of inspiration, and I wanted so badly to see what my dad could. So I tried harder. I looked at the sky, longer and longer, hoping to reveal the magic he told me was right before my eyes.

"I wish she could be here today," I finally said to my dad. This was the first birthday I would celebrate without my grandma.

My dad wrapped his arm around my shoulder. "Me too. But you know she'll always be with us."

"How?" I asked my dad, not ever understanding what happens when the people you love are suddenly gone.

My dad took his arm from my shoulder and turned me to face him. He bent down to be right at my level. He brushed his thumb across my forehead and then gently tapped the center of my chest.

"Just because someone passes away doesn't mean they're gone. A part of Grandma is now inside of me and inside of you. Especially on days like today, you can feel her. Here. Right in your heart."

I studied the sky again, then scanned the lookout once more. A trashman with dark, sunbaked skin hunched over to empty out a nearby bin. He looked old and exhausted as he reached toward the garbage to add to his already overflowing pile.

I felt my dad nudge me, offering his support.

Softly, I swallowed as I walked toward the trashman. Before I closed the distance with the final two steps, I glanced back at my dad. He stood at the point of the overlook, and for a moment, the clouds drifting behind him looked like a pair of wings.

"Ex...excuse me?"

The trashman didn't even hear me as he was still preoccupied, so I repeated, "Excuse me...sir?"

The trashman looked at me, his eyes kind.

"Oh, hello. What is it, young man?" he began. His voice was old, like a grandfather clock. "Is there a mess around here that needs my attention?"

"No...nothing like that. I'm...sorry to bother you. But..." I trailed off, unsure of how to ask or even what further to say.

The trashman gave me his tired eyes. His doubt and his ease. I could feel the wisdom behind him. I was seeing a real person.

I looked back at him once more and began, "I'm searching for the Key of Courage. It's supposed to be with the king."

He didn't say anything for a long moment, but slowly the trashman answered, "I'll give you the Key of Courage, but you'll need to give me something in return, Phoenix."

Somewhat startled, I looked right at him. My attention was suddenly much sharper than before.

"Does that sound alright with you?" he asked.

All I could manage was a nod.

The trashman gently placed his bag down and continued, "You must give me your fear of being uncomfortable."

I had no idea what he was talking about, so I didn't say anything. He had to be some sort of crazy person.

"Repeat after me," he said.

I stared blankly back at him and was getting the sense that he really was just someone who had no idea what he was talking about. What he'd asked for was something I couldn't give him. He had to be crazy.

Although, despite my clear confusion, he just repeated once

more, "Repeat after me…I will not be afraid of what I do not know, for what I do not know is the only thing keeping me from the place I would like to go."

I looked back at my dad, but the instant my attention wandered, the trashman called back at me.

"Don't lose focus. You must decide to trust me for yourself."

I looked back up at the sky. It didn't move around me at all. It was simple.

Carefully, I repeated, "I will not be afraid of what I do not know, for what I do not know is the only thing keeping me from the place I would like to go."

Then, he reached into one of his trash bags and pulled out a small box. He handed it to me, and I slowly peeled it open to find a chain necklace with a key at its center. The glimmer reminded me of some sort of sterling silver family heirloom. It really was the key after all.

While admiring it, I looked up to thank him, but the trashman had already picked up his bags and retreated toward another garbage can down the hill.

2

As Shay came humming down the slide, she laughed like mad. Her ice blond hair trailing behind her small ears. I was sitting at the bottom, in the sand, waiting as she ran right up to me.

"What's that?" she said, pointing down at my necklace.

"The Key of Courage," I began proudly. "I found it here with my dad this morning. It has special powers."

"Special powers!" Shay burst back.

"It gives me the power to do great things. My dad says," I answered with a humbleness that made me blush.

I'd been doodling in the sand and had just finished drawing some stars from the sky my dad had told me about.

"Super cool!" Shay said, now joining me in the sand. She climbed in and tucked her pink Converse under her, sitting crisscross next to me. Our knees touched.

Her hand then went to the key on my neck. Softly, she ran her fingers over the design—letting her palm absorb its grooves and details.

At a bench, surrounded by balloons and snacks, were our parents and a bunch of our other friends. I turned back to see my dad and Shay's dad, Marcus, both drinking sodas, wearing their matching police uniforms. They'd been partners for as long as I could remember. Marcus brought their cruiser to the park, too, which was always really cool.

The sun shone down in specks as it poked through a tree above. The different flashes gave a shadow of all the leaves—each shape. Shay let her head rest on my shoulder. I looked over at her blue eyes.

"Are you having a good party?"

I smiled and laughed. She did too.

"My mom told me you had a story you wanted to tell me?" Shay asked. Her hair was windblown from her trip down the slide, some of it curling slightly, and some of it hanging in straight, white-gold strands below her shoulder. Pink flushed across her cheekbones, and her lips puckered slightly in expectation. A shiver went through me.

"Yeah!" I choked back a bit too loud, trying to knock myself out of it. "This story my mom reads me. She reads it to me at night, or sometimes during the day. It's a really great story."

Shay kept her head on my shoulder, her eyes looking straight on. I could hear her breathing slow as she settled next to me.

I began. "It's called 'The Elephant and The Giraffe.' And the story starts with an elephant, all by himself, walking through the forest, looking for friends. He walks and walks and walks until he sees a monkey. He asks the monkey, 'Can we be friends, Monkey?' The monkey says to the elephant, 'You are big and can't swing on trees like I do, so I cannot be your friend, Elephant.' The elephant goes back to walking until he finds a rabbit. He asks the rabbit, 'Can we be friends, Rabbit?' The rabbit says, 'You are too big to fit inside my burrow, so I cannot be your friend, Elephant.' Then, the elephant meets a frog, and he asks, 'Can we be friends, Frog?' The frog says, 'You are too big and heavy, so you cannot jump like me, so I cannot be your friend, Elephant.' This all made the elephant very sad."

I looked at Shay then, as she had turned to fully face me. She pushed her hair behind her ears. I could see her full face.

"Elephant continued to ask all the animals in the forest, but they all kept saying the same thing. 'I cannot be your friend, Elephant.' Until the next day, a giraffe, all by herself, walks by. The elephant sees the giraffe but is too sad to even ask if she would be his friend, so he doesn't say anything, not even hello. But the giraffe looks at the elephant and asks, 'What's wrong, Elephant? Why do you look so sad?' The elephant answers quietly, 'None of the animals in the forest will be my friend. I can't swing on trees like the monkey, I can't fit inside the burrow like the rabbit, and I can't jump like the frog. And now I am all alone.'"

Shay frowned.

I continued. "The giraffe understood. She says to the elephant, 'Well, I can't swing on trees like the monkey, I can't burrow like the rabbit, and I can't jump like the frog. Would you like to be my friend?' The elephant answers, 'But I don't have spots like you, I don't have a long neck like you, and I am much heavier than you.' Then the giraffe says to the elephant, 'That's okay. Just because we're different, doesn't mean we can't be friends.'"

I finished and looked at Shay, wondering what she thought. Tears pooled in the corners of her blue eyes. She didn't say anything. She just reached over and took my hand.

We sat like that for a while.

I was about to finally say something when I heard my mom's voice call out.

"Phoenix!" my mom called from the picnic table. Then louder, "Phoenix!"

But when I turned to look back at my hand in Shay's, she

wouldn't let go. She just squeezed my hand even tighter.

"One more time down the slide?" Shay asked with a small smile.

I nodded, adding, "I'll race you to the top!"

I took off first toward the jungle gym and first ladder I could find, but Shay made her way up the other side. Because her ladder was a more direct route to the slide, she beat me to it. We were both crying out in laughter as she stuck her tongue out at me while flying down the slide once more.

I stood there, watching her hair fly around her again when I heard her call out in a sudden pain. She curled over herself at the bottom. Something was wrong.

I raced down to get beside her.

"Are you okay?"

Shay sat back on her heels and looked at her arm. Blood welled up from a ragged tear just above her elbow. It ran down and dropped onto the sand.

She pressed her hand over the wound, her pink face pinched in pain. There was a small nail sticking out of a wood protecting beam. The nail head was bent back.

"I bet my mom has a Band-Aid in her purse," I said quickly. I felt bad that she got hurt racing me.

She lifted her fingers away from her arm. It was bleeding good now, running in a little stream off her elbow, red smeared all over her hand.

"Shay, I'm so sorry."

Shay responded in a small warmth. "I'm okay, Phoenix. It's just a bad scratch."

As the summer sun moved through the sky, Shay and I got up and ran back toward the party. By now, all our friends had shown up, and I had a pile of presents taller than me. My mom was organizing everything.

Shay's mom saw her arm right away and had Marcus grab the first aid kit out of the patrol car. In no time at all, Shay was bandaged up and eating a hot dog with the rest of us.

"You two need to be more careful," my mom said while putting out plastic plates and cutlery.

"I know. I'm sorry," I said. Now that Shay was alright, my mind was on food.

Plopping down on a blanket, I noticed my dad and Marcus were back to sipping Cokes in between laughs.

"Okay, everyone! Food's ready!" my mom began, getting everyone's attention. "Time to eat!"

"Thank you, Diane," Marcus said to my mom as she handed him and my dad their hot dogs. The deepness of his voice stuck out amongst a collection of my friends. "I wish it was always Phoenix's birthday."

Everyone laughed as we sat down around all my other friends. Most of them ate, while the adults yapped and yapped, but it was fun. I loved having everyone together at Logan Park.

The plates cleared quickly, and while I wasn't looking, suddenly the entire party was singing "Happy Birthday," and a giant brownie cake was headed my way. The candles sparkled right in front of my eyes. I continued to look ahead, and behind the cake I could see all my friends and family. But looking on longer, I saw that my dad was talking into his shoulder radio and looked serious. Marcus was right next to him, listening to it too. I tried to focus on my candles, but suddenly, all I could see was the two of them.

"Blow out your candles, Phoenix! Hurry!" my mom said, cradling the cake right before my lips.

I shut my eyes and blew them out, but when I opened my eyes again, my dad and Marcus were gone. The cruiser sped off, with the lights blaring, down the road. The entire party then turned to watch their cruiser fly down the residential road, blazing off with their siren screaming. All their heads gawked as the flameless candles over my cake stood pointless, lifeless. Each them carefully whispered to one another.

"Did you make a wish?" my mom asked, trying to take my attention away from the obvious disappointment.

I forced a smile as I looked toward her. I could feel a quiver in my eyes that I quickly stifled. I was thinking then that I hadn't wished for a pony, a rocket ship, or even a cool family car, like most of my friends would have.

Shay looked just as sad as I felt, like a deflated balloon. She gave me a sad smile, the two of us the only ones there who knew what it was like to have your dad drive away in the middle of your birthday party.

I tried not to act sad as I opened my presents, but it was hard to celebrate once my dad was gone. I felt incomplete and empty. I didn't really care much about my gifts, but I knew I had to act grateful with all my friends there. But after my dad and Marcus left, it seemed like the entire party was somewhere else too. Nobody was nearly as interested in what was going on around us any longer. All of them were wondering what was so urgent that had called them away.

Peeling each of my presents open as my mom handed them to me, I watched the colors in the sky shift, growing darker and darker. Each of the clouds seemed to grow, and pretty soon, the sun was gone. The trees shook as the breeze came through the park. We'd made our way through most of the presents in the next half hour. I opened several train sets and sports cards, but thankfully, we were now coming down to the last few.

"What's this?" my mom asked, sounding confused. She was holding a plain manila envelope that had been at the bottom of the last pile. It had a number written in pen on the front. She turned it over several times in her hands.

"What is it, Mom?" I asked.

Still confused, she said to me, "It says it's from…from Grandma?"

Carefully, my mom handed it to me. With my pointer finger, I peeled it open. Inside it was a handwritten letter. I pulled the letter out and started reading it at the top. But suddenly, I was stuck. I couldn't move. Not my head. Not my eyes. I had no control of anything. I tried to keep reading, but I felt my body freeze. It began in my hands and then moved throughout my entire body. My eyes were locked onto the page. I couldn't breathe.

"Noodle?" I heard my mom say at first with confusion, and then moving to my name a second and third time with a rising fear. "Phoenix? Phoenix?"

I wanted to burst into tears, then, I was so afraid. My eyes felt like they were growing blurrier and darker. I tried to say something, anything. I even just tried to scream, but nothing came out. Not even a sound. I wasn't sure if what I was feeling was actually happening or not. Because suddenly, I was on my back, shaking violently. Turning my back over and over.

"Somebody call an ambulance!" I heard a voice scream, but it sounded far, far, far away. The voice that said it seemed like it was from a different place altogether.

I'm in flurry of dark red, black, dark red, black. The colors zoom by me like I'm flying through a tunnel. The length of the colors is long, endless. I'm going faster and faster.

The colors leave behind a thick tail that trails in the darkness. The red beams over me as a flicker. It comes in and out as I fly.

Suddenly, everything stops. It goes completely black. No other colors. No sound. Nothing to see. Just a pit of black darkness. A deep, fallen abyss.

I look down, but I don't have hands, feet. I'm floating, weightless. There's nothing here, but somehow, I know I am.

Then, that same dark red flickers above me once more, only this time it's not moving. It comes in and out right over me. Like a stop light, car light, or sign.

I try to say something, but no voice comes from my body. I then try to scream, something, anything. All of it remains silent.

The dark red beam flashes on and off. The buzz of the light is like the slowing flutter of a bug's wings. It comes in and out but stays a little bit longer each time. On, off, on for a little bit longer, off, and then on again.

Things begin to zoom by below, but they're going too fast for me to see what exactly they are. Going each direction, I can feel the heat of them flying by under the light. In between blows of the wind, I try to focus on the light above. Its flicker is suddenly becoming clearer. I'm staring at it, waiting for it to reveal itself fully. Knowing then that it's coming. The fuzz of the light starts to disappear.

A gust of wind whooshes by my cheek. Everything else stops.

A cascading white figure floats gently down from the light, a bright white glow that washes out the red altogether. Suddenly, it's as if this glow is everything now. All that I can see.

Through the glow, a person appears—an older woman. She looks normal, fair, but old. Her movements are slow and calculated. I can't see her face, but her presence is somehow familiar. She's wearing a sweeping black gown and a white belt, hovering above me like an angel. Watching her slowly come down from this darkness, I somehow feel less afraid, less confused, and less out of sorts altogether. She's mystical, yet crystal clear. I can see the wrinkles in her forearms and the ease in the creases of her cheek. Her soft, white hair curls at her neck. Her fingers are intertwined like the alternating stitches of a quilt. But it's as if she has no idea I'm there and only I can see her. I have to get her help.

I yell for her, this time as hard as I can, with everything left I've got. But still, nothing comes. No sound at all.

She turns so slowly toward me, as if she can't believe she isn't alone in this place. She looks right into my eyes.

I don't move.

"Phoenix? Hello? Phoenix, can you hear me?"

Then, suddenly, I drop to the ground. My hands and feet are back. I go to feel my face, I'm here.

But before I can answer her, she continues. The old woman begins again in one, long breath, "Phoenix, my child. Carry the light that shines in the darkness. And the darkness shall never overcome."

Peeling my eyes open, I saw flashes of white drywall. The sharp lights made my eyes shut again. People in masks and bug-eyed goggles hovered over me.

"Phoenix? Hello? Phoenix, can you hear me?"

I could still hardly keep my eyes open, and I had no idea where I was or what was going on. Suddenly, a creeping knot of pain pulled at my back. My whole body hurt. I screamed.

"Stay with us here! Stay with us, Phoenix. You're almost through it, just stay strong."

I felt my body retching. I was at war with myself, my body against my mind. One was in agony, and the other was in panic. As each wave of pain moved through me, my eyes shut and my hips arched forward. I couldn't get any sense of where I was. I couldn't think. I screamed again.

"Keep his arms down!"

My upper body went one way and my lower body the other. I felt trapped beneath a wall of wet concrete that was quickly drying over me.

As the agony continued, I felt a rush of warmth. I opened my eyes to a team of hands pushing me down—holding me still against a hospital bed.

"My baby! That's my baby!" I heard a familiar voice scream. "That's my son!"

It sounded like it could be my mom, but something didn't feel right about the pain and agony in her voice. Her voice sounded less like a voice, and more like a shriek from hell.

~

My eyes came open slowly and delicately, as if I'd just woken up in my own bedroom, but as I looked out, I saw my feet wrapped in a blanket that wasn't mine. The door was open to a hallway that wasn't in my house. There were nurses, doctors, all in white and other cream colors, flying by.

I turned my neck slowly to see a whiteboard with my full name written on it beside today's date. It was still my birthday, 6-10-1994. A monitor was beeping over me. Flashing, dark red lights came in and out.

On the other side of the room, my mom was curled up in a chair just below a window, asleep. Her head moved up and down, resting against her left arm, which, in turn, was braced against the wall. It was dark outside the window, the lights of Darling blinking in the distance.

I looked down and flexed my fingers, then I lifted the blanket. Instead of my jeans, I was in a blue hospital gown, and my feet in cushioned socks. I looked intact, with a tape and cotton ball wound tightly beneath my right elbow, but there were no needles or IVs.

I had no idea what happened or how I got here.

My head slipped back against the pillow for a moment before

I pushed myself up and peeled off the blanket. I slowly swung my feet off the side of the hospital bed and slid gently to the floor, then pushed myself off the bed. I took one more look at my mom, but she was still asleep.

And alone.

The lights were dim out in the hallway, and it didn't seem like too much was going on. So, I just started walking. Aimlessly. Slowly at first, letting my feeling and sense come back.

The hallway was dotted with the windows of other hospital rooms. I looked through each of them, and I couldn't believe how many other kids there were. Some of them looked my age, but many of them looked even younger. Their eyes followed me as I walked. It put the pain and fear I thought was gone right back into me. A few nurses passed by, but most of them just looked too busy to notice. They were the only other people I saw outside the rooms. My feet in socks continued to slide against the tile as I walked along, looking at all the others in here with me.

Then, on a bench, sat what looked like a man. A broken-looking and bent-over man, who was bumping up and down in tears. He was sobbing like he was so hurt and so broken that it made me want to do the same. His head was on his knees as he slumped over. The noise of his cries was the only sound in the hallway then. He was all alone on that very long bench.

The lights were still dim, and it was growing harder to see, so I decided to try and walk past him without him noticing me there. But as I grew closer, I noticed that this sad man was in a police uniform. His badge glistened in a familiar and unmistakable way.

"Dad!" I yelped in excitement, wanting to run into his protecting arms and hear him tell me that everything is okay. That he'd just arrived and found out that nothing at all was wrong.

But I stopped walking and just stood there. It was, indeed, my dad, but he didn't say anything. He looked up, lifting his head from his hands, his expression full of shock and misery.

And his police uniform was covered in the dark red-black of dried blood.

"Phoenix?" he belted out in a broken rasp, traveling through the thick air toward me. "What are you doing here?"

My body started to tremble as I felt like I wasn't looking at my own father, but some monster.

My dad looked down at himself to see what I had seen. He attempted to quickly wipe the tears off his eyes with his hands that were covered in cold blood. The same hands that had raised me, held me, now trembling too, in agony.

"Phoenix, buddy. It's okay. Come here. It's okay."

He looked into me with a fear that nearly sent me to the floor. I didn't even recognize him at all. So, when he stood up and took his first step toward me, instead of running into his arms, I took off back toward my hospital room.

I never turned back.

1999

3

My mom and I walked up to the lady behind the check-in desk, and I exhaled. Most of my nerves settled, and I was able to focus, but it took a moment. The road had been so long. I was as prepared as I could be, but something about being here now struck me differently. All of the work had been put in.

The lady behind the counter quickly asked for my information.

"Name."

"Phoenix Iver."

"Age."

"Fifteen."

"City."

"Darling, Colorado."

"Guests."

I turned toward my mom. It was just us.

Most of the other kids I'd seen had large groups with them: teachers, family, and friends. The planning and preparation each of them had put into coordinating each posse was obvious.

The lady handed my mom a pass as she added in a sympathetic tone, "I'm sure all of Darling will be cheering for you back home, then."

As we walked down the hall, I stopped. My mom did too. She

gave me a hug.

"You're going to do great, Noodle. I'm so proud already."

I squeezed her tighter. The fabric of her clothes grazed my cheek.

"He'll be here. He's just running a few minutes late, that's all."

I tried to nod.

"Trust me, he wouldn't miss this for the world."

"You guys will be in your normal spot?" I asked.

She smiled. "Two rows up from the left side of the front."

She kissed my forehead and turned to move down the hall. I had to get on stage. But as I took a few more steps closer to the final door, I heard her call out for me once more.

"Phoenix!" she cried.

I turned to look back at her and waited. She never said anything, but there was a different type of smile on her face then. One that let me know, despite all my anxieties and fears, it was all going to be alright. Everything was going to fall into place.

She turned and headed to her seat in the audience. I moved into my seat on stage and sat there quietly. Then, the loudspeaker came on, and we were all welcomed to the 1999 Colorado Annual State Spelling Bee. The other contestants stood up, and we were greeted by a loud and boisterous audience.

I did my best to stand up tall, but suddenly I felt alone. Nobody could see what I could. It was always different in my head.

Ever since that day at the park on my birthday five years ago, I'd had these visions. Visions that appeared almost out of nowhere. I'd lose myself, and that stuck feeling would start, where I couldn't move, and then those colors—black and dark red—would come zooming by. Then they'd stop and flash over me, and just before I would come into focus, that old woman in the white belt would appear and it would end. Something would snap me out of it, and they'd always remained preternatural—not long for this world.

The doctors diagnosed them as mini seizures, but none of them could figure out why. I went to see all sorts of specialists and did all kinds of tests, but the only thing that they kept telling me was that I should start seeing a therapist. They told me I was dealing with trauma. My therapist, Mrs. S, was alright, I guess; she'd helped me to slow down my mind by thinking of my words. I could paint words in my mind.

"Think of your words, Phoenix. Think about how they fit together," I could hear her repeat to me. "Think of all the rules you've mastered."

I could see their definition, origin, and spelling. I could see the letters that were floating in some ether, pull together to give birth to a word. Zestful or vivisepulture. A finite number of letters in the alphabet that could create an infinite number of words. But I couldn't always use it like that. It wasn't always that simple, and sometimes I would lose control—my own self vivisepulture.

Over the years, Mrs. S helped me learn to focus on my triggers. Usually, I could spell my way out of them if I caught them quickly, but sometimes it was too much. Sometimes I got so lost, I started falling through that darkness. I got so lost, I had no control. I felt it all collapse under me. My entire being prematurely buried by itself.

The letters came. I slowed down. I was able to escape the vision that sought to suffocate me. S...U...F...F...O...C...A...T...E. Breathe. *Breathe.* With each letter, I felt my vision widen once more.

The audience slowed their clapping as we all sat down.

The head judge came over the loudspeaker. "Congratulations

to all our contestants. For each of you to make it to this stage today means that you have proven to be some of the best spellers in the entire state. That, alone, is an amazing achievement."

The audience clapped.

"But only one of you who wins today will advance to the Scripps National Spelling Bee."

It had always been a dream of mine to make it to Nationals. But as I looked to my left, I caught a glimpse of a Superman cape. James Jamson, also known as "Super Jimmy." He wore the same Superman costume to every competition. I'd even seen him wear it at Nationals when he was on the television.

"It's single elimination," the judge continued. "If any word is misspelled, you will be eliminated, meaning that the last contestant standing will be our winner."

Suddenly, my nerves got tighter. My mouth more dry. Eleven letters. I slowed everything down. E...L...I...M...I...N...A...T... I...O...N.

"Now. Let's start spelling!"

I took my seat. It was always easier for me to just focus on my toes inside my shoes.

I'd looked at them so often that I could see even the tiniest little details in how they filled the interior of my shoes. My right pinkie toe poked out further than the left. A crease had started to form at my right heel. My laces used to be white, until they'd gotten muddy.

"Phoenix Iver," the loudspeaker blared.

But now, my shoes had a new crease, right at the forefront of my big toe. It was huge. It was terrifying to me how I'd only just noticed it, and now it was all I could see. My eyes flew to it like a pair of nasty flies on fruit.

"Phoenix. Phoenix Iver from Darling," the loudspeaker repeated. Startled, I got my feet beneath me and approached the microphone. "That's me."

The audience laughed. My nerves had taken hold. My chest was pounding.

One of the judges announced my word. "CRUSADE."

I shifted slightly as the word quickly tattooed itself to my brain. I knew that one well. I'd written it down the previous night during my second evening session. I'd break down my days, minute by minute, to maximize my spelling time. When spelling, I wouldn't have to think about how all of the world was bad—that there were no rules and that no one cared about each other. I wouldn't have to think about any of that.

I pushed my glasses back onto my nose that had been sliding on an errant bead of sweat. I tried for one more breath before calmly starting.

"Crusade. C...R...U...S...A...D...E. Crusade."

I stepped away from the microphone and looked down. The new crease was still there.

"Correct."

A slight clap followed by a quick cheer. Without thinking about it, I turned toward my mom to see if my dad had arrived. But the only eyes I recognized were hers. She was sitting alone. As the clapping subsided and the cheers ran out, eventually it was just her hands clapping. But because the auditorium was so big, I couldn't hear her for long. After a while, even she, too, gave up applauding.

We started to move quickly, and contestants began dropping out after each new word. Every other kid that went up to the front to spell their word had the bell ring, signaling their folly. The bell just continued to ring. Until, eventually, it was just me and Super Jimmy.

We were the last two contestants standing. I made my way up to the microphone after he had just completed a tough one. I tried to think calmly, but still, the spotlight was so very bright.

"CAVALCADE," the loudspeaker blared, booming so loud that it startled me once more.

"May I hear it in a sentence?" I asked, giving myself more time to think.

"From afar, I watched all eight men and women proceed through life, despite having gone through such catastrophic events, appearing as though they were a part of a royal cavalcade."

I couldn't see it at first, but just as I thought the word would arrive, something else did. It was the same thing that I'd been able to keep from happening earlier, only this time I wasn't so strong.

The dark red and black come in and out over my eyesight. I feel the wind in my face as my cheeks absorb the strain. My vision goes narrow, and I can hardly see a thing. I'm back in this dark tunnel.

I see now that, this time, I'm not just falling endlessly through some darkness, but I'm stopped. My body is stationary. I'm at a place. Somewhere new. It's different than it's ever been.

I'm on a street corner, the sidewalk cracked. Trash pools at the edge of the block. Mushy snow melts into the gutter right beside my toes.

The feeling of zooming continues to stop, then, as I become still. But the feeling of a wind coming toward me continues. The dark red and black alternate with a growing ferocity.

I look up toward the flicker for the old woman, hoping she can help. But I don't see her, not where she would normally be. I don't see anyone at all.

Looking toward my feet, I examine this sidewalk I've now found myself on. It looks badly weathered and aged. As if I am standing upon the oldest sidewalk on the planet, sloppy graffiti and sharp divots cut into each slab. I begin to tiptoe along it, then, hoping to find something, someone.

But what must be ahead of me, then, are cars. If I'm on a sidewalk, then the zooming before me that I feel is cars. A street or highway has got to be close by.

I look up again and the light shining above flickers in that deep red and it's starting to become clearer. I want to know what this is. I want to understand.

The old woman comes slowly from the same dark sky, as the dark red fades. I can see her now, just as obviously as she can see me.

I watch her with a growing curiosity, as the stress of all that's around me evaporates.

Her white hair falls gently behind her as she smiles.

"Phoenix," I hear her say.

I try to speak, but no words come out.

"Phoenix?" she says to me, only this time, it's with a fear and foreboding that startles me.

I try to answer her another time, but I still can't hear my own voice.

"Where is your father, my child?"

The previous warmth of the old woman's expression shifts. She slowly fades from my vision.

I look down, and the cracked sidewalk falls apart right beneath me. I reach and grab for anything I can, then I fall, deeper and deeper. The old woman says my name over and over again, her voice growing softer and softer.

"Phoenix…Phoenix…Phoenix…"

"Phoenix?" the judge repeated my name louder a second time. "Phoenix Iver?"

In a flash, I came back, "Yes, sorry…may I hear it in a sentence?"

"You've already asked that. You have ten seconds to spell your word, or you will be disqualified."

In a panic, I started spewing letters, "Cavalcade. C…A…V… A…L…C…A…Y…D…E. Cavalcade."

They waited a moment before saying anything, but I could tell. When you'd been spelling as long as I had, you always could.

"I'm sorry. That is incorrect."

The bell rang. The audience paused as a sweeping breath came over them.

"Congratulations to Mr. James Jamson. Our 1996, 1997, 1998, and now, officially, our 1999 Colorado State Bee Champion!"

The audience clapped so loud that it instantly made my ears itch. I did my best to try and look up, but now it felt like the light was even brighter. It scrambled my brain. All of these years and all of the practice I'd put in to get here, all to be lost on one misplaced letter. And even worse, I'd let *him* down. I looked toward where my mom sat once more, but still, he wasn't there. It was just her—the adult who'd forgotten how to be anything other than an adult years ago. It felt as though it was only then I noticed that my mom was dressed in droopy colors that appeared more appropriate for a coal mine. She'd decided today to spice up her usual gray sweater and gray sweats with a gray scarf. Although that had little to do with my being cross. For how much time I'd spent to get here, *he* couldn't even sacrifice a few hours. To celebrate with me in success, but more importantly, sulk with me in defeat.

"May we please have all friends and family gather on stage for a photo with our first, second, and third place contestants?"

Mom tried to look happy as she joined me—giving me a sloppy kiss on the cheek—but it didn't make much of a difference.

"Great job, Noodle! Second place is not so bad! You did fantastic."

She probably didn't even remember that she'd said the same exact thing last year.

"Here," she said in a much softer voice, handing me a bouquet of sky blue flowers. "From your father."

Then, they all started coming up, so many people. Too many people. My skin itched and burned. I had nowhere to hide my eyes. My ears were telling me that people were all around. A crawling feeling slowly enveloped me. I didn't want to be on stage. There were so many judges all of a sudden—hot bodies that were recklessly breathing all over the place. While holding the flowers, I opened my eyes to see one of them bending down to place a ribbon around my neck with a heavy silver medal. I was nearly certain I was choking. I snapped my eyes shut again and tried to calm myself.

B...R...E...A... ... ...

The letters dropped as my mind dropped with them. Nothing was coming. I swallowed hard.

B...R... ... ...

The tiny conversation I was trying to have in my head wasn't helping. Everyone kept interrupting me.

"Everyone, please give another warm round of applause to all of our contestants. And let's especially bring our hands together for our now four-time champion, James Jamson. Good luck as you represent the state of Colorado, once again, at the Scripps National Spelling Bee! Bring home the gold!"

Since they were all looking at him, nobody had noticed yet, but I wasn't here anymore. I stood in one place as if I were instantly paralyzed.

My arms and legs flail like mad as I continue to fall through this endless dark. Past nothing at all. I turn over and over and over.

I let my body continue down as I wait to reach the bottom. Tiny lights shine around me in the dark as my falling begins to slow. They look like stars.

"Are you ready to see now?"

"We should get you home," my mom said, snapping me out of

the vision and bringing me back once more.

I was finally able to nod, but I wasn't even sure she noticed. Nobody could ever understand what I was going through. My brain and body were always operating separately. Neither was ever really in control.

For as long as I could remember, something else had always just been dragging me along.

~

We named our house "Metropolis" because of how intricate and unusual it was. Each room, desk, light, or even shoe, had a specific purpose and helped contribute to Metropolis's ability to function. My dad named it because he said it was like our house was a booming city. Sometimes I liked to think we were enormous monsters that bowled around the city streets inside and bounced off of skyscrapers. Creatures that had finally been set free.

"What happened to him tonight?" I asked my mom as soon as we were inside.

"Work," Mom responded while putting her scarf down on a nearby building (a clothes hamper).

"He said he was going to be there. You said he wouldn't miss it for the world," I said with some obvious disappointment.

"I know, Noodle, but you know how hard your father works to care of us."

I really wished my dad could have been there.

"Can I make you…" my mom began, but that was all I heard as I stormed up the stairs and crashed into the Bird's Nest (my room).

Inside, I quickly hopped in the shower and cleaned up. Right after

I'd finished drying off and getting changed into my favorite clover-print pajamas, I found my desk next to my window, popped a few of the remaining M&M's into my mouth, and went back to my cards.

I only had fifty-three more words to memorize before bed, and then I would have completed all of A Semester's national words 127 days early. I wanted to be able to start on all of B Semester's words before the summer was over. My first day of high school was tomorrow.

My desk was pretty messy, although I seemed to know where everything was. But then I thought about what my dad always told me, "Looking the part is always half the battle. You could be the smartest man in the world, but if you're sloppy, then nobody will ever take you seriously."

My dad always had a way of saying things. This or that or about anything really. Little words, phrases, and little items even. He'd give me small things to remind me of lessons he wanted me to hang onto, and each of them lived on my desk.

I had a tiny cactus from a trip he'd been on to see Arizona, and beside that was a bottle of earth and grass from the day of my first hit on my baseball team.

I put my cards down and organized my desk a little bit, just in case my dad came home to say goodnight. Thinking he'd want to see I'd taken care of the blue flowers, I neatly arranged them on my windowsill. Most nights, I'd wait up for him if I could, but sometimes it was hard for me to stay up so late.

But as I was tidying up around my room, the lights in Metropolis briefly faded. Shining in and out, they flickered. I stopped moving as I was caught in this partial darkness. The lights faded slowly at first, and then they flashed in and out in quicker intervals.

My dad took a break from work after my first seizure five years ago. He said he wanted to be around Metropolis more to look after me. And once I started going to therapy with Mrs. S, he decided he didn't want to be a police officer anymore. It all just seemed like it was too much for him.

For a while, it was just the two of us in the house a lot. He spent most of his time reading, and mostly reading from this weird book that had a pair of wings on the front. It seemed like, suddenly, that book was the only thing he cared about—I hardly saw him without it. Then, he finally told me he got a new job, a better one. I was really excited for him, but then I found out that it was to be a high school security guard. I tried not to ask him about it, though, because I could tell he was much happier.

In Darling, we'd also always had problems with our power. Something about the city growing too fast and our old power grid not keeping up. So, once my dad felt like I was doing better, he began moonlighting as an electrician on the side. Most of the time, though, the power would get bad, and he'd need to leave in the middle of the night.

Since he now had two jobs, he was gone for work all the time. But I knew that he wasn't getting paid very much, because a lot of things in Metropolis were starting to break, and we weren't fixing things like we used to. He and my mom fought about that a lot.

My mental wandering stopped when the lights inside Metropolis fully powered back on. Then, I looked out of my window and saw my dad's headlights shine on our grassy knoll. I watched him sigh as he opened his car door, grabbed his wings notebook, and walked inside. I was about to run downstairs to give him a hug when I heard muffled yelling, so I put my ear to my door and listened.

"Herman, it's nearly midnight, and we haven't seen you all week."

"I'm sorry, honey. Work has been crazy. You know how it is this time of year." His voice was deep. His sharp tenor sounded like a campaign-exhausted politician.

"You're running yourself into the ground. I can see it in your face…your eyes. You're drained."

"I'm fine, Diane. Everything is alright."

As I kept listening, my head started to pound, and my hands suddenly got sweaty. I tried to wipe them on the side of my legs, but that didn't help.

"Fine? You call this fine? Our bills are piling up to the ceiling, and I've hardly got enough food to feed Phoenix. But that doesn't really matter anyway, because he won't eat anything I make."

My stomach lurched. Now my hands weren't sweating, but my eyes. Of their own accord, they dripped.

"We're out of meat and milk, but I'll stop by the store next time and bring home some things. I'm sure Maya won't mind."

There was a silence. I thought they might've suspected I was listening, but then I heard my dad ask, "How is he?"

It was the way he said it that made me cringe. Like I was some sort of invalid.

My mom went silent for a moment before she continued, "It… it happened again."

"During the competition?"

My mom said something I couldn't hear, but then I heard her say, "He won't say more than two words to me, and the only person he will talk to is out half the night."

"I'm sorry I—"

"No. No, you're not. I know you'd rather be out there, but he needs a father, Herman. I can't do this alone."

Then, it went silent again. I heard someone pass by the Bird's

Nest, and then a door click shut. I was still stuck to the side of my door and couldn't calm down my eyes. They were starting to get so tired, despite how much they were crying.

Another pair of footsteps came. A note slid under my door.

How did it go tonight?

My hands were shaking as I reread the note over and over. I wanted to write back to my dad that I'd won, that I was strong and that I'd made him proud. But I didn't write anything back at all. After another moment, a second note came.

Hey, don't worry about it. You did all you could. Now get some rest. You only get one first day of school, and I'll make sure you get the VIP treatment.

Dad

I fell asleep against the door with the note clenched tightly between my fingers.

4

"And second place in the bee last night? That's amazing, son," my dad started as we walked to school, then added, "That means you automatically qualify for state again next year."

"I guess that's nice," I began half-heartedly, before asking, "What were those flowers you had Mom give me?"

My dad put his hand around my shoulder. "The Colorado blue columbine. The state flower of Colorado, son. For good luck. I'll be there next year to give them to you in person. And did you hear where they're hosting the state tournament next year?"

"Where?"

"Denver. But because it's going to be at a different venue, it's actually not for about a year and a half. I think that's going to be the one, Phoenix. Just keep working at it, and I know you'll win gold. And I promise that I will be there to see it. No matter what."

Looking up at my dad, I noticed the salt and pepper stubble that seasoned his chin. His broad smile beamed back at me, despite tired eyes.

"But it happened again on stage..." I trailed off. I was so embarrassed that I felt like I was shrinking.

"Chin up, Phoenix," he began. "You know, one time when I was in high school, I took this public-speaking class. And our final was to give this ten-minute speech in the auditorium in front of our entire school. I was a wreck; I couldn't eat or sleep for days. When eventually I went onto the stage, I felt like I was ready, but I started to sweat, and then I looked down at my speech, and I felt nauseous. I threw up in front of the entire school. They called me 'Hurling Herm' for the next four years."

My dad let out a chuckle, so I tried to humor him with a bit of levity on my end by forcing a laugh.

"Trust me, son, it happens. No sense in losing sleep over it."

We went back to walking along in silence before my dad added, "I've been looking forward to this day for a long time."

"Will I be able to see you a lot?"

"Some days are busier than others, but don't worry about that. Focus on making some new friends."

"But what if I just want to see you?"

My dad stopped me, placing his hand on my shoulder.

"Here, I brought you something." Reaching into his pocket, he pulled out the Key of Courage and gently dropped it over my head, letting the silver key fall to the center of my chest.

I hadn't seen the necklace in years, but just the sight of it somehow made me happier. My hands went to it.

He smiled again. "Believe me, I would rather just hang with you all day, too, but remember the power this key gives those who have it in their possession."

I nodded as I tucked it under my shirt. The cold of the key landed against my bare skin.

"Besides," my dad began again, "I have to keep watch over all of you kids. It's my job to make sure every student is safe on campus… and that includes you." He let his hand land on my shoulder and then added, "And that, son, is as important a job as any."

As we got closer, my dad gave me a hug and reassured me that he wouldn't be too far. He'd be patrolling campus until after lunch and would be back to pick me up in the Ferry so he could drive me to my appointment later. I think he could sense, like always, that I was nervous.

Walking into Darling High for the first time, I had the feeling it would be somewhere I would hate. It kind of made me think of what goes through an inmate's head as he walks down the halls, carrying his secondhand pillows and blankets. I was taking a look around the cell I'd be sequestered in for the next four years.

They call it the "Darling bubble" because nothing important ever really happens here. We all tend to stay close by, without ever venturing off too far. Nothing of any noteworthiness had ever happened in our quiet town, except when our water tower toppled over. We'd made national news that day, and it was the most exciting thing that had ever happened to this place.

I came in through the side entrance to avoid the oncoming tide of all the other freshmen. Also, that's where I'd told TT I'd meet him. Sure enough, there he was, all awkward and gangly. As usual, he was also wearing his Denver Bronco's belt buckle and even tucked his t-shirt into his jeans to give it a pop.

"H-Hey, Phoenix!"

"Let's get this over with," I greeted him.

"D-Don't be like that. W-We're gonna love it here!"

"I have no idea why we decided to sign up for Honors English," I said once I got close enough to him to lower my voice.

"W-We want to challenge ourselves!" he said as he let out a long smile.

He'd acquired the name TT because of his stutter. He always

started out saying the first letter twice, which is how he got the nickname, "Two-Time Tommy." Some people called him Triple T, but he told me once that he wanted to be called TT, so I've only called him that ever since. Although he talked funny, he did have his height going for him. He was tall and was thinking about going out for the basketball team in the winter.

TT and I slipped into Honors English without being noticed. Just as we'd taken our seats, the loudspeaker began.

"Goooooood morning, Darlings! I hope you all had an amazing summer. To those of you returning, welcome back. To those of you who are new, my name is Principal Roman, and let me be the first to welcome you to Darling High School!"

Most of the kids kept talking and poking one another as our warden continued, making it hard to hear much of anything.

"Here at DHS, we hope you'll create some amazing friendships, memories, and bonds that you will carry forever. As an alumnus here myself, I take a great amount of pride in being a Dragon, just like all of you."

Mr. Creason, our English teacher, attempted to quiet down the class, but nobody listened. To be honest, I'd already sort of tuned out the announcements, too, until I saw that TT was hanging on to every word.

"Tickets for the Snowball have just gone on sale at the gym, cafeteria, and library, so be sure to pick yours up for our annual welcome-back dance. Let's carry on our school's great legacy by having an amazing, fun, and safe school year. Be excellent and see you at the dance, Darlings!"

In class, we learned all about F. Scott Fitzgerald. He sounded like a nut. We would be starting *The Great Gatsby* soon, which I wasn't really excited about. I wasn't much of a reader, but I'd convinced myself that I'd at least, maybe, be able to learn some new words from it.

At lunch, TT and I found seats at a long, empty table in the back. Even though it was just the two of us, we were the only ones sitting there. He pulled out a salami bagel sandwich and talked as he ate. I wasn't very hungry. I just took out my cards to go over the rest of my A Semester words that I hadn't been able to finish.

While chomping away, TT talked. "I-I don't think high school will be too bad. I-I just hope that the mean kids from middle school went over to South High. B-But I know Pounds is here. H-He is the captain of the football team, and he's only a junior. S-Someone told me he's probably going to go to Duke."

TT ripped off another bite of his salami.

"M-Maybe since I've gotten so much taller, Pounds won't be mean to us like when we were younger."

Pounds tore us to pieces when we were in middle school, which was a big reason why I wasn't really looking forward to starting here. But he bullied most kids, so I doubted he would remember a couple of nerds from his past anyway.

"W-We should try to find dates for the Snowball," TT said.

"The dance?" I asked, still only partially listening.

TT laughed. "Y-You work too hard, Phoenix. W-We have to party while we still can."

I joined him in laughing as TT carried on, "W-We get to be young and dumb right now. A-All the mistakes in the world are out there waiting for us. I-I want to get in some trouble!"

"Trouble?"

"Y-Yeah, trouble. Y-You, know. L-Like girls and stuff."

Startled, I responded with a look of disgust before replying,

"That's just stupid. What girls would want to hang out with us?"

"H-Have you seen Shay yet?"

I looked up from my cards momentarily and shook my head.

"M-Me either. I-I wonder if she's going here."

If I was going to look up from my notecards, it was to talk about Shay. That was an opportunity I rarely missed.

Shay was forever a year ahead of me in school, but she was the kind of girl who made me forget that bad things ever happened. Just being around her was somehow magically inspiring. And for as long as I'd known Shay, that was always who she was. But ever since our dads stopped being partners, we suddenly stopped seeing each other. Our families had been super close, but after my birthday party, it seemed like everything changed. After that day at Logan Park, Shay never looked at me the same again.

"She is. She's a sophomore though."

I went back to my notecards, but then felt a hulking shadow over me. Then, I saw it.

My vision falls onto all the stars around me. They're sparkling brighter and brighter in the darkness.

My body becomes rigid as I hear the light of the stars echo in a fierce laughter. They're all staring at me, laughing.

It's getting louder and louder as I fall. I start shaking, and with each sound of laughter, my body pierces in pain.

I try to yell and scream, grab hold of anything to make it stop, but I just keep falling.

All my notecards were slapped out of my hands and onto the floor. I didn't turn around to see who did it. Instead, I tried to pick them up as feet piled around. Then laughing, lots and lots of laughing.

A voice silenced them, and I looked up.

It was him.

Wearing a purple jersey and backward cap, Pounds stood over me with a mouth full of bubble gum being sucked on by his big, crooked teeth.

He then bent down into a squat to get right beside my face. "Still staring at words all day, freak?"

I didn't say anything as I just tried to reach back down for my notecards, but Pounds trampled all over them, this time mangling them beyond return.

"Give it up already. Spelling doesn't mean crap anyway. I'm basically doing you a favor or something."

While still looking down at the wreck that was now all of my cards, I muttered, "Please. They…They mean a lot to me."

"Why?" he asked with a laugh.

Because focusing on my words was better than focusing on people. But I couldn't possibly explain that to him. I couldn't possibly explain that to anyone.

I fell into a deeper silence, upset I'd even engaged him in any way.

Pounds repeated himself more powerfully. "Tell me, or I'm going to do the same thing that I did to your little words to your precious little face."

I answered him, even though I didn't want to. "Be…because my dad taught me how to be really good."

The whole group of feet shuffled as everyone burst out into a laugh. Pounds continued to lead the charge.

"Aw, you're a daddy's boy? Well, that makes a lot of sense."

They continued to laugh as I fell to the floor to scoop up the mess.

Pounds continued, "Too bad your daddy is just a useless bum who can't even protect you."

I tried to stand up tall and look him in the eye. "He's not a bum. He's a hero. He…He…" But I trailed off. I had nothing left. I had no idea what to even say.

The whole group howled in laughter even louder than before. Pounds started in on me again. "I've got news for you, freak. Your stupid dad was never a hero. The whole town knows it. Maybe he used to be a cop, but now his job is to make sure seniors don't ditch class and to pick up trash after lunch. He's basically the school maid!"

I couldn't help it. My shocked facial expression must have said it all. My anguish was on full display.

He put his hands on my shoulders. "I can't believe it. This loser didn't even know his dad is the biggest loser in all of Darling. Nobody must have told him. But I guess it makes sense. Being a loser runs in the family."

"Y-You leave him alone!" TT chimed in.

Shifting his stance, Pounds turned toward TT. "Oh boy, if it isn't Two-Time Tommy back at it again. Freak *and* Triple T. Say, can you repeat that for me, Triple T? I didn't catch it the first time."

TT went white as a ghost, but finally, Pounds felt as though he'd had enough for the day.

"Well, I thought I'd just stop by and welcome you both to DHS. It's good to have the gang back together. I've missed you guys!"

TT tried to help me up, but I stormed out alone in a whirlwind of tears. They all continued to howl in laughter as I took off in a full sprint for the bathroom.

~

I whipped open the first stall and locked it tight behind me. My breathing continued to pulse, even though I was alone. I snapped my eyes shut, attempting to black it all out.

I let the horrible thoughts of all I wanted to happen to Pounds and his posse run wild in my mind. How I wanted to watch someone hurt them. At first, it frightened me the things I imagined, but after a while of sitting there in my own darkness, I decided I didn't really care. They were just harmless, private fantasies.

A knock came at the door, which startled me up and out of my haste. I kept my eyes closed, hoping to return to my dark thoughts.

"Go away, TT," I said toward the sound of the knock.

But a second knock came.

"I said go away. I'll meet you in speech therapy. I'm fine. I just need another minute."

A third knock came, and this time I was upset.

"I said go away!" I yelled, letting my eyes burst open this time. But looking up then, I saw the scars of dark messages cut along the walls of the stall. Each of them came right at me.

Death to them all.

I folded inward even more.

One day you'll know why.

My eyes felt stuck wide open.

Time is running out…

Turning away from the horror, I saw the same pair of feet in front of my stall door. I pulled my knees to my chest to keep from falling over.

"Who are you?" I asked.

Through the door, a voice returned, "I saw what Pounds did to you. I want to help." I swallowed again as the boy added, "I want to help you make sure he never bothers you again, Phoenix."

I could hear the fear in my own voice as I struggled to reply, "How?"

The boy's feet shifted slightly, as if he'd adjusted how he was standing. I waited for some time for him to finally respond. "Can I trust you?"

I unlocked the door, and a boy lugging his backpack, with long hair falling over his shoulders, stood before me. He wasn't very tall or recognizable, but he was dressed in very formal clothing for a high school student. He was wearing a wrinkled white shirt and tie. The cuffs were folded, stained, and unbuttoned.

"I'm Tyler," he said, holding out his hand for me to shake. "I'm a senior, so I know all about Pounds."

I tried to smile, but my eyes left him and stuck to the graffiti on the walls.

"Oh," he said, "a lot of that was me. I come in here sometimes too."

"Really? Don't you get in trouble for that?"

Tyler laughed. "Only if you get caught. Plus, all they'd do is make you wash it off anyway."

Tyler then tossed me something, and I caught it without thinking what it might be. Opening my hands, it was a thick, red Sharpie.

"Try it. It helps."

I wasn't sure at first, but almost without thinking, my hand opened the cap and began writing. The blue metal of the stall bled quickly in my font.

My hand pulled away, and I capped the Sharpie once I was finished. I exhaled as the sudden rush left me.

"Better?" Tyler asked.

"Yeah," I said and meant it.

"Good," he replied. "But let's wash that Sharpie stain off your hands so it doesn't look too obvious."

Looking down, I saw my hand that had been gripping the Sharpie was stained in red ink. The prints of my fingers were rubbing against each other.

We both laughed as Tyler helped me out of the stall. I flipped on the faucet and let it run for a while in order for the water to heat up. Tyler stood just beside the sink holding some paper towels.

"I needed to get that out. Thanks," I said to him as I tested the water with my pointer finger. It was slowly warming up.

"No problem," Tyler said, then he shuffled his backpack forward, toward his feet. "Pounds had been giving me problems for years, but I finally stopped him, you know. Now, he won't even come near me."

"How did you do that?" I asked, placing my hands into the warm water. It sent goosebumps up my back as the warmth surged through me. I let the water run through my fingers, knuckles, nails.

Tyler didn't say anything, but just opened his backpack and lifted it toward his chest, so I could see inside. Beneath his calculus homework and Spanish textbook, was a gun. It looked heavy.

"Is it loaded?!?!" My heart sunk deep into my chest.

He nodded. "I would never use it. It's just to scare him off, you know?"

"How did you…? Where did you…?" I felt like I was losing all the blood in my body. I could hardly think.

"My friend got it for me. I could get you one, too, Phoenix. It's really easy."

My whole body surged in a hot sweat. In a panic, I scanned the bathroom again to make sure we were alone.

"You believe me, right? I told you, I would never use it," Tyler asked looking deeply into my eyes. He zipped his backpack shut, concealing the gun once more.

I nodded.

"I knew you would. But let me know if you want Pounds to leave you alone for good."

Suddenly, my hands burned deeply in pain. I hadn't realized it, but the water coming from the faucet was now scalding hot. I yanked my hands away violently and let out a screech.

"You alright?" Tyler yelled after me as I stormed out of the bathroom.

I didn't look back, trying to shake the feeling back into my burnt palms, before limping into speech therapy class.

Class was a blur, as my mind couldn't keep from replaying the image of the gun at the bottom of Tyler's backpack over and over again. I thought to tell my dad, but I wasn't sure if I would get in trouble or not. I also thought about what Tyler would do to me if I told anyone.

At the sight of the Ferry after school later, my anxiety calmed. It wasn't completely off, but it was coursing through my body with much less vigor.

I kept my head down as I paced toward the car and tried to remain unseen. I needed this day to be over.

Then, a voice called out and stopped me from running. It stopped me from doing anything.

"Phoenix."

I tried to look up to see who it was, but once I saw her shoes, I realized I didn't have to. I remembered that she always wore those hot pink Converse sneakers.

"Hi," I bubbled to Shay.

5

Her voice was soft. "You look so nice. I really like your hair longer like that."

I ran my fingers through my hair and tried to keep from exploding at her compliment.

Thankfully, before I could say anything back, she asked, "How was the first day? You adjusting alright?"

I glanced up at Shay and saw her washed jean jacket wrapped over her small hoodie. Her hair was the same color it'd had always been, but now she was wearing glasses. The dimples of her cheeks poked as she smiled.

"Yeah. It was…good," I said slowly.

"Good," she replied.

Silence fell, but it didn't seem all that bad. My heart was racing. Just the sound of her voice put my brain into knee-deep mud. She fidgeted with the strings of her hoodie as she bounced back and forth. I felt my hands beginning to sweat.

"I should get going, but it was nice seeing you. Maybe we could have lunch together? I could show you around a little bit after?"

"Okay…yes," I started, but each letter in each word was a mission for my vocal cords to speak. "That's…a plan."

I looked up again, but she'd already turned and was headed in the other direction. All I could see was her soft blond curls bouncing on her back just atop her starry night JanSport backpack.

"Hi, Officer Iver," I heard her say as she passed my dad.

"Shay, great seeing you. Give your father my best."

My dad walked toward me and smiled. "It looks like you're off to a strong start here."

He gave me a hug before opening the passenger door to the Ferry.

"I haven't seen Shay in so long," I said.

My dad didn't look at me right away as he continued to focus on the road. Once out of the parking lot, he asked, "So, did you make any new friends?"

I gulped as I began to feel the burns on my palms. I wiped them up and down the side of my legs. "Yeah, I guess. Pounds is here, though."

My dad could hear the angst in my tone. He was hurting for me. "Have you ever heard of Plato?" My dad asked.

I shook my head.

"He was a famous philosopher who taught Aristotle and is thought to be one of the founders of Western religion and spirituality. Have you ever heard of something called, 'platonic love?'"

I nodded. "Yeah. Non-romantic love. Right?"

"Correct. It was named after Plato. He was very wise, Phoenix, but he has a famous quote that I want to share with you. And promise me to never forget it, okay?"

I nodded. I'd never show it, but secretly I'd always loved his little nuggets.

"Be kind. For everyone you meet is fighting a hard battle." He then added, "Don't let Pounds cause you any nonsense. Nobody has it as easy as they make it look, so we mustn't ever judge another, just like Plato was attempting to point out."

The sun shone over his cracked hands, closely gripping the Ferry's steering wheel. He was still in his security outfit.

It amazed me how easily it seemed the exact words always came to him. He had aged quite a bit in the last few years, though. Sleepless nights had begun to accompany his gray streaks. I'd always wished I could see my dad more than I did, but our car rides were where we'd done the most of our chatting. Where we'd make up for lost time.

"Why weren't you there last night?"

"I'm sorry about that, son. I promise I won't miss your next bee. I had a last-minute job I wasn't expecting."

"Stuff with the electricity?"

He nodded.

My mouth suddenly became very dry. It had a foul taste. I wanted to get out of the car. The words then exited without my permission. "Why don't we see Shay and her family anymore? Is it because of me?"

My dad quickly started while keeping his eyes on the road. "No, son, not at all, and I don't want you to ever think that. You couldn't control what happened. Nobody could ever be upset at you for that."

"Then why? Is it…is it because you aren't a police officer anymore?"

My dad looked at me deeply as we pulled up to a red light.

I continued, "It's okay if you're too embarrassed to tell me."

He smiled and released a breath that came from a deep place inside him. "Phoenix, I love what I do. And I do it to provide for you and your mother. The most important thing a man can do is take care of the people he loves. There's nothing more important than family."

I looked up at him for the first time since occupying the passenger seat in the Ferry and forced a smile.

"And families get busy, which is the only reason we don't see

Shay and her family like we used to. I promise it had nothing to do with you, son. But, sometimes, life gets ahead of us, that's all. Don't get down about it, okay?"

"Okay," I replied with some anguish, fear. Sometimes none of it seemed to make any sense. I thought about how something was wrong with me and wrong with this world. I thought about how lonely my mom looked all the time. I thought about how they fought when I wasn't around.

"Maybe this would be something good to bring up with Mrs. S this afternoon?" he added.

I continued to stare out the window then, wondering if any of this would start to make sense.

"Besides," my dad began again, sensing my discomfort, "now that you've started high school, maybe you and Shay can become close again."

~

"Find a seat."

It was quiet, but when Dr. Sabintter (more commonly referred to as Mrs. S) spoke, the words felt about as boring as the local news on the lowest possible volume.

"How are you feeling today?"

I felt like I was in a room that was slowly getting darker. Like I was falling through tasks with little passion at all, and that I was the only one who realized there was no way out of this.

But I just sat there and said nothing. I looked down at my feet, putting all of my attention into the subtleties of each lace.

"Well, how about the State Bee then? Why don't you tell me about that?"

My vision passed on to her office around us. Framed papers she'd published; a photo on her desk of a man with a mustache, who looked like a firefighter; a diploma from Boulder for clinical psychology. Everything was too neatly organized and set in place. The unlimited set of editions of what looked like the same exact book made me nauseous.

"Now, I understand you had one of your mini episodes. Your mother let me know. Did you try to visualize your words like we practiced? Did that help?"

"It helped at first," I started slowly, while still staring down at my feet. "But it doesn't always work. I just want to make it stop."

"And this time, when it happened, what did you see?"

I exhaled and left my hands at my sides as I closed my eyes. I tried to not think about any of it, but I guess Mrs. S wasn't going to just let me sit here silently this appointment. Mrs. S perked up a bit as I gathered myself. She slowly arched up in her chair and clicked her ballpoint pen.

"It was how it always is, the dark red and black colors and then that sort of zooming feeling, you know? Like your head is out the window of a fast-moving car. Then, all the lights go away, and I see that same old woman."

"The one in the white belt?" Mrs. S interrupted me.

"Yes. Her," I answered as she wrote everything down. "And even though the whole thing is terrifying to me every time—the dark and the feeling like it will never end and this time I will never escape—for some reason, I feel like she's there to help, even though she never does. And then, that's usually when it ends. No matter what I do, or how I visualize my words, that's it. I can't ever say anything to her, either, even though I try. But she talks to me. Somehow, she can see me, even when I can't see myself."

Mrs. S scribbled each word I'd said down fiercely. She was intentional about putting all the pieces together.

"But I can't function. I can't...I can't go anywhere or do anything without feeling like something's wrong with me, and nothing we do helps."

Mrs. S looked up from her notes sharply. "Phoenix. I know it must be frustrating, but believe it or not, we've made plenty of progress. It's easy to forget how far you've come, but you've improved tremendously with all the work you've done on your own and the work we've done in here, every week, together."

"I feel like I'm getting nowhere."

I was stuck in this paralyzing fear that I was the only one dealing with this problem—seeing the things I saw. No words could describe what it was like—the terror I felt.

We didn't say anything else for a while, as Mrs. S read through all her notes. She was quietly scanning them once again right before me.

"Could you try and remember what it is that...that this woman in the white belt said to you?"

I replied slowly, "She usually just says my name. Something short. But she was asking me about my dad. She asked me where he was." I waited for Mrs. S to respond, but she just kept writing things down. Finally, I asked, "What does that mean?"

"I think," she began, lifting her glasses gently from her nose, "I think this woman in the white belt you're seeing is the embodiment of your grandmother. In some way, I think she must be. Her asking about your father sounds like something that's coming from your own subconscious. And because your grandmother has passed, that's why you can't speak to her in these episodes when she appears. And because of this, it explains your agitation is simply due to your desire to communicate with someone who's gone. You can't speak with her in your vision or here, in the real world. You can only talk to people who are here, like your father. Like me."

"But she...she doesn't even look like my grandma. It's not her. Wouldn't she look like her?"

"Not necessarily. It could be your own mind simply painting the image of someone insignificant you saw on the street or in town. You may not even remember ever seeing this woman before," Mrs. S explained. "Phoenix. Death has a profound effect on our psyches. Especially when it comes to us at a young age. And most of our lives, we struggle to understand, with this certainty of life, that death will eventually come to us all."

I let my head sink between my knees. It was a deep heaviness atop the crown of my skull.

Then, a thought came into my mind and remained there. It came from somewhere deep inside me, as if this was the question I'd been pondering all along.

"But if she's really gone, then why can I hear her so clearly?"

"Our minds are more powerful than we realize, Phoenix," Mrs. S began in a different tone. "They can sometimes hang on to memories and bring them back to us when we least expect them and without our permission."

I asked her what I really wanted to know, slowly, deliberately. The question that maybe only someone like her could answer. "But Mrs. Sabintter. People die every day. Why is *this* happening...happening just to me?"

Mrs. S put her notebook down, letting her attention float out the window. She looked at me.

I watched a deep, honest chill go through her.

6

After my dad finished walking me to school and stopped at his post, I ran into TT. I'd forgotten to tuck the Key of Courage under my shirt, and it had been bouncing around the outside of my coat. I'd been wearing it to school for about a month and had always remembered to hide it away.

"W-Whoa! Wh-Where'd you get that, Ph-Phoenix?"

Looking down at the key, I covered it with my palm as I quickly answered, "It's nothing. I sort of…rediscovered it."

We were both at school early that day, which wasn't particularly normal. We had about ten minutes to burn until first period.

I could tell TT was hoping I'd tell him more about the necklace just as Shay approached us.

"Hey, guys."

TT could hardly keep it together, so he decided to look at me, thinking I'd know what to do, which I absolutely didn't.

"H-Hi, Shay. H-How have you been?"

As she looked over at TT, I knew she wasn't looking at me any longer. I could finally look up with no chance of catching her eyes on mine.

She smiled so easily as she talked. I noticed small freckles that kissed her nose. Shay was wearing the same glasses from the other day, but somehow hers—unlike mine—made her even prettier. Summer yellow frames. Her bottomless blue eyes behind the even glass made me think that's what seeing cresting waves in the Pacific must be like.

I'd been so lost in her air that I'd only caught the last part of what she'd been saying.

"I only thought I'd ever see something like that in the movies. I'm working on a story about the entire thing right now."

"You write?" I chimed in.

She smiled as she explained, "Yes, I want to write a full movie someday. Telling a story through pictures…it's my passion, kind of like you and your spelling."

My shoulders lurched, and I felt queasy, but in a good way at first. I quickly looked back down, to ground myself, by focusing on her pink sneakers.

"How's that been going?" she asked.

I thought I was going to fall over. My eyes started to dim. Grays became blacks.

I heard Shay turn away from me slightly as TT asked her something to cover for me, but I was so stuck in a trance that I hardly noticed. My hands moved quickly and then became violent, moving completely of their own accord. They started to ache deeply, and then my entire arms, chest, and, eventually my legs, locked. I could feel it coming down over me. I snapped my eyes shut.

While attempting to break through and ball my hands into fists, I went for deep breaths. I searched for my letters.

S…P…E…L…L…I… …

But I couldn't finish the word. I was still shaking.

S…P… … … … … …

Then the sensation grabbed hold of me, and that was when I realized there was nothing I could do anymore. It was happening again.

The wind flies by me as I narrowly dodge something going fast. The zooming feeling slows, and the lights around me stop moving. It's still now.

My feet are on that same cracked sidewalk as before. The mushy paddle of snow and mud carry errant trash around me. All of the cracks are filled with this mixture.

With my hands buried inside my pockets, I find myself walking. But this time when I look around, I'm not alone. The old woman in the white belt is floating beside me.

I want to say something, but no words come out. And I try to stop walking, but I can't control my feet or my legs. I'm following her somewhere.

I try to look around to see what else is around, but it just looks like a beaten-up neighborhood. Another sidewalk across the street looks just as trashed as the one we're on, and rundown shops populate the outer sides.

The lights above then become clearer—losing their fuzz—to the point where I can nearly read them. I squint my eyes to follow the letters. They're shop signs in fluorescent lights.

"Stop."

I look beside me, and the old woman commands a presence. My feet stop moving and I jolt in her direction out of fear. All else fades, except for her. Her white hair floats over her ears.

"Phoenix," she begins more softly, "you're searching for your father in the wrong places. You cannot waste any more time, my child. You cannot. You are more important to those around you than you know. Do you understand?"

I swallow sharply as I attempt to nod. Panic crawls over me. But as I continue to stare up at the old woman, the dark red and black flickers into a fluorescent focus. It's a sign, and I can almost make out what it says.

"You, like all of my children, have less time than you think. None of us can continue to wait for the answers we've been put here to discover."

It takes more out of me than I thought anything ever could. It takes all of the energy out of every joint and muscle in my body to finally say just one thing. The exhaustion flattens me like a truck.

"Who are you?"

But before she answers, I fade out as I can read the fluorescent sign we've stopped in front of. It's a sign in that same deep red writing. A name. A simple name.

Maya's.

"Who am I? Phoenix? It's me. It's me...Shay," I heard Shay say to me in a confused jumble of panic and fear.

I then felt TT come to my shoulders to calm me down.

"H-He's been doing very well. S-Sorry about that."

I continued to look down fiercely, trying to shake off what just happened. Slowly, I said, "I don't know. I don't know."

I peered up, and Shay looked like she felt bad for me. Startled and unaware of what else to say in response.

But my mind wandered on to what she had to be thinking. What I knew she had to think of me. That I was some freak.

I watched her pink shoes turn and glide away as I looked over at TT. He was a good enough friend to try and cover for me, but this was different. I had no idea how either of us could have possibly talked our way out of that.

"C-Come on. W-We should get you a sip of water before English."

~

I did well on our quiz about the first four chapters of *The Great Gatsby*, scoring a 98%. I only got one question wrong, and I realized it right after I'd turned it in.

The question was "What sits in the valley between the East and

West Egg?" I'd quickly answered that it was Gatsby's mansion, being that it was symbolically caught between two worlds. But I was wrong. The correct answer was an ash heap.

At lunch, TT and I sat down at our normal table in the back. He quickly demolished a hot dog with chili-cheese that he'd bought at the cafeteria. The bun was bursting with roasted onions and green peppers. I got started with my new B Semester notecards.

"I-I wish my dad worked at the school. I-It would be so cool to see him all the time."

Without looking up from my cards, I said pointedly, "It's not as cool as you'd think. He's pretty busy anyway."

"O-Oh," TT fumbled slowly. I instantly felt terrible and realized why I should have never said anything like that.

"How are your parents doing?" I asked, hoping to undo some of the damage and show him my interest in carrying on our conversation.

TT's mother had died a few years ago, but his dad worked a lot and was never around. His dad remarried too. TT was close with his dad and stepmom, and they were really nice people, but he and his mom had had a different relationship. It really messed him up. I didn't know him when she was alive, but he'd explained to me that he developed language problems after she'd passed. That's also how he and I met.

"Th-They are good. Th-They travel all the time, but you have to come over soon and check out our new house."

TT's dad was loaded. He owned a bunch of hotels all over the state and made a killing.

"Maybe once I can catch up on some of my spelling."

I continued to flip through another couple of cards, while TT was busy licking the chili off his fingers, which made a disgusting slurping noise. I looked up quickly to scold him as he broke my concentration.

"TT, stop—"

But then my eyes stopped my tongue. I looked past TT and saw a clear view of Shay sitting next to Pounds. They were having lunch. Together.

The two of them laughed and exchanged casual banter back and forth. I did a double-take and TT could tell something was up.

"Wh-What is it?"

Like watching a distracted driver roll into a busy intersection, the obvious catastrophe was hard not to watch. All I could do was just sit and hold my breath. I couldn't take my eyes off them. He smiled at her, and she smiled back. Their hands and knees touched under the lunch table. He would look away, and she would look into him. His attention would drift, but she remained locked onto whatever spewed out of his throat. But none of that was the worst part. The worst part was that, for as long as I'd known Shay, I'd never seen her look happier.

Then Pounds got up for a moment, and I thought about going over to her and saying something. Warning her. Letting her know that she'd been misled. I wasn't mad; I just felt like someone needed to tell her.

I stood up. I could do this. I could protect her. But as I rose to my feet, she looked right at me, deep into my eyes, and her disgust was impossible to miss. Revulsion. As if she'd just seen a freak.

"Hey, everyone!" Pounds began as he leapt onto an empty lunch table. The entire cafeteria stopped and looked toward him.

"I've got an announcement to make!" he screamed.

My heart throbbed. I began to sweat all over. I felt sick and helpless. The whole cafeteria instantly went quiet. Every pair of eyes in sight focused right on him, except mine. I couldn't stop looking at her.

"I have a very special question to ask a very special person. Mind helping me out, boys?" Pounds boomed.

A whole slew of football players appeared from out of nowhere, holding flowers. Bouquets of all different types were in each of their hands.

"Shaylin Alex Stexton, will you be my Snowball?"

The entire cafeteria *oohed* and *awed* at Pounds and his show. Then they all shot to Shay, who was blushing like mad. She was overwhelmed by the attention. The other football players walked toward Shay and gave her all of the flowers.

But she didn't immediately say anything, which was all I needed.

"No!" I shouted at the top of my lungs, then I shouted a second time, "No!"

The cafeteria went even more silent than before. All of the eyes that had been on Shay shot toward me. Everyone in the entire cafeteria was looking right at me. Everyone but her.

"What?!" Pounds yelled, turning toward me.

But I kept staring right at her. Expecting Shay to somehow thank me for saving her, I instead received a look. A look I'd seen on her face only one other time before. The last perfect thing I'd ever seen in this broken world.

"Hey! Phoenix! I'm talking to you!" Pounds said, standing atop the lunch table I'd been sitting at. It yanked me from my memory. He repeated, "I'm talking to you, freak!"

I stood up to find Pounds and his clenched fist inches away from my face.

"Did you really think you could get in the way of me and Shay?! That I wasn't gonna have a problem with it?!"

He got even closer to me, ready to crush me in one drop of his fist, when Shay screamed from afar, "Leave him alone!"

Pounds let his guard down only for a moment. Then he caught a glimpse of my necklace with the Key of Courage and ripped it off my neck, admiring it in his filthy hands.

"Fine. Only 'cause she's watching. I'll just take this instead of beating your face in."

He then jumped off of the table and started to walk away when Tyler came out of nowhere and stopped him. He took his hands off his backpack and said to Pounds in a snarl, "Give that back to him. It's not yours."

"Of course, you two are friends. Now it all makes perfect sense." Pounds laughed.

Tyler went for his backpack and began to unzip the top. My heart dropped.

"What?" Pounds simply laughed Tyler off and looked around the cafeteria, which was now packed.

But Tyler stopped and didn't say anything else.

"That's what I thought."

Pounds just laughed and kept walking. He only took one more step before Tyler shoved him with both hands. Pounds went hard to the ground.

All of the kids around us laughed and pointed at him on the floor. Pounds got to his feet and pulled his fist back, winding up to smack Tyler, when a coach showed up.

"Knock it off! Are you kidding me with this?" The coach grabbed hold of Pounds. "What are you doing?! Don't be stupid, Pounds. You're the one with everything to lose."

Pounds nodded slowly and tried to play it off as cleanly as he could, dusting off his jacket.

Once Pounds saw the coach was gone and the crowd dispersed, he turned to me and Tyler with a smug look on his face. "You want this stupid necklace so bad? Meet me at my house tonight. I'm having a party. You freaks ever been to one of those? Come, and I'll kick your ass where there aren't any parents to protect you."

He shoved Tyler hard in his chest and stormed off with Shay. The crowd that had gathered around the cafeteria was now completely gone.

I turned toward Tyler, struggling through a shiver in my voice. "Thanks."

Tyler's long dark hair hung over his eyes. He looked toward me slowly. "Next time, I won't be there."

I nodded as TT stood beside me. We both looked at one another and didn't say anything else.

In speech therapy class afterward, I tried to forget about everything that had happened. I couldn't believe what an embarrassing start to high school this had been thus far.

I frivolously jotted down my notes when I was interrupted by a student next to me.

"What you and your friends did to that guy was so cool. He's the worst."

I thought he was talking to someone else when he then added, "Sorry... Name's Ronnie."

TT joined in. "H-He's lucky that coach stepped in. I-I was going to pummel him next."

Ronnie laughed, and TT put out his hand. "T-TT, and this is Phoenix."

Ronnie looked like a nice kid and all, but I didn't recognize him, which is odd for Darling. He had a huge smile and seemed to laugh at everything. It was kind of annoying.

"Where are you from?" I asked while continuing to take notes.

"Chicago. Me and my mom just moved here. I live over in Westchester County, but my mom really wanted me to go to Darling High."

Ronnie gave off the impression that he was harmless. His braces were hardly intimidating, and with all that metal in his mouth, it made you feel like nothing he said could really be all that serious.

"And what's your problem?" I asked, probably cutting a little bit too deep, so I elucidated, "I mean, why are you in ST?"

"I'm a pretty slow learner, especially with words."

Ronnie looked around the class again and asked, "Say, I don't have anyone to eat lunch with since I'm new and all. Do ya mind if I eat with you guys from now on?"

TT and I looked at each other, perplexed, not having understood why he was asking us. We'd never had anyone ever *ask* to be our friends.

I spoke up. "We're not really the cool kids, you know. We don't normally do stuff like that."

Ronnie just looked up at me and smiled. "Since when are the cool kids actually cool?"

TT and I couldn't help but laugh. Easily and openly, the three of us laughed together.

~

Back at Metropolis that night, I thought about going to Pounds's party, but I didn't even know how I'd get there. Mom met me after school that day, which meant Dad was out working. We didn't talk much as we walked home.

It was Friday night, and I spent it doing what I normally did on Friday nights, practicing. After starting my new B Semester words this morning, I began working my way deeper into the pile.

When I was inside the Bird's Nest, at my desk, going over my words, nobody could hurt me. My tunnel vision would come, and the focus would bring me one step closer to my goal. The bad people couldn't find me, and life became simple—fair. A vowel, a trick, a word to describe an action.

The letters would fly in, and I could put the pieces together. Chrysanthemum, idiosyncrasy, demitasse, and logorrhea. All these words that—when in my mind—brought me quietude. A secret method of peace that, if I practiced enough, I could access anywhere. At a moment's notice, I could use. A place I'd long wished I could just live in forever, hiding from the rest of the world that seemed to constantly be on fire.

There were rules that I'd been able to memorize and make sense of. Each rule came with a specific set of guidelines, and the one who worked the hardest came out on top. Life wasn't at all like that.

People with money got jobs, pretty girls only dated those guys, and together they made mean kids, who never had to work hard or get good grades. People didn't look out for each other. There were no rules or guidelines to live by. Most people only remembered all the bad things that happened to them and forgot all the good.

People thought that the world was out to get them, when really, it was people who were out to get the world.

If I'd learned anything in my life, it was this—that the sick remained sick, the rich remained rich. That nothing was fair, and then, after all of that, and once you finally crossed the finish line, you died. You became nothing. You did all this suffering your whole life to become ashes, dust even. And that was if you were lucky; some people didn't even live long enough to become that.

But spelling wasn't like that. Words came into our lives to define a situation. Words were used to provide clarity. It didn't matter how smart you were, because anybody could become good if they worked hard. You could practice anywhere, and if you practiced a lot, you could maybe even become memorable. You could maybe become good enough to inspire someone. Maybe even help someone. And if you could do that in anything, then, well, I think you should.

So, rather than spending my time doing things that didn't make much sense to me, I decided I'd stick with what did. A Friday night, at my desk, spelling, and away from anybody that could hurt me, sounded like a party. At least here, some of it made sense. At least here, I had some control over what happened.

But I thought about how stupid I'd looked in front of Shay today and how I couldn't even stand up for her in front of Pounds. How, when he approached me, all I could do was sink into myself. But not Tyler. Tyler was strong enough to scare Pounds back, and if he could do it, then so could I.

Something inside of me started to change. I think when you get mud kicked into your face enough, you get sick of hiding. The wounds were getting so deep they couldn't properly heal, and even at my desk, I was beginning to feel less and less safe. The change came quick and hot. It was an emotion that I'd never felt so strongly. It was *anger*. Anger so bright and hot there was only one way to quench it.

The Ferry pulled into the driveway late that night, loose gravel dancing beneath its bow. The headlights cut off quietly, and my dad did his best not to make a peep.

When he walked in, I heard his keys jingle on his waist as he lifted them up and placed them on the Banking District Skyscraper (the mantel) beside the closet door. Without thinking about it, I rubbed the spot on my chest where the Key of Courage used to call home.

As my dad entered the second story of Metropolis, I heard his usual deep sigh. His bedroom door swung open, shut, and then locked behind him. The shower started. I heard the errant droplets tapping the tile.

The lights flickered. Making a soft crackling, they came off and on.

I sat quietly with my cards for another moment as the lights returned to normal. I decided that, tonight, I was going to make my mark. I wasn't going to let that bully poison Shay or anybody else. Those days were about to be over.

Reaching for my jacket, I stepped out into the hall. The lights were on but dim. Step by step, I crept until I saw the keys atop the Banking District Skyscraper. With my eyes closed, as if to give myself plausible deniability, I grabbed them and exited Metropolis.

Outside, I looked back and already felt a sense of longing for the Bird's Nest. Longing for the warmth that even its flaws provided ached inside of me—the scratch on my nightstand from a rogue pen that had stabbed it months ago. The missing third handle on my drawer that we lost transferring it from Goodwill. Scars of a place lived. But I had to do something. Sweet revenge was at the tip of my fingers. With each step, I was conflicted with both the rush of warm blood through my cold veins and betrayal for having forgone my studies.

I unlocked the Ferry and hopped into the captain's seat. It smelled like him. His musk brought with it a sort of comfort, despite my swirling insides. Then, a light inside the house. There was movement.

My hands were still sore from the burns of hot water. Suddenly, they began to ache in pain. I couldn't hang onto the keys. I didn't have much time. Then, I dropped them, and my feet kicked them underneath the seat. I was going to be made any second now. But when my hands crawled under the seat in search of the keys, they felt something else. Something that I couldn't believe until I had it right before my eyes. As if my hands were trying to prove to myself that they hadn't been lying.

As my fingertips traced its exterior and brought it out from beneath the driver's seat, there was no denying what it was. It was what I had hoped for all along.

A gun.

7

My hands were gripping a machine made for killing. I didn't think it would be this heavy. The cold steel burned my skin. I wondered as I studied each corner and structural design, had this gun ever ended a life?

It came in a flash.

The deep red, fluorescent sign of Maya's flashes so brightly into my eyes it burns. I can feel each individual letter of this bodega shine at me—coming in and out of focus. The fuzz around them abates, then returns. Maya's is all that it says and all I can see.

I try to put my hand out in front to shield myself from the harshness of the light, but then I hear her voice again above.

"No matter the pain, we must all see. These are things we cannot hide from, Phoenix. Not you. Not me. Not your father."

Her booming voice startles me, sounding like it's coming from a place beyond the clouds. Somewhere otherworldly. My hand comes down to my side, and I stare at the sign until it finally comes into focus without any more pain. In front of me, a chiming door swings open on its own. A bell above the trim sounds.

Inside, it's a normal-looking corner store. A random assortment of goods populates the shelves of the aisles. But for being such a small shop, it looks as though they sell literally everything. Scotch tape, hand sanitizer, a sack of potatoes, and books are all in the same aisle closest to the door. The building feels just as old on the inside as it appears on the outside.

Picking through aisles, the intricacy of the store reminds me a lot of Metropolis.

"Yes, this is your home. Because it's everyone's, my child. Eventually, Phoenix, we all come home."

But I'm alone. No one else is inside.

Then, the power inside, all of it, shuts off in a loud whoosh. All, except for the red glow of a large vending machine inside remains. The buzz of the machine is now the only sound inside the store, its glow the only light.

I walk toward it and stand before its red glow. I stare at it, searching for something that I cannot find. All the buttons look like regular vending machine buttons, but I'm drawn to it. Like a heavenly call from above.

I gasped. My eyes shot open, and suddenly I was still holding my dad's gun behind the wheel of the Ferry. I tossed it onto the passenger seat beside me as if I'd been bitten by a wild cobra, my hands throbbing from the venom.

Pulling the Ferry onto the road, I feel the darkness still. Everything feels heavier, my fingers on the leather, my feet in my shoes, my lungs in my chest. It was getting harder. Gravity became thick. At the same rate, I thought about Tyler and protecting myself. As terrified as I was, when I'd had the gun in my hands, I felt powerful, invincible. I felt brave. I felt it and it felt good. Nobody could push me down and stomp all over my notecards if I had that in my possession. Something needed to change. Somebody had to do something, because bad things were happening all the time everywhere. I'd sat on the sidelines long enough, waiting. Waiting for someone else to tell me what to do. Waiting for it to be my turn. Waiting for girls to like me. Waiting to make friends. Waiting to have nice things. Waiting, it seemed, was the only thing I'd truly done in my life. Waiting day and night, waiting for everything to happen for me, waiting that had gotten me nowhere.

Arriving at Pounds's house, something kept pulling me forward. Telling me to carry on, even though all I really wanted to do was go back home. But you can't always be in control all the time. Too many things happen for that to always be the case. All sorts of unnatural and unexplainable things happen each day. Sometimes something stronger than yourself takes hold. It pushes you, even when you don't want it to.

I stepped out of the Ferry, and tucked the gun into my coat pocket, leaving my finger on the trigger. Even though I'd parked a few houses down, I could hear the bass from down the street. The closer I got, the more red Solo cups I saw polluting the neighboring hedges.

The weapon felt heavy in my pocket, and as I walked, I felt like everyone could see it inside the fabric of my clothes. But nobody said anything.

Walking through the doors of Pounds's house, my heart began to race. The music was so loud I could hardly think. Bodies now flew all around me. There was a strange smell in the air that was really strong. My nose stung. It was dark, but it looked like everyone else couldn't see either, because they were all knocking into each other. As I walked through the crowd, my eyes began to adjust. I didn't look up as I walked and just stared at the floor beneath me, but I was slowly starting to recognize everyone's feet. I was in the right place.

Although there were people all around me, I slowly started to feel alone again. The darkness was closing in on me. The smell was so strong that it made me feel sick. The breath of the hot bodies around me made me nauseous. I felt wobbly. I couldn't tell, for a moment, if I was still walking or standing in one place.

It was all becoming too much.

Pounds.

I closed my eyes and rubbed the steel of the gun.

Pounds.

Internally, I was about to combust. I was so terrified at how trapped I was starting to feel.

Pounds.

Everywhere I looked and everywhere I went, he was all I could see.

Pounds.

Snapping my eyes shut to hide was my only option. The letters flew in.

P...O...U...N...D...S

But it was so loud and so dark that no one could see my internal cry for help. My eyes flashed open, and I was surrounded.

"Yeah?" a body I'd bumped into said to me in a warped tone.

I was so lost I couldn't say anything back, but the person got closer to me, looking into my eyes—close enough to examine every pore and follicle. My finger tensed around the gun.

"No way...Phoenix? What are you doing here? Let me get you something to drink."

I shook my head. I knew who this person was. Elliot, a sophomore at Darling, who was always pleasant to me in private but acted like he didn't know me around everybody else.

I finally responded, "Pounds."

"Oh, it's his house, you know. Check his room upstairs. I'll bet he's in there." And he pointed at a winding staircase off to the side of the living room, then added, "But make sure to knock, if you know what I mean."

I headed up the stairs and down the hall. Pounds wasn't anywhere I could see.

Somehow it felt even darker up there. From my vantage point, now atop the staircase, I looked down at the party's rhythmic tide.

Swaying to the music, all of them came and went as the lights bounced off their shoulders.

Before taking another step, I carefully peeled my pocket open to make sure the gun was still there. My pointer finger still rested over the trigger. It felt cold.

There were several bedrooms upstairs, a few of them with lights on. People were sparse, but everyone upstairs looked like the older kids from school. Their eyes looked empty, the smell on their breath even stronger. People all over the place were acting strange. Talking and laughing louder than usual.

The first room I came across was nearest to the staircase on the left. As I creaked open the door, I felt my hand on the gun begin to shake. I flipped on the lights, but no one was inside.

As I took my first step, my eyes tracked up. The room was perfectly set. So perfect it looked almost staged—as though nobody had stepped foot inside of it for years. Almost every single thing was pink. Pink walls and pink pillow covers. Photos adorned the shelves, and medals hugged the walls. This wasn't Pounds's room. This room belonged to a girl. Probably a little girl.

My fingertips left the gun for the first time and made their way to a photograph. Pure joy was captured within its frame. An encapsulated memory. It felt strange to be in this room and even stranger to be looking so deeply at this photo. It all just felt a little too private.

I exited to hear a commotion going on down the hall. As a result, I carried on with a bit more caution.

The next room was also empty, but it was the polar opposite of the first. A tornado of clothes found themselves tossed into each spot of the bedroom. The space smelled like a sweaty gym sock. This had to be it.

I took another step inside when I saw the pants that Pounds had been wearing earlier at school. In his back pocket was the Key of Courage. I quickly slipped it into my back pocket and placed the pants down.

But as I softly put them back, I saw a glimmer of something else that I'd seen earlier that day—Shay's pink sneakers. I let out a deep exhale. Second-guessing everything, I pulled my hand off the gun and rubbed them both against my sweats. I then picked up her shoes and realized I had no idea what I was doing or why I was even here. I wanted to cry. I felt instantly cold and dark. I fell onto the bed and just sat there, breathing. My head was in my palms as I tried to slow everything down, realizing I'd had no plan whatsoever.

I looked around the bedroom again before eventually leaving to see if anyone had been close by, but no one was in sight. The hall outside was empty.

With my necklace in my pocket and the key back, I walked out of Pounds's room when I heard a shriek—a cry for help. The noise came from what was probably the master bedroom several feet away. As I got closer, I heard the same voice call out again.

Once close enough to the door, I slowly pressed my ear up against it to get a better listen to what was going on. I heard the voice again, only this time I could recognize that it was Shay's. A voice I'd come to know better than my own.

"Stop," she repeated, then got quieter. "We shouldn't. You've had too much tonight."

Then a laugh, a girl's laugh, that sounded like her, followed by another "Stop" once more.

I paused and thought again about what had happened at school earlier that day. I didn't want to make the same mistake, but I let my hand go back to the gun in my pocket. Knowing that it was time to put an end to all of this, I heard her say the name that had been haunting me for as long as I could remember.

"Pounds. You gotta stop."

I didn't wait another second before bursting through the door.

It was Pounds and Shay lying beside one another with their clothes on in his parents' bed. Even though I'd startled them, Shay appeared to be totally fine. I quickly realized nothing was going on that warranted my barging in.

Shay recognized me before he did. "Phoenix?! What are you doing here?"

I quickly stumbled over my own words. "I heard…he was hurting you…"

Shay was still shocked as she said, "What? Why would you…?"

"I…you said stop…but…"

Pounds sat up angrily, adjusting his shorts. "Is this kid serious!?!?"

My hand clenched the gun, wrapping around the grip. I kept my eyes locked on him as he got out of the bed and made his first move toward me. My wrist flexed.

I took one more small step back when I saw the anger in Pounds's eyes. My breathing quickened. My heart pounded. He was about to make a move, so I went for it. I pulled the gun out and pointed it right at him.

But just as the gun left the safety of my coat pocket, all the lights snapped off. In one loud whoosh, the power went completely out in the entire house. It was pitch black.

"Phoenix!" I heard Pounds force his way through the darkness toward me.

I couldn't see anything, and behind Pounds's heavy breathing, the party downstairs groaned. Through the black, my fear grew.

"Phoenix, I'm going to kill you! You hear me, freak!"

I had no idea where he was in the darkness, but I could feel the heaviness of the gun aimed his general direction. A trigger-pull away from all my problems disappearing for good. Ending the worst person and saving the best.

As Pounds continued to snarl, I trained the gun in the direction of his voice. With each noise that came from him, I focused the gun in the dark, through the instinct, drive, and pain that had been building inside me for so long. I was living out the fantasy I'd imagined in that bathroom stall. I took another deep breath as I contemplated the decision, hanging onto what I could and wondering how I would get out of here alive after I did it.

But it was Shay's voice that shocked me back into reality. "Phoenix…don't listen to him. Don't listen to anyone, Phoenix. No one is going to hurt you."

In the complete darkness, I slid the gun into my pocket, and took my finger off the trigger.

A wave of guilt flooded over me. I started to panic in a mixture of blurriness and tears. I started to profusely cry. I slowly backpedaled toward the direction of the door, and the power snapped back on. At first, it startled me, but then I saw Pounds. His eyes were trained on me. He was ready to attack. I took off in a storm of tears, frantic, running as fast as I possibly could. He wasn't trailing far behind me, his breathing heavy, as we tumbled out of the master bedroom and down the spiraling staircase.

"This ends tonight!" he growled between breaths.

With the power back on, the madness of the party resumed. I pushed through the tide of people downstairs as quickly as I could, blasting through what felt like thousands of shoulders and elbows until I was at the front door. I burst through, coughing and wheezing in the cold air outside. But despite my lungs feeling like they were on the verge of exploding, I kept running. I ran harder and harder, without looking back, until I finally made it to the Ferry. I juggled the keys in the door until I got it open, then I started up the Ferry and peeled onto the road, the tires screeching behind me.

I was breathing hard, fogging up the windshield, my hands on the steering wheel. For the first time, I turned to see the house on my left as I drove by, but it was strange then, looking at all of them. It seemed none of them had noticed my frantic exit, because it seemed none of them had noticed anything, ever.

There was nothing there; even the people seemed absent.

~

I didn't live far from Pounds, but I decided to drive around and cool off. As I eventually caught my breath, I thought a lot about what had happened.

I thought about how, in trying to do something brave, I'd only made everything worse. My anxiety, fear, and depression had only entrenched themselves further into my body, digging in and making their long-term stay even longer. I was running out of options and fearing that, pretty soon, there would only be one option left. Because, eventually, something had to change, and somebody had to make this stop.

I thought about how I seemed to be the only one who could see how screwed up everything was and how I was the only one trying to do something. It made me sink deeper into my seat as I drove, realizing

I was also the only one on the road. Not a single other car was in sight.

But you're all alone in life. You're the only one who experiences those pearls of good that come and go like the Christmas holidays. But like those days at the end of each December, they are just that—days. The rest of the year, you're all alone to put all the pieces together and deal with the reality that there is more pain, suffering, regret, and hurt than anything good. And it's just you to deal.

It was nearly three in the morning by the time I arrived back at Metropolis. I inched up the driveway and placed the car in park. My eyes shot toward my parents' bedroom window, but the blinds were closed, and all the lights were off inside the house. Metropolis looked still in the night.

Carefully, I peeled open the car door and slid it shut behind me. I made sure to pick up my feet with each slow step through the gravel to the front door.

But suddenly, it didn't matter how quiet I was. When I slowly creaked open the front door, the lights burst on. My dad had been sitting in the dark, waiting. He looked deeply at me; his eyes froze me in place. My dad was wearing a dark suit and an even darker tie. He appeared to be wide awake.

"Where were you?"

I couldn't say anything. I couldn't think. Because when I saw him, my hands fell into my coat pockets. And as they felt around inside them, I realized my dad's gun was gone.

8

I was still so startled that I didn't have his gun, in a panic, I just told him the truth.

"I took the Ferry out."

My dad stood up, emptying out his cold coffee in the sink and filling his mug with water. "You cannot take my car like that, son. I need it for work."

I nodded. I could tell that he wasn't upset. He remained stoic and calm—per usual. Somehow his demeanor upset me.

"Maybe I wouldn't take your car if I knew what you actually needed it for," I said with more anger than I'd intended.

There was still so much about what my dad did at night that I didn't understand. I didn't know why he left so late, or even where he went. I didn't know why he wouldn't tell me, and I didn't know why he couldn't just go back to being a police officer. But, worst of all, I didn't know why he'd always seemed so happy to leave.

He placed his mug down on the counter. "I've told you countless times, Phoenix, I help people with their power. You know how bad our electricity gets."

"But you used to be a cop!" I shouted back. "Now you...help fix people's power in the middle of the night? I don't believe you. I don't believe that's what you're doing."

It came out of me so quickly that I hardly realized all I'd said. To hear my own voice admit these suppressed insecurities shocked me. My dad looked back at me without saying anything.

Then, I added more softly, "Dad. You are too smart to do such a pointless job. It doesn't make sense."

My dad sighed and scratched his cheek before bringing his tone to a gentler level. "If a man is called to be a street sweeper, he should sweep the streets, even as Michelangelo painted, or Beethoven composed music, or Shakespeare wrote poetry. He should sweep streets so well that all hosts of heaven and Earth pause to say, 'Here lives a great street sweeper, who did his job and did his job well.'" He paused, catching me even more deeply with his eyes. "Martin Luther King Jr. said that, not too long ago, when he wasn't much more than a street sweeper himself." My dad continued, "Son, no man or woman is too stupid to do any job. No job is pointless. We're not above anybody, and it's a mistake to think as much. I've raised you better. We're all just…people. People who love. People who laugh. People who…die."

My dad's feet shuffled, and I could see the book with the wings emblem he'd always kept with him on the counter. He protected it with his hand.

"Most people forget that."

"And how do you know…all of this?" I asked accusatorily.

He smiled. "Your grandmother taught me. And someday, I will teach you."

Somehow that made me feel better, I guess. I wanted to believe there was more to it. More to him, more to what he was doing and, honestly, more to everything in general. Although, lately, life had been disappointing me the more that I stopped to look around.

I was about to walk up the stairs when my dad called out my name. It sent a quick terror up my spine when I remembered his gun was missing. I had no idea what I was going to do about that. I slowly turned toward him.

"You're not going to get much sleep tonight, are you?" he asked.

I shook my head.

"Why don't you come with me then? I can show you what I really do."

I stood there silently for a moment, contemplating what my best course of action would be. At least then I'd be able to keep an eye on him.

"Yeah, sure," I said, hoping to sound normal.

Grabbing his hat in his left hand and his notebook in his right, he walked toward me and ruffled my hair. Then he continued to walk toward the front door of Metropolis and open it. But he stopped in the doorway and turned to look at me while saying out of the corner of his mouth, "Well, come on then."

~

It was strange being out on the road. There was an eeriness driving around town at this hour.

As my dad and I drove, he reached for the radio and turned our favorite Harry Chapin on, but he never went under his seat for the gun. Every time he shifted his weight slightly or let his hands move at all, though, I gulped.

Cutting through the streets, eventually a fresh excitement replaced my fear—this was going to be it. For so long, I'd wondered about my dad and what he was up to. Why he was out every night and what doing his other job really looked like. A part of me couldn't wait to find out.

I figured I'd keep his mind occupied, though, just to be safe. "Why do you have to work so late…or is it early?"

He laughed. "I work all the time, Phoenix."

"What about sleep?"

"You'll see as you age. The older you get, the less you sleep. What happens is you start to realize how little time you actually get."

"What do you mean?"

He happily continued, "Time. When you're young, you feel like you have all of it in the world. But nobody does. Not even you. As you get older, son, you start to realize all that you'd like to do, and eventually, even sleep becomes something that gets in the way of all of that."

As we drove, we pulled to a stop outside Darling High School.

"Wait here. I'll only be a minute." He jumped out of the Ferry and headed toward his office at school. It was on the outskirts of campus, so even when the school was locked up at night, he could walk right over. Shuffling his key into the door, he pulled it open. He wasn't gone long, and we were back in the car driving again.

"Sorry," he said, once we'd pulled away. "Forgot something."

"Is this what you always wear to work?" I asked.

He nodded.

"And why, out of all the jobs, did you pick this one? Weren't there plenty of other cooler jobs you could've been doing for extra money?"

My dad looked at me and smiled, as if it was the simplest question he'd ever been asked. "Have you ever heard the parable of the three bricklayers?"

I took my gaze from out the window and wiped my eyes. "No,

what's that?"

My dad reached down toward his window to roll it up before he began. "Three different bricklayers are asked, 'What are you doing?' The first says, 'I'm laying bricks.' The second says, 'I'm building a church.' And the third says, 'I'm creating the house of God.' The first bricklayer has a job. The second a career. The third a calling."

My dad paused before finishing his sentiment.

"When you're lucky enough to be alive, your occupation is irrelevant. Anything you do, no matter the pay, you do it, son, and you do it well."

And I could see it now. My dad moved through life with a freedom I'd never seen in anyone else before. As if each small task was building toward something even greater.

"Why?" I asked.

My dad turned toward me before etching something into my memory. "Because. Think of a world where everyone acted that way."

After driving for a half hour, my dad pulled the Ferry onto a side street and parked along the sidewalk.

"Here. Come in with me."

I looked around from inside the safety of our car. I saw how rundown the neighborhood we were in was. We were all the way on the other side of town.

My dad let out a small laugh. "Trust me, son, it's safe. We'll be fine."

But as I followed my dad around the corner, the cracked sidewalks closed in around me. The trash in the street made me feel a déjà vu so deep in my bones they twitched in pain. Like a bolt of lightning just went through me. Because across the street, in the direction we were going, there was a sign. A sign with wooden infrastructure jutting out of the top of the roof. A sign that flickered in red fluorescent light in front of a small convenience store.

Maya's.

My heart began to beat in my chest so violently I nearly fell over. All the blood in my body rushed to my head, and I fell into the side of my dad's leg.

"Woah, woah. What's the matter, son? You look like you just saw a ghost."

My dad got close enough to my face that I could feel his hot breath on my cheek.

"Phoenix? Are you having another episode?" he asked.

I blinked my eyes again and again, but this wasn't any episode, this was real. I was here. We were here.

I swallowed hard before finally replying, "What...what is this... place?"

My dad turned toward Maya's again and then looked back at me. "What? Maya's? It's an old hangout of mine. I've been coming here for years, even back when I was a police officer. Which is why I wanted to take you here, show you how I start each of my days."

My dad waited another moment as I slowly collected myself. I was still so shocked that it was hard for me to listen to anything he was saying.

"Here, let's walk in together. Okay?" he said, slowly taking my hand.

The same bell I'd heard in my vision chimed when my dad opened the door. Inside, it was the same small shop that looked as though they sold everything. The building felt the same as when I'd been here the hundreds of times in my head.

Following my dad closely, I saw a few others picking at shelves.

"This place...this place is open right now?" I struggled to ask.

My dad put his hand around my shoulder as we continued to walk. "Maya's is always open. And it's really like a secondary home to most of the people here, Phoenix. A haven. A safe place where all are welcome."

Uneasiness returned then as I remembered all the years of visions and fears that had occupied my mind since my birthday party five years ago. That woman I'd always seen and how afraid I'd been. But to be here, now, with him, only made me even more confused. Because, despite my fears, there was nothing special about this place at all. This was no haven, as my dad said, but a place that sold all the things you'd forgotten to buy.

I was getting dizzier the longer I looked around. But then, my dad took us right up to the same red vending machine I'd been drawn to in my vision just hours ago. Standing before it scrambled my mind. I felt like, for some reason, the vending machine could hear everything I was thinking.

"I'll be right back, okay? Don't worry, you're safe here, I promise. Now, go and pick something out for breakfast if you'd like."

My attention wandered for a short moment, but when I turned around, my dad was gone.

My eyes found the others walking around inside. Each of them moved with an energetic pace, but that wasn't the strangest part. As I continued to look at each of them, I noticed that they were dressed in the exact same clothes as my dad.

Pacing around the store, hoping to occupy my mind, I moved from aisle to aisle—looking at several items. Eventually, I wandered into an aisle of all different sorts of CDs. I saw *Abbey Road* by the Beatles, *Tattoo You* by the Rolling Stones, and *Every Picture Tells a Story* by Rod Stewart. But *Verities & Balderdash* by Harry Chapin immediately caught my eye. Reaching for it, I took the CD in my hands and read the track list on the back.

Putting the CD down, I kept walking through the store as I waited, hoping the woman in the white belt would appear and explain to me what it all meant. But as I moved closer to the front door again, this time, I noticed what looked like a memorial. It was a framed photo of a little boy. In the photo, his smile spoke. On the wood of the frame, it had a silver plaque that read, "Aloanso Woodle. 4-22-1982 to 6-10-1994." Flowers sat on the floor beneath the frame, and a small candle burned. But I reread the date a second time as my eye caught it, and then a third. The day he died was my birthday.

"Ready?" my dad said, startling me. "Sorry buddy, but we should get going, we've…"

My confusion only grew when I turned toward my dad and saw that he, too, looked like all the life had suddenly been sucked out of him. All the color from his face drained, and a lost look came over his eyes. He stopped talking and went blank, overwhelmed by something.

I kept looking into his eyes to see that glimmer I'd known so well return, but in an instant, it seemed his light had completely extinguished.

~

It started to rain. A light drizzle. Back in the car, neither of us said anything for a while, until my dad began to nibble on a tuna sandwich and a bag of Starbursts. To wash it all down, he had another mug of hot coffee.

Repulsed, I exclaimed, "That's your breakfast?"

"Breakfast of champions, son." He smirked.

"I didn't even see you pay for that or even anyone working the cash register," I said, fishing for more information.

"That's because everything at Maya's is free," he replied, taking a large gulp of his morning roast.

"What? Everything is *free*?"

My dad smiled widely. "Yes, sir."

"And…why do you always go there when it's such a…well, just sort of rundown place?"

My dad reached across the center console and placed his hand on my shoulder and said carefully, "Because, Phoenix, Maya's is the house of God. And I am one of the bricklayers."

As we slowed to a stop in front of a massive house, my dad reached into the glove box just above my knees and pulled out a radio. It was a massive contraption that had antennas and screens on it. He plugged it into his dashboard.

"What's that?" I asked.

"A radio scanner. I get traffic updates and police signals about what's going on in our immediate area."

"That's so cool," I said in awe.

"It's really cool." He flipped through some of the channels to show me. "Keep this secret between you and me…don't tell Mom."

I tried to smile—act normal, really—but then the thought about the gun missing from beneath his seat made me afraid again. My mind careened at the explanation I'd have to provide once he figured it out. I wasn't sure if I should just admit it now or continue to play dumb.

The sun gently began to rise over the horizon. It was still early, but glimmers of yellow and oranges hues washed across the windshield.

My dad got out of the car and opened the door to the backseat. Then, I looked closer at the house and realized that I'd been at this exact place just hours earlier. This was Pounds's house. Red Solo cups still polluted the street around us. The wreckage from the party last night had managed to harshly stain suburban life.

Behind the cover of the car door, my dad took off his coat and tie, and put on a greased mechanics shirt and toolbelt. Buckling it to his waist, I could see that he had wrenches, screwdrivers, and a tape measure. Aside from a few pens in his shirt pocket, the shirt looked worn and frayed at the left shoulder. As if he'd been using the same one for years.

Out of the house came a man in a blue blazer and raven black tie.

"Good morning, Mr. Francis."

"Morning, Herman," Mr. Francis said to my dad before going on. "Damn thing's busted again. My son thought it would be a good idea to have a party with half the town. Mind taking a look?"

"Sure thing."

Mr. Francis looked toward the car to see me in the passenger seat. I slid down below the window.

"And this is my boy, Phoenix."

I tried to act natural as Mr. Francis said to me, "Ah, I've heard all about you. Your father's told me that my son knows you well."

I kept my head down as I replied, "Yeah. Hello."

"Well, I'll be inside if you need anything. You know where it's at, Herm?"

"Yes, sir." My dad nodded. "I'll be right in."

Mr. Francis walked back toward his looming mansion. My dad shut the back door and came up to my window. I lifted my chin.

"I won't be too long, son. Just hang tight."

My dad could tell my mood had dropped. He added before walking off, "I'm really glad you're here."

Once my dad was inside the house, my heart began to race once more. I couldn't believe we were at Pounds's house, but now would be my only chance to try and find the missing gun. If I was lucky and found it, I could sneak it back under the seat before Dad returned.

I opened the door and frantically scanned the front lawn.

Throughout the wet grass, there were empty liquor bottles and cigarette butts everywhere. It was mostly just trash, but as I continued to retrace my steps from just hours before, my memory slowly returned. I was able to find the path I'd taken back out to the Ferry when I'd parked down the street. My footprints were still in place because of the rain and ice on the grass from the cold night.

Through trees, rocks, and all the trash, I went step by step as my dad continued to work inside. My breathing grew heavy as I searched as thoroughly as possible. Then, beside a small bush, I saw a glimmer of silver. In a bed of flowers, looking more like a shiny pipe than a steel barrel, was the gun. I looked around to make sure no one else was watching before I sank into a squat and scooped it up. I hurried back toward the Ferry. Once inside, I dried the gun as best I could with my shirt before slipping it back under his seat, just as I'd found it.

After the initial wave of relief faded, I began to feel a deep cloud of disappointment. Not just in myself, but in my dad too.

I wasn't sure what I was expecting to find out about my dad today, but thus far, it had been incredibly underwhelming. Because I sat there for another hour before my dad finally came back to the car and we left. I didn't even care then if he noticed the gun or not.

The rest of the day, we stopped at house after house all over town. Every time we arrived, my dad would put on his belt, and I would patiently wait in the car until he was done. That was what I did most of that day. Sometimes I would wait in silence, and other times I would watch him talk to whomever he was working for.

But as I watched my dad, I noticed that he found a fresh energy and warmth with each new person. He smiled, said hello, grabbed his belt, and greeted them as if they were family. He looked each of them in the eye as he talked and knew, not just their names, but all about them. The connections were genuine. One of them even started to cry when we got there. It was an old lady, and she hugged him like she'd never been happier to see anyone in her entire life. However, despite my dad's glowing positivity, my initial energy and excitement for the day arrived at an abrupt undeniable pile of disappointment.

It turns out that my dad was no bricklayer, but just a simple electrician. A school security guard by day and an electrician by night. And it turns out that my episodes were not of some holy house of God, but just of a simple corner store. A rundown bodega marred with trash and gutter water on the bad side of town.

I'd held out hope for so long that there was something more to, not just him, but everyone. Everything. There had to be something bigger and more important going on in this world; the hope couldn't be dead. But as I took my gaze out the window, the more buildings I saw that looked exactly the same. There was no hope, just stucco walls. But to me, that's how life had always been. My dad was wrong about the older you get. If he had asked me, I would have told him that the older you get, the more disappointing you find out all of it is. For the longest time, I'd never understood why it was that my dad had kept me from coming with him to work all this time, but now I knew. My dad understood that I wasn't ready to know until now—a truth he'd wanted to keep from me for as long as he could. The disappointment was true. I'd always held out the hope that he was different, but even my own dad hadn't been immune to the world's most infectious disease.

With age comes an unshakable lack of desire to become something. My dad was just another example of an adult. None of them much different from the other. A cycle that our world had been going through long before he'd even taken his first breath and was clearly showing no signs of slowing down.

All kids remember the time when they thought their dad was a superhero. All kids also remember the time when they realized that wasn't true.

9

I woke up before my dad and decided to walk to school alone. Outside, our first snow of the year had begun. It had let up just in time, but without looking, I stepped right into a pile of mud. My tan boots and laces were dripping from the mixture of soft snow and dirt.

My feet left a trail behind me. The seasonal shift brought with it a host of thoughts. Things in my head that had long been repressed, I flushed once more. Not now.

I arrived at the library an hour before school was set to start. It was my first time inside this part of the school. Walking through the entrance, round tables were individually set at each spot, and most of them were empty. But in the corner, I watched Shay—she was ferociously turning the pages of a book.

I'd always enjoyed watching people when they didn't realize anyone could see them. It wasn't to try and catch them in the act or anything weird like that, I just took a keen interest in seeing who they really were. You really are your truest self when you have no one to impress. When you see people with their guard down, it makes you feel like you may have some things in common. Perhaps they are as strange as you.

With the flurry of the world totally around Shay, she was undetectable. Lost in the Galápagos Islands or the Swiss Alps. The typed words on the page were her cheap escape—something she could call upon at a moment's notice to vanish in plain sight.

I took a table in the back so as not to disturb Shay and her escape. We all have our thing, our own world where we can be anyone or anything we want. Old people don't really care about that stuff, but it was important to me.

My attention wandered to all the other students in the library plucking at shelves. Quietly, everyone was up to something productive, it felt like. There were other freshman and even seniors too. Picking one of the aisles lowest to the ground, I saw Tyler. He and somebody else were all the way in the deepest corner. His long hair was tucked over his shoulders, a tie dangling from his neck. They were moving quicker than everybody else.

Looking toward him, I met Tyler's eyes. I immediately looked down. I felt my breathing accelerate.

Ronnie sat down beside me. I was about to let him know that I was in no mood to talk when he began loudly, "Heya, Phoenix! What happened to your boots?"

"Mud walking here," I said quickly. I turned to see if Tyler was still watching me. He was. The sight of his face made me look down again. His eyes felt like knives. I, instead, decided to focus on Ronnie's shoes. I noticed he was wearing red Timberland snow boots.

"Oh," Ronnie said, seeing I was looking at his feet. "Just got these. I'll try to be careful then myself."

He could tell I'd forced a smile. I just went back to reading my words.

"What are you looking at all of those cards for?" he asked.

"My B Semester words. I'm getting ready to compete in the Colorado State Spelling Bee next year."

"Woa...Woah. That's super neat!" Ronnie had gotten a little bit carried away. He quickly noticed and brought his volume back down. "I had no idea you were so smart. Is it...really hard to memorize *all* of those words?"

I smiled. "Not really. I've won our City Bee two years in a row, but—"

Ronnie cut me off. "What! That's amazing! Phoenix, two years in a row?"

I laughed before adding, "But...I've never won the State Bee. That tournament is pretty tough. It gets harder the further you get."

"I'll bet," Ronnie responded, still in visible awe.

Ronnie was sweet. Awkward? Sure. Acted like we were best friends too quickly? Probably. But I rubbed the Key of Courage, whose chain I had repaired after taking it back from Pounds, as I thought more about that old trashman from all those years ago, his chapped hands wrapped around the cans of garbage. For some reason, I never forgot the phrase he'd had me repeat. About letting go of my fear of being uncomfortable. About what my dad had always told me about talking to strangers.

In a calm then, I closed my eyes and silently recalled the phrase. Hoping to unlock some of the key's power.

I will not be afraid of what I do not know because what I do not know is the only thing keeping me from the place I would like to go.

Opening my eyes, I noticed the lights inside the library glimmered for a moment. They flickered off and then back on.

After the lights settled, I gathered myself and turned to meet Ronnie's eye. I saw a chance to open up to someone. "So. What are you doing here so early?" I asked simply.

Ronnie looked at me, surprised. "Oh. I...uh...had to get out of my house. My mom was getting mad at everything this morning."

I sighed. "I know the feeling."

Ronnie's expression suddenly grew darker. He looked as though he wanted to say something but wasn't sure if he should. It was strange to see someone I'd just met shift so abruptly. My mood, too, went darker as his spirit waned.

I placed my hand on Ronnie's shoulder as I explained, "My parents, they fight too. Well, mostly, it's my mom. She gets mad at my dad, but he usually never says anything back."

Ronnie was now the one looking down as he slowly responded, "That's why I'm here, in Darling, ya know…my parents just split. They started fighting a lot when I was sick in the hospital. I wanted to live with my dad, but my mom wouldn't allow it. He left Chicago the same time we did, and we can't really afford airplane tickets anymore because of all the medical bills. I…I don't know when I'm going to see him again."

"You were sick?"

Ronnie nodded. "Common variable immunodeficiency. Nobody's heard of it, but it's something I was born with. I lost all of my hair and everything from the medications. I was in the hospital for four months of isolation, too, when I was eight. I'm doing better now, but…but it's hard."

Initially, I didn't know what to say, but then, I knew what I had to. "I'm sorry. I'm…I'm much closer to my dad too." He looked up before I continued. "I always have been. He makes it all less confusing to me. I never feel like I have to wear a mask or try so hard. My dad makes me laugh and disguises cool life lessons for me in games and stories. My mom, she…she just doesn't get it." I stopped. I couldn't believe how much I'd just said, and Ronnie could tell.

"Don't worry, I'm like that also. But when she says mean things about him, it makes me really sad…that's why I'm here." Ronnie opened up his arms and motioned toward the large library around us. "Nothing bad can find us here. Libraries have always made me feel better for some reason, and I can never figure out why."

"It's the quiet for me," I said.

Ronnie continued to look around in awe. "For me, it's an escape."

"Yeah, and the bullies are too stupid to find it." I laughed.

I looked up toward where I'd last seen Tyler, but instead, I saw Shay. I could see that she was looking at me too. I wanted to wave and apologize about the other night at the party, but I told myself that I'd just see her tomorrow.

~

After school, I tumbled into my weekly appointment with Mrs. S. In my same chair, I felt pulled by the same sadness, the same unanswered questions, and the same lack of any sort of explanation from anyone.

Looking at her, thinking about Pounds and the gun under my dad's seat, Maya's store, the look on Shay's face whenever she saw me, it hit me just how pointless all of this was.

"So, how's everything?"

I had no idea what to say whenever she, or anyone really, asked me that. The words never came. Terrible? Like giving up? Were those the answers she was looking for? Or I guess I could've lied and gone the other direction. Everything's fine, how about you? Pretty busy but good? No complaints? I decided on nothing. Silence would explain it better. I just kept looking around her office.

"Now, Phoenix," she started, as she sat up at her Victorian desk and took off her glasses, letting them fall as the faux pearl strap around her neck cradled them like a necklace. Her breath smelled terrible. "We can't get much out of these appointments if you don't talk to me. That's the whole reason for all of this. So you and I can talk."

As I tried to look back at her, suddenly, I was angry—vicious even. I'd been coming to see her for years, and nothing had helped. All we did was talk about the same bad memories, and then I would leave, only to go out and make the same mistakes again. Round and round we went.

"Phoenix? We need to be open with one another."

"Why?" I shot back, startling myself with my own voice.

"Because talking helps us make sense of things. Life can be… complicated."

How could she possibly understand what was going on in my head?

"Phoenix, I—"

I quickly cut her off. "What!? Do you want to hear about how every time I try and put myself out there, I just get laughed at? How my parents hide the truth from me like I'm some child? How, when I get nervous, I see visions of some random street corner? Or…how about this? How about that none of that even matters anyway, because when we get older, we just get uglier and uglier and uglier until we eventually get so ugly and broken that we just fall apart. Then, there is…nothing. Just black. Like we were never even here at all."

Mrs. S was shocked. She didn't have anything to say, and she always had something to say. I'd been seeing her for years, and I'd never said more than a single sentence or two at a time.

"And why are you so certain that nothing happens to us when we pass on?" she finally asked.

"Look around! Is it that hard to believe nothing happens? I think you'd have to be crazy to believe in anything other than the truth. Nothing happens to us when we die. Dirt. We become dirt. That's what I think."

"And why this realization now? Today?" Mrs. S quickly quipped, with her usual yellow legal pad resting on her crossed knee. "Why today for this philosophy?"

"This stupid place. My dad took me there when I went with him to work, and all he talked about was how amazing it was, special, when really, it was just a rundown store. I used to think he was doing something meaningful or important when he was away from us all the time, but I learned he's spending all his time at some dump he calls the house of God. Time he could've spent with me…"

I trailed off then, remembering all the memories I'd created without him all these years. All the milestones I'd hit. How many times I'd wished he'd been there, and how, after a while, I'd given up on wishing for much of anything.

"But I don't know why I get my hopes up anymore. It's all just make-believe, just like God. The fake story we all hold on to so we can sleep at night." I finally finished in a heavy drop.

Mrs. S continued to write on her notepad, scribbling down my rant only to use it against me later.

"And what about your grandmother?"

"My grandmother?!" I shot back with both vitriol and confusion.

Mrs. S leaned forward. "For claiming not to believe, it doesn't make sense that you've had this crisis in 'life after death' only once she was gone. You began with your visions right after she passed. Explaining your desire for a belief in something more…more than the finality of death. Although, with your father's early departure the afternoon this all began, it *does* make sense why you've harbored this aggression. That much adds up to me. He wasn't there for you in the most vulnerable moment of your life." Mrs. S took a quick glance at her notes before she continued once more. "I think you're suppressing the belief in something more, Phoenix. I think your mind is telling you something different that you're attempting to ignore."

I looked directly into her eyes. I kept my focus there as I responded, "So, if I'm wrong, then what do you believe in?" Mrs. S didn't say anything right away, so I asked, "Do you believe in God?"

Mrs. S quickly backpedaled. "I'm afraid I'm not to talk to you about my own beliefs. I'm sure you can understand that there are professional limits, Phoenix."

I grew red-hot. "Tell me! No, I want to know. You said it yourself, we have to be open with one another, so why am I the only one who has to be open between us and not you too?"

"Phoenix. I didn't mean—"

"Tell me!" I cut her off and shouted so loud it startled her once more. I didn't realize I'd bursted out of my chair and to my feet. I sat back down and waited.

Mrs. S took her glasses off and placed her pen and notebook on her desk. "I'm…I'm afraid that you are, in fact, right." She spoke so slowly that it seemed as if each individual word took her a full minute to say. "I suppose it depends on who you talk to. Plenty of people think there's an afterlife, but most think nothing happens. That when you pass, well, that's it. Just as you said. So, it's important to live a full life, because it's more likely the latter, I'm afraid."

"And that's what you believe?" I asked.

She stopped and took the photo carefully from her desk into her hands. "I wish I didn't." Mrs. S placed the photo back onto her desk before finishing, "But everyone has their right to believe in something."

~

Back home after my appointment, I walked into Metropolis with my mom. My dad was sitting at the kitchen table. Surprisingly, the early snow had stuck. The storm wasn't over, but it had let up and left an icy woodland that was visible through the window above our sink.

I looked at both of them and was disgusted. Their boring looks made me want to run my fist through a cement wall.

"How was your appointment today?" my dad asked.

"Good."

"Early for a first storm," my dad began, letting his attention wander out our window. "Did you walk to school by yourself today in this weather?"

"Didn't feel like waiting around."

"Nonsense." He paused. "I'll get up earlier and walk with you tomorrow then. Nothing wrong with being first in the morning line."

My mom added, "Tomorrow's Tuesday, Herm. I have that job interview early, and you've got two stops before getting to the school in the morning, and then you're working the Snowball all night."

"Ah, that's right. How could I forget? I need to see Mrs. Haddley and then go by the crafting store. They've been having a ton of wiring problems lately, more than usual," he responded, before turning his attention back to me. "Say, will I be seeing you at the dance with someone special tomorrow night?"

By this time, my anger had grown heavy. I was tired of them both talking to me like I was still a child. The older I got, the more I started to feel like I was more of an adult than either of them.

"It would be nice for you to spend some time out instead of studying your words, Phoenix. Everyone goes to the Snowball.

Besides, you could make some new friends," my mom added, sounding as if she just wanted Metropolis to herself.

"No. I'm not going to any stupid dance. And I went to work with Dad. You don't need to try and make what he does sound important. I know what a worthless job he has."

I didn't need games anymore. I needed parents.

My mom looked shocked. "Phoenix? What's this anger about?"

I threw my hands down by my sides. "You're both losers! All Dad does is drive around to people's houses all night and sit around at school all day. You used to be something! You used to be a cop! A hero! Now we barely have enough money to live! And all you do, Mom, is just cry all day for him to come home, and then when he is home, you two just fight! What's wrong with both of you?"

"Phoenix? Your father, he…he takes care of us. He gives us a life to live," my mom began as I looked on at her with aggression burning in my eyes. "Apologize to us both."

I waited for my dad to say something, but just as you'd expect, he rolled over and acted as though nothing was wrong, which, to me, was even worse.

"Go on, say something!" I screamed at him. "Tell me what happened that night of my tenth birthday! Tell me why you were at the hospital that night covered in blood! Tell me why you froze up when you saw that memorial of that little boy at Maya's! Tell me… tell me what the hell is wrong with me and why no one will tell me what happened!"

My mom went completely still before looking at my dad. I waited. I waited some more. But he said nothing. He was as calm as I'd ever seen him.

"That's what I thought. You have nothing to say, because you know! You're just an electrician, Dad. No matter how many people you smile at, make happy, or tell great stories to, that doesn't change what you really are. Both of you are just like everyone else."

My mom spoke in a hushed voice, "You should never talk to either of us like that. We're your parents—"

"I wish you weren't my parents! I wish I never knew you!"

I stormed up to my room.

Finding my way into the Bird's Nest, tears streamed down my cheeks. I slammed the door behind me. I wanted to cry harder, yell more, punch something, anything. My anger and frustration oozed out of me with a violent fragility. I ran over to my bed and hid myself in a pillow, screaming into it. My tears created a pool around my face. As I lay in bed, I turned over and saw the dying blue flowers on my windowsill, reminding me again how worthless my dad truly was.

I wondered what tomorrow would bring. It really was no different from any other late-night thought. But, while continuing to cry, I realized that tomorrow would probably just bring more disappointment.

I wasn't sure I could believe in much of anything anymore. The more I saw, the less I understood.

10

7:44 A.M. THE DAY OF THE SNOWBALL

The flowers were dead. What were once vibrant, soft blue petals were now shriveled, gray skin—wrinkled flesh, popping off the stem like wind carrying ashes of a lost loved one far, far away.

Every morning, I'd turn over in my bed to see them warmly check on me from my cracked windowsill. At first, they stood young and stiff. Proudly, like stout young soldiers being sent off to war, waving their caps, they smiled at me. But as time went on, they began slumping inward, losing their muscle and lumen. They slowly began to disintegrate. Frowning at me. Now, returning overseas, hardly more than skin and bone. Famished. Pale. Lost. Unraveling, until there would be nothing left.

Their smell had grown rotten as I'd watched them fall into nothing.

"We're running late."

I pulled the blanket over my eyes. "I'm tired."

"I can't miss my interview this morning. You know we need this. Up."

As I let my eyes creep from out of the top of the covers, I could see that she'd opened the blind over my windowsill. Nothing about the day looked sunny. A deep fog cloaked the morning sky.

"Come on. Up, Phoenix. Breakfast for you downstairs." She walked out of my room and shut the door.

Moisture had begun to populate the top of my bare window. I got up and slid it open.

The gust pushed in, and the vapor patted my face. My cheeks, nose, neck, and ears at once got colder. My skin pricked in sharp goosebumps.

I grabbed the dead flowers. They were meek between my fingers. The petals were carried by the fog like ashes. The poignant smell of death awoke me once more.

I tossed them out the window without waiting to watch them hit the ground.

7:47 A.M.

I slid to my closet and pulled on a long-sleeve shirt, hoodie, sweats, and a warm vest. But I couldn't find my tan L.L. Bean boots. It looked like it might start to snow.

My desk was still a mess from last night, but I threw a couple of my cards into folders. After pushing my desk chair in, I flicked off my light and made my way downstairs in my socks.

"Cereal?" my mom asked as she unfolded the collar on her shirt. She looked nicer than usual.

"Not hungry."

I took my gaze off her quickly and, instead, focused on trying to find my boots. Jumping under the sofa, they weren't there either.

The wind patted the side of Metropolis, carrying with it the beginnings of a storm. Like spiders' legs, a tapping sound crept around our kitchen window and walls. The hiss came and went from the outside chill.

I opened our side closet, looked by the front door, and behind the TV, but there was still nothing.

"Here." I heard my mom laugh. "Your dad was putting clean laces in this morning before he left." She handed me my boots and, while fixing her earring, went for a kiss on my forehead. "I've got a bus to catch, but wish me luck."

I nodded as I started to tie my boots and pulled up my socks.

"Listen, I know you're still upset about last night, but no matter what, our love is the most important thing we have. Nothing changes that. We both love you so much, Noodle. You know that."

My mom stopped my hands as she could tell I wasn't paying attention. She stood in front of me and waited.

"Good luck," I said in a quick breath.

But my mom just shook her head as she continued to keep her hands over mine. I sighed.

"I love you too," I finally added.

My mom smiled over her shoulder as she walked out.

From the kitchen window, I watched her head against the wind in the direction of her bus. She tucked her hands, once over mine, into her armpits from the cold. Her hair flew behind her like a flag.

The clouds above her parted, and the sun came down.

8:01 A.M.

I walked into the library and saw Shay reading again in the same spot. This time I felt like going up and bothering her, instead of keeping to myself.

"Morning."

She gently looked up as she closed her book.

I took a seat next to her as she pushed some hair out of her face. "Why didn't you come and sit next to me yesterday?"

The way she said it made me forget about my normally more terrifying thoughts. It was a sweetness that was effortlessly purging.

I started talking, but it was so loud in the library that morning, because of the abnormal number of people inside. It was now snowing hard outside, so everyone flooded in in the last five minutes. It looked like the storm had caught most of them by surprise.

Shay grabbed my hand and said, "Here, let's go somewhere quieter."

She pulled me to a corner of the library. We sat facing each other on the ground in between two bookshelves.

"Now." She smiled. "We were saying?"

Shay and I laughed and caught up easily. She told me all about the book she was reading, which, to my surprise, wasn't much of a book at all. She was reading a poem called "Ode on a Grecian Urn," which surprised me. She'd explained that it wasn't for anything related to school, but just that she was so fascinated by John Keats.

"It's just…we always look for the greater meaning in *everything*. That's what we always do, but how about…I don't know…let's say… even this conversation we're having right now." Shay stopped for a second and looked away as if to think more. "How insane is it that you are right here listening, and I am right here talking. Out of all the other things that could be happening, and places we could be, this is…this is real," she finished.

"How could it not be?"

She just smiled as she attempted to simplify further. "It's not about you, and it's not even about me. It's not about what you're thinking about when you're listening to me, and it's not about what I'm trying to get across, but the real beauty is in this…" She stopped.

Shay slowly brought her finger almost to her nose and then moved it toward me. It was so slow at first, I almost couldn't tell if she was moving at all, but she was. Waving her finger enchantingly in the air. Feeling nothing, but acting as if she was feeling everything.

She then softly finished, "The beauty is…is in this little space in between you and me."

But as she'd lifted her arm to wave her finger through the air, the fleshy, rubicund-colored scar she'd gotten in the tower on my birthday peeked out of her sleeve. The long, jagged scratch of fleshy skin made me wince at first, but then it made me remember that day. At first the good, then the bad.

We just sat and looked at each other. The silence didn't keep me from continuing to think.

I looked into the space between her and me, but I couldn't help but think about what it was like back then—back when I got to see Shay almost every day. When, each morning, I'd wake up, and she was the first thing I thought about.

"We can waste a lot of time thinking, talking, studying, researching, preaching, praying, and wondering, but I guess what this poem reminds me of is that this space between us right now is the most wonderful thing imaginable. It's all we need to be able to know. That's it. The attempt at life is enough of a miracle," Shay said.

In great detail, Shay continued to explain to me the poem's ability to capture the moments in life and the simplicity of everything.

It wasn't so much what she was saying that had begun to ease my anxiety, but just exactly how she chose to say it. I'd forgotten until then, that there had always been something especially calming about the way she could put together a sentence.

Shay repositioned how she was sitting to be crisscross apple sauce right in front of me, so I did the same.

She was right. To me, the purity of having her back, sitting in front of me, was like a miracle.

8:12 A.M.

Somewhere in talking to Shay, I got lost in her eyes and felt incredibly present. All of her was before me, and I sank into a mud of calm. Watching her talk and smile was so soothing. I was here in a way I didn't know anyone ever could be.

But like a knock at my internal door, I felt the shadow slowly come back over me. The storm was headed my way, and then it came on fast. Just as easily as my relaxation arrived, it vanished. I couldn't think, all of a sudden. I could see it all.

I'm back at Maya's. The red sign flashes in and out above me as I hear the jingle of the door.

"Phoenix, come in, my child."

I look up and see the old woman in the white belt behind the counter. She's wiping down where a cash register sits alongside fruit and packets of gum.

I walk through the same aisle with all the different CDs from the different generations of music. Just below them, it looks like different car accessories are sliding on the floor.

"I apologize for the mess, my child. Normally, I have everything organized better than this."

Looking around, I notice all the others around me, this time dressed in black suits and ties. All different types of people. Men. Women. Some tall and some short. But all of them are dressed exactly the same. All of them, except me.

The old woman comes from behind the counter and stands right beside me. She places her hand on my cheek.

"My goodness. You're really starting to look just like him. Say, where's your father? Have you found him yet?"

I don't say anything at first as I start to try and look around for him, but my dad's nowhere to be seen. I scan all around the inside of Maya's, but my dad isn't with me. He never has been.

"Phoenix? Phoenix? Where is he? How did you get here without him?"

I start to panic as I turn around in circles, looking for him. But it becomes impossible to find anyone at all in here, because everyone looks exactly the same. Nobody is different any longer from the person to their left or right.

"Phoenix? Hello!?"

Suddenly, Shay was snapping my name as I came back into focus. "Phoenix! Phoenix? Hello? You in there!?"

I quickly blinked.

"Was that…?" she began, concerned. "Was that another episode?"

I nodded my head and tried to apologize. She didn't say anything but decided to just wrap me in a hug. After the moment of shock wore off, I hugged her back even tighter.

Then, it just sort of came out of me. Maybe it was because she had been there that first time it happened, maybe it was because I'd just seen Shay's scar from that day, or maybe it was because I simply felt like, after all these years, finally saying something meaningful to her again. I sat up straight, meeting Shay's blue eyes.

"I'm sorry about what happened the other night at the party. And…I'm sorry about what happened…what happened at my birthday when we were little. I'm sorry I'm different."

Shay took my hand like she had that day at the playground.

"Phoenix, it's okay. It wasn't your fault. You don't have to apologize to me, ever. And sure, you may be different from most people, but who wants to be like everyone else? Not me."

I smiled a little bit, and she did too.

"It's like the story you told me that day. The really sweet one about the elephant and the giraffe," Shay said.

"You remember?" I asked with a smile.

"Of course, I do," she said as she smiled, too, then added, "Just because other people don't understand you doesn't mean that's a bad thing. You're different, and that's okay. Being different means you won't be forgotten."

I cracked open with a smile. Shay could always cheer me up, but one question was more important to me than anything else. I knew that, if anyone had any idea about what happened, it had to be her.

"That day...five years ago. What...what happened?" I asked with some doubt in my voice.

Shay looked back at me sharply. "You had a seizure while you were opening your presents. One second you were reading a birthday card, and then the next, you were on the ground, and we were all running to get you help. We were so scared."

I swallowed hard, slowly second-guessing myself, but realizing that I couldn't keep hiding. And if I was going to trust anyone, it had to be her. Maybe she could help me finally put this all together.

"Not with me, Shay," I began slowly, thinking about each and every single word. "I meant, what happened to...to us? Our parents? They were partners. Because, ever since then, I feel like everything's been different. That night...I saw my dad at the hospital and...well, he wasn't there to see me. He was alone. And when I saw him that night...he was covered in someone else's blood."

Shay locked up. She looked like she had no idea what to say. She turned away from me then.

"Why isn't my dad a cop anymore?"

"Phoenix, I…" Shay began with some trepidation, but trailed off and didn't finish what she was saying. She just shook her head in silence.

I was starting to get upset. I could instantly tell she knew more than she was telling me.

"Hey. Stop already. I know that something happened, and I'm not some baby. I deserve to know, and I'm sick of everyone trying to protect me all of the time…acting like I can't handle it."

She turned and looked at me like she was about to cry. I felt bad about raising my voice.

Shay answered me quietly. "I wish I didn't. I know that my dad he…he was never the same. They told me to never talk to you again. That it was all Herman's fault…but I didn't want to believe them. I…"

She stopped. Seeing her sad hurt me more than I could have possibly imagined. I felt horrible, but I really didn't know what else to say.

Then, something happened. A loud bang. Several jolting pops. Shay lurched toward me. We were both instantly shaken.

The library went deathly silent, and we didn't hear anything for a moment. The quiet was almost worse than the noise—the not knowing what was under the bed.

Then, after a short while, people slowly went back to what they were doing. Regular life just as easily resumed.

"That was weird," she said.

8:15 A.M.

An even louder bang rumbled into the library, shaking the books surrounding both Shay and me. Crackling—like fireworks—sounded even closer. Screaming noises outside. The library went silent this time, and this time, it stayed that way.

The crackling continued, getting louder and louder. I couldn't tell if we started to hear laughing or screaming. It would start and then stop, but it was hard to figure out exactly what *it* was.

The librarian's eyes crept over each of us. She came out from behind her desk and went to the window in the library door to see what was going on outside.

Shay squeezed my hand.

The librarian panicked. Suddenly, she bolted the heavy door shut.

"Everyone! Under your desks now!" she yelled out to all of us.

The fire alarm screamed through the library as everyone fell into cover. Shay pulled me to the ground, and we laid down on the floor in between the bookshelves.

I don't remember what I was thinking, because I don't know if I was thinking about anything at all. When you're being uprooted that abruptly, the only thing on your mind is what you're doing in that exact moment. All I could focus on was lying on the floor.

The blaring of the alarm burned so deeply into my inner ear that my brain twisted and turned. My hands shot up to the sides of my head to protect my ears, but it wasn't helping. It was too close. My ears felt like they were starting to bleed. I was in agony.

The crackling was still going on outside. Fire and snow. The kids screamed and cried inside the library. The librarian didn't say anything else. She was also now under her desk.

I was so scared. My breathing quickly increased, and my heart pounded through my chest. I went to feel it with my hand. I was going to have a heart attack. My toes and fingers scrambled, and I felt like I was now bleeding, not just out of my ears, but everywhere. Burning into a pile of ash.

8:17 A.M.

I couldn't stop coughing. Quickly, my coughing turned to wheezing and my wheezing to sobbing. It was all happening so fast.

Shay pulled me in toward her, but that didn't make it any better. I was trying to hide us both by holding onto her tight, feeling as though, if I squeezed hard enough, I could make us disappear. If I couldn't keep quiet, though, what I was going to do was get us killed.

I was never going to leave this library. The last conversation I'd had with my dad was running on repeat in my head. I was embarrassed. I was never going to see him again, but I was also starting to miss even the things I didn't like. Another dispute with my mom or getting shoved in the back by Pounds. I wasn't going to do anything ever again.

Despite staying out of trouble my entire life, being a good person, and always trying to do what is right, I'd still ended up in this place. Each step had taken me right here. None of the good things I'd done had mattered at all; it was always supposed to come to an end for me today. And there was nothing I could do to stop it.

Shay started to rub my head.

"It's probably nothing. Don't worry, we're going to be alright."

I was losing it, and Shay could now see that her efforts weren't making much of a difference. Her reassurance had only heightened my anxiety.

"Don't let your mind play tricks on you."

But it was too late. I jolted Shay off of me. I had to run—be anywhere but here. If I stayed in one place any longer, I was going to implode in front of Shay again.

As I struggled to my feet, Shay quickly ripped me back down to the floor. Hard. My back shot with pain, and my elbows barely braced my fall. The tears shortly followed the sting.

"Phoenix. Listen to me, okay?"

I tried to nod, but the tears in my eyes made her blurry.

"Do you remember that Thanksgiving when we were kids, and we played hide-and-go-seek at your house? When you disappeared and none of us could find you because you had the best hiding spot?"

I remembered the spot well. It was in the Arts District of Metropolis. The inside of my parents' walk-in closet, between a rack of my dad's jackets with a cabinet beneath me. It was like lying in a cornfield—nobody knew where I was. I disappeared without a trace for what felt like years.

"We are going to play the same game right now. We're going to make you invisible."

I tried to nod my head, but I didn't know if she could tell if I had done so or not.

"I need you to hold your breath and close your eyes. Like you're in that same spot of your house, and you don't want any of us to find you."

I nodded, and this time she knew I'd understood.

"On the count of three."

I closed my eyes and put both of my hands over my head.

"One."

Slowly, my world got darker and darker. Even though my eyes were closed, through my eyelids, I could still tell we were in danger.

"Two."

My heart slowed, and I started to gradually feel better. I was back between the jackets.

"Three."

With my eyes still closed, I could hear Shay's voice getting progressively softer.

"Good, Phoenix. Good…now take another big breath in."

I did, and I felt safe. It had finally passed. I could feel my dad's wool jacket against my cheek. Despite the maelstrom around me— the fire alarm and the crackling outside—all I could hear was Shay's soothing voice. It would all be over soon.

8:21 A.M.

The fire alarm continued to scream, although Shay and I had become accustomed to the noise. The rhythmic pattern had now been burned deep into our subconscious to the point where we almost didn't notice it any longer. Shay kept talking to me, close enough to my ear so I could hear her over the alarm. As I remained invisible, it was hard to think.

Using the strongest magic Shay had, she told me all sorts of stories. She helped keep me from having another episode with the way she was able to make me ignore the screams or make me forget the sirens. I went to a different place while listening. Almost like being at the movies with your eyes closed.

But then, loud knocking and banging came at the library door. My eyes snapped open of their own accord—I wasn't in my parents' closet any longer. I wasn't in the Arts District. I could no longer feel my dad's sleeves against my skin. I realized that what had felt like his wool were actually pages. I was under a pile of books from the shelves around me. I could see that Shay had emptied out the rows of books, exposing herself yet remaining by my side. Piles of them were blanketed over me. Pages and pages of old and new texts were here to protect me.

The banging continued at the door, but no one moved. The less we did, the louder the banging seemed to get. Then a massive relief swept through the library—the fire alarm shut off. It was all finally over.

I could see that a few kids shuffled out from under their desks, but Shay told me not to move. Concerned faces looked around at one another as I peeked out from a gap between the books at my eye level. Luckily, my eyesight wasn't hindered.

It was silent. No one said anything as the banging on the door stopped. With the alarm now off, exhales followed. Beside Shay, and underneath the pile of books, I felt safe again.

She moved a few more books from my face so I could now see the entire library. Calm started to return, and tears gradually slowed.

"Nothing can hurt you," Shay said to me.

But as I looked around, I could tell that, still, nobody had any idea what was going on. I was no more lost than anyone else, but I didn't want to ask Shay as she sat beside me. I didn't want her to know I was still afraid.

The longer the silence continued, though, the safer I felt. But then it came back harder than ever before. The same vision became just as clear again. I was back in that place I seemed to never escape.

I'm still looking for my dad inside of Maya's, but he isn't anywhere I can see. I'm running through aisle after aisle, turning my head side to side as I look across the endless shelves of stuff. Pens, books, snacks, candy, and clothes, but my dad isn't here, and for some reason, he's supposed to be.

I'm back at the counter beside the old woman in a disappointed heap. She gently lifts my chin.

"It's okay, Phoenix. Just breathe, my child. Just breathe. Focus your mind on only one thing—the rising and falling of your chest. In and out, in and then back out again. There isn't anything to worry about other than the breath in your lungs—that's it. Count them in your head. Count each individual breath, my child. Now, when you're ready, and only when you feel certain, imagine a place. A safe place. This is where you are now. You are there. He can come later, but for now, it's only you. This place has no name, because it doesn't need one—you know it well enough to not require such branding. You've been here countless times. All of the things around you are good things—happy things. They are simple beauties, and they bring an easy warmth to your heart. You are outside now, and the weather is great, but you'd hardly notice. Time moves slowly, and everything is calm. Everything is where you'd like it to be. A gentle tapping of water is close by. A breeze ruffles a tree. You hear these things as you start to notice someone with you. A person you know better than you know yourself. It's him. Give him a hug. He's so delighted to see you. Beside one another, you sit on the ground, and you swear that you never knew natural earth could be so welcoming. As you sit now, you don't talk. Words are not necessary, because you're sharing the exact same thoughts. The comfort with each other makes you feel safe. You are not alone, because you never really were. Now, focus again on your breath, notice its new rhythm. Its cadence is slow, but your breathing is not labored; it's perfect. The rising and falling is gentle in your chest. Now, open your eyes, Phoenix. You're exactly where you are supposed to be. This journey that you have been on is all coming together. It's time. There are no mistakes in this life. Your feet have taken you here for a reason, my child. Now allow your mind to follow."

Through the door of Maya's, I can see that it had started to snow.

I instantly left my place of escape and crashed back when I heard a voice scream, "Help! Please! Can someone help!"

I wanted to save everyone. I wanted to protect all of them. I wanted to be uplifting. I wanted to be remembered as a good person.

I wanted to be brave. But I didn't do anything. I didn't say anything. I didn't even move. I didn't even flinch.

The banging at the library door was back. It was louder this time. I could see the door, and through the little window, it looked like it was a girl. A girl not much older than me. She was trying to get in.

Initially, nobody moved, maybe hoping that, by doing nothing, the voice would just go away. That the girl would give up.

Shay remained by my side, but I could see that she was fidgeting.

"Help! Let me in!" the girl screamed as she hit the heavy door with a closed fist.

Then, someone rose from out of the cover of their desk. It was Elliot, the sophomore from the party.

"We have to help her," he said to nobody in particular.

Elliot was now the only person standing up as he looked around for approval, but he was completely on his own.

"Help! Please!" the girl cried.

Elliot took another breath before deciding to act. He moved toward the door, but the librarian stood up. "There is nothing we can do."

"We have to open the door for her!" Elliot screamed. "We can't just leave her out there!"

The librarian looked at him firmly. "I'm sorry, but I cannot allow you to do that. I cannot put all of you at risk."

Elliot was emotional. Scared. He looked at her. "We have to be better than them."

The librarian looked out and could now see that everyone was staring at her—waiting to hear her final decision. We were all awaiting her next move.

We make decisions every day. There really isn't anything foreign about them, as we all understand what's at stake. More than we'd like to admit, life and death really are, in one way or another, always waiting. Waiting for us to decide. Getting into the car every morning or crossing the street, those are decisions that we make. Even then, there is risk.

We get nerfed by life. What starts to happen as a result is that, over time, we forget that there's the potential for things to go wrong. We don't see that the possibility is still right in front of us. When, in reality, it always has been and always will be. To live, or to live in constant fear.

I watched as the librarian contemplated this decision. A decision that would forever change the course of all our lives.

Eventually, the decision was made. When it comes to human life, the loss of just one, is too many.

8:24 A.M.

The librarian moved toward the door and looked out of the window once more. Together, we collectively held our breath as she peeked outside. I wanted to close my eyes again and focus on my breathing, but we were beyond that. My safe place, where I could escape to, had now been infiltrated by thoughts too horrid to silence.

We studied every small movement as she looked out. Every direction. Every degree of motion. What she did with her hands. The shift of her weight.

She turned one more time and looked at all of us as if to apologize, as if to take a mental picture of the youth in the room and get one more look at all the lives she was now potentially putting at risk to save just one.

I wanted to go home. I was so scared that I wanted to take off and run. I'd had enough. I got up to escape when Shay reached for me. She stopped me in my tracks by yelling, "Phoenix! No!"

The door opened, and a gust hissed in. The girl stumbled onto the librarian in a panic. She panted like a wild animal and clambered on top of her.

The cold air invaded the room just as quickly as the girl did. Snow fell at an angle into the doorway.

The librarian found her footing and had moved to shut the door when three loud cracks came toward our direction. They were so quick, yet so loud, you could somehow hear each individual one. Louder than the others that had come before them. The vibrations through the cold air painfully swept through all of us. They were close.

At the fright of the noise, I slammed my eyes shut. It was ringing deep in my head. My palms were sweating.

Once the echo of gunshots stopped ringing, I opened my eyes and looked toward the door. The librarian was on the floor.

Two men walked in holding guns.

8:25 A.M.

At first, they didn't say anything. Semi-automatic rifles rested at their hips, they both held handguns, and masks concealed both of their identities. But once one of them spoke, I could tell that these were not men. The pitch of his voice let me know these were boys— boys not much older than me.

"Everybody up!" one of them called out.

Not a single person moved.

"I'm not going to ask again!" he yelled a second time, but still nothing.

He pointed his gun into the air. Rounds were randomly dispersed all around the library, shattering the windows surrounding us. Glass sprayed, and it almost looked like bullets were raining down from the sky as a result. With all of the windows down, the snow fell into the library like a flurry.

The window gone behind me was just above a small bookshelf that was about at my eye level. Cold air slapped the back of my neck.

I adjusted myself underneath the pile of books, so I could better see what was going on. Glass slid off the books, falling to the floor like shards of ice.

"This is your last warning!" the boy screamed out.

But before he could open fire again—unleashing a torrent of catastrophic magnitude—something happened. Ronnie stood up.

"Finally! A brave one!" one gunman yelled to the other over the drone of the storm.

All I could initially see was that Ronnie's legs were aggressively shaking as he walked toward them. He was doing his best to stand tall, but the gunmen started to laugh as Ronnie's terror increased.

"I thought he was the brave one!" one gunman said to the other once Ronnie stood right in front of them both.

"Look at him go!" the other said, while mimicking Ronnie's trembling legs.

Like gnarling hyenas, they picked at him, first with their words and then graduating to their fists. They started softly, and then their punches got harder and harder. They laughed the entire time. But Ronnie didn't say a word until one of the blows brought him to the ground. I watched as he was now on the floor. His hands slowly inched together in prayer.

"He can't be serious," one of them said, looking at the other.

The laughing dramatically picked up, and the boys kept exchanging comments as Ronnie looked up for help.

"Some belief he's got. What a good kid!" the other gunman added.

"I almost want to wait and see if something will happen."

But nothing did. After a few moments, no clouds parted above. No shining light came down. After a few moments, snow still came storming in through the windows. And Ronnie continued to silently ask for help from someone who didn't exist.

Ronnie looked down when one of the gunmen suddenly stopped laughing and pointed his weapon right at Ronnie's head. With the gun pressed up against his temple, the boy behind the trigger simply asked Ronnie, "Please, tell me, what is it that you are so sure can save you?"

Ronnie's legs stopped shivering. His body calmed. He raised his chin. Slowly, he rose to his feet as if he had simply tripped and was getting back up. He looked like he was in no pain and no agony. A clearness became of him.

The gunshot echoed through the library, and the vibrations sent us all into a pure and unsettling shock.

All I could see were Ronnie's feet. They were hugged by his beloved red Timberland boots.

Gasps went through all the students as they huddled together even closer.

My eyes started to water, and it was getting even harder to think straight. I was going to die. We were all going to die.

"Nobody else is brave enough as Red Boots here!? Fine! Have it your way!"

The two gunmen tucked their handguns in the backs of their pants and swung their rifles up from their hips.

Bullets flew like metal sleet. Pieces of wood from desks splintered into the air, and smoke from the barrels clouded the ceiling above, giving it the feeling that a dense fog existed atop us all. Life after life was lost before my eyes. Some kids I had hardly even known, and others I had known my entire life. But all of their faces I would now never forget. They would be the last faces I'd ever see.

The hellish barrels continued to howl, and eventually, fewer cries were heard.

Smoke clouded around us all as the casings bounced off the library floor like piano keys. As the two gunmen reloaded, the silence was even more terrifying than the noise. We were in the eye of the storm we knew wouldn't last long.

"Stop!" someone yelled. "Stop, I'll stand up! Just stop!"

But the voice sounded oddly familiar. The voice sounded close by. It was the voice I'd thought about saying my name every night just before falling asleep. A voice I'd heard in my dreams—a voice that was normally less of voice and more like a song. Instead of now singing, this voice was screaming. This voice was saying something much different. Something that belonged, not in my dreams, but in my nightmares.

"Stop now! Please! Just stop!"

The boys kept reloading. Sirens wailed in the distance.

Shay stood up, her t-shirt sleeve covering half of the scar above her elbow. Beside me, she whispered, "The window, Phoenix. When the moment comes, you run."

I wanted to yell at her to stop. To say that we could just hide in the books together. That we would be safe. That I could protect her, but I didn't. I didn't say anything at all.

Shay walked toward them as I, cowardly, laid idly by.

Once in front of the shooters, one grabbed Shay by the hair and pulled her close. Holding onto her, he said, "Who do we have here?"

"It's her," the other shooter said calmly. "It's his girlfriend."

Shay stood beside them both as powerfully as she could, but she looked petrified.

Watching her get treated like a rag doll tore me apart. All she'd wanted to do was read her poem.

"Ahh, don't be scared. I promise we don't bite!"

Shay looked at the one grabbing hold of her and spat back, "I'm not scared of anyone who hides behind a mask!"

The shooter pushed her, and she fell to the ground. She didn't get up.

Then, they both laughed, and the one who was holding Shay gently slipped off his mask, proudly looking down at her.

"Happy now?"

A gentle face. Soft cheeks rested atop his teenage skin. His nose red from the bite of the cold. His eyes were a sharp gray. My heart sank into my stomach when his long hair came tumbling out of the back of his mask.

Tyler.

Lying with her cheek against the floor, Shay, instead of looking up at him, looked right at me. She tried to smile but was in too much pain to do it for long. I could tell. Then, she mouthed the word, "Now."

My breath quickened, and before I knew it, I was moving. Now would be my only chance.

I slid out of the back of the pile of books and didn't look back. Each movement was careful. Once out of the cover, I slowly climbed over a small bookcase and looked out the broken window. I turned to take one more look at Shay. Tyler took the gun from his waistband. The wreckage around her was hell on Earth—once a place of quiet thought, now a flurry of blood and smoke. I desperately wanted to do something, but I was afraid.

She laid on the ground beside Tyler and his accomplice. But

DARLING, YOU'RE NOT ALONE

in an accidental swoop, I fell atop a bank of snow and out of the broken window.

After falling onto my side, I noticed my leg had gotten caught on some broken glass. I couldn't even feel it as my heart continued to pound in my chest. Blood slowly pooled beside me in the snow.

I found my way to my feet, and out of pure fear, I started to move quickly. Faster and faster, I ran. I approached an open field, where I saw groups of other kids running beside me. Several police cars zoomed by us, going the opposite direction we were running. The snow flew right into my face.

My lungs began to sting. Snow covered my eyes and mouth. My feet were freezing. I was losing it and losing it quickly. But I knew I had to keep going. If I didn't get help soon, she wasn't going to make it. She—and everyone in there—were relying on me to save them. Now would be my only chance.

I was running with everything I had until it happened.

Three shots.

I looked back at the library, where I saw flashing lights of cop cars and paramedics flying in.

Then, I couldn't move no matter how hard I tried. In the snow-covered field around me, I cried. My hands sank into the white powder, and I searched for any strength I'd had left, but it was all gone. There was no hiding from this. She was gone, in order to save me. This sad world didn't need me; it needed people like her.

My tears became heavier and heavier, so heavy that I felt like I was falling through the snow and through the surface of the Earth.

It had all collapsed underneath me. Tragedy had struck in a place where hardly anything ever happened at all.

8:48 A.M.

I crumbled into Metropolis. By now, the entire city was on fire. Sirens blared all around, and the constant noise wouldn't go away. The gunfire still rang in my skull, as if I was still trapped inside the library.

My leg continued to bleed, so I grabbed a towel to slow, and eventually stop, the wound from dripping. Then, through the kitchen window, I saw that the Ferry wasn't in the driveway.

I ran to our home phone to call him. To let him know that I had cut my leg, but I was okay. That I was home now at Metropolis and safe. That he should come home too.

But when I reached for the phone, I noticed it had a voicemail on the machine. I pressed play. His voice began. His breathing was heavy.

"Honey, it's me. Listen, something's happened at the school… don't turn on the news. I'm going to get Phoenix. Everything's going to be alright. I'm at school. I got here as soon as I could."

His voice started to trail off, and the crack of gunshots in the background was easy for me to recognize.

"Phoenix! Phoenix!"

I started to cry as I couldn't believe it.

"Dad! I'm here! I'm home! I'm home…" My voice trailed off as I realized I was talking to no one on the other side of the phone. I hung on to each second as the voicemail crawled on.

"I love you both very much. Okay? I'm sorry…I'm sorry…I am going to get him. I won't let anyone hurt him…I'm coming…I'm going to bring our boy home."

He started to run, the sound of his steps increasing.

I knew that he wasn't on the other line, but I yelled back, "Dad! Dad! I'm okay! I'm here!"

I lost control of myself and melted into tears. I wanted to be with him so badly. I wanted to run to wherever he might be.

The speakerphone on his voicemail continued to play, even though I was no longer listening. "Everything is going to be alright... I'm coming. Everything is going to be alright."

Suddenly, it all drove me into the ground. Everything that I'd known and loved had been ripped out of my life in the blink of an eye.

I tore the phone out of the wall and took it with me. I started calling out again, "Dad! Dad!"

I ran into my room, but he wasn't there. I opened the door to his bedroom, nothing.

With the phone still in my fingers, I crawled into the Arts District. Inside their closet, I fell between my dad's jackets and let his clothes protect me. His scent hide me.

I played the voicemail once, then twice, and then a third time. It was the only thing that could keep me from falling apart, so I played it for the next hour straight, until eventually falling into a state where I wasn't sure if I was awake or not.

3:30 P.M.

I woke in a panic. I heard the Ferry roll into the driveway and park. When I heard the front door swing open, though, it wasn't his voice.

"Phoenix!" my mom yelled as she scrambled into Metropolis.

I heard her go into the kitchen first, then head toward the stairs.

"Phoenix! Phoenix, where are you? Are you here? Are you home?"

I was so frightened I couldn't move.

I heard my mom swing my door open as she continued to cry. "Phoenix, where are you…I'm home…I'm home…I'm…I…"

Their bedroom door opened, and I could see my mom's feet turn left and right, left and right. She was crying.

My body started to tremble. Hearing the anguish pouring out of her. All of the shock reminded me that this was still real.

I curled up into a ball in their closet and covered both of my ears with my hands as she screamed. It only got harder to stay quiet as she ebbed and flowed with her bouts of fear.

She turned on her TV, and the news channel blared out the following.

"The worst mass school shooting in US history has taken place today in the town of Darling, Colorado. We now know that at least thirteen students and two adults have been confirmed killed."

She screamed again and then, much more softly, started to say to herself repeatedly, "Why God? Why God? Why? Why?"

The news channel came back through. "With chaos surrounding the area, many students are still missing or unaccounted for after fleeing to—"

Black. Silence.

The TV snapped off. The power, all of it, blacked out. All of the lights went dark, and all of the sounds were gone. It was completely still, other than my mom's cries.

"Not both," she cried in the dark. "Please, not both."

I held onto my shirt with my mouth, gnawing on it while I listened to my mom cry. My ears were the only thing that could prove this was happening. Her helpless prayers continued, though, despite no light, no sign, or call to action. Then, as her tears returned, they came even heavier and even hotter. The sound of her crying was, by far, the worst sound I'd heard all day.

"Why God? Why God?" she repeated again.

But she was calling out into thin air, into darkness—to a God who surely wasn't in that library this morning and a God who couldn't hear her now. Nobody was listening but me.

2000

11

Initially, we had TV and press from everywhere flooding into Darling—we were all anybody wanted to talk about. All over the world, everyone knew about what happened here. There were endless memorials, marches, vigils, funerals, and ceremonies. But then, as the weeks went on and on, fewer cameras showed up. The world stopped tuning in. People changed the channel.

Adults had to go back to work. Kids had to go back to school. Somebody had to take Ronnie's old desk, and eventually, somebody had to read our morning announcements.

"Good morning, Darling High School. My name is Principal McGugan, and it's great to finally be meeting all of you. It's an honor to be here, and I cannot wait to get started."

None of it made any sense—the fact that something so seemingly temporary as a desk could still be here and something so alive as a person could not.

"The Snowball is just one month away, so be sure to pick up your tickets soon for a special night in the gymnasium you won't want to miss."

Despite it all, the metal book cradle at the bottom of Ronnie's old desk hung strong, the arch at the back was still curved, and the flat piece of wood with pencils and paper looked as clean as ever. Yet, someone as harmless as Ronnie was now dirt. The desk had survived in this plastic world longer than he had.

"Let's make this school year special, everyone. Let's work hard, look out for one another, and most importantly, let's never take a single second for granted. Let's soak up every second we get to learn, grow, and mature."

But, for me, not even sitting here now could be pleasant. The desk chair my body tried to rest in was tight. Even my breathing seemed like something to think about. My body had forgotten how to do so on its own.

"Thank you for listening, and have a great day, everyone. And never forget, my door is always open." Principal McGugan concluded the announcements. The microphone clicked off, and the speakers crackled for a moment before they left us in silence.

Mr. Patts talked and talked that morning, although it seemed as though even he didn't care what he was saying. It was my second consecutive year in his speech therapy class, and I felt like we were still on the first lesson. We were literally reading the same exact book as freshman year.

Not like I was listening much, though. Most of the time in class, my attention would just fall onto where Ronnie used to sit. His desk was just two in front of me. Now some new student was sitting there, which certainly, in a calamitous way, felt fitting.

Today, Mr. Patts was teaching us about the importance of appearance as it pertains to positive socialization. He explained that how a person thinks of you during a first impression is largely based on your physical appearance. He didn't just mean how you dressed, but also how you looked that person in the eye and if you smiled when introduced to them. It made me sick how fake it all sounded. Shouldn't the content of your character far outweigh whether you have green or brown eyes? If he was right, then "people" sounded like some of the most superficial creatures imaginable. It was all just one jumbled waste of time because, clearly, if you weren't born with the correct physical attributes, then you were screwed no matter what.

I wasn't ready to fake a smile or dress nicely for anyone. You'd have to be fake to meet a stranger, and the first thing you do is smile. To do so would mean that you were ignoring the fact that all of this is bad. The entire human experience is just one great big disaster, falling into tragedy after tragedy. No matter what you do or have, nothing will protect you. Money, family, fame, youth, health—it's all fleeting. So, to go up to someone and instinctively smile means that you are either fake, or perhaps just too stupid to realize that we're all leaving soon. When you're a kid, people just don't tell you that the whole world is plastic.

But as the blabbering continued, my gaze fell back onto Ronnie's chair. Then, instantly, all of the kids disappeared from all of the chairs. They evaporated into thin air. Imagining my words and putting together the letters in my head no longer did the trick. I was spinning. I was headed back to the eternal place my mind had trapped me inside of. The place where I lost all control.

Inside Maya's, the woman in the white belt is just ahead of me at the same counter. A rumbling—like we're below a train station—shakes dust off the ceiling above. The lights flicker. My vision bounces side to side, but no one does anything or says anything about it.

"Did you bring them?" the woman asks me, then repeats, "The boots, Phoenix. Did you grab them for me, my child?"

I shake my head as I look down at my hands and see that I'm carrying nothing with me.

The woman in the belt shakes her head in disappointment as she looks out beyond me for a moment. I turn to look in the direction she is, but no one is there.

Eventually, she says, "Well, they're not going to grab themselves."

Before I know it, I am voraciously searching up and down the aisles of Maya's, picking through piles and piles of clothes and random collections of things. I scan more and more quickly, feeling the stress of forgetting weighing on me.

"You have to keep looking. They're in here somewhere, and he needs them, my child. He needs them."

I start throwing things over my shoulder as I dig into piles and piles. I'm sorting through everything as fast as I can.

"Hurry, Phoenix, hurry."

I feel my heart rate increase as I pick through it all, but I'm running out of time. I'm letting everyone down, and somehow, I know I won't find what I'm searching for.

But suddenly, I hear a different voice say something. It's not the lady in the white belt, but a boy. A male voice just behind me says my name.

"Heya, Phoenix!" I hear over my shoulder.

Turning quickly, I see Ronnie. Healthy and smiling as wide as ever, he looks right at me. He's waving at me.

I wave back.

Looking back down at the same pile before me, I finally uncover the boots I'd been searching for. I reach down, and it's Ronnie's bright red snow boots.

They have some good weight to them, the leather a bit worn. I look up to give them to Ronnie. But where Ronnie was just standing, now stands Tyler. He's wearing his white shirt and tie, his long dark hair mussed up like he had just pulled off a ski mask.

"Ronnie!" I scream. "Ronnie, where are you!?"

But I'm too late. Tyler pulls out his gun and points it right at me.

"Ronnie! Please! Ronnie!"

The gun cracks.

Down…down…down…

"Phoenix! Phoenix!" I hear Ronnie's voice scream out for me.

"Ronnie! I'm sorry! I'm sorry!"

"Phoenix!"

The first thing I saw were my hands. They weren't holding his boots any longer; they were banging against the walls of my classroom.

Mr. Patts grabbed hold of my shoulders.

"Phoenix. Calm down. You're in class with all of us right now. Try and breathe. Try and slow down."

I could hear in his voice that he sounded terrified.

"Just breathe. You're with us in class. You're here."

I finally turned around to see the rest of my class. They, too, looked at me with fear. Jaws were gaping.

Mr. Patts looked me in the eyes. "How can I help you, Phoenix? Please, if there's anything, just tell me. Tell me, and I'll do it."

But he and I both knew that there wasn't anything he, or anyone, could do.

I couldn't keep going on this way.

~

"So, it's happened again, has it?" Principal McGugan frowned. "Everyone's growing even more concerned than we already were, Phoenix."

Principal McGugan was a gentle woman, but she didn't know what it was like. She'd gotten hired once Principal Roman ran for the hills after the shooting. I'd never quite trusted her when we talked.

"Mr. Patts informed me that you were yelling the name of a student that we lost that day. Ronnie Laxlel."

I looked up, and beside a small lamp was the school's intercom on her desk. There were photos and ornaments all around her workspace. It reminded me a lot of my desk in the Bird's Nest.

Principal McGugan was someone who really was trying to help, but I wasn't sure if that really made much of a difference.

"To help deal with grief, it's best to occupy the mind with a goal. Using something to work toward as a productive distraction." She paused, briefly shifting her weight. "Your therapist tells me you're a magnificent speller. One of the best in the state."

"You talk to Mrs. S?" I was shocked.

Principal McGugan nodded. "Think of us as your personal team."

I looked down again.

"But your spelling, Phoenix. You're quite well known for it amongst all the staff. Have you been preparing for the state tournament? It's coming up in little less than a month, and I've been looking forward to seeing you in action myself, after all of the good things I've heard."

While staring at my feet, I sighed. The truth was, I hadn't looked at a flashcard in a year. I couldn't focus on it anymore like I used to. I couldn't focus on anything anymore.

Principal McGugan and I just sat there in silence. The quiet of her office sank deeper into me, and I felt the enduring scars of my chronic terror ache. Nowhere was safe anymore. Then she interrupted my haze of pain by adding, "I know you'd do your father proud by competing in the tournament. You're an Iver, after all."

At that, I lost control. I couldn't take it anymore.

"He wasn't even there! He never was! And now...now he won't be anywhere ever again. I don't care about making him proud."

Principal McGugan gave it a moment before responding. "Your

father was a good man, Phoenix, and no matter what, he'll always be proud of who you are. I'm sure of it."

I shot out, "He's not some hero, you know. He was just a security guard."

I had grown tired of all the stories that had circulated about him after that day of the Snowball last year. Everyone talked about him like he was some saint, but I knew who he really was. He was the furthest thing from perfect. Everyone else, it seemed, had decided it was best to just forget about all the other stuff.

Principal McGugan slowly began, "I never said that he—"

But I cut her off. Hard. Saying the one thing that seemed to constantly remain on my mind. "If he is such a hero, then how come fourteen other people died!? Would a *hero* let that happen? It was his job, wasn't it? To protect us? You can tell yourself whatever you want, but I don't owe him anything. He's gone! Besides, don't act like you knew him, because you didn't. I knew him, and he wasn't any hero at all."

"You don't mean that," she started. "Your father gave his own life to save the lives of hundreds by storming into the library that day. What he did was brave."

I was about to cry. I knew the feeling all too well after all that had happened.

"A hero would have come home. I…" I started to choke and sputter. "I don't care. I really don't anymore. It doesn't make any of this better either way. It…it doesn't change the fact that I will never hear him or see him again."

Principal McGugan appeared as though she didn't have an answer for me. She knew that nothing she could say would bring him back.

"But that's life," I said with an exhausted drop of my arms. "People…just die."

She took a long exhale before saying, "I really wish I could have known him. But I'm sure he misses you, too, Phoenix. I'm sure he misses you every day."

"No. No, he doesn't," I started as I got up to leave. "My dad can't miss anyone ever again."

I hobbled over to my table during lunch to try and stomach something. I sat down, feeling curious eyes glance at me. Everyone knew about my dad and what he did that day, how he'd run in, alone, and stopped them. He became all anyone wanted to talk about after that, so people started looking at me. Now it seemed I couldn't hide anywhere.

I was going to wait for TT until I looked up and saw that he was sitting with his new teammates at the basketball table. He'd made the varsity team this school year and had started hanging out with those guys most of the time. He'd asked me once at the end of last year to come and eat with them, but I could tell he just felt bad. He was happy he didn't have to be a loser any longer.

I peeled open my brown bag and unwrapped a peanut butter and jelly. It wasn't much, but I wasn't very hungry. Plus, the quicker I ate, the quicker I could go and hide in the bathroom. At least there, I couldn't feel all of the other students looking at me. It was a safe place to wait until marching into my final class of the day.

My teeth chewed. My saliva softened. My tongue swallowed. But the whole time, I wasn't focused on any of it. Each bite was worse than the last, and each breath was more difficult than the previous. While sitting alone, I finished a third of my sandwich and tossed the rest. Standing up, I zipped up my backpack and headed for the bathroom.

I turned the corner and saw her—the only person in all of Darling who still looked alive.

Shay was standing around with all the seniors on the football team and a couple of her friends. Pounds had his arm around her. All of them leaned against the wall by the doors to the gym.

She no longer wore her signature pink Converse sneakers. I could see that, instead, she'd chosen to wear a pair of dark jeans and Pounds's deep purple Darling Dragons football jersey. They had a home game tonight.

As I walked by them, I looked up and could see that only she had seen me. The quiver in her eyelashes was undeniable.

I slowed myself almost to a stop. I looked back up at her more directly. She'd changed. She didn't look like a girl anymore, but a woman. Older, but in a good way. Since I'd hit puberty, I'd only welcomed more acne into my life. She'd welcomed more beauty into hers. I'm sure her voice was still a song, while mine was caught between a baritone and a squeaking pitch.

Even though I was sad. Even though it was his arm around her and not mine. Even though I wasn't sure I could keep going. I did my best to make a good social appearance, just like Mr. Patts said.

I was plastic.

I waved, as friendly as I thought possible, and was even able to trick myself into a smile. She didn't wave back, just looked at me, then her friends turned, and so did she. They all just looked right through me before turning away. Like they could see how empty I really was.

Shay met my eyes and then glanced back down at her shoes before she turned.

All of them walked away.

I scurried toward the bathroom, threw open the stall door, and melted. My body began to shake, and the cold was getting stronger.

I sat on the toilet, the stall door locked and the bathroom empty, but I no longer even felt safe here. It was all closing in.

I looked around the stall. Nothing but the scarred blue *clair de lune* walls were around me.

Tyler's old graffiti had still remained cut into all the walls. Serving as a paralyzing omen—a cry for help that had been ignored—seeing them here now felt as though they had a new meaning. Each of Tyler's messages was somehow shouting at me in his voice. A warning for what none of us had realized was coming. I didn't want to read them, but my eyes continued to dart from one to the next.

Death to them all.

My knee's rocked back and forth. My teeth chattered.

One day you'll know why.

I was getting colder.

Time is running out...

But then, my eyes came across what I had written. I turned my head quickly, as if to shake off the truth, but there was no denying that was my own handwriting next to his, next to the writing of the person who had gunned down my own father. The sharp red ink dripped down the blue of the stall like blood.

Kill Pounds.

I panicked. I bolted out the door. There was only one place I could think to go that might be safe any longer. I desperately wanted to be there as quickly as possible, holding out hope that it would still be safe. I needed it now more than ever.

~

Flying through the front door of Metropolis, I saw my mom sitting in the kitchen. I hadn't been expecting anyone home, so to see her caught me off guard. But she hardly looked surprised. In fact, the way she stared back at me was as if the fact that my face was marred by tears was of little shock to her. She didn't even flinch.

Sliding my backpack from my shoulder, I noticed the declivity in her face. The skin on her cheeks looked sucked inward. The bones were protruding. If I hadn't known better, I would've thought she was terminally ill. She was still in her bed robe.

"It's just you and me," she croaked. "No matter how much we cry, it's still just going to be you and me."

But all I could do was try and look back at her. My eyes had been so clouded with tears that it felt like I could hardly see. I wiped them once more.

"You have school, Noodle. We cannot keep like this."

"I can't keep doing anything!" I screamed at her, then adding even louder, "All you do is cry all day, so why can't I?"

She looked back at me fiercely. "He's not walking through that door."

My tears came back hard. I wanted to just simply combust into a million pieces before her—divvying up my pain into manageable fragments. The more we talked about it, the less sense it made.

"He was my best friend," I choked out.

Her eyes glazed over as she turned toward the window. "Mine too."

She and I looked at each other and then looked away. Two strangers, forced to work together to solve the same problem. The issue being that our solution to every problem before this one was gone. He was gone. All of this was gone—whatever *this* ever even was.

"He was the only person who ever really knew me," she said. "I felt like my life started when we met. I hardly remember anything before then."

I wiped my eyes once more when she reached for her rosary

beads with a steel cross attached to its end. They were just before her on the table.

Slowly, she closed her eyes. I watched her lips move as they whispered a quiet sermon.

Since he'd died, faith had found its way into her life. It felt incredibly ironic because, when he was alive, she'd ridiculed anyone who believed in such a thing. Now it seemed, religion was the only thing that kept her going. God was the only person she would speak to, even when her own son was standing right in front of her.

I was boiling with anger as I watched her pray. The way she just stopped our conversation in an instant.

I slapped my hands on the kitchen table. "He can't hear you! Nobody can! Nobody!"

Her silent prayer stopped, but her eyes remained closed. Tears ran down her cracked cheeks. Her fingers trembled on the beads.

I didn't know what else to do but just go and hide from everything. After saying that to her, even I didn't want to be around myself.

I ran into her bedroom and slammed the door behind me as I tucked myself into the Arts District. Once inside, my crying turned violent. But as I stood inside of the closet in an eruption, I was suddenly burning. It was all getting much too hot. Sweat dripped from the back of my ears, my neck was sticky.

I jumped out of my clothes and stripped completely naked. Standing barefoot directly on their linoleum floor, I shook my arms and legs to try and ease my anxiety, but nothing helped. The cold shot up quickly through the bottoms of my feet into the remainder of my body. I fell into a pale ball on the floor. My teeth began to chatter once again. None of it was helping much at all, and I had nowhere else to turn. I didn't know what else to do. So, in a moment of pure weakness and no other options, I did something that I would have never imagined. I turned to the one thing I said I never would. I started to pray too. Naked and in the fetal position on my parents' closet floor, I beckoned for a higher power.

I thought about what a catastrophe my life had been and asked God the simplest question that I could think of.

"Why?" I struggled out of my throat.

Why did he choose to make my life so dark? How could he have given me so little, yet taken so much?

The only thing I'd ever truly wanted was to be normal. I just wanted to be able to have friends, go to school and not get bullied or worry about being shot at. To have a dad that could throw the baseball with me and teach me how to talk to girls. To have a mom who understood my pain and wanted to talk to me instead of some myth in the sky.

I asked God why he would do all these things to me, to someone who had never done anything to him except fail to believe.

Then I prayed for all of it to stop, for brighter days and happier moments.

When I was strong enough to rise to my feet, I opened my eyes and saw how dark it still was. How cold it still felt. How alone I really had become.

The light was gone, and it wasn't because God had taken it—it was gone because it had never existed in the first place.

Defeated, I crawled into the shelf of my dad's clothes, which hadn't moved since the day of the Snowball. My breathing eventually slowed. My tears eventually dried up. But the pain remained. The stain on my tongue from what I'd said to my own mother was impossible not to taste.

I shifted my weight slightly when I felt something. Typical, I thought, even here, I couldn't be comfortable. But after looking beneath my right knee, I found something. I reached for it.

The feel of it in my hands was strange. Heavy.

It was a small pocket notebook with a pair of wings on the front.

12

Between the sleeves of my dad's jackets, I carefully studied this book. After quietly turning on the light so I could see, I went page by page. Partially because I was interested, partially to distract myself from everything else.

In the silence of their closet, I could intently focus.

I could immediately tell that it was his handwriting. A handwriting that was the voice I'd always known. The pages were old, the ink weathered. My hands ran over the characters, attempting to unlock some of his spirit.

But it wasn't the journal or diary I'd hoped it might be. The book, it seemed, was just a list of different addresses. It was one hundred pages of unmarked addresses with no names. I couldn't initially identify any of them. Their only similarity was that they were all to places around Colorado, from Grand Junction to Telluride. There were addresses to places across the state.

The only strange thing I did notice, though, was that the first ninety-three were checked off, but the final seven were not.

Eventually, my confusion cleared, as I'd finally concluded that this was probably just a list of all the people he worked for at night as an electrician.

I was ready to discard the book entirely, as it represented all that was wrong to me in this world, when suddenly, I read a strange phrase in the front. It was in some other language. Written on the opening flap. But it somehow reminded me of my dad and all his thoughtfulness. It had to mean something; I just had no idea what.

Το φως λάμπει στο σκοτάδι.

I looked back down and could tell that it wasn't his handwriting, though. It was curvier—like it was written by a girl.

Then, just below that, there was an address that was more specific than any of the others. It was on the very first page, and it was the only address in the entire book that had a name and an exact location.

WINGS
4421 S. Springfield Rd.
Darling, CO 80105
Locker 8½

Then, it came to me. I knew this address. It was the address to Darling High School.

With the book tucked beneath my arm, I got my clothes back on and waited in the closet until my mom fell asleep that night. Once I was certain she was out, I slowly snuck back to the Bird's Nest.

Carefully, I looked over everything again to make sure that my eyes were telling the truth. But each time I read the address, it didn't change. All of the letters stayed the same. The words didn't disappear like in one of my visions, and the numbers didn't bleed away. This was real.

I still hadn't the slightest clue as to why this address had a name, when all of the others didn't. But there had to be a reason. Whatever it was, it had to be important. Whoever "Wings" was, I was going to find him or her. And I was going to do it tonight.

~

Once the dark had fully blanketed the night, I found my heavy jacket, yellow beanie, and a flashlight. But as I ruffled around my closet, I watched the Key of Courage fall to the floor. I'd stopped wearing it since the shooting and hadn't seen it since. I guess, after that, I just sort of gave up on that kind of stuff.

But seeing it on the floor, shimmering in the dim light of my closet, I decided that I wanted to have something with me. I scooped it up and threw it on over my head. I tucked the book in my pocket, grabbed the flashlight, and was out the door.

It was late. The night yawned around me as I walked, and there wasn't a sound for miles. The deep air in my lungs initially made me cough. I realized, as I took another deep breath, that I hadn't been outside in over twelve hours. It was after midnight.

The walk wasn't all that bad, as it gave me the time to acclimate. With each step that I took, I felt more and more myself.

Arriving at the school, it suddenly became much darker. All of the lights were off this late at night. I couldn't see a thing.

They locked up all the halls and classrooms at night, but because all the lockers were built into the walls on the exterior of the buildings, the school left the campus open. I knew because, when TT had forgotten his chemistry book last semester, the night before our final, we had to come back around this time to grab it. Nobody stopped us from walking right through the center of campus to his locker.

I wasn't sure what I was doing, but then I saw it. The library on my right.

Fifteen painted hearts.

When the art students had first made them, they'd looked vibrant along the wall of the library. The pinks, yellows, and reds were alive. Each one bore a name. We all placed signatures on the wall around them, their favorite hat, a photo, or sometimes even a personal note. But as more time had passed, the elements had significantly weathered them. Dulled their lives. Now it was hard to read any of the names. Hard to tell what colors they used to be.

Ghosts moved in the reflections on the dark windows. I could hear them again. The cracks. The cries. Shay's gentle voice in my ear. Tyler's shouting. Ronnie hitting the floor. I wanted to forget it all, but over time, I'd realized that it only became easier to remember each minute detail. While the memorial hearts had faded over time, those memories became more vivid to me, more colorful.

I knew I'd never be able to get it all out of my head for the rest of my life. Even now, after all this time, it felt like a part of me was still trapped beneath those books. And I was starting to accept that a part of me always would be.

I stopped walking and just stared. It was a graveyard. The longer I looked at it, the more the cement corners of the library looked like headstones, and the long black windows looked more like coffins. Nothing about this once shining symbol of creativity would ever be bright again. After looking at it for too long, I didn't want to keep going. I remembered why it was so hard to smile nowadays. Why it seemed like it should always be dark, with none of van Gogh's swirling stars.

But I went on. I had no idea why, but I did. I walked deeper into the school. While looking at the library, I was reminded why all of this really didn't matter, but I kept walking anyway—one foot in front of the other.

I shined the flashlight onto the book as I cracked it open. I was standing in the middle of campus, but it was still too dark to see much of anything.

I peeked at the address once more, thinking about where to find locker eight and a half. It seemed like it should have been easy enough, although the number itself seemed odd for a locker. I'd never before heard of such a thing.

I knew that lockers one through fifty were tucked away past the old soccer field and on the backside of the bus drop-off. I never really went back there, since I always walked to school. The lockers were hidden by a small bridge that served as a walkway to the school's second story. Because of the cover, it was shielded during the winter from the elements.

Making my way through campus, I found lockers five, six, seven, eight, nine, and ten. There was no locker eight and a half.

I stood there with my flashlight and closely attempted to examine the entire row, but there wasn't anything special about them I could see. The closer I looked, the more it appeared to be a row of normal, dull, high school lockers. A little bumped and scratched from use, but other than that, not a single one stood out.

Another disappointment. I'd given one more shot at hopefully discovering something fantastic, but instead, discovered, yet again, another healthy dose of reality. That nothing is as enchanted as it appears.

A shiver went up my back, and I got the feeling of heat crawling all over me. It was my anxiety again.

I ripped off my jacket, tearing the buttons loose, and slid to a seat against the wall below the lockers.

In a heap, I wondered what it was I had been hoping to discover. I was starting to get the sense that maybe it had all been my fault. I had always been responsible for thinking there must be more to everything, when, in reality, there wasn't.

I was perpetuating my own cycle of fear, then anger, then anxiety, finished with depression. To stop it from happening anymore, I decided that I had to stop swimming upstream. I had to fall in line, or else I wasn't going to be able to function much at all. I had no other choice.

With age comes more knowledge, but with age also comes more disappointment. The more you start to taste and experience the real world for what it truly is, you start to miss the times when you truly couldn't. Ignorance most definitely is bliss, and it was that sweet bliss that I could taste no longer. My palate had matured faster than I'd desired. Parents are scared, and kids don't realize it. But when your parents weren't around anymore to control what you take in, it was right in front of your eyes. It was waiting right on your plate.

The world is black.

I wasn't sure what all of this was for, but I'd settled on the fact that there probably wasn't an answer. I guess, over time, you just start to become okay with that.

Getting up to leave, I slid my way back through the center of campus, my head hanging low and my eyes tracking my steps. I had no idea where I was going anymore.

Wandering and following, wandering and following, is what most of us do. We wander until we find something to follow. Ideas, dreams—some of us even follow people—but, like all things, ideas, dreams, and people, they all die. Ideas get disproven. Dreams don't come true. People pass away. We then go from followers to wanderers once more, walking aimlessly through life, having gained nothing of any real value. In the same boots as before, walking through life with our eyes on the same ground, suffering from the same anxieties and the same disappointments. Wandering again until we find something else to follow. Until we, like all things, die ourselves.

Beyond the library, a light shined from an open doorway. Something about it looked familiar.

I sighed. I took one look at the light, then one look in the direction of Metropolis. I was tired. I didn't want to keep myself in the pursuit of hope.

With my anxieties still burning, I stopped to breathe again. I was feeling overwhelmed, but then I felt the key against my bare skin. I thought about it and all that he'd taught me. I thought about the trashman and the park. I closed my eyes and focused on my breathing.

Softly, with my eyes still closed, I said, "I will not be afraid of what I do not know because what I do not know is the only thing keeping me from the place I would like to go."

And slowly, when I opened my eyes, the light from the doorway flickered. Then it came back on, shining as brightly as it had been when I first saw it only a moment before.

I stared at the light—my eyes wide open. "I will not be afraid of what I do not know because what I do not know is the only thing keeping me from the place I would like to go."

As I spoke, the light flickered again.

"I will not be afraid of what I do not know because what I do not know is the only thing keeping me from the place I would like to go."

Like a dam, my voice continued to control the current. Light, dark, light, dark, all the way until I finished speaking and it remained bright, glowing magnificently out into the harsh, shadowy night.

The open doorway belonged to an office. My dad's old office at school.

Taking a step inside, I saw a weathered desk with notes, old mugs, cups, and books atop the surface. Nobody was inside, despite the light being on. I pushed aside a mop that was leaning against the front door and started to look around. Then, just beside his desk and beside a waste bin, almost like a safe, was a locker with a wings decal that matched the one on my dad's book. Locker 8½.

It shone brightly. It looked completely different from the other lockers on campus. But then, I noticed that this locker didn't have a dial like all of the others, either, but a lock for a key. I carefully took the Key of Courage off my neck and placed it into Locker 8½. It clicked open.

Surprisingly though, there wasn't much inside. I wasn't sure what I'd been expecting, but what I saw certainly wasn't it. It was just a plain manila envelope with the number "94" written on it. The handwriting, though, was the same curvy female handwriting from the inside flap of my dad's book. There was nothing else.

I grabbed the envelope and could feel something inside of it. It was sealed tight.

Standing in front of the open locker, I began to slide my finger through the envelope to peel it open, when a light shined right into my eyes. Someone was coming.

"Hey! You're not supposed to be here!" a voice called out. "Stop right now! Don't move!" the voice yelled again before I could even think to respond to the initial call.

The light was blinding, and I couldn't see anything. It was

extremely disorienting.

"You shouldn't be here," the voice repeated.

But then I realized who it was, who it had to be. The one person who could tell me what all of this was.

Wings.

13

The light was so mighty and angelic I was convinced it was the rapture. With the darkness of night around me, it provided a warmth that I so desperately needed, like morning sun.

The voice got closer and closer, the light brighter and brighter. I closed my eyes.

"This place was built by everyone, for everyone. A place that would keep people safe, but also, provide both the messengers and the recipients with a purpose. But no place is always safe from everything, everyone. Do you understand now, my child?"

I do my best to nod. I'm not sure if I look like I understand or not, but I finally figure out who the woman in the white belt is. Who she must be. This book and this letter belong to her.

"You have something else to ask me now, don't you?"

The state I've entered is a place that I am certain must be real this time. For so long, I'd just felt as though I hadn't yet found it until now, even though I had searched for it in every single place imaginable. But, entering Maya's this time, made it all worth it. The journey finally meant something more.

Her voice gets close enough to feel. The warmth of another is right before me.

I use everything inside of me to ask her a simple question. A question I now know the answer to and understand that it is all going to fit together. What this place is and why I can never escape it. Because now I know her name.

"Wings?"

But suddenly, it all stops. She doesn't say anything in return. Just as quickly as it came, it ends. The light disappears, and the woman in the white belt slowly dissolves from my vision. The store and the aisles around me begin to fall. It's dark again, just as dark as before.

"Wings? Wings? Wings?" I repeat again and again and again. She fades, and now I could hardly see her. Then I can't see much of anything. But that name continues to wrap around my mind.

I opened my eyes, but the aftershock of the light temporarily blinded me.

"Phoenix?" a male voice said. "My goodness, kid, what on Earth are you doing here at one in the morning?"

His light was now off and at his side. My bliss turned off once the darkness returned. My journey, it seemed, was far from over. I hadn't been called yet.

"Wings?" I asked with less conviction than before, tucking the half-opened envelope in my back pocket.

But then my eyes began to properly function again. I was in my dad's old office. Before me, stood a man in a deep blue police uniform with badges attached at the breast and a belt full of supplies around his waist. A police officer. It was Shay's dad, Marcus.

"Wings? Who the hell is Wings, kid? It's me…Marcus. Phoenix? What are you doing here?"

I hesitated, realizing he knew nothing about Maya's store, the locker, the book, or Wings. The disappointment was neutralizing. Seeing Marcus standing before me made me sad again. It reminded me of *him*. How many nights he'd spent in this space. It made me think of how I would never again see him standing on his two feet.

Marcus suddenly changed his tone. "I'm sorry I scared you. I… had no idea that it was you. That's all."

He put his hand on my shoulder, which I guess made me feel a little bit better.

"What are you doing here?" I softly asked, turning the question back on him.

He adjusted his cap. "Ever since the shooting, our station has kept the school under twenty-four-hour surveillance. Since the news took off with the story, pretty much everyone and their mother has tried to come and see the school after hours. You'd think it would be the opposite, but I've learned that, in tragedies, that is rarely the case. People…they feel like they need to see it." He slowed down before adding, "I think people are trying to learn the lesson without actually experiencing it."

I looked up at Marcus to see that he wasn't just wearing any normal badges on his breast, but several gold stars. He must have been recently promoted to chief. It struck me then as odd that it was him watching the school at night and not one of the more junior officers. Surely, a police chief had better things to do.

"Are you here every night?" I asked.

"I haven't really slept much since. So…yeah. I figure, if I can't sleep, then I'll let someone else off the hook. Put this insomnia to use."

He looked tired as he said it. It was late anyway, but it wasn't a sleepy tired that pulled at Marcus's face. It wasn't the kind of tired that a couple of good nights' sleep, or even a long vacation, could fix, either. I'd seen this type of tired before. It was the kind of tired that became a part of you—the kind of tired you carried.

"Me either," I piped up. "Most nights, I think about it a lot too."

As Marcus and I stood in my dad's old office, our mutual

heartache was palpable. But in a lot of ways, it was scarier for me to see such a strong man so routed. Someone I knew for a fact was better equipped than I to deal with tragedy. Both of our eyes scanned the room. The mess of what my dad's old office—now that he was gone—was as close as I'd ever get to him again. Inanimate objects were the closest I'd ever get to having a father again. I brushed my hand across the top of his desk, dust clinging to the tips of my fingers.

"Come on, kid, let me get you home."

I followed Marcus back out of the school and into the parking lot. The darkness had settled in more calmly. It began to seem slightly less unnerving. Although I was beginning to grow even more tired of this seemingly endless unknown. I could feel the unopened envelope in my back pocket and felt as though he wasn't telling me his full truth. Everything had just been one consecutive black hole after another—somebody had to know more than they were admitting.

In the parking lot, we approached his squad car. He'd fixed the scrape on the door, but the top corner of the siren still had the same crack from six years ago. It was the cruiser that he and my dad used to drive together.

That night after my birthday party flashed in my memory—the blood on my dad's uniform, the pleading look on his face— and my emotions got the best of me. Questions that I'd suppressed all these years bubbled to the surface. Not knowing just simply wasn't going to be something I would settle for anymore. I had nothing more to lose.

With the night around the police cruiser, it hardly looked like a machine built to maintain the peace.

"Listen." Marcus stopped me once we arrived beside the car. "I'm sorry I wasn't there sooner...that day. You and my daughter should have never had to see any of that. I'm sorry...I'm sorry that you had to. I'm sorry that I couldn't protect you both."

Somehow it didn't make me feel any better.

"But Shay told me how brave you were. How you kept each other safe. It's over now. It's over now, and you're both safe."

"But *he's* gone," I started softly, gradually becoming louder. "He's not okay. Everything I ever did was for him…and…and now that he's not here, I don't want to do anything. It doesn't matter, because he will never see any of it."

Saying this to Marcus, I hadn't realized I'd thought any of it until my very own voice confessed. To speak these words felt foreign.

"And…and it feels like I never even knew who he really was. And now that he's gone, I know I never will."

I turned from Marcus and looked back at the library.

"He was the best man I knew," Marcus said. "He taught me everything I know about living a happy life."

I faced Marcus once more as he said, "I've been on the force for twenty-two years now, Phoenix, and I've never had a better partner than your father."

"Then what happened?" I asked sharply.

Marcus looked down at me with skepticism in his eye. "Phoenix. Listen, I—"

"No!" I cut him off. "Stop trying to protect me! Don't be like Shay or like him or like everyone else. Tell me why he lost his job. Tell me why we never saw your family again. Tell me why you both left my party that day. Tell me why my dad was at the hospital covered in blood. Tell me why…Tell me…Tell me…"

Eventually, I just ran out of breath. My arms fell to my sides. I had no patience anymore. I already wasn't sleeping.

He didn't answer.

"I get it," I said once I'd caught my breath in the silence. "You're just going to tell me the same thing that everyone else does. To forget the past and just move on."

Then a wind came that was stronger than a breeze.

"Not here," Marcus finally said firmly. Then he added, "I'll tell you. But just not here."

He opened the passenger door to the cruiser, and I fell in. With Marcus now in the driver's seat, we peeled out of the school's parking lot.

~

Six years were gone. Some days it felt like that night had never happened. Other days it felt like that was the only night that ever had. What I did know was, that was the night everything changed.

Driving down the roads, I wanted to feel safe, but the cop car didn't quite offer the respite I'd hoped for. The beeping screens and armored interior kept me jagged. There was a shotgun pinned just a few inches over my head.

I kept my eyes on Marcus as he drove. The way he confidently maneuvered the streets. Even at this hour, and despite his tired eyes, he appeared at home, his hearthstone a steering wheel.

Lights went by and by and by. He didn't say anything more as we drove. I kept quiet. The only thing I was able to gather about our journey was that we were headed toward the bad side of town. The distances between each house were getting smaller and smaller. They also looked less and less like places people could live. Trash piled up in the gutters. House pets roamed the streets. But, even with all of that, the strangest part were the people outside in the middle of the night.

As our police car rolled along, each person stopped and turned to look at us. They appeared as though they weren't stopping out of fear, but disgust. Despite all of that, Marcus appeared hardly fazed. To me, it felt like all of their eyes had been tearing me apart.

Slowly, we pulled into a parking spot along an inner-city neighborhood street. Despite the odd hour, lights were on in a few of the homes. Looking around outside, I didn't see much of anything that I would've liked to look at for long. We sat inside the car.

"There." Marcus pointed at a house over on the left. "Theo Bridges. I've arrested him twice for armed robbery."

Marcus then pointed to another home across the street and continued. "Junior Sal and Big Sal, everyone calls them. Your dad and I arrested them both on a first offense for aggravated assault. The second time...the second time was for kidnapping."

I swallowed hard. I began to regret my asking about what had happened more each second we sat beside one another. I wanted to go home.

"But there." Marcus pointed again. "The blue house."

It was a rundown old home. The washed blue paint had started to peel on the corners. The stairs that led from the sidewalk to the front door were short two steps. The fence around the modest property appeared trampled.

But Marcus didn't say anything else. It was silent for so long that, eventually, I turned to look at him instead of the blue house. I saw that Marcus was attempting to stifle tears, clenching his jaw. He was laser-focused on the property, although his emotions were starting to get the best of him.

"Gloria Woodle. Record as clean as a kindergartener."

Looking closer at the blue house, I could see an old woman with white hair. She was on her knees in the cold dirt of what looked like some sort of garden in their front yard.

"Is…is that her?" I asked.

Marcus nodded.

"What's she doing gardening this late…this time of year?"

Marcus was still emotional as he responded. "The same thing you and I were doing at the high school."

Hearing him say that made me turn away. I just couldn't look at him, or anyone really. My mind raced with grim possibility.

Marcus rubbed his eyes before he continued. "She comes out here every Friday night, every season no matter the weather, rain, snow, hail, or shine, at the exact same time, to replace what flowers she can. It's never for very long, and she usually picks them right from her garden."

As Marcus explained, I watched Gloria carefully shuffle around her urban meadow. Her movement was so dawdling that you could tell—even from this far away—she was very old.

"But in *this* neighborhood and with *these* neighbors at *this* hour… it's too dangerous for anyone to be out…especially for someone with a condition like hers."

"So, you come here to look after her?" I asked.

Marcus was still looking at her as he nodded. "That night of your birthday," he began heavily, "in '94. It was something your dad and I talked about. We couldn't get the entire day off, so he told me he'd take you to the park early, you know, so the two of you could have some time together. Just in case something came up later. We were lucky most of the day. We didn't get any calls, and the party was great, so even I was able to come by too. Everyone was having a really great time. But it all began when your dad and I got a call for a broken fire hydrant on Ladamere Road. The thing exploded and was leaking into the street. Normally, firefighters would handle that sort of thing, but your dad insisted we check it out, since we weren't far away. We knew your party was winding down anyway, so we left. When we got there, I was freaking out, but Herm just looked at me and laughed. He pulled out our wrench and had the thing fixed in seconds. He gave me so much crap for it that he made me promise to buy us both pizza and sodas after."

As Marcus spoke, I watched Gloria. She picked an errant weed or two, gently tending to the surrounding plants.

"After the fire hydrant, we stopped at Maya's so I could make it up to your dad for saving the day. It was this small convenience store that was your dad's favorite place. We went a lot because they had all kinds of stuff. It's not too far from where we are right now."

Gloria wiped her forehead clean as she started to dig.

"But when your father and I walked in, we heard people yelling and screaming. It was an armed robbery. Two guys with weapons were holding up the place."

An automatic light from Gloria's patio clicked on, and I could see her face for the first time. Worn pale skin. Deeply canyoned cheeks. Tan gardening gloves. Loose dirt smudged below her eye.

"The first guy took off the minute we entered the front door, so I chased after him. Your father stayed behind in the store. Herm tried to talk the other guy into giving up. We could tell then they weren't really grown men, they were just kids, kids who didn't know what they were doing. The second assailant panicked and took the storekeeper as a hostage instead. He had him at gunpoint. It escalated quickly. Herm told me he pulled his gun to see if he could get a clear shot, but it was impossible. I don't know…he…he really did everything he was supposed to do. He followed our training. He kept his weapon on the suspect the entire time."

She continued to dig until adequately unearthing enough ground for her new flowers. Carefully, she surgically pruned the old flowers—using only the tips of her fingers.

"With his weapon still trained on the suspect, he was able to slowly inch toward the hostage. It was all exactly by the book. Humanizing himself and the situation to put the assailant at ease. It was a tense stand-off, but we both had everything under control."

Gloria took a long breath and stopped to look out. Further beyond the street, you could tell her eyes were staring off. Then, she returned to her task at hand.

"But then, the suspect took his gun off of the hostage and fired at your father. Your dad...he...he quickly dove for cover, but the suspect continued to fire. It was a semi-automatic weapon. Behind cover, your dad waited for the gunman to reload before Herm fired several shots back. The two went back and forth with neither sure if they'd hit the other."

With her hands so carefully wrapped around the base of her flowers, Gloria cradled them like a child—fresh white tulips.

"I had just returned from arresting the initial suspect and calling in for back-up when I heard the shots. Taking cover beside the front door, I was able to get a clear shot on the suspect. I took him out. I thought it was all over, but then I saw your father. I turned and saw him holding a small child. In tears, he told me that one of the bullets he'd fired...one of the bullets he'd fired had ricocheted and...and hit...this boy. We didn't even call an ambulance as we rushed him to the hospital ourselves. He was losing a lot of blood. Your dad flew into the emergency room with the boy in his arms. They took him into surgery right away...but this boy...died. The boy died on the operating table that night. Her boy. Her…grandson. A completely innocent bystander. A twelve-year-old boy inside of the store, who was just shopping with his grandmother. Aloanso Woodle."

The light aiding Gloria automatically flipped off, but she didn't bother to turn it back on. She just carried on planting the tulips in the dark.

"I tried to help your father live it down, but he wouldn't forgive himself. We got so much public blowback that your father was forced to resign. I…I begged our chief at the time to not be so hard on him, explaining that it was just a terrible accident, but she wouldn't budge. She told me I was lucky that I was still able to keep my position. Our boss even told me that if she ever saw me around your father, I would never wear this badge again."

It was hard to still see Gloria in the dark, but somehow, I could tell she was there.

"It was on a night, just like this, that Aloanso was killed. So, for the last six years, Gloria comes out here every Friday, at two in the morning, and changes the flowers on his headstone. He's buried right there where she plants those flowers. And the reason I know all of this is because, without them knowing, all those years and countless nights, your dad would come out here to make sure that they were okay. To make sure that Gloria could safely mourn in the middle of the night."

With all the flowers finally set, Gloria rose to her feet. She slowly climbed back up to her house, avoiding the missing steps. She slid open the screen door and entered the blue house. Alone.

"I know it stayed with him," Marcus concluded. "How could it not?"

My breathing slowed, and my heart rate dropped. I wasn't sure if finally knowing what had happened was a good thing. But I'd come to learn that bad things happen all the time. I guess this was no different. I just never expected it to be because of him. An innocent human life was lost at the hands of my dad. The same hands that had once held me, raised me. Those same hands, in my mind, would now be forever covered in blood.

I'd been sitting quietly for so long that I wasn't sure I could speak.

We sat there a while longer, until I finally just said it. "But you weren't there."

"What do you mean?" Marcus asked.

"You weren't there," I continued. "You don't know if he followed everything by the book. You don't know what really happened in that store when you were gone. You don't know if he told you the truth or not."

Marcus responded with conviction. "But I do. Your father, he... he was not that kind of person. Herman was a helper. He always wore his heart on his sleeve. I trusted him with my life. That's what he told me, so I know it's true, Phoenix."

I swallowed hard. My head hurt. My body went hot. I was all twisted and turned.

"Phoenix." Marcus sighed. "Herman is the same helper who saved my daughter from those monsters...saved all those other kids... saved you. If Herman hadn't shown up that day...I don't know if I would have ever held my baby girl again."

Finally, I looked up at Marcus and said, "But if he hadn't left my birthday party six years ago, Gloria would never have had to let go of her grandson."

Marcus looked back at me, but I just went down to my feet. It was all coming in around me again.

"Aloanso Woodle is up there with your dad in heaven."

But I just shook my head. Back and forth, I just shook my head.

I guess you can choose how you want to look at it. Good or bad, religion or science, hope or reality. But to me, there's no debate. If you just take a second to look around at your past, at those around you, in the end, only one wins out. Only one is real. In the end, it is only you. You, to deal.

Marcus drove me home to Metropolis. As the pavement sped by, I couldn't stop thinking about Maya's, about Aloanso Woodle, and how suddenly it all was starting to make sense.

Marcus pulled up in front of Metropolis and shifted into park. "I'll be here for you, Phoenix. I know that your dad would've done the same if anything ever happened to me. Whatever you need, just know you can ask."

I looked at him and tried to smile, but I didn't have much else to say.

"He was a good man."

Stepping out of the car, I knew I was getting closer. I knew where I had to go. I'd desperately wanted a moment to think, but I was also starting to get the sense I'd almost found what I'd so long been searching for, what had been pulling me.

I carefully crept back into Metropolis and slipped the keys to the Ferry off the mantel. They were in the same spot as always.

I had three hours until my mom would be awake for work.

14

The sun still wasn't up, but I knew they'd be open. I was headed to Maya's, the only place I could think to go, the place where I'd first seen Aloanso's full name in relic. I still wasn't sure what I was hoping to find, but I couldn't be inside my house. It seemed to just remind me too much of the tragedy of it all.

Driving through the streets, the occasional morning commuter moved beside me, but other than that, I was entirely on my own.

Despite being away from Metropolis, even in the Ferry, it wasn't long before I was overwhelmed by grief. The thought of my dad's atrocity made the center of my chest heavy. Thoughts of hope and doubt collided. One moment I was convinced I'd proven the existence of something fantastic, the next, I was certain it had been staged. With the destruction of my true north in my dad, I was simply wandering. And wandering, it seemed, was what I was still doing.

Suddenly, I was caught on a loose string of memory, a recollection triggered by the grief of finally learning the details of the tragedy that had cost my dad his job. All of it started to flood back as the pieces had finally come together.

Six years ago, and some weeks after my dad had the accident, I remembered being in Metropolis one morning. I was padding around the house—still recovering from my stay in the hospital. I could feel the bits and pieces of my past falling into place.

~

I'd stopped seeing my parents together as much. They were hardly ever in the same room, and they looked away from each other when they crossed paths. I'd only noticed, because we'd stopped eating together. Sometimes we wouldn't eat at all. That day, though, I couldn't take it any longer. I didn't care what was going on, or how scared we all were. I was so hungry.

I crept up the stairs to my parents' door, my stomach growling. I heard my mom on the phone, crying. I stopped outside to listen.

"I need to get out…I need to be out of this…this house. I need to be away from him."

I started to feel a growing sadness slide over me like a winter chill. Every part of me was pricked with goosebumps as I froze in place, not out of desire but anguish.

"I don't know. I…something must be wrong with him. I don't know what it is…but…but something just isn't normal."

My eyes, lips, and entire body felt heavier now. I was slowly collapsing inward. My shakes were quickly becoming more severe.

As I listened, my mom stopped talking and cried. No more words came from her. No more admissions or elucidations. Just painful, bottomless tears. A language I was becoming increasingly more familiar with.

I rubbed my elbows with my hands as I tried to reaffirm to myself that everything was going to be okay. That I wasn't alone in being afraid. That I wasn't alone in being cold. That I wasn't alone.

But continuing to listen to my mom cry through the paper-thin walls of our home she now felt trapped in, I started to believe less and less.

My eyes went down to my shoes. Through my mom's tears, I counted all of the different threads, stars, stitches, and stripes. Every little one I could find. I told myself that I was going to count as many as I could until she stopped crying.

I gave up after one hundred and forty-three.

~

I pulled the Ferry into a parking spot beside Maya's, the fluorescent sign flickering above me. Dawn painted the drifting clouds in the sky rose pink.

A feeling of emptiness came, but I reminded myself that I needed to be brave.

Inside, I was startled to see both how little had changed since I'd last been here, now over a year ago, and how it looked exactly the same as it did in my visions. As if the two were both just as real. The random assortment of shelves with countless aisles of items were stocked. Everything was still imperfectly perfectly organized. Aside from an occasional shopper, the store was empty.

I attempted to move with some purpose, as I knew I hadn't much time. I just wanted to see it all for myself. I shuffled to the front of the store to try and find Aloanso's shrine and almost find some way to apologize. Then, before me, I saw the wood. The framed photo hadn't moved. The same candle burned. A year since I'd last seen it, and not a single thing had changed. I picked up the photo, hoping to tell him how sorry I was.

He looked so young. His smile told me that he was alright, but what hurt me was to think about how I knew he wasn't. He looked like the kind of person who had tons of friends, the kind of person everyone knew and loved. The kid that you could ask people about, and they'd laugh and tell you a sweet story. Eyes that thought they had a full life ahead of them.

The pain of this place crept through my hand and into my organs like poison. An otherwise ordinary place that, much like the school library, had morphed into a graveyard. As much as I wanted to hide from the pain, I allowed my mind to try and find it. I allowed myself to let go and find it all. Then, it started happening.

I'm at Maya's as a line begins to build before me. There are plenty of people ahead and behind me. I look down and see I'm wearing my boots from when I was little.

"Did you find it?" The woman in the white belt stands next to me. I'm not surprised to see her.

I feel as if I've missed her so much, but she doesn't seem to return the feeling. Her demeanor is calm and patient, as if we've been standing in line beside one another for some time.

In one hand is hers, and in the other, I'm holding a bag of sugar.

"Oh good, good. Now we can have our treats. I know you've been waiting for them. These cookies are going to be the perfect way to end the perfect day."

I smile. I've missed her so much that I could start to cry. She looks so happy now.

I stare back at her and begin to feel her spirit with me, her light and her tenderness.

"We're almost to the front now."

But the line continues to build and build, and we don't seem to be moving at all. The building shakes again, the rumbling comes much stronger this time than it's ever been. It's strong enough to knock all the shelved items to the floor. Pretty soon, all of us in line are lying on the ground across the debris too.

I'm on top of boxes of cups and broken plates. For some reason, the woman in the white belt, along with everyone else who had been in line, doesn't seem startled that we've all fallen. It's only me who appears afraid.

"Don't miss it. He'll be here soon."

As I attempt to rise to my feet, Tyler storms into the store, past the jingle of the door, past the line of people, to the other side of the counter. And for some reason, it appears only I can see him.

I watch Tyler's anger build as he scans around the register frantically, searching and clawing at everything. His tension is fierce, adding a stress to the air around me. I'm locked to the ground as I'm forced to watch his uncontrolled aggression.

In a panic, I look over at the woman in the white belt. Again, her calm disarms me. It's like she knows what I'm thinking.

"Don't worry, Wings is coming. He's here now. Look."

I turn and look toward the door. Walking into Maya's, in full police uniform, is my dad. It's the same uniform, badges, and belt I'd seen him wear for years. The blue of the fabric and the glistening of his badge is unmistakable. It's really him.

I look toward my dad and feel the tears begin to well in my eyes. I want to yell out his name, to let him know that I'm here with him. But as my dad walks into the store, he passes right by me, unaware. As if I'm invisible. Only the woman in the white belt can see me.

My dad and Tyler lock eyes.

"Here, let me help you up, my child."

I'm crawling up until I see it—the hand of another—her hand. No words were spoken, but I knew.

At the touch of her hand, I'm shocked back into reality. I shake my head and blink my eyes, but she's still holding my hand.

It's her. The woman with the white hair in the sweeping black gown. The woman in the white belt.

"W-Who...who are...you?" I struggled to get out, my heart

pounding in my chest.

"Maya," she said tenderly, in the same voice I'd been hearing in my head for years. As if we'd known each other my whole life.

I blinked again.

She was still there.

I jerked my hand away from her, hard. I fell to my knees.

But when I looked up, she was still actually there. Other people were now standing beside her. I hadn't realized it had happened again; I panicked.

"You're…You're not real. You can't be. You're not real! This isn't real!"

"Phoenix, it's alright. Don't worry, you're safe."

"What is this? Who are you? All of you!" I stumbled quickly, raising my voice in a panic. I wasn't sure what was reality and what wasn't.

"Breathe, my child. Breathe. You're home now, Phoenix. I'll answer all your questions, but first try to breathe."

"How do you…why do you know my name?" I asked, stumbling to my feet.

But she just repeated once more, "You're safe here. You're safe, my child. I promise you this. You're safe."

It was overwhelming. Now others began to gather around. I could feel all of their eyes.

At first, I thought I was fading out again when I then realized everyone else could see her too. This was not a vision. The power snapped on and off, dimming slowly at first and then more quickly. Inside the store, everyone looked at one another as it began to happen.

Slowly, I regained my composure, but as I looked out at all of them, I saw something that struck me as incredibly odd. Except for Maya, all of them were dressed exactly the same: dark suits and black ties. It was the same exact outfit that my dad used to wear at night when he worked as an electrician. After a moment, all of them stopped looking at each other and then went back to me.

Maya turned to all of them still huddled around us. "All right, everyone. You know what that means. Now let's get back to it. You'll have plenty to do."

They all dispersed, and I rose to my feet. It was now just her and me.

"Are you feeling alright?" she asked.

Aside from the eerie flip between my visions and the real world, I was starting to return to a sense of my normal. But I wasn't even sure what that really was anymore.

Maya calmly put her hand on my shoulder, as if she could sense my unrest. "I can imagine you have a lot of questions," she said delicately, then added, "I've been expecting you for some time now, my child."

I turned once again toward the photo and looked into Aloanso's hopeful eyes. "It happened...here?"

"Yes," she responded simply, before elucidating carefully, "It was how your dad and I met. That was the night your father began his walk."

"And you..."

She smiled as she cut me off. "Maya. I'm the owner. It's a simple trade, really, but it means the world to me, all of my customers. I have plenty of regulars that have, over the years, come to be family. The Woodles come in all the time."

I sighed as I thought about Gloria, her knees in the dirt.

"Your father also did. He was family. He was a good man, Phoenix. I know that his loss has weighed heavily on you. I'm so sorry, my child."

My lip quivered, and the complexity of the question I was about to ask frightened me. Carefully, I pulled the notebook out of my pocket. "And what is this…this book…this book of places…the addresses and the locker?"

It was easy to tell that she wasn't exactly sure how to answer right away, but I didn't care. There were so many things I still didn't understand.

"Who is Wings?" I asked again before she'd said anything in return.

"May I?" She gestured toward the book.

I gave the book to her, and she went quiet as she began flipping through it. The way her fingers gripped the skin of its cover told me more about the book, though, than words possibly could. At her touch, the magic had been revealed. Her eyes teared slightly, and her smile got wider with each passing moment.

I stopped talking. Suddenly, it all felt okay. All of this had finally been for something.

Her eyes gently rose to meet mine. For what felt like an hour, we just stared at each other, her gaze probing.

Then, she asked me something. "How far would you go to save a stranger?"

Her question came into my mind in a way that made me think, unlike any question I'd ever been asked before. An answer that I wanted to get right more than I'd ever wanted anything. I had to dig deeper, further down than I thought possible, to unlock a place that I didn't know existed within me.

But as I continued to search, I felt her hand come again over my shoulder. Her fingers wrap around me in a building warmth. At her touch, I searched no longer. It was as if suddenly formal language had become archaic, and words were no longer necessary.

I looked up at her, and she smiled—not just with her lips, but with her eyes, nose, forehead, mind, and heart. Every part of her being was smiling.

She turned and started walking.

I followed her.

~

Aisles of food and supplies surrounded us. I felt something almost under my feet as we walked, as though I wasn't the one responsible for picking up my knees and pushing myself forward.

"Do you feel ready?" she asked.

But my tongue couldn't find words. I settled, instead, for a nod.

We approached a larger vending machine, and Maya walked right up to it and punched in a code, as if she were just grabbing a Coke. But, instead of a soda, the vending machine swung open like a door.

Beyond it was a massive expanse of white marble. It looked like an underground city.

I took a hesitant step forward.

Maya stopped me. "Phoenix."

Standing straighter, I looked at her.

"Everything you're about to see…you mustn't speak a word of it. To anyone. Not a single thing, my child. This is more important than you're able to understand, but still, you must hear me clearly now. Nobody, Phoenix. Nobody."

"I…I understand," I promised sheepishly.

"Good," she said. "Now, follow me."

Carrying on, there was a cascading double staircase that led to a large central corridor. Flags from every country in the world hung along each wall in eyeshot. Fifty or sixty people were buzzing around the main area, with foot traffic going in each direction. Peering over the stair railing, it looked even more like it was an underground city that was fully capable of self-sustainment.

Maya stood at the top of the staircase beside me.

"What is this place?" I asked.

She looked at me. "The axis mundi."

"The what?" I asked, quickly jumbled. I'd never heard of such a thing before, but I also had never seen anything like this.

She simply continued to look at me before smiling. "Why don't we start by showing you around."

We climbed down the spiraling staircase and out toward the massive central corridor. People of all different shapes, ages, and colors buzzed around. Some looked old, but all of them looked busy, humming around from place to place. But one shocking similarity remained—they were all dressed in the same dark suit and tie.

I followed Maya through the end of the large corridor toward what appeared to be a massive postal service. Mail flew into cubbies and was sorted at an exemplary pace. Then, she directed my attention toward a large map that had stickers on locations all over the world. It made me feel like an ant.

Watching everyone continue to fly by, I finally asked, "Is this place like this all of the time?"

"Twenty-four hours a day, seven days a week. No holidays or breaks. Death takes no holidays, Phoenix, so neither do we."

"Death?"

"Every year, you pass an anniversary unaware. Every year you do, we all do. Now, do you have any idea what anniversary that is, my child?"

I looked up at her and shook my head. The more she said, the less I understood.

"The anniversary of your own death," Maya said, then added, "Your father told me that once, and it's stuck with me all of these years. He said that he'd gotten it from the English writer, D.H. Lawrence. Your father would always share these sorts of things with me." Maya stopped, able to sense my confusion. "In one way or another, Phoenix, all of us are working against it. Ready or not, we all have a 'final' day." She stopped and then put her hand on my shoulder before adding, "But that is also what connects us all."

"And how does...how does everyone work so hard all of the time? Stay awake?"

Maya laughed. "Well, coffee mostly. But..." She then added slowly, "Belief. We run on the prayers of everyday people; that's what keeps our lights on. Without that, none of this that you're seeing right now would exist. There would be no need for all of these souls you see here. There would be no need for me. There wouldn't have been a need for a soul like your father."

We continued to walk until we arrived inside of a small office that appeared more like it belonged in the real world rather than this dreamscape. A stack of yellow legal papers and a worn-down coffee mug adorned the surface of her space.

"Sit," she said, gently taking the chair across from me.

As I more closely examined her study, I noticed that it was overrun with books just like the one my dad had. They ran wildly on her shelves.

"It's a wonderful place, isn't it?" she prompted.

I was still so shocked by all of this that I said simply, "Yes...it's... it's amazing."

"It truly is the most amazing place I know."

Everything about her demeanor was still so calm. She was so easily at peace that it appeared to be a permanent state. Nothing could move her off-kilter.

Maya carefully handed the book of addresses back to me. I took it in my hands once more.

"Open it."

With the book back in my hands, I slipped it back open to the first page and looked down. Softly, I heard Maya's voice as a guide.

"Page one. That's the address of Kyle Canterbury. He died from a heart attack at forty-one. His letter was delivered by Wings to his wife, Michelle."

I turned the page.

"Page two. That's Deborah, 'Debbi' Kilculen. She died from a sinking boat at thirty-three. Her letter was delivered by Wings to her eldest son, Stellio."

As she spoke, I ran my finger over the handwritten text on each page.

"Page three. Mikey Young. He died while playing in the park at thirteen. His letter was delivered by Wings to Mikey's mom, Georgia.

"Page four. Miles Blonder. He overdosed at twenty-one. His letter was delivered by Wings to his girlfriend at the time, Claire."

She stopped, collecting herself before adding more carefully, "When a person dies, Phoenix, there is so much more pain for the loved ones that person has left behind than the actual pain that person felt in dying itself."

The way I looked back at Maya let her know that I had no idea what she was getting at.

She carried on. "So, my boss devised this system."

"Your boss?" I asked with supreme confusion.

Maya smiled, saying one word. "God."

I couldn't look straight at her then, so I looked back down at the book. All of the handwritten addresses and all of the different places. I felt them once more with each of my fingers. Then, I flipped to the front and saw the different handwriting.

Το φως λάμπει στο σκοτάδι.

"The system of delivering the light," Maya finished.

I looked up at her, filled with confusion and awe. I didn't want to stare, but I hadn't the slightest clue what to say. I didn't know where to begin.

"So...you...you aren't just a store owner," I began with some trepidation, hoping she'd fill in the blanks for me.

Maya responded, "'Do not neglect to show hospitality to strangers, for by this, some have entertained angels without knowing it.' Hebrews 13:2."

I looked down again, trying to put it all together. "Did you make this? Or your 'boss'?" I asked, holding the book of addresses.

"No. Wings made that," she said and reached for the book once more.

Finally, I asked again, "Who is Wings?"

Maya smiled before carefully carrying on. "My very best messenger," she said with the book in her hands. "This book, Phoenix, it's a map. A map of all the addresses to which your father, Wings, delivered the light."

My mind was in a pretzel. "My dad's name was Wings?"

"All of my children are given delivery names when they start with me. When they begin delivering the light. Although, some just prefer to call it mail from heaven."

"Heaven?!" I said to her, with so much confusion and lack of understanding that I thought I might pass out.

Maya slowly explained, "It isn't like you'd think, of course. I'm afraid nothing is as good as our imagination makes it. But do believe me when I tell you that there is a place. A place where you feel no pain, no regret, no sorrow, and no sadness. Where you fully understand who you are and what your time here meant."

"But my dad was a security guard and an electrician...I saw it. I went with him. How could he have done all of this without me..." But I trailed off without finishing my question. My mind was spinning.

Maya answered in an even more delicate tone. "Your father was many things, Phoenix. But as I explained to you when we walked down here, this is a sacred place. As much as your father wanted to reveal to you what he was really doing when he wasn't around, he couldn't. But I'm here, telling you now, what he was really doing was delivering the light."

"What...What is delivering the light or... What is mail from heaven?" I wanted to fully understand everything as soon as possible.

"The night of the robbery, when Aloanso was killed, I knew how torn apart your father would be. He needed something to help restore his faith in the good of human life. But really, this is no different from any of us. We all need to be reminded of this beauty at times, as it is easy to forget. Most of my messengers, when I find them, are struggling to see. They've lost the faith. Some life-altering event, perhaps, and your father, I'm afraid, was no different. He knew he wanted to do more but didn't know how."

She continued. "Mail from heaven is the opportunity to leave them with your parting words. As you make the transition into the afterlife, you can communicate one last time to your loved ones. *One* letter you're allowed to write to *one* person. My children here, such as your father, take these letters and deliver them to their intended recipients back on Earth, using this book as their guide to help find for whom each letter is written."

Maya gently closed the book in her hands as she finished.

"The day after the robbery, in the kitchen of your own home, I gave your father this book. He was one of my very first messengers. That was the day he became Wings."

The way she looked at me, it was as if she could hear my wheels spinning, which was terrifying. Intimidating at best, I was instantly sure she knew every doubt I had been thinking about what she'd just explained.

"And these letters…people write them…after they…die?"

"Yes. That's exactly right. They come straight from heaven. And they are written to husbands, wives, brothers, sisters, sons, daughters, best friends, and sometimes, even strangers. People back home to whom they want to say one final goodbye."

I was trying to listen as hard as I could, because Maya didn't strike me as the type of person used to repeating herself.

"Why are there one hundred addresses in my dad's book and only ninety-three checked off?"

"Each one of the messengers is a part of a grand scheme, as am I, Phoenix. We all are, and it's for the greater good of humanity. We all have a duty to fulfill, and it is an extremely challenging burden these messengers each vow to shoulder. I know it was hard on your family. Therefore, all messengers agree to deliver one hundred letters. No more, no less. They do it on their time and their time alone, and I am here to help in any way I can. I, like you, am one of God's children. But once they complete their one hundred deliveries, they are to return back to a normal life. They are all able to ultimately carry this light with them for the remainder of their days, knowing that they were able to make their neighbor smile. But your father, I'm afraid, was unable to complete his one hundred." She took a moment to change her pace. "He was an incredible person, my child. I consider myself lucky to have known him as well as I did. I know it seems hard to understand now, but your father lived a happy and full life. That is more than most, I'm afraid."

For so long, he'd worked without reward and without recognition. To come up this short hurt me more than anything else I'd learned thus far.

"Here." I reached into my back pocket and gave Maya the envelope. "I found this in his locker at school."

But Maya didn't take it. She just looked back at me sharply. "Open it when you feel like you are ready."

"What?" I asked, confused.

She stood up out of her chair and walked toward me. "I know you have doubts about everything that I've just explained. Your father did too. But like him, you're stronger than you realize. I know you can be doing more than you think."

"But Maya, I'm...I'm just a kid."

"A kid who knows more about the fragility of life than most adults," she said strongly.

I looked down at my toes. I couldn't possibly do this. I wasn't as strong as my dad. I wasn't as brave.

Thinking about it all made me question so much. I thought about how knowing of this place, and these letters, made me question a lot of things. I thought about decisions, dreams, and feelings. How powerful this could be, but how unbelievable it still felt. Far away.

Maya showed me out of her office and started walking me back toward where we'd entered.

Back in the main corridor, I looked at all of the same people I'd seen earlier much differently. How many bakers, teachers, pilots, doctors, coaches, and other professionals, who appeared as though they led normal boring lives, were now standing beside Maya and me, in the middle of the night, in this magical place? On the outside, I'm sure every one of them appeared as though they would have never done anything like this.

Maya and I made it back to the vending machine.

She looked at me, and I looked down, afraid that all of this had already come to an end. Then, she reached for my necklace and lifted the Key of Courage with her finger as she said, "You must choose. Nobody can for you. Just you, my child. Just you."

Then, Maya turned quickly and was almost off when I called out to her, "Wait! How will I know what to do? How will I talk to you?"

From afar, Maya called back to me, "The same way you always have. This journey is the only way I can explain to you why. I'm always with you, Phoenix. Do not forget that." Then she turned and was gone, just like that.

With the book and envelope with "94" in my hands, I walked out of the shop and back to the Ferry.

It sounded like I was going to have to start getting used to drinking coffee.

15

Mom,

It's me! Can you believe I actually get to write you something? I really hope you can read this, because I miss you so much. I think about you all of the time. I wish you could be here with me. I know you're sad, but try not to cry too much. Tomorrow is going to be easier. I have good reason to believe that will be true. I know it will be.

Although you're angry, sad, tired, and confused, try not to let those feelings control you. You have every right to feel that way, but now I want you to think about how often you would tell me to remain positive. Allowing love to overcome any other emotion. Convincing me it will always win.

Think about my favorite day. Because if I can remember right, when times were tough, that was how you would help me get through it.

The smell of popcorn and cotton candy. The great arches looming above. The sun on my shoulders. The heavy feeling I'd always carried with me, gone.

You'd told me that, since Dad worked for Disneyland, you'd

take me for my ninth birthday, but you didn't tell me that we would have the entire park to ourselves. That we wouldn't have to worry about me getting sick, because nobody else would be there. That, today, my compromised immune system couldn't stop us from having some fun.

We walked up to a clerk, and he knew my name and yours. He showed us to a special cart that would take us around for the entire day. We needed that, since I couldn't walk very long with my oxygen tank. It was like riding on a magic carpet.

It was January, but you'd always told me that California was like a fairytale. You said it was always beautiful, and I couldn't believe it when you told me that it was hot enough to drink lemonade there, even in the winter.

Looping rollercoasters and waterfalls were all around. It was even better than all of the pictures on the website. Each person that helped us that day had the biggest smile. I think that makes sense, though, the more I think about it. They got to work at the happiest place on Earth.

I remember smiling a lot too. The entire day was smile after smile for me, and that's something I will never forget. I smiled so much my cheeks hurt.

So, just like you would always tell me about our day at Disneyland to cheer me up, I thought I could do the same. To help you remember how pretty life can be. How lucky we really are.

When those shooters walked into that library, I promise you I was strong. I didn't let them scare me. But once I heard them coming, I knew. I knew right away that I didn't have much time.

It all happened so fast, but parts of it, to me, also happened so slow. My heart raced, but as I tried to slow myself down, I realized that I had the only weapon I needed to stop those boys. It was the one thing that you'd always given me. The strongest weapon I knew. The thing you'd told me, ever since I was little, that would win.

I closed my eyes, and let your voice tell me about Disneyland. I knew your love would protect me no matter what. And on that day, I promise it did. Your love was stronger than those bullets. They may have killed my body, but because of you, the love never ran out.

I love you, Mom. I love you, Dad. I love all my classmates who are now here with me, and I love those boys who ended my life and the lives of everyone else. There isn't a single person who deserves to feel hate, not even them.

Because maybe they weren't as lucky. Maybe they knew someone they'd lost to an inherited immune disease. Maybe they didn't have a mom who could take them to Disneyland. Maybe they did that because they didn't think that anybody loved them.

There is no hate where I am now.

But something is even cooler in heaven that I wanted to tell you about. It is even better than that perfect day. Because here, I am not sick. I have all of my hair again. I don't need a machine to help me breathe. I don't get tired after a full day of being on rides. But, even with all of those things, there is still something even better. The best part is that, now, this is every day for me. Every day in heaven it is looping rollercoasters and cotton candy. Every day I'm at Disneyland.

So I am writing you to tell you not to be sad. Now, instead of thinking about how we aren't together anymore, think about how, every day, I'm forever in the happiest place on heaven. And don't ever feel hate in your heart. Feel love, just like you told me. I forgave those shooters the second they pulled the trigger, so you should too.

I have to go now, Mom, but I love you so much. Tomorrow will be better than today, and the day after that will be the best. Now when you get sad, remember that, even though I never did graduate from high school, I still got my dream job. I'm a professional Disneyland rollercoaster rider. How sweet is that?

Love,

Your Little Baldy

Ronnie

It had started to snow on my drive home from Maya's. When I got home that morning, I sat in the living room and just stared at Ronnie's letter for what felt like years. I'd made it home minutes before my mom woke up for work. She walked right out the front door without saying a thing.

With the letter in my hands, my eyes tried to focus on the words, but it was hard to read. Not because of how he curved his j's or how he only used lowercase t's, but because of how he dreamed. Seeing his own personal handwriting in black ink was enough to make it all just feel too personal. Like I'd been reading something that didn't belong to me.

The story itself made me feel hopeful and doomed all at once. The whole time I was reading, I could picture Ronnie sitting across from me in the library, his voice happily telling me this story. His red boots and chrome braces.

As my mind played with the words, my body was paralyzed. I was glued to the position I'd taken on our couch while reading. Hours came and went with no change. I was so terrified of the power and responsibility now in my hands. The words of a kid gone and the duty to deliver these dying words to a person in need.

Once my legs had regained the strength to function, I slid up to the Bird's Nest and passed out in my bed. The exhaustion of it all just took over, and I slept. Fully clothed and atop my bed, I knocked out.

Waking up later, I turned toward my desk. The letter was still there. Staring at me.

I could hear Ronnie's voice in my head again, pushing me. If I didn't act, I was afraid it would never leave me alone. I don't know what I was hoping for when I woke up, but it seemed there was no escaping this responsibility. Ronnie was relying on me.

With my mom home from work and in her room, I could surely sneak out and deliver this tonight. No matter how terrified I was, I told myself that Ronnie's mom needed to see this as soon as possible.

I found my dad's notebook and tracked down the address on page ninety-four. It was only about twenty minutes outside of town. If I left now, I'd be back before my mom even knew what happened.

I slipped on my heavy jacket and grabbed the letter. The keys were in the usual spot.

The slippery roads skipped off the tires of the Ferry. Some of the snow from the previous night's fall had started to melt, leaving behind a mushy puddle. The mixture painted the outside of the car doors as I drove.

My mind wandered onto the many nights my dad must've made similar drives. An argument with my mom, followed by a game to calm me down. Although, when he'd felt like we were both okay and settled, he was surely off to make a late-night delivery while we were sleeping. Once he knew we were alright, he knew he could freely move toward what he needed to do.

I arrived at a house that hardly looked like a home. It wasn't far from where Maya's was—the rougher side of town.

Pulling the car to a stop, I sat there for a while as I just looked at the place.

A small, rundown townhome. It was mostly broken concrete out front, but where I could see grass, it appeared mostly unkept. The earth around the property had started slowly taking it back. Whoever lived there, it appeared, had just accepted this evolutionary reality.

Judging the place from afar, it wasn't somewhere I wanted to walk toward. This sleeping bear of a mission was best left unbothered. I had no idea what was going to be on the other side. Against my better judgment, though, I got out of the car and moved toward the gated fence. All the flowers in pots on the front porch were dead. It was a little after one in the morning when I opened the fence gate and approached the front door.

I was about to knock, when it was suddenly too much. I was overwhelmed by grief as I looked down at the letter again. Nothing I said or did would bring him back, back to her.

I wasn't as strong as my dad. I may have understood the importance of what he did, but that didn't mean I could push through like him. He was stronger than me. This was his destiny, not mine.

He was a man; I was a boy.

If I'd learned anything from the shooting, it was that, clearly, I wasn't brave. I just didn't have it. Doubt can be a crippling thing. Maybe I could just leave the letter on the doormat or in her mailbox and go home.

I turned around and made my way toward the gate to put the letter in the mailbox when a voice called out.

"What do you want?"

I turned.

A feeble woman. Her hair frayed. She looked like she had no life left inside of her—a broken mom who'd died along with her only child.

"I'm...sorry. I didn't...I didn't want to wake you, miss," I muttered back haphazardly.

"I haven't slept in a while." Her voice sounded like a broken harpsichord. Something that, at one point, had made beautiful music, but was now no more than just a warped splinter of wood.

I wasn't sure what to do, and she didn't appear as though she was going to say anything further.

We stared at one another for a long moment. I swallowed hard.

The distance between her and me somehow felt like it was getting smaller, although I knew I wasn't moving.

I tried to look down at my feet to calm myself, but I could see I was now shaking. My eyes started to water, and I fell to the ground. I was crying harder than I ever had before.

When I looked up, the old woman stood right before me. What, at one point, appeared to be a scary old stranger became a friend. Her broken eyes still contained remnants of soft blue. She smiled down at me with a full smile. Reaching for my hand, she helped me to my feet.

With my strength back, she carefully said, "Whatever your bother is, don't worry."

Then, she turned around and headed back toward her front door, but I just watched her, as I wasn't sure if I should follow. Once she arrived at her doorway, she turned to me and added, "Come in. Please. It's too cold for this nonsense, anyway."

~

Old newspapers and dirty dishes rested on every visible surface inside. Clothes were scattered everywhere. A broken photo was lying face down in a bed of glass.

"Coffee?" she asked.

Somehow startled, I responded, "Please, thank you, miss."

The house was a tornado, and I wondered if it had always been like this.

In Ronnie's letter, she sounded so warm and loving that I felt like I was meeting an entirely different person. I'd seen a glimpse of it outside, but just as quickly as that spark arrived, it flamed out. She looked like love was no longer possible in her heart. I don't know how I could really blame her, though. She looked about how I'd felt since all of this had happened. A part of me had appreciated the mess, as I could relate to it. At least she wasn't afraid to visibly portray her struggle.

Ronnie's mom returned with two cracked mugs of coffee and handed me the one without a handle as I took a seat across from her.

"You knew him, didn't you?"

I slowly nodded my head. My first sip of coffee made my stomach turn.

"A couple of kids have come around, but it's mostly reporters. The cameras and lights make me want to punch 'em dead. Looking for their next big story or whatever. Ruthless, bothering an old lady like me. But eventually, even they stopped showing up. Now, nobody comes around…nobody cares longer than they have to."

I remained by as she unloaded all of her pain and hurt. Her voice now sounded more like a dying wind, getting weaker the longer she spoke.

"It's like all of the support in the world is right at your feet one minute and gone the next…another innocent kid dies…or another totally different tragedy, and then that's all we're talking about. People move on too quickly, but how can you blame them? There's too much tragedy going on to focus on one for too long." She looked away, anger twisting her features. "But what about me? What am I supposed to do? Just move on like everybody else? Forget about my boy, just like everyone else?!"

She tired herself out, and I wasn't sure how to respond. I didn't say anything back.

As the silence settled, I continued to look around her house. The wallpaper was only colorful in small specific rectangles.

"Can I see his room?" I asked.

She looked at me and got up, so I followed.

Opening the door, I looked inside Ronnie's small bedroom as she said, "It's the only room I won't touch…won't…change. When I want to live with some detail about him one more time, I come in here. I…come in here anyway. Most of the time, it comes back, but…yeah…most of the time."

The room was simple—a small bed. Jackets and jeans hanging. A desk with pens and papers. It looked like Ronnie still lived here. I took another step in and let my hands scan his desk. At the top of a pile was a set of half-finished geometry problems. I instantly recognized Ronnie's handwriting.

"His math homework due that week," she explained.

Turning toward where he slept, I saw a frog green Buzz Lightyear toy on his bedside table.

"What was that day like?" I asked.

"What day?"

Still looking at the toy, I said, "His favorite day. The one that you used to tell him about. When you went to Disneyland."

She came into his room and took a seat atop his bed. "That day…wow. I haven't thought about that day since he was just a boy. I guess all I really remember was that he had a great time. I'd never seen him happier. He was a happy kid, but that day was different, and I never knew quite why." Then she looked at me and asked, "How did you know about that? What was your name again?"

"Phoenix," I answered and shook her hand. "He…I was with him that morning."

She looked at me solemnly and nodded. The pain in her expression was impossible to miss.

"That morning. Our last morning together…I didn't even get to tell him I loved him before he left." She started to cry softly. "I don't even remember the last thing I said to my son."

It was uncomfortable to watch, so I just stood there. I had no idea what I was supposed to do.

She then reached for the toy on his table. "If I'd have known...I would've had more days with him like that. I would have spent more time with him." But her tears overcame her. She stopped talking and just wept.

It was so hard to watch her cry like that. To watch her unravel made me want to do the same.

With her letter in my hands, they started to shake again. While looking down, I said to her, "But...he's...he's better. He's...in a better place now."

She looked up only to say to me, "I'm glad you can believe in that sort of stuff...because I can't. Even if I wanted to." And then she went back to crying.

While still looking at my feet, I carefully walked toward her, closing the gap between us an inch at a time. If I didn't look up, then I couldn't stop. I just kept inching along. I handed her the letter from her son.

~

As I walked into Maya's store afterward, Maya was standing close by, stocking a few shelves.

Without turning around, Maya asked, as if she could sense that I was right behind her, "Phoenix, my child. How did it go?"

I tried to act like I wasn't surprised by her candor. "It was... too much."

She turned toward me, and I could see that she didn't look very prophetic at all. She was wearing a collared mechanic's shirt with her name stitched onto the shoulder.

"The first one always is. There's no protecting you from that. Sometimes you must walk right into the storm."

Maya reached into the shelf and handed me a bag of peanut M&M's. "To celebrate."

I handed her some, too, which she gladly nibbled on.

"Are they usually like that? The…the letters. If they are, Maya, I…I'm not sure I am the right person for this."

"It's different for everyone," she began. "It makes each person reflect differently on their time here, I've found. Some write about lessons they've learned, and others write about regret. No letter is like the last. They are snowflakes, and all should be handled as such."

"But, finding a way to tell them…"

"Is hard," she answered for me. "I know, but it's up to your discretion. That's up to you each time." She placed her hand atop my shoulder. "And you are the right person, Phoenix. These letters, they are not just for the recipient."

"Who else could they be for?"

"Each night, I make sure that I come out here and walk the shelves. I reorganize a pile of chips or say hello to a passerby, but most of the time, I do nothing at all. But I always make sure that I walk the aisles of my store." She then added simply, "Pain can be both enemy and friend. It's a waste to go through life thinking of pain as just a bad thing."

"The next one, is it…?" I started.

"Waiting for you in the same place you found the first." She smiled.

I couldn't help but let out a small smile too.

16

Dear Milan,

I apologize if this is a little strange. You might not remember me, but when I was given the chance to write to anyone, I could only think of you. I haven't stopped.

I used to wake up at the same time every day. 6:10 a.m. I'd lean over and tap on the alarm clock, but I would always snooze for a few more seconds. During this time, I would play out my entire day in my head, most of the time imagining the worst possible outcomes. A yawn or two later, I'd already be late.

After showering and getting dressed in a sloppy shirt and the first jacket I could find, I'd get to the office one minute before my boss could, with reasonable cause, rip my head off my shoulders.

The man I'd become was this monotonous routine. Tuesdays bled into Wednesdays that bled into Thursdays. The drinking would come and go. It all just came one after the other, and I'd started to wonder if it was ever going to change.

Then, one Saturday, one summer morning, I met you.

I walked into the Corner Deli and sat at a table three up from the entrance, closest to the window. Prepared to just order some toast and a cheese omelet from the first server that walked my way, instead, it was you who came by. You were wearing a patterned purple hair tie with your ponytail bouncing in the back. I swore you were the most perfect thing I'd ever seen. When you smiled at me that morning, I knew there had to be something beautifully offbeat about you.

We'd struck up a conversation that day, and nothing out of the ordinary happened. We talked about where you were from as you brought me my food. Cincinnati, Ohio. You mentioned you loved to square dance, and you told me your name, so I did the same.

"Max, huh? Good thing your Mama taught you how to dress, Million Bucks Max," you said, which almost felt like an insult. But for some odd reason, it made me laugh so freely that I nearly lost my ability to remain suave.

That day I was wearing a suit and tie, which never seemed to happen anymore. But something else happened that day that never seemed to happen anymore.

Most of my days had been built around the skill that I'd acquired to be able to blindly fall from one task into the next. I'd become accustomed to steeling myself to get through just one more meeting, one more report, one more day, but with you, I wasn't thinking about any of that. I wasn't thinking.

My breath was in my lungs. My eyes grabbed hold of you, and never wanted to let go. My mind was trained on you and nothing else. You reminded me that there is more to who we all are.

Soon after that, I was coming in every Saturday, for months. You would sit me at my table, and we would have our time together before you had to get back to work. Each second was a love letter, and each time that I saw you, I made sure that I was in my suit and tie.

Over time, waking up every day for work became easier, my job enjoyable again, and my coworkers and I got along incredibly. I wasn't late anymore, and my drinking subsided almost overnight. It was like my life gained an entirely new perspective.

I'd told everyone at work all about you. The way you looked me in the eye when you asked me how I was doing. The manner in which you said hello and goodbye. The warmth you effortlessly shared with the cheeks of your smile. It was a sincerity I hadn't even known I'd been lacking in my life.

But the more that I talked about you, the more they continued to ask the same question.

"When are you going to ask her out?"

It wasn't that I didn't think you were attractive—that much was obvious—but it seemed that how you looked had little to do with my infatuation. I'd rather listen to you than kiss you. I'd rather talk to you than sleep with you. It was different than I'd ever felt about anybody else.

But when I got in my car that next Saturday morning to tell you, I was in such a hurry that I didn't put on my seatbelt. That morning, the rain had made the roads especially thick. That morning I didn't see the other car that ran that red. That morning, well, that was the last morning I ever had.

If I had gotten the chance to see you one more time, I would have sat at my normal table and said hello. But at the end of my usual meal, I wouldn't have just paid the check and told you that I'd see you next Saturday. I would have told you that, one day, I'd like to go on a walk together. Through a park or around a pond, maybe.

I know all of this must sound a bit crazy, because it still does to me. But no matter how it may sound, I wanted to make sure that you knew. I guess it's been easier for me to be honest about how I felt, because I know that we will never see each other again.

Although, I still must thank you. You made my life whole again with just your smile. I'd fallen in love with you long before the day I died. I knew it the moment you said hello.

Never change, Milan. Someday, another fellow in a suit and tie surely won't make the same mistake I did. You're too perfect to miss.

Love,

Million Bucks Max

Corner Deli was all the way on the other side of town, but because it was so early in the morning, there wasn't any traffic. The streetlights were awake with me.

I drove down a residential road to get onto the highway, when the sun cracked over the windshield. It was a subtle orange as it peeled off its sheets and rose in the west. As the sun fully got out of bed, I was just pulling into the parking lot.

It was early, but there were certainly plenty of people inside. A cozy breakfast nook with folks from young to old starting their days together. It smelled of eggs and bacon.

A man approached me. "Good morning. Can I get you seated...?"

"I'm Phoenix," I began, "and may I have the table three up from the entrance, closest to the window?"

The host gave me a look of confusion before allowing my odd request. I took a seat and looked over the menu.

I was drawn in by all the patrons' faces. Each one looked delighted to be sharing this small moment in time with the person across from them. Drinks were slowly sipped, and laughs came in between bites. Dogs rested at feet. Everything and nothing were happening inside.

The sun was still keeping me company, and the smell of breakfast made me forget I hadn't slept.

"Thank you for taking the time to start your day with us. What can I get started for you?" a tender voice asked.

I turned around, and I saw her like Max had. She had dark caramel skin and gorgeously curled cola hair. In a ponytail in the back, her hair was tied together by a patterned purple hair tie. Her name tag: *Milan*.

But she looked...sad. Her energy was warm, but it came off as a forced warmth. Pain wasn't at the forefront of her eyes, but it was certainly behind them. You just had to look a little bit harder to actually see it.

"Toast and a cheese omelet, please."

She wrote down my order, and when she looked down, I could tell how young she was. Twenty-two maybe. Her youthful glow came as a surprise, but the pain looked like it had matured her too early. She'd forgotten about the light.

"Coming right up."

With Milan gone, my mind wandered upon a question.

How easily could I have come into this restaurant and looked past her? Not a second thought of her potential pain? But because of the letter, I knew to take a deeper look. To not let my initial judgment color who she was in my mind.

I waited for her to return as I thought about what I was going to say. I was trying to remain strong, but her sorrow had infected me in a way that I knew she couldn't even help if she'd wanted.

Milan returned with my food and asked, "Is there anything else I can bring you?"

"Are you sad?" was all I could think to ask.

Puzzled, she looked down at me. "Excuse me?"

"Are you sad?" I repeated, not losing sight of what I knew I had to do.

She stopped shifting her weight back and forth on each foot and just looked at me. Her deep eyes revealed her pain, and I could see more of her true self. Twirling her hair nervously, she looked down, appearing as though she were now afraid.

"Is it because of him?" I asked.

"Who?" she asked, even more perplexed.

"Million Bucks Max."

She now looked intensely at me. "How did you...how did you know him?"

I didn't know how to respond, so I didn't say anything for a moment. The look she gave frightened me, affected me in a way that I hadn't even known possible.

"Did something happen?" she asked.

I nodded my head, as I couldn't help but get emotional. The exhaustion had finally caught up to me. I was so tired, I could have fallen asleep sitting upright in front of her.

I felt like I'd known him so well, and seeing her made it that much harder. He would have done anything to just be sitting across from her, as simply as I was at that moment. In a place where he could've wished for anything, all he wanted was to be here.

She quickly came to my side, and I watched her eyes shift once more. The sorrow was overwhelming me. Her embrace came.

"It's okay. It's okay. It's going to be alright."

A coworker saw what was going on and, while still holding me, Milan asked if he could cover for her.

Milan took the seat next to me. I'd slowly regained some level of composure.

"This was where he always sat," she said. "He probably didn't even realize it, but it was the thing I looked forward to the most each week. It was the way he looked at me. It was like I was the only thing he could see. I'd always had something going on, or something on my mind that had been bothering me, but when I felt his eyes on me, somehow it all went away."

I looked up and saw her sneak a smile. Knowing her pain, I felt more inclined to look her in the eye or be warm instead of trivial. Knowing her story made me want to leave her with something more than just a generous tip.

"I liked who I became around him," she added.

"Did you love him?"

She smiled even wider and nodded. I could see why he had cared so much about her. She was angelic.

My nerves had finally calmed to the point where I could breathe and think clearly again.

"How did you know him?" she again asked.

"I didn't," I explained, "but I do know something about him."

She adjusted herself in her seat as I reached into my coat pocket and pushed the envelope toward her.

I said in a breath, "I know that he loved you too."

~

A week went by where the only thing I had any time for was attempting to catch up on all the homework I'd put off. Although, despite going through the motions of my geometry problems and history flashcards, all I could think about where the letters. They dominated every waking thought. It was getting harder to see the reason for such pointless schoolwork when I had light to deliver.

That next Monday, drudging through the snow, I arrived at school ten minutes late to first period.

Lunch that day was spent like all of the others that had come before it—alone.

As I tried to sit and eat as quickly as possible, I saw TT sitting with his basketball teammates. He was busy laughing with them.

With my new task at hand, I rarely thought about him anymore. I had more important things to worry about.

After school was over, I was excited to get back to the letters. I snuck back to my dad's old office and Locker 8½. I made sure no one was in there before using the key to get my next one. Carefully, I placed letter "96" in my back pocket.

Walking home, out of nowhere, I felt hands on my back. I was pushed to the ground by Pounds and his two buddies.

"Get up," he said, looming over me. I rolled around in the snow and tried to find my footing when he pushed my face directly into a bank of white powder.

His friends laughed as I did my best to try and breathe with Pounds's hot hand tightly gripping the back of my neck.

"You're so soft, I always had the feeling you'd liked snow, but I had no idea you liked it that much!"

"Get off me!" I yelled, but they just continued laughing like beasts, barking back and forth.

I tried to squirm my way out, but I stood no chance alone.

"Careful, Pounds. His daddy's ghost might haunt you!" taunted one of his cronies.

"Yeah, you don't want to mess with a dead guy's kid."

As I fought to get free, my backpack popped open. My dad's notebook fell out.

Pounds let go of me for a second and scooped the notebook up off the snow. I lunged for it, but my effort was quickly thwarted by Pounds's heavy foot.

"Look at this! The freak has a diary!"

"Give that back!" I screamed.

"Oh, of course, you want your little diary back. I can imagine all your secrets that you write about in here. Maybe I'll just have to keep it and read for myself. I haven't read a good book in a while."

One of his buddies shot back, "By a while, do you mean never?"

Pounds playfully shoved him, which gave me a final window to try and reach for it once more. But Pounds quickly saw my attempt and shoved me again. This time I landed right on my shoulder and banged it hard against a rock hidden beneath the snow.

"See ya, freak. Can't wait to read!" Pounds said before they all ran off.

I tried to shift my body weight to get up and chase after them, but as soon as I brought my arm up, it stung all the way to the tips of my fingers. My cheeks were ice cold. After limping the rest of the way home, I waited for my mom to go to sleep before sneaking out to go and see Maya.

When I arrived at her store that night, Maya again appeared as though she'd been expecting me.

"You look tired," she said.

I approached her fiercely, as if she was the one with whom I'd had a bone to pick. "I wish he'd been the one who got shot! He deserves to be dead!"

She came calmly to my side. "Relax, Phoenix. Breathe. You don't mean that."

"He took the book, Maya! He took it! All of the places my dad went! Everything he worked for!"

"I know, sugar. I know that he did."

"And that doesn't matter to you?" I asked with a ferocity that was even alarming to her.

Maya let out a deep exhale. "That boy…he has pain, Phoenix."

She fixed my matted hair by securely tucking it behind my ear. "Now, you don't mean what you said. I know that isn't true. Just like Ronnie, and just like you, he, too, is one of my children."

"But he is so mean! So…evil! Why would God take someone as innocent as Ronnie, but not someone as terrible as Pounds?"

Maya sighed. "Life has nothing to do with how much time you are given, but everything to do with *what* you do *with* that time. Pounds still has much more of his journey to complete. Ronnie—despite how young he was taken—completed his."

"It hardly seems fair," I said, losing my hope in it all.

"You're right," Maya started as I looked up. "But life was never intended to be. No life is the same, for we all have different journeys than our sisters and brothers. Some are always going to be harder. And the true beauty is that pain is the best teacher. With a tougher life comes even more responsibility."

"But what about the book? Without it, I won't be able to finish what my dad started."

Maya calmly looked at me and asked, "Letter ninety-six. Do you have it?"

I nodded.

"Read it. The answer will be there."

I looked up at Maya. Then, without saying anything, I headed for the door.

"Phoenix!" she called out.

I turned slowly just before walking out.

"Get some rest, child. The coffee will still be hot in the morning."

With the night now closing in around me, I knew being near the light would protect me from falling back in. If life were a hellish cave, then my mission was my celestial candle. But like any candle, I needed to get to where I was going before it burned out. The darkness wasn't going anywhere, and it was only now—for the first time in my whole life—I'd finally been able to see.

17

Big Brother,

I'm sorry I didn't write sooner. More than anything, I realized writing to you would mean forever saying goodbye. I don't want to let you go, but I've only now come to terms with the fact that I never will. So, here I am.

I had to remind you that I know who you really are. You're the kind of boy who would dress up in a pink Barbie costume to make me laugh. Even though the dress didn't really fit you, I still thought you had the best legs in the family. In fact, I'm actually pretty jealous.

There aren't many things as cruel as that ugly c-word. All that talk about stages, growths, tumors, and experimental treatments made me sicker than any of the chemo. The word itself just looks, well, ugly. I don't know who came up with it, but I'd bet he's pretty ugly too.

I was just a young girl when we got the diagnosis. But it was you who kept me upright. It was you who only talked to me about it just one time and then never spoke about it again. You treated me as you always did—pre-leukemia and post-leukemia.

The day we found out, all you said to me was, "Knowing how tough you are, I sorta feel bad for the cancer." It was one of the last times I laughed.

When we were together, I could forget I was slowly slipping away. But even that, too, was just one of the many ways that you helped me in my final days.

If there was something that I had to give up because of my treatment, well, then you gave it up too. When I had to shave my head, you shaved your head that very same night—even allowing me the honor of doing so.

Aside from all of it, though, I also knew how much pain it was causing you. It was something that—in addition to my nausea—kept me up at night. When I was in the hospital and you didn't think I could hear you, I could. When you were at home and you tried to hide your pain, I knew. You were starting to smile less and frown more—say less and cry more. To put it simply—I realized I wasn't the only one my cancer was changing.

So, I sat you down and told you to believe that I would be going to a better place soon. I tried to convince you to find solace in a place beyond the clouds, but you lost control. You refused to believe. You told me not to think like that. And when you screamed at me for giving up, it crushed me. But what broke me even more than that was what followed.

Then, I heard about those older boys who made fun of you. Saying things about the wig you'd worn and making fun of you for allowing me to paint your nails. My already-weakening spirit waned and it made me realize that I had been selfish. Which was when I made the mistake of thinking I had to do it alone.

As my time quickly slipped away, I wanted to see you less and less. I didn't want to put you through what I had been going through any longer, so I pushed you. Even still, you persisted and then, eventually, I got so sick that I had to stay in the hospital. A place that I forbade you to see me in.

I was in my final moments when you came to my side and tried for one more laugh. As a last effort, you showed up by my bedside in that pink dress. I screamed at you. I called you names. I'd never seen you cry until that moment. Little did I know, that would be our final moment.

I made an unforgivable mistake. I should have laughed with you one more time. I shouldn't have called you what I did. I should have explained that, without you, I'd have given up living long before I did.

Now, I see that, for me, dying was the easiest part. A slip of my breath. Allowing my eyes to close. Quick and nearly painless. There truly wasn't much else to it.

What has been even harder than all of the pain that cancer brought, is watching what happened to you after I left. Watching the aftermath from up above. Helplessly watching it all unfold.

But it is never too late to change, to go back to who you really are. The world is changing every day. You don't have to do the things that people used to do. You don't have to fit the stereotype to fit in. You don't have to pretend to be happy when you're sad. You don't have to pretend to like one thing when you like another.

People will accept you for who you really are. Dance in whatever clothes are your favorite and sing your favorite song as loud as you can. Just like you used to always tell me, don't be afraid. Boys are allowed to cry. Girls are allowed to be mean. Boys are allowed to be pretty. Girls are allowed to love football. Boys are allowed to like other boys, and girls are allowed to like other girls.

I know that I didn't get to live long, but you made my days the brightest. Even at our worst, we are lucky to be given a body to live life in—all that I want for you is to be happy in yours. No matter what they might say, you would make me the proudest little sister. It's the only thing I want now. I want to return the favor—I want to give the person who gave me the freedom to live the same.

As much as this is goodbye, I hope this can also be hello. Hello to the person I knew. My favorite person. My best friend.

Anybody can put a mask on and pretend to be someone they are not. True, genuine energy isn't easy to capture, but I know who you really are. I know that you may go by Pounds, but to me, you have always been Paul. And even if you like to wear a pink dress, you will always be my big brother.

All my love,

Rose

"And what do you have to say for all of this?" Principal McGugan said to me from across her desk.

It was the first thing I'd heard her say since I'd sat down.

The truth was, I had no idea what I was supposed to say. The line between right and wrong had become so blurred. I wasn't sure if I was sad, or if I was just confused, or if I was really mostly just tired. Tired of it all. But I did know one thing I *was* sure about— my anger. Anger that even an inch of my being cared at all about Pounds after reading his sister's letter. Anger that he didn't die in the shooting instead of Ronnie. Instead of my dad. The letter didn't fit with the relentless bully who had ruined my cards, pushed my face in the snow. The thug who had sucked beautiful, kind Shay into his twisted world. Even Tyler had been Pounds's fault. Although I had cooled down enough from last night to understand why I'd have to keep that to myself.

"You went from being one of our brightest young students to failing almost every class. Most of your teachers let me know that what few assignments you've turned in have made little to no sense. Some even went as far as mentioning to me that you have been regularly dozing off during lessons."

"I'm sorry," was all I could think to say in response.

Looking up, I caught a glimpse of the school's intercom beside the same small lamp on her desk.

"I know you are, Phoenix, but that isn't good enough anymore. I'm trying to help you. We're trying to help you, but we cannot do that if you don't talk to us. If you don't tell us what's really going on."

I knew I had to play this exactly right if it was going to have even the slightest chance of working. But it seemed only then that I'd finally figured it out.

"But whatever I say," I started sheepishly, "it can stay just between us?"

"Of course. I can't help you if you don't feel like you can be open with me," Principal McGugan answered.

"But...I don't know..." I trailed off, looking down.

She sighed. "Please, Phoenix. Whatever's going on, I promise that I'll do whatever I can. We all have lives outside of this place, and I understand those lives can get...can be...complex. That's why you need to understand that you can talk to me. No matter what it is."

She'd fallen right into it.

I rubbed my eyes. "At home, I...I have had to deal with a lot since it all happened. My mom has taken all of this even harder than me. But to be completely honest, ever since that day, it's been really hard for me to be there. The whole house just reminds me of him. During the days, it's okay most of the time, but it's the hardest at night. I can't sleep. I just can't anymore in that house. Now, I'm just...I'm just...tired."

Principal McGugan slid back in her chair. "That can be extremely difficult. Not having that sense of home can shake up your entire life."

She was sucking it right up.

To drive it home, I looked down as I added, "I'm just not sure I've found a place to rest. Because that place of peace and quiet outside of my house used to be the library, but...now nowhere seems to feel safe."

I watched Principal McGugan turn and look at a full-length couch under her window. It had two throw pillows and a day blanket on it.

"And I can only imagine how challenging it has been to not have your father around," she responded.

"I guess. But sometimes, I just feel like I need a quiet place I can stop. Where I can be alone and reset. Think about everything. But with her there all of the time and the library…it just doesn't work for me like it used to. Like I haven't been able to stop since."

I scratched my eyes, letting out a deep sigh. Then, I yawned. I hoped it wasn't too obvious, but it was still just after nine in the morning.

She looked at the couch again. "Well, how about I make up the sofa for you, and you take the next hour to try and get some sleep here, in my office. I need to go and meet with a few teachers in their rooms anyway. I'll draw the blinds. No one will even know you're here."

Bingo.

I continued to remain coy. "No, that's alright. Thank you, though. I…I probably shouldn't miss any more class."

But she stopped me once more. "Listen, I'm the principal. I'll let your teachers know you're busy with me. There is no sense in you going back to class this depleted. Please, take a moment to get some peace and quiet."

Principal McGugan stood up, walked toward the couch, and threw the blanket over the top.

Standing over it, she added, "Trust me, we adults take these little rest naps too."

"Are you sure?"

Principal McGugan walked back to her desk and grabbed something from a drawer. "It's why we do what we do, Phoenix. To *help* our students. And surprisingly, I've found in all of my years of education that help has little to do with the actual schooling and more to do with just simply listening. Thank you for allowing me to listen."

I looked back at her and faked a smile.

"But, Phoenix," she said quickly.

I was afraid she'd realized I was lying. "Yes, Principal McGugan?"

"You have to pick it up. You are too smart to be having these problems. I don't want to hear from your teachers about this again. Deal?"

Internally, I sighed. "Deal."

I could see now that she'd grabbed her keys. Closing the blinds, she stood in the doorway before reaching for the light.

"On or off?" she asked.

"Off," I said.

Then Principal McGugan flipped off the lights and locked the door behind her as she left.

I slowly went to the couch and couldn't help but shut my eyes for just a short moment. It hadn't been a complete lie—I was exhausted. I took a moment to calm my head and reset, collecting my thoughts. The thing that I'd lied about was exactly what those thoughts were.

It wasn't long before I jumped up off the couch. In the darkness still, I slid over to Principal McGugan's desk. I knew I wouldn't have much time once I got started. I had to get to work.

Ever since I'd panicked at Pounds's party last year in front of him, I'd thought about getting a second chance. I'd dreamed about the day when he'd finally pay for all he'd done. Over the years, he'd done so many bad things that I'd convinced myself this would be payback for it all. Not just for myself, but for driving Tyler to do what he did and for all the people affected because of that. For all the others who had paid for simply crossing his path. All of the other lives he'd ruined. I just never expected to be provided with an opportunity as good as this. I'd been thinking of some way to not just get back at him but to take something equally as valuable. But this? This was going to crush him.

Sliding into Principal McGugan's office chair, I felt my heart rate increase. My eyes shot in all different directions—checking around the room to see if I was still in the clear.

I set my backpack beside my feet and took a long deep breath. I looked at the button at the base of the microphone that would broadcast my voice to the entire school.

I pushed it down with my thumb.

"Hello, everyone, it's…it's Phoenix…Phoenix Iver. And…for those of you who don't know…I'm a sophomore here…"

I stopped and quickly took my thumb off the button. My breathing was heavy. I couldn't see much.

I stood up and did a quick pace back and forth before sitting back down. I pressed the button again.

"And…I…I have a very important announcement to make today. One of our fellow classmates…he…he isn't who he says he is. He isn't the tough football player he appears to be. Pounds. You… you're a liar. And I can prove it."

My heart was now beating so hard that I could feel it in my chest. I was so proud of myself for getting this far that I was almost too excited to keep going. I could feel the smile on my face. To finish him once and for all. For all the innocent kids he'd harassed.

"I have something that I would like to read to everyone."

I took my hand off the button and reached for my backpack. It was slightly unzipped. It was time.

Reaching down, I slid my hand into my backpack—feeling past the normal things that lived there. I'd placed Rose's letter there this morning, after reading the entire thing. Once I'd finished, I knew exactly what I was going to do. I could hardly keep it all to myself as I bounced into Principal McGugan's office this morning.

But as I continued to fish around with my hand, I couldn't feel it.

I started to sweat as my breathing increased. The microphone on the intercom was off, but I could still somehow hear everyone in the school holding their breath, waiting for me.

Panicking, I tipped the entire backpack onto the desk. I was running out of time. I turned the whole thing over onto Principal McGugan's desk, the contents to spraying everywhere. From my pack of colored pencils to my math binder, they poured out like a waterfall onto the desk. It was all of my normal belongings, except for the one thing I'd been searching for.

"Phoenix! You open this door right now!" a voice screamed through the locked door.

I pushed the microphone across the desk in fear. I had to find the letter. Right. Now.

Continuing to sift through my things, I couldn't believe it. I'd put it inside my backpack right before I left for school. I knew I had. I would have never been this careless.

"Now!" the voice called out again.

But I kept looking. It had to be here somewhere. I started going through my backpack again just to be sure.

The office door shook. It was still locked, but I heard the key jingling on the other side.

I had to find it, and I had to find it quick. I wouldn't give up; I had to start reading the whole thing this second. Everyone needed to know his secret. Everyone needed to know the truth about Pounds.

Then, I stopped looking. Not because I finally found the letter, but because it was all over for me. The door to Principal McGugan's office flew open.

~

I walked home alone the second the final bell rang. If Metropolis wasn't going to be safe, then I didn't know where else could be.

I'd received sufficient scolding from Principal McGugan when she'd returned. She unleashed on me unlike I'd ever thought possible. She basically only let me off on account of all that she knew I'd been through, which somehow didn't make me feel any better. It was as if, in her eyes, having to be me was adequate punishment.

I knew, though, that she must have called my mom the second I left her office. Now *she* was going to kill me. Walking through the door was going to be another nightmare. But as I neared Metropolis, the most important thing was finding the letter. It had to be on my desk or somewhere stupid where I'd forgotten it this morning.

When I walked in, my mom didn't even hear me. She was on the phone, in tears. At first, I thought she had to be on the phone with the school, based on her reaction, but after a few moments, I could tell she wasn't.

"But you can't…I can change my hours," she pleaded. "Gregory, I won't be able to take care of my son. Please. It's just him and me now. I…"

There was a deep fear in her voice. I felt filthy, disgusting.

"Please…just until I can find something…"

The phone cut off, and my mom placed it down before she sank to the floor, melting right before me.

Knowing then that I could be of no help to her in that moment pricked an even deeper pain. If anything, I'd only made all of this harder. Brought more pain and more trouble with my actions. We were both broken.

Without turning around, my mom slowly made her way up to her room. I could already hear her emotion from her bedroom.

I wanted all of this to be over. I hadn't any clue as to the potential of things becoming worse, but here we were. I was even more lost than before.

But the hope of finding the letter kept my feet moving.

Looking around the Bird's Nest, the letter was nowhere to be found. My room looked exactly as I'd left it this morning. I checked all over, but it wasn't anywhere.

"No. No. No." I started quietly at first, getting progressively louder.

I searched inside of my garbage bin, under my bed, inside my closet, and in every pocket of every pair of pants I owned. It wasn't anywhere. My whole room had been torn apart, and it hadn't turned up.

Not giving up, I then started looking around the house. I checked our living room, the kitchen, inside the Ferry, and even our trash outside. But it wasn't anywhere. There was no letter. None of it made any sense at all.

Lying on my carpet, I ran out of ideas. I was stuck somewhere between confusion and denial.

I knew I'd placed the letter in my backpack this morning. I could remember it so clearly—the feeling I'd had when doing so and my entire plan. Suddenly, I thought of one more place to look.

It was nearly pitch black when I ran out of the house. The cold night air woke me back up as I reached for my flashlight.

I followed my feet all the way back to the school.

Leaves flew over my head, and a dog barked, but other than that, it was quiet when I finally came up to my dad's old office. The door was slightly ajar, dancing in the wind. The office felt darker for some reason, but everything was still in the same place.

I came up to the locker and closed my eyes. As I held the key in my fingertips, I said, "I will not be afraid of what I do not know because what I do not know is the only thing keeping me from the place I would like to go."

I'd said the phrase now so often that I normally repeated it with much less conviction than when I'd first discovered mail from heaven. It had become a bit monotonous as I was already aware of what was on the other side. But when I opened my eyes and pushed the Key of Courage into the lock, nothing was inside. The locker was completely empty.

I repeated the phrase once more, saying it this time with more fervor. When I opened my eyes again, though, the locker remained empty. Like a skeletal corpse with a bequeathed soul, I was gawking into an empty casket. Nothing at all. The leaves continued to float around me, the dog carried on its barking.

Not giving up yet, I repeated and repeated and repeated the phrase until I couldn't breathe. Until every gallon of light in my tank had been burned. Until my tears were so strong that I couldn't see the locker anymore. Until *I* couldn't anymore.

But over time, the painful reality of it all settled in. The well had run dry.

This was just an office. An office holding cleaning supplies and reports, not handwritten messages from the angels. An office that only heard the wind that gently blew through it, not my words. And I was just a high school kid, not the man who could deliver the light.

18

"Please. Please," I pleaded. "Please, God. I know now. I know."

I'd prayed only a handful of times, but never once out loud like this. Usually, I'd get it all out internally, but this was different. I had nothing. I was on my knees, begging. A plea for some sort of life raft so I could eventually climb back aboard.

I was drowning and only He could save me.

"I let you down. I let…I let all of them down. But please…" I trailed off once more.

Then I snapped back into reality. I was in my room. In the middle of the night. Yelling at the ceiling.

I closed my eyes again. "Please…I need them…I need them too."

I silently concluded the remainder of my prayer by pleading to God. On my knees, begging Him to put all of this back together. For me to be able to find my feet in this sinking loneliness. For the chance to, once again, make my dad proud. For an opportunity to arrive.

But when I opened my eyes, my stomach pulled at me. My body was rigid. My muscles strained. I could still barely stay afloat.

Faith comes, and it goes. I couldn't handle the current wave of emotions alone any longer, and something needed to change. The only thing I'd received after my plea was another helping of doubt.

It kept me company as I attempted to find sleep that night—sleep, which I didn't end up finding much of at all.

Day came abruptly. Through my window, the sun slapped me right in the face. I'd been so restless that the arrival of the following day crept up, as if it were waiting around a corner. Limping downstairs, I noticed my mom wasn't home. I was already late for school. The enervating disappointment made my body feel like mush. I could hardly move.

At school, they were all probably already talking about it, laughing at me. Pounds and his crooked smile would be waiting. Nothing but more *bad* was ahead.

I had nowhere to go.

After attempting to stomach some cereal, I went back into my room and just sat. I tried my best not to think about it, but I didn't know. It seemed like it was all potentially going to get better, but maybe that was my fault again for thinking it could. For believing in something more, when it always just got worse.

Not out of inspiration or idea, but out of fear, I fell into the Ferry and started driving. Through the roads and out into town. Without a destination in mind. I drove around. I didn't really notice anyone or any of the other cars around me. I was so lost in my own thoughts that it hardly felt like there even was a world outside of my own. The tunnel vision was collapsing in around me. I was filled with anger, frustration, exhaustion, betrayal, and pity. I sank down deeper into my seat as I let all these emotions infect me. I wanted to feel them all, hoping they could finally win. I didn't need to keep playing this tug of war.

I came up on a red light. Other cars stacked in front and behind me, filing into an orderly line and pausing together before resuming our lives. I looked out of my window and saw someone—a street sweeper. He was an older man with a scar on his cheek. He carefully swept the street from the inside of his truck, leaving a freshly scrubbed road in his wake. Not stopping even for a moment to examine his finished product but pushing his vehicle forward. I watched this old man slowly inch his machine along, as it gently spun its broom at the bottom, both cleaning and sucking up errant trash. He was in no rush at all.

Looking around at the other cars, it seemed nobody had noticed him but me.

All too quickly, the light turned green. Our lives were taken off of pause, and I was lost again in the tide around me. Moving closer toward a destination that none of us wanted to admit we all had in common.

Driving on, I thought more about that street sweeper. His patience. His persistence. His near invisibility.

I made the last few turns before eventually arriving at Maya's. It was the only place I could think to go. I parked the car and walked in. Even though it was the middle of the day, the fluorescent light out front still flickered.

I thought less about all that had transpired and more about what was going on in this very moment. My feet in my shoes. My hand on the doorknob. My breath in my chest.

Inside, I didn't see her right away, so I carefully slid through a few of the aisles, not really looking at much. But it was again the simplicity of the store, the other people inside, that made me feel at peace. All my worries and all my fears were lost at the sight of a little girl bouncing beside her mother. As pure as that rush of happiness was, that, too, was short-lived. Because at the sight of Aloanso's photo, I fell into myself once more. I was reminded again just how serious this was. Aloanso and his smile held nothing but guilt. His photo— still in the same place—told me that, as much as I'd walked, he never again would. That every letter I'd read was written by someone who would never walk. And even with this golden opportunity, I'd taken it for granted. People as innocent as him were still gone.

As I moved through the store, my anxiety began to build. Maya wasn't here. She wasn't anywhere inside. I'd just wait. I'd just sit there until she showed up. No matter how long it took, I was just going to wait.

I quietly stood up and pressed the code into the vending machine, but no door swung back. Instead, a Coke just rolled down the machine's belly and popped out at the bottom. The most unsatisfying, yet most probable, result.

Returning to the floor, my back against the vending machine, I saw again that it really was just a normal corner store. Normal people shopping for household items, coming, and going. For hours, the cycle continued. The longer I sat there, the more I was convinced that Maya's store had simply returned to its original function.

I'd been searching my whole life, doing the right thing and doing my best to keep my ear to the ground. Despite all I'd seen, I believed. But then I was given my chance—this chance—only to lose it all again and be back searching once more. To lose him, and to now, lose this.

The brutal finality of this realization was unsettling yet undeniable. Everything that I'd seen in my life, like the blue columbines on my windowsill, was the only proof I'd needed; anything beautiful doesn't last long.

It's hard to build anything. It's easy to destroy everything.

~

The aisles of Maya's close in around me as I walk. It's cold inside and a chill creeps its way up my back. My head turns. I rub the back of my arm in a nervous tic.

My confusion, fear, and isolation build the longer I walk up and down aisle after aisle. But no one else is inside her store. There are no messengers in suits and ties. No regular customers shopping for regular items. No sign of my dad, Wings. But, worst of all, there's no sign of the woman in the white belt. No sign of Maya.

My body begins to shake as the cold gets stronger. The skin on my arms pricks like knives. It cuts into me as a crawling feeling comes over. It's taking me over.

I start to run, looking for an escape out of the store. I fly through the aisle toward the front.

But the door is gone. It's just the walls all around me, caving me in. I'm stuck here. I'm stuck everywhere. I'm stuck nowhere.

"Maya, please! Maya!" I scream as loud as I can.

A male voice booms back over me, sounding as if it's coming from the sky above.

"You can't be here."

"Maya!" I yell out a second time.

"Are you lost?"

Suddenly, my eyes snapped open.

A person stood over me. "Are you alright?"

I manage a nod.

"Listen, we're closed. You can't sleep here. Can I call your parents or something?"

Blinking awake, I made out the blurry edges of a long, rail-thin man with copper hair. I couldn't immediately place how old he was. Quickly, my eyes shot down as he looked back. I was still sitting inside the store with my back against the vending machine. It was colder now. It had to be late.

"Let me at least help you up." He reached toward me.

Getting back to my feet, I tried to look at him again, but I couldn't.

"I really am sorry, but like I said, we're closed."

I was ready to give up. I would be able to find my way again somehow. There was probably more out there somewhere. I was ready to return to my padded life and just forget. Forget about the store, the book, and the letters. Forget it all. But there was this pull. An extremely powerful pull. It came from deep. And all that I felt was that it had everything to do with the fact that I was here, and people like Aloanso never would be again.

Still looking down at my feet, I said, "But Maya's is always open."

The man took another step toward me. "Well, I suppose I can keep it open for a few more minutes if you need to grab something in particular, but be quick."

But I didn't move. I didn't move at all.

"And…what is it you need…?" he trailed off.

"I need to see the owner. I need to see Maya," I said.

The man looked confused as I watched his hand move from his side to his face. "I think you must be mistaken, kid. This is my store. I'm the owner."

I looked up with broken eyes. "What are you…?" But I trailed off again. My throat felt like it was getting tighter. I couldn't say anything more.

"I'm sorry, I…I've owned this store for nearly ten years now. What did you need to talk to the owner about?" the man asked simply.

My legs shook. I thought they might give up on me, and I would just crumble. I was at a complete loss for words.

"But…you…you don't understand…you don't…" My tears overcame my voice. I probably wasn't making any sense.

"It's alright. Whatever your issue or worry is, kid, I'm sure it'll be alright."

"No…No, it's not. I messed up bad…real…bad," I choked out.

The man continued to stand before me as I attempted to collect myself. I was just trying now to calm down.

It was all over. With Maya gone, I couldn't even tell her how sorry I was or how bad I felt about what I'd done. Even the chance to apologize was gone.

"I'm sorry," I finally said back to the man, while wiping my nose.

He stood there firmly. "No need. Is there…is there anything I could possibly do to help?" he asked.

But I just shook my head. I had nothing left.

I followed him to the door, and he held it open for me. I shuffled by, keeping my head down.

It was late outside. There weren't any cars on the road.

Looking out, I was startled by the man's voice beside me. "Whatever happened that you're so worked up about, just remember that we all make mistakes. But it's how we respond after we make them that matters, not so much the mistakes themselves."

Then the man turned and closed the front door. He reached into the back pocket of his jeans and pulled out a set of keys. Taking one of the several attached to his full ring, he pushed it into the lock and deadbolted it.

"Have a nice night," he said to me and walked away.

My eyes lingered on the door for a moment after the man was gone. It wasn't much longer before the flickering red fluorescent light from Maya's sign powered off.

~

Sliding into the driver's seat of the Ferry, I tried to silence everything. The more I thought about it that night, the more confused I became. Eventually, I just settled on the fact that the best thing I could do was forget about it all and start over. Find a different way.

I wasn't ready to step back into Metropolis, so I drove instead to Logan Park. Sliding the Ferry into a parking spot near the pond, I shut off the headlights and took a walk to cool down.

It was incredibly still. The water, the trees, the stars—everything appeared calm. It was late, and nobody else was there, but the calm was oddly unique. I was the only thing making any noise.

I made my way to the lookout point where my dad and I used to watch the stars. Because the night was so still, the stars were magnificent. Their gleam and sparkle would normally have been healing, but I felt nothing of the sort. I thought about how this was where it all began. How here, in this place, my dad had made me feel like I was something. My memory of him was normally strong when I came here, but it somehow now felt less powerful. I couldn't feel him here anymore. It, too, was now just a lookout point at a neighborhood park.

Empty glass bottles clinked. Out beyond the pond then, I saw the outline of a man. He was alone, his hunch significant, but I noticed he was reaching down over a trashcan. A waste bag hung in his hand.

"King. He knew your father, too, you know. He has been with me nearly since the beginning. He started with me after his brother passed."

I swung my head around instantly when the voice behind me finished.

Sitting on the bench behind me was Maya. Sitting, reading, appearing as though she hadn't a worry in the world. Like she'd been there all along.

"Maya?! What are you…?"

Maya closed her book before she continued. "King has been through more pain and suffering than he would ever let you, or anyone for that matter, know. But it is that pain that he uses, not to seek revenge, but to spread only the good. He knows that we already have enough pain and suffering out there. He's seen it. He's personally experienced it. But because of that pain, Phoenix, he understands that he must use it to fuel his endless pursuit to spread the good."

"King? Maya...I don't understand."

"And it was King who pleaded on your behalf to me. He begged that, in your case, I offer you forgiveness. Knowing how much I trust him made me more sympathetic than I originally intended to be with you. Because King reminded me again what it was like for him when he began working with me. How confusing it could all be at the start."

I swallowed hard, doing my best to keep from talking and, instead, pay close attention.

"I know you have plenty of pain, more than most, but that is your superpower, my child, your gift. That pain is the reason I chose you."

Eventually, I was able to respond. "I am so sorry, Maya. I...I don't know what I was thinking. I—"

She cut me off. "No. You knew exactly what you were doing. You were attempting to use something that was meant to heal, to hurt. Because that person hurt you. And for the first time, you felt strong enough to hurt them back."

I looked down again.

"When someone does something mean to you, child, it has so much more to do with that person's own personal pain than something that you've actually done to them. We people get caught in our own worlds; we often fail to remember that another is sitting across from us. A person who wants to be heard. A person who wants to be accepted. A person…a person who wants to be loved."

"But Pounds has done so many bad things. And he always gets away with them. Always."

"It may seem that way, but you do not know that for certain. You do not know what he does when he goes home. You do not know if he has trouble sleeping at night. What you see is what he wants you to see, what he chooses to allow others to know about him, which is never the full picture. Not even close." Maya then looked at me calmly as she finished by saying, "'Do not repay evil with evil or insult with insult. On the contrary, repay evil with blessing because to this you were called so that you may inherit a blessing.' 1 Peter 3:9."

Maya relaxed in her seat. I tried to unravel some of the stress on my shoulders.

"I've ruined everything," I admitted.

Maya sighed as she stood up and reached for my hand. Gently, I reached mine toward her. She grabbed hold of my palm, and instantly I could breathe more easily.

Looking up at Maya, I could see now that she was smiling. She looked fully alive.

"This really is a wonderful place, this park. I can see now why you and your father always came here. It's also where you and I met, my child. That very special birthday party of yours."

In her eyes, I could see hope but also sorrow. She was open, vulnerable. Somehow it made me do the same.

"This book and those letters, Phoenix, are no small responsibility. Perhaps I have made the mistake of giving you too much too soon."

I looked back into Maya's eyes, determined. "I'm ready. Please, Maya. I am. I'm ready to make this right."

The look she responded with made me feel even stronger.

Hopeful even.

She started in a different tone than before. "You must understand now, Phoenix. You can never make this mistake again. It can be you and you alone who takes the remainder of these letters forward. Under no circumstances at all may you break this trust, or all of this that I have shown you will come crumbling down. No one can know but you."

I nodded. "I promise. I promise I won't tell anyone."

Maya then released my hand as she reached into her pocket.

"When someone does something bad, they don't realize how deep it goes. It sends an endless number of ripples throughout the world, causing more pain than they thought they were ever capable of causing."

Then, she stopped. Maya handed me a plain manila envelope with the number "96" on it.

"But, when someone does something good, what they don't realize is how the same thing happens in the exact opposite way."

I carefully took the envelope in my hands and studied it. The simplicity, yet power, of the letter back in my hands was both healing and inspiring. My eyes devoured every inch. But when I looked up, Maya was gone. Looking back out over the railing, the trashman was gone now too. I was alone again at the lookout—nothing but me, the letter, the night.

Without wasting another moment, I ran back to the parking lot. In the Ferry, I turned onto the highway toward Pounds's house.

~

Their great lawn went on and on, the wet grass soaking the cuffs of my pants. I knocked on their ten-foot door. I heard footsteps, then whispers, and then someone cracked open the door. A man stood tall as he struggled to will his eyes open.

"Can I help you?" he asked, then quickly added, "Do you have any idea how late it is?"

He looked terrifying above me. His voice was deep and raspy—his jawline razor sharp.

"Hello, Mr. Francis. May I come in?"

He looked down more closely. "Phoenix? Is that…?"

But before he could say anything further, I walked in and took a seat on his sofa. He was too shocked to do anything but simply fall into the seat across from me.

"What's going on?" he asked, appearing now to be more alert.

I looked around, and on all of the walls, there were mostly just football photos of Pounds. Trophies and ribbons he'd won from all of the teams he'd competed on. But the more I looked, the more I noticed that there weren't any photos of Rose. Not a single one. Appearing as though she was never even here.

Few things are more difficult in life than finding a balance between honoring those who are gone and moving on. But more often than not, it's better to lean toward remembering the people we've lost. Doing so helps us act accordingly when in the presence of the living.

"I'm here to see your son. He's taken something from me, and I need it back."

"At one in the morning?" Mr. Francis asked.

"It's important."

I looked up and saw his wife standing in a nightgown at the edge of the railing. I recognized the master bedroom behind her from the party.

She called out, "Honey…what's going on?"

"This is, uh…Phoenix. Herman's boy. He says that he's here to

DARLING, YOU'RE NOT ALONE

get something from Paul. That it's important."

She shuffled down into the living room. Once she was able to get a better look at me, she said, "You're one of the boys who grew up with our son. I'm...I'm so terribly sorry about your father. He was a sweet man."

Somehow that upset me. My dad wasn't a *was*, but an *is*. Just because he was gone didn't mean that he still wasn't all those same things. Who you are doesn't disappear when you do. Not for him, not for anyone.

"Thanks," I said. "That's actually why I'm here."

Both Mr. and Mrs. Francis sat quietly before me, arm in arm. I could almost feel their daughter with us, telling me that it was okay. That it was safe to tell them.

"Your son has something that belonged to my dad. He took it from me."

Mr. and Mrs. Francis looked at each other and could now understand my initial distaste.

"What did he take from you that's so urgent?" Mrs. Francis asked.

Before answering, Pounds stormed out of his room, "Why are you...guys *yelling*...what's...what's going on?!"

He quickly noticed me. Standing up taller, Pounds, instead of being alarmed by my presence, belted out in laughter.

"*You!* Oh my God. It's the biggest joke in all of Darling!"

"Paul, shut your mouth," Mrs. Francis scolded. But he just went back to laughing even harder.

"Mom. You should have seen it! This idiot broke into the principal's office and embarrassed himself in front of the entire school today! It was brilliant! The whole place was dying laughing."

Both his parents went back to silence as Pounds disappeared

back into his room and then returned and bulled down the stairs, now standing across me.

Pounds chuckled. "Here." He tossed my dad's book across the living room table at me. "Nothing cool in there anyway."

Somehow just the feeling of the book back in my fingertips instantly calmed my nerves. I could think more clearly again.

"And what do you say to Phoenix?" Mr. Francis asked his son.

Pounds looked at me and complied with little conviction. "Yeah, I won't take your book anymore. My bad."

They all stood up, and Mr. Francis finally said, "Well, sorry again about all of this, Phoenix, but it is late. I'm sure you'd like to get back home yourself and get some sleep. I know I would."

But my body wouldn't leave the sofa. To stand up, to move, to think about anything other than Rose was somehow painful. To watch all of them move on. To watch them without her now almost made them appear incomplete, missing their *good*.

"Phoenix?" Mrs. Francis asked. "Is there something else?"

I wanted to look up, but it was just easier to keep looking at my feet while I spoke.

"You can't...do this anymore. You can't do this to her."

I felt all of them over me. I could see that their feet had stopped moving.

Pounds eventually jested, "It's late, bro. I won't take your book anymore, alright?" Then his feet turned, "Mom, can I just go back to sleep now? I have practice in the—"

"Sit down," she shot back. "Both of you."

Out of shock, Mr. Francis and Pounds both took seats again across from me.

Mrs. Francis spoke softly, "Go ahead, Phoenix. We're listening."

I felt my knees start to jump and my ankles shake. I was getting more and more nervous, but I tried to be strong.

"I'm...I'm sad too. About my dad...but I try not to let that make me sad all the time. That's no reason to be mean to people. We...we should try to never be mean, but that is no reason to be...to be mean..."

I trailed off, but I could feel them listening closely.

"But...now...now I know."

I stopped. I couldn't keep going. It was completely silent then.

"Know what?" Pounds burst out. "What the hell do you know?"

I closed my eyes. "I know what happened to Rose."

I opened my eyes and watched them for the first time. They tried to have a sensible reaction—an audible response of any kind—but I'd completely taken their breath away, robbed them of the opportunity to think clearly, because they were right. There was nothing even remotely sensible about what I'd just said. Nothing at all.

"How do you know what happened to my little girl?" Mr. Francis finally asked.

I reached into my back pocket and handed the letter to Pounds. Carefully, he looked at both of his parents before opening it.

He took a deep breath, then slowly began to read aloud. In front of all of us.

I watched the looks on his parents' faces shift.

But as the painfully real words hit all of their ears, one thought remained true. So true, that I could clearly see the letter's true power unfold right before my eyes.

For the first time since that ugly c-word, they were a family again.

19

To my dearest Sally,

Oh, my goodness, Salamander, how much I miss you. From your cooking to your dancing to even your silly laugh, I would do anything for just one more day. I would do anything to find you again in my arms. The only thing missing in heaven is you.

When I think back, though, I still don't understand how it all happened. I really was just a guy. I didn't need much. In my opinion, life had spoiled me plenty. If you don't have big dreams, then you can never be disappointed with how it all turns out.

My story has been written more times than one could count, but there was one special thing about my life. Somehow and some way, I got to be the guy to kiss you at the end of the night—just a regular old fella like me who married a princess.

Life can be kind of funny like that, I guess.

It was our dream life we'd always talked about. We were in New York City, where I could fight fires, and you got to go to school to pursue your passion. I was so happy, and you were too. We were so damn young.

But despite our youth, we had to grow up quick because a miracle came. A bun was in the oven.

Taxi after taxi lined the streets as we drove to our regular ultrasound. It was amazing to me how many people lived around us. Lives that were happening everywhere.

The appointment went well, and we'd learned together that we were going to be having a boy. We were thrilled. A boy was what we'd agreed we'd be better suited for.

As I did my best to manage that crazy downtown traffic on the way home, we went back and forth on potential names. I wanted Christopher after my grandfather, but you were settled on Gabriel after your brother. Back and forth we went when, eventually, I decided to just throw in the towel on the name.

After battling through all of the cabs, I dropped you off at the house and left for work.

"I love you," you said to me as I helped you out of the car.

"Love you too. See you for dinner."

Work was work, but it came like a wave that afternoon, a flash that knocked me onto my back is how I remember it.

My team and I were all in the truck responding to a fire on East 32nd. It had reportedly started on the tenth floor of a high-rise that went up five more stories. Over seventy people were trapped inside.

I was the first one in as I trudged through the rubble and up the stairs. Each step I took was on shaky ground. The walls crumbled beside me, and with each forward motion, the screams became louder. But once you get past the first few floors of a collapsing building, you can't avoid it. The only thing you can think about is your loved ones. Experience had taught me that it was impossible not to. With each step I took, I could see your face as clear as the day I asked you out—every detail.

One by one, we lifted all different types of rubble off struggling people. But as I moved from person to person, I heard final wishes coming from all of them. Each civilian that was in bad shape kept repeating the same thing.

"Tell them I'm sorry."

For hours, it felt like we moved broken bricks and cement off people—the injuries were severe. It looked like a war zone. But then I heard a woman call out that a young boy was stuck. I bolted toward her.

He must have been no older than six years old. I could tell he was young from the hope in his eyes. I was beside him and his mom as, together, we tried to free her son from a portion of the ceiling that had collapsed, crushing both of his legs. With all of the strength in me, I tried. I tried, and I tried, and I tried. We pushed and pulled, trying everything that we could possibly think of, but nothing worked. The whole building was starting to crumble.

I screamed at the woman to go—that I would grab the boy and meet her downstairs, but she wouldn't leave his side. One of my guys had to carry her out kicking and screaming. I remained by the boy's side without her.

The building was going to fall any second, but the floor we were on had finally been cleared. It was just him and I.

"What's your name?" he asked.

"Captain Sabintter...but everyone just calls me Captain S. What's yours?"

The boy smiled back, and amidst the chaos, the last thing I heard was him say his name.

"Christopher."

I may have never gotten the chance to meet our baby boy, but I like to think that, because of my final moments, I did become a father.

In those last seconds, I drifted off to the beginning, when we met and how lucky you made me.

Even though our boy will never know his father, I hope he knows that I am thinking of him every day. I hope our boy grows up to meet someone just like you because that would mean that, no matter what, he will be alright.

Because of you, I lived the perfect life. Each one of my days, all the way up until my last, was full.

It's time for me to go now, Salamander, but keep forward. Life rolls on. Don't stop living yours. And I'm sorry that I never made it home for dinner.

Love,

Andy

Walking into her office that next Monday for our appointment, I *saw* the woman in Andy's letter. She looked younger—free of some of the normal pain. I wasn't looking at Mrs. S, I was looking at Salamander.

"Sit, Phoenix."

I plopped down, and she looked on with intrigue. "So, how's everything?" she asked.

When she asked me that this time, I felt a different type of warmth rise out of me. I couldn't help but think about all the places I'd now gone with the light.

"I think everything is starting to make some sense, finally," I admitted.

Mrs. S sat up a bit in her chair as she looked back at me. I could tell she hadn't been expecting that. "How so?" she asked.

I looked up at her. "I guess…I'm starting to realize that bad things happen, and good things happen. We can't control that. But we can control the choices we make. How we take these things."

"And what's helped you figure that out?"

"The people. Meeting them. Getting to know their stories," I said, following along myself with intrigue in my own admission.

Mrs. S began to write something down on a notepad. "Your episodes. Have you been able to manage those alright?"

I thought about Maya and her store. About how long she'd been trying to reach me, to bring me here, to this moment. I thought about how, for so long, none of it had made any sense, but now I was able to start seeing how connected we all were.

"Yeah, I think so," I answered, "I think those have been alright."

"That's wonderful," Mrs. S responded, then asked, "And this mishap at school. Why did I get a call from your principal the other day about you causing trouble?"

I swallowed hard, looking down for a moment. I had to just

come clean. "That was stupid. It wasn't me, really, but I did it still. I don't know what I was thinking."

My voice trailed off at the end, and we both went silent. She was still writing stuff down.

"What made you want to do something like that?"

"Anger," I said quietly.

Mrs. S explained, "Good. Good. Anger. We all have it, Phoenix. A lot of people try to act like they don't, but that simply isn't true. We all do. Now, that doesn't mean that we should, but it's human to lash out. Forget reason." She placed her yellow pad down before finishing, "But it's important, when you feel overwhelmed by this anger, that we find an effective way for you to deal with it."

"How do you deal with it?" I asked.

Mrs. S smiled. "I think about my family."

I collected myself in a way that I never had before. I'd sat in this office so many times with little interest in the hour that I knew all too well was ahead, but today was different. I was happy to be there. I was happy to be doing my job.

"Do you have a son?" I asked.

She waited a moment before reaching for a photo on her desk. Mrs. S turned it toward me to reveal a boy in her arms. The two of them looked as happy as a mother and son could be. It made me think how strong we really are. How resilient family can be.

"Christopher," she sang. "My everything."

I thought about how many memories she'd made without her husband. All of the nights it was just her and her son. The last thing her husband had given her.

His parting gift.

As I watched her with the photo, for the first time, I stopped judging her. My idea of who she was all of these years was blown up. Hearing that she had lost someone so important to her explained so much. To picture her as a young adult seemed impossible, but I suppose everyone—even people like her—were young at one point. Immaturely loved at one point. Danced like mad at one point. Dreamed at one point.

"It was tough losing my dad," I began. "I think about the millions of other scenarios that could have played out that day every time I close my eyes. And still, to this moment, all of the other scenarios seem much more likely. If the police had gotten to school just a few moments sooner. If I'd just decided to stay home that day. If the librarian had just kept our door locked. If the Ferry had broken down on his way toward us. If he'd jumped one more inch to the right instead of the left. If somehow, that morning, he'd decided even just something as stupid as not ever getting out of bed. To take a day off for once, and for once to put himself first, instead of behind everyone else. Instead of giving his life to a roomful of kids he didn't even know. All of the other ways it could have turned out. If any of those small, tiny things about that day had been different, my dad would still be here—a small change in the universe.

"But that is no way to think about it. Not at all. That is no way to think about that morning, and that is no way to think about life in general. Because small changes in one thing could negatively impact all the other things that have been really good.

"If you think about life like that, then you also have to think about how all of the good things that happened before that might not have. How if my dad would have never met my mom, then I wouldn't even be sitting here right now. How all of the tragedies he avoided as a cop allowed me to get to spend fifteen years with him in my life. How the whole time I got to know him, he was warm, despite whatever he was going through. How we got to walk to work every morning before the shooting together. How he stopped one of the largest tragedies in US history from becoming an even larger one. How all of the lives he saved are lives that will grow up now and fall in love one day, give birth to lives themselves one day, make this world a better place one day. Lives that, if one of those small things about that day had been different, or millions of other scenarios that could have played out had happened, may not be here now, either. Those other small changes in the universe too.

"Without bad, there is no good. And another thing. We can go crazy trying to imagine how things may have been different if one small bad thing hadn't happened in all of our lives. But, when we get stuck doing that, we have to also remember the same thing is true for that one small good thing. That one small good thing that also changed our lives for the better. That one small thing that may be the reason we are still here today," I finished.

Mrs. S smiled, and I saw it again, briefly. For a short moment, she was that young lover I'd read all about.

She looked on proudly as she asked, "So, we're here today to talk about your loss, I presume?"

"No," I answered simply, "we're here to talk about yours."

~

At school later that night, I made my way to Locker 8½.

It was a little after midnight, but I'd become accustomed to being around the exterior of the campus at this hour. My routine was becoming more comfortable.

With all of the main buildings and hallways locked up, it was quiet. Walking beside them all, there was this sort of peace that accompanied each step. Like walking around my bedroom in the dark…I still knew where everything was.

Once I had the next letter, I held it tightly between my fingers. I only had three more to go.

With each deliberate step, I headed back through the back side of campus toward my house. But as I was walking, I heard someone. I jumped to get behind a wall. Quickly, I looked around but couldn't see anyone. I thought it had to be Marcus again, but then I heard something, soft but unmistakable.

Soft tears I'd hoped to never hear again. A sound that I'd thought about more than anything.

Shay was sitting in the parking lot—in front of the fifteen painted hearts—softly weeping into her hands.

Suddenly, I thought about how, now that I'd known what had happened with my dad and Aloanso, I'd finally understood why I wasn't able to see Shay. Why all those years between us were lost.

My mind shot back to a memory from six years ago right after it happened. Feeling the moment when it was, instead, *my* face that was dripping in tears.

~

My dad's hand quickly wrapped around my tiny shoulder.

"Phoenix, buddy, what is it? What's wrong?" he said when he found me crying beside his bedroom. We could both now hear my mom through the paper-thin walls.

I brought my eyes off the laces of my shoes as I sort of just fell into him. I let my whole body unravel in his arms as he held me close, pulling me into his chest and heart. But it made my tears even heavier.

My dad didn't say anything further but just continued to pull me in tighter. Rocking me side to side and allowing it to flow out of me. All of my pain, confusion, and sorrow. First a little, and then a lot.

I was blue about many things, but there was only one thought on my mind. "At the park...how come...how come I don't see Shay?"

None of the other adult stuff mattered. At the end of the day, I just wanted to be with her at our favorite place. Talking and playing in the sun.

"I'm sorry...I'm sorry. I did something wrong, didn't I? I'm sorry, Dad. I'm..." I struggled to say in between tears.

After saying it out loud, my tears came on even stronger than before. To lose her felt like a pain that would never fully go away. I knew it even then. That I wasn't going to be able to meet anyone as special as her for the rest of my life.

My dad held me and rocked me as I continued to cry.

"I'm sorry. I'm so sorry."

I wrapped my arms around him as tight as I could. Hoping to pull as much of his strength he'd always carried with him into me.

He knelt to my level and smiled as he looked into my eyes. Slowly, I saw the corners of his eyes start to pool in tears. "Everything, Phoenix. Everything is going to be alright."

~

Shay looked every bit of the same girl I'd cared so much about since we'd met. Her hair was longer now, and she was wearing a purple hoodie and sweats. But even from afar, and in the dark of the night, the second she lifted her face, I could still see those blue eyes. No matter how many years it had been, those never changed.

I carefully left the cover of the wall I'd been behind and approached her.

"Hey, are you alright?"

Shay was partially spooked as she looked toward me. She said nothing but quickly ran toward me and wrapped me in a hug. It was so tight I could hardly breathe. I let my eyes close. I became putty in her arms and felt like I had melted right into her.

We slowly let go.

"If there's anyone I would want to sneak up on me crying in the middle of the night, it's you," she said to me with a subdued smile.

I tried to smile back as best I could.

"I was just…I…" But she trailed off as more of her tears came back. She fell into my arms once more.

"Don't worry. I know…" I tried to explain.

"Are you here, too, because…because of what happened?" she asked, suddenly confused.

I quickly locked up. Feeling the letter in my back pocket, I immediately realized what would happen if I told her. How easily it would all disappear again. Although, I desperately wanted to tell her why I was here, more than anything really.

"Yeah," I lied.

She wiped her eyes. "I just still can't understand why…I can't understand why someone would do something like that."

I thought then about Tyler and what he'd been pushed to do. How he'd been spinning, but how I'd been spinning too. How if, maybe, something good, instead of bad, had happened to him the day before the Snowball, maybe none of this would have taken place. How, really, when you think about it, we're all spinning, so it's important to love instead of fight. You never have any idea who's that close to the edge.

"I don't think we'll ever know why," I eventually said. "And we have to be okay with that."

We looked back at one another in the simple night. The air was cold. She then reached for my hand. "Come. I want to show you something I think you might like."

At the start, we were just walking. It really didn't seem like she had much of a destination in mind, which was fine by me. I was still adjusting to the fact that we were even here in this moment together. But then, as we walked, suddenly it turned into jogging and then, eventually, we were running. In full sprint, I took off after her. Like we were kids again, we ran and ran, smiling all the while. Like we were playing a game. My nerves were suddenly gone.

We arrived at a small wooden bench atop a hill and stopped to catch our breath. We were now out past the football field, by the old science building. I'd never been back here before.

She took a seat on the bench, so I did the same.

"What was that all about?" I asked, still breathing heavily.

She just looked at me and laughed.

We sat there for a few moments before she said, "I come out here sometimes when I have writer's block. It helps me think."

"Did you ever finish that movie you were working on?"

She laughed. "Yeah, well…I did, kinda. But I actually decided to turn it into a book instead last summer."

"A book!?" I said, surprised. "A whole entire book?"

She nodded. "It's not very long, though."

Unsure if she'd be interested, I tiptoed. "I'd love to read it, if you want?"

"Really?" She jumped up, her hair bounced. "Would you really read it?"

I hadn't expected her to be thrilled at my asking, so I smiled and nodded.

"Well, okay," she said, taking a breath. "I'll let you read it. If you love it, please tell me, but if you hate it, I don't want to know. Just lie to me or something."

We both started laughing.

"Shay, I'm sure it's amazing," I reassured her.

A soft silence settled between us. The night breeze came in, but thankfully didn't stay long.

With darkness all around, I felt a little less scared, a little less afraid of what was ahead. My internal checklist in my head, of all the things I needed to do, seemed a little less important. Just being nearly close enough to have our elbows touch was all I could think about—her sui generis glow.

The trees around us were short so I could easily look over them and see a view of the entire school. It looked small from up here.

"You know why this is my all-time fav spot?" she asked.

I waited for her to tell me why, but then Shay just pointed up into the sky and said, "It's got the best view of the stars."

I looked up into the sky. There wasn't a single cloud for miles.

While looking up and quietly getting lost in the depths of the universe, I felt Shay's head gently rest atop my shoulder.

2 0

To the Singer,

They say you hurt those you love the most, but they say a lot of things.

You turned what would have been my worst moment into my greatest memory. I knew once I was given the chance to write, it had to be to you. It had to be.

The only reason I knew I wasn't dead that night was because I could hear your voice. It was like church bells.

A flood of pain. I couldn't move my legs. Strapped to the bed, I woke up in critical condition in the ICU. I was told that I'd just been in a terrible car accident. The last thing I remembered was leaving my son's apartment. A conversation that had turned much too quickly.

My pain was growing more and more severe by the crawling moment. Pain like that aches deep in your bones. It drums low within. Despite my declining spirit, my hands gripped the side of the hospital bed with tremendous strength. I'd lost a ton of blood. Syringes were stabbed into my legs, but I could only feel them with my eyes. My legs were entirely numb—not even a tickle. Nothing around me seemed to make much sense. Although, properly judging a situation had never quite been my strongest suit.

An evil realization slithered through my mind: when all you want to do is die, everyone is there, but when all you want to do is live, no one is.

Fighting with myself, your voice served as my only reply. A tender sound that gradually wrapped me in its warmth. It crawled through the curtain. We were suitemates, and I was gracious enough to be in the audience of your performance.

Once they were finished stabilizing me, I called for your name.

"Teresa," you said gently.

I could picture you through the sound of your voice. A distinguished yet elegant woman who had many talents. A happy learner and someone who didn't categorize herself by the job she had or status she held, but by how she made people feel. A soft complexion that became rose in mid-June. A wonderful snowy smile and caramel blond hair.

"Are you alone?" I called out as I surveyed the seclusion of my private space.

Your response came slower than expected.

"No," you began. "I have you."

Through the night, we talked and talked. We talked until our cheeks were blue. The way that you looked at life was so incredibly fascinating. Your optimism despite your journey. Your story, it seemed, was all laid out like chapters in a book. Every detail—down to the sentences of each paragraph—had its perfect place. You read it aloud to me as if the pages were right at your fingertips.

Then, what began as a tiny crack, burst open. I was running yolk all over the floor. The pain that the hospital had put me through eroded my usual guard, and as a result, I was more vulnerable.

I told you my entire story, the pain and the hardships that I'd gone through with my son. My first divorce followed by my second. The constant misdirections I'd suffered on my journey. My pity party that had led me to this very predicament I was now in. I told you how, earlier that very same day, I'd tried to end it all. I wanted it to all be over. I was rubbish.

But you patiently listened to my garbage, piece by piece. No judgment and no sorrow. Returning only with pure love.

You started to tell me about a place where none of these things would matter. The grass always blew in the wind, and the water in the ocean was always crisp. Deep pain and regret had all but been gone and replaced with only pure love and hope. Nobody and nothing could ruin this place, and now it was going to be my destiny to go there—you were sure of it.

You made it all sound so certain that I actually started to believe. For the first time in my life, I really did. The detail in which you described this place made it seem as though you'd been there before. But it almost started to sound maybe less like a place and more like a mind state.

"How do I get there?" I asked.

Your reply came slowly. "Close your eyes."

It started slow. The blanket of your song warmly slid over me again. At the sound of your voice, I fell into a gentle sleep.

But when I woke up, I was no longer in my hospital bed. I looked down, and my legs were working. I could feel no pain. My pounding headache, gone. I felt rested for the first time I could remember. I was young again. I was in that place you had described. It was exactly as I'd envisioned.

I looked all over, but you were nowhere to be found. Searching everywhere I could, I found the answer to something I couldn't believe. That same moment was when I found out. I guess they were right.

The reason you were in the ICU that night was because I'd swerved into you. You were in critical condition because of me.

Teresa, I am writing to not only tell you that I am sorry but to tell you that you were right. It is just like how you described. The grass always blows, the water is always crisp. Every day that you wake up is like the first all over again.

I know that your light on Earth will forever shine. In just one night, you were able to alter my entire perception of the importance of life. I can only imagine what you have been able to accomplish in a lifetime.

Love,

Your Suitemate, Grace

Just as I'd finished reading, Shay snuck up behind me. "What's that?"

I quickly folded the lined paper as fast as possible and placed it back into its envelope. Shay slid into a seat next to me. I was sitting in the hallway just outside of my first class that morning.

"Hmm, you're a writer, too, are ya?" She reached for the letter. Quickly, I pulled it back.

It frightened her. She backpedaled. "Woah. I didn't mean to…"

"It's not that. It's just…not what you think it is," was all I could think to say.

Shay was rigid and didn't say anything else. The silence was nice, but I could tell she was looking for more. Normally I'd be more concerned with how I was making her feel, but nowadays, I couldn't focus on much of anything other than my mission.

"I'm glad I ran into you last night. How come I don't run into you more often?" she asked with some disappointment.

"I…I've just been busy," I fumbled in response.

Then Shay asked, "And TT? I don't see you two together anymore."

I blurted out my answer. "He…He and I just have different schedules now. That's all."

I looked around, concerned that possibly other people could've seen the letter while I was reading it. I didn't see anyone who looked suspicious, but you never know.

"The school's going to do the Snowball this year," Shay said quietly and looked away for a moment.

I'd suddenly clammed up. "Oh…Uh, that's great."

"So…do ya think you're gonna go?" she asked.

"Probably not. I'm…I'm pretty busy."

She nodded slowly. "Yeah, me either."

"What? What about…?" But I trailed off. Remembering suddenly what had happened last year and how I'd embarrassed her in front of everyone. But Shay just looked back at me and tried to offer a smile. It was hard to see how, but for some reason, it made me sad.

"You busy with your spelling?" she asked.

I stumbled over my reply, not wanting to sound too suspicious. "Ye…yeah. I'm getting ready for the State Bee right now. Lots of words. I have so many."

"That's right. I'd love to see you in action one of these days," she said.

I just tried to smile back, despite my uneasiness.

She gave me a strange sideways glance. "You're acting kinda funny, you know that?"

Then she nudged me playfully, and I tried to laugh. I was afraid she was starting to catch on.

"Oh!" she handed me a folder. "I almost forgot. Here. It's the first two chapters. As promised."

"First two chapters?"

"My book, Phoenix! Remember?" Shay shot back, playfully affronted.

Inside the folder was a stack of pages held together by golden round-head fasteners. Flipping through it quickly, I smiled as I saw with my own eyes that it was actually real.

The details came back to me. I fumbled, "Yes, yes, I remember. Thank you…thank you so much for letting me read it."

Looking down at her book again, I almost couldn't believe she was serious when I'd asked. But before I could apologize further, she wrapped me in another hug. A hug that quickly put me in my own little heaven.

"Gotta go, but keep me posted." She was off down the hall, then she turned and walked backward, yelling toward me, "I hope you don't hate it!"

~

The address for the delivery was an old retirement home just a few blocks from school. I could get there on foot in just ten minutes. I walked with my head down and my hands on the strings of my backpack. The weather hadn't rolled in yet, but I could tell that it was just on the horizon. The cold swell wasn't far.

The automatic doors to the White Oak Assisted Living Facility slid open, and I was greeted by a young man working at the front desk.

"Can I help you?"

"Hey, uhh…I'm here to see Teresa?"

He looked me up and down, as if to question my reason for being there. Maybe he knew her well enough to know that she didn't get visitors often.

After another moment, he handed me a sign-in sheet with a pen attached to it.

"Name and date there. Do you know what floor she's on?"

I shook my head.

"Two zero two. It's on the second floor. The elevator is over there to the left."

As I walked toward Teresa's room, I was drawn in by all of the residents. Wrinkled faces smiled in my direction, and each of their stories captured me. Their eyes were a time capsule. I realized that these were the lucky ones in the end. If you were old enough to spend your final days in an assisted living facility, then you'd survived plenty worse.

I approached Room 202 and was drawn in by the earthy smell.

Fresh flowers. The door was cracked open. I peeked in. An old woman sat at a desk, looking out the window with sunglasses on. She looked just as beautiful as Grace described, with flowing blond hair and a youthful glow, despite her age. I'd never been able to more easily place a stranger as happy.

"Teresa?" I asked softly, still standing in the doorway.

"Who is it?" she responded without turning around.

"I…uh…Phoenix. My name is Phoenix."

She continued to remain focused out the window. She spoke to me with some restraint in her voice. "You…you sound so young. Come in, Phoenix. Find yourself a seat."

Even with me sitting across from her, she remained focused outside the window. Her nostrils flared as she took deep breaths.

"We haven't had the pleasure, have we?" she asked.

"I'm afraid we haven't."

"Well then, this is a treat. A stranger has come to visit." I laughed softly before she continued, "How are you then today, Mr. Phoenix?"

She spoke as if she knew me, which somehow seemed fitting. It made me feel generally welcome.

"I'm good, I guess…it's just been a long week," I admitted.

"I can hear that," she began slowly. "Your youth is a priceless thing. You've got the rest of your life to be an adult, but you only get one childhood crush, one school play, and one lucky date to take to prom. And those are things that you will carry forever. Until you are even as old as me." She turned to face the birds once more as she laughed. "Don't let life stress you all that much. That is the secret to living a long while; it can't always be serious."

I watched as she intently listened to the birds that chirped outside her window.

"Do you know what kind of birds those are?" she asked.

"I have no idea, ma'am."

"Ruby-throated hummingbirds. They don't normally come around this time of year. Generally, they spend their winters in Central America, Mexico, and occasionally Florida. But each time I hear them, I am more often than not brought good fortune. Listen to them. You can tell the type of hummingbird by the high-pitched tone in the flap of their wings. It's a beacon call."

I turned my attention out the window as she talked. The hummingbirds quickly zipped around each other from tree to tree.

"Or by their red necks," I said in response.

She laughed. "Yes, I suppose that is a fair point of reference for some."

"Do you bird-watch every day?" I asked.

She shuffled into her seat, getting even more comfortable. "Not quite. I bird *listen*. But, yes, they teach me, and Phoenix, they can also teach you. Say, the ruby-throated hummingbird. They remain vibrant and energetic because they never stay in one place long. They do not allow themselves to be confined to one place or even one flower."

I looked out the window as I watched the little birds flutter about. Remaining in motion and only stopping for a moment to drink from each flower before floating to the next. Floating along in the still air.

As I continued watching Teresa, I noticed how she appeared to be perfectly content. There was no place she needed to be; she was in no rush at all. She savored each breath and enjoyed each blink. To her, life moved at a different speed.

"What brings you to me today, little hummingbird?" she asked.

Without saying anything, I reached into my bag and extended the letter out toward her. The envelope startled Teresa, as if she hadn't seen me handing it to her. It was all very strange, really. It grazed her wrist, and she almost didn't even take it.

She slowly opened the letter and felt it carefully with the tips of her fingers—the handwritten characters on the page and each individual stroke of ink. As I watched her struggle, my confusion washed away. Each of the books and things on her walls were written in braille. A white fold-up cane with a red tip was tucked behind the door.

She handed the letter back in my direction. "I'm sorry, Phoenix, but would you mind reading it for me?"

"Of course," I said quickly.

I took the letter back from her and started to read. Slowly and carefully, I attempted to relay Grace's message, not missing a single moment or place of emphasis.

Teresa listened with every part of her. Her chair became the most important object in the room as it promised to hold her upright. She cried so softly behind her sunglasses that I hardly noticed, but you can always tell. Tears are an impossible thing to hide.

I gently placed the letter into Teresa's hands once I'd finished. She ran her fingers over it once more. This time, her touch appeared as though she was somehow writing her back.

"Grace," Teresa said powerfully. "What a wonderful name."

"Do you remember her?"

"December sixth, nineteen seventy-three. I remember every single moment. The last day I was able to see."

I froze. "I…I am so sorry…I…"

She reached her hand out to touch mine. "Don't be. I wouldn't have changed a single thing about it, even if I could. In many ways, I've never seen more than I do now. It is not a burden, but a gift."

Silence came just as quickly and left at her next words.

"And do you know what else Grace gave me?"

But instead of taking her attention back out toward the ruby-throated hummingbirds, she tuned into her room once more. The little birds behind her danced in the sun.

"My new favorite bird to listen to."

Watching Teresa, I was again drawn in by her allaying stillness. This moment was perfect, and everything inside Room 202 was clear as day.

~

Walking home that night, I passed by Darling High to grab my next letter.

The parking lot wasn't full, but there were more cars than usual, which caught me by surprise. It was around eight p.m., which meant nothing should have been going on. But was I walked by, I heard people clapping and shoes squeaking from our high school gym floor. Occasional yells echoed into the rest of the school.

I felt terrible almost instantly—it was TT's first varsity basketball practice.

Rather than going by the door to look in, I just kept walking toward Locker 8½. Something inside of me wanted to step inside and wave, but I couldn't. I didn't want to embarrass him in front all his new friends anyway.

With the next letter in my hands, I thought about how things used to be. When times were much simpler.

The rest of my walk home was terribly lonely. The further along on my journey with the book I'd gotten, the more isolated I'd started to feel. Traveling from place to place, delivering letter after letter, only drove me further from those I'd once felt closest to. I knew, then,

I really was all on my own. I could not share this burden. Not only all of the tough moments, but even the good ones. No one else was seeing them or experiencing them. No one but me.

At home, I opened the door to a cold house. The heater wasn't on, and I shivered the minute I entered the kitchen. I hadn't eaten anything all day. I realized it when my stomach growled upon opening up the fridge and seeing close to nothing edible.

I looked over at the sofa to see my mom fast asleep with the TV on. I walked over and shut it off before heading up to my room, alone and hungry. The only two things I could come across that night.

I was busy providing warmth for others when I couldn't find much warmth myself. I hadn't checked on me, my mom. My own home wasn't in order.

21

To my son,

Sadness does not exist where I am now, but that does not mean I don't miss you dearly. There are many wonderful things about where I am, but I wanted to take the time, instead, with you, to remember our beginning. I will forever love to relive the times when you were just the size of a teakettle.

My sweet boy, I have not known a stronger love than the moment my eyes met yours on April the 12th. It rained a bit that morning, but when the sun arrived, so did you.

Your smile reminds me of the best possible day. And your laugh, now that gentle noise is my symphony, and I considered myself lucky to have occasionally been your conductor.

When you were just a baby, I would take you to the park and watch you chase the butterflies. Orange, gold, and yellow specks danced in the air, and you happily danced alongside them. Albeit you could hardly walk, but this was but an insignificant detail, for when you saw those beautiful monarchs, you, too, flapped your wings. Before you could walk, you could dance. Before you could talk, you could laugh. And before your life had even started, you'd already made mine.

I watched you transform from that beautiful baby boy into a handsome young man. A transformation that any mother would dream of witnessing. Gosh, you grew so quickly. You were almost translucent, because your skin could hardly keep up with your body. But unlike the other boys, you always knew who you were. I was your momma, and you never forgot to kiss me. You were never too embarrassed to care.

But even the bad days I have made sure not to forget. The days when yells were exchanged instead of kisses, screams instead of hugs, and silence instead of music. For those are the moments we mustn't ever let go of, but, instead, allow to teach us that we must always be careful.

Your father and I were not meant to be forever. I know it has been hard on you, but this is how it is, baby. I cannot protect you from all of life's pain.

And even though your father and I were not together long, we made the most wonderful thing. We made a boy that I believe will one day champion a worthy cause. When the world will point fingers, we made a boy who will, instead, help show them how to focus on the rhythm.

Your father hasn't taken all of this well, but go easy on him. I know my passing weighed heavily on him, as I, of course, know it has on you. But, my boy, this is something you share.

Grief is the hardest on those we leave behind. Your father is hurting, and he needs the healing power that only you can provide. Be gentle, for age does not better help you in dealing with this pain. That, unfortunately, is something that you can find light in or not. It is a gift that you have. You must help those who cannot freely dance as you so wonderfully can.

I say all of this because I want you to rest easy knowing that I am okay. I am all better now. It hurt when I had to leave, but the physical pain was only temporary. To leave you was the hardest part of my transition.

But as I look back on the life I was given the privilege of living, I realize one thing—my reason for writing.

The reason I was put on this Earth was to be your mother. You were my greatest achievement. Everything I did in my life was building toward April the 12th. The good, the bad, they were all lessons that I got to pass on to you. Then, once you were born, well, everything after that was extra. By then, you were already well on your way. I was quite happy to be your cheerleader with my little remaining time.

But understand that you will come across moments of doubt. There will be times when the darkness appears to be closing in. People will try to keep you from flapping your wings, and people will refuse to listen to your song. These are all things that will happen. Knowing this truth, I want you to never forget that you must still—even then—push on.

Do not forget to not only embrace all of the good that will surely come your way but also the bad. These terrible things that come to you in your life are what will help you grow the most, my child—hang onto that tight. Fallen fruits grow into magnificent trees.

Even though I won't get to watch you graduate high school, get married, or have a baby boy of your own, I'll still be by your side. And I know that, sometimes, you still cry, but don't worry, even then, you are not alone. We are all full of tears, but the lucky ones are able to let them flow. If you can cry, then you're still able to laugh. Able to love.

My tiny dancer, keep chasing butterflies. Momma is still making sure you don't fall.

Love you forever,

Mom

I scanned down at the address at the bottom of page ninety-nine. I couldn't believe I hadn't realized it sooner. It was TT's.

I'd pushed myself away from my greatest friend—someone who'd known loss—real loss—far longer than I had. A gripping pain shot through me. I was in a heap when I'd realized who this letter was for. The message contained nothing but pure love. There was no pain on these pages—none at all.

As I tried to gather myself, I looked around the cafeteria. There he was, sitting around his new group of friends with his lunch. But the longer I watched him, the more I felt like I could see some of that pain I'd known he harbored. Perhaps none of them knew about it, but even from afar, I could still see it. Although, as I'd come to learn, most people do.

It had been a year now since the shooting, but the energy on campus was still somehow subdued. Each student looked over their shoulder a little differently. What was already a lonely place, became a lonelier one.

I'd been working round the clock to try and bring some light back into the darkness of Darling, but I was starting to feel like I was losing the war. I was staying up each night to deliver notes of hope, only to come back and see that nothing had changed. The only thing that really had happened was more time had passed. They'd painted over all of the bullet holes, but if you ran your finger over them, you could still find the deep scars.

Just then, Shay carried a handful of books toward a table on the other side of the hall. She plopped herself down and started reading.

The pain had started to catch up with her too. The colors she had worn nowadays weren't really colors. Just like her smiles weren't really smiles. I hadn't seen her wear her pink shoes since it all came crashing down. She looked tired all of the time.

I wanted to do something, but I had no idea what. Her warmth seemed permanently extinguished. I had to do something—say something. But as the moment continued to also wear me down, I felt a crippling doubt speak to me. Nothing I could say or do could possibly make it go away.

The rest of the day at school was much more of the same. People walked around like the world around us didn't exist and acted like their time here would last forever—all in a hurry to do nothing.

But despite it all, I knew I needed to see TT. The letter would serve perfectly as my olive branch. I needed to make things right and close the distance that had grown between us. Even if it was just settling on fixing a small thing today, I would have to just start with that.

I dropped a note on his locker after third period. I told him to meet at our old spot after school. There was a small classroom that shielded a table from the outside cold. It was a usual hangout for us during our freshman year, because it had our favorite vending machine close by. But on my way over to meet him, I saw he was at our spot already with a girl. They hadn't seen me. From the corner, I watched the two of them.

I couldn't believe it. An actual, real girl. I didn't even think it possible, but the longer I watched, I guess the more real it had to be. Together they sat with his arm around her. They looked like they fit perfectly together.

Realizing the time, he gently shuffled from his seat, and I watched her scurry to kiss his cheek. His hand slipped to the small of her back.

As the girl left, I waited another moment before slowly walking over and acting like I hadn't seen any of that.

"Hey, TT."

He turned and didn't look entirely pleased to see me. "H-Hey, Ph-Phoenix."

I sat down across him as he reached into his pocket for some change. He walked toward the vending machine, and I watched him punch in a number to grab a bag of chips and a root beer.

"How's basketball been?" I asked.

TT took a sip of his bubbly drink. "I-It's good. I-I like all the guys on the team more than I thought I would. Th-They aren't actually all so dumb after all."

I laughed, but I saw that TT was serious still.

"S-So what are we doing here today?" he asked, quickly changing the subject.

"TT, I'm sorry. I just really haven't been myself lately," I admitted. As I said it, I felt uncomfortable. Not because I didn't mean my apology, but just that so much had happened that he didn't know about.

I studied TT closely. He seemed surprised. He wasn't sure where to begin.

"I-I know that all of this has been hard since...th-the... B-But you should never push people away like that, Ph-Phoenix. E-Especially me. I-I'm your best friend. W-We are supposed to always have each other's back."

"I know, and I was wrong to not open up to you sooner. I just didn't know how to...but I am now. I'm sorry."

TT slowly replied, "N-No...I-I'm sorry. I-I should have tried to talk to you sooner too. I-It's both of our faults. W-We all have different ways to cope. I-I know..." He trailed off, upset with himself for his stutter. "I-I've missed you. I-I'm sorry about what happened with you and Pounds. B-But..." Then, he stopped.

"What?" I asked. I was afraid. I had no idea how to talk to someone I'd once been able to share anything with.

TT finally carried on. "Th-That was pretty cool when you broke into the principal's office and used the announcements. I-I thought that was so awesome."

We both laughed freely. I was so glad to see him smiling again.

"Thanks." That was all I could add after we'd quieted back down.

"A-And...I-I have something...I-I need to tell you," he added.

"What?" I asked a second time, startled, as I'd been the one who was supposed to be telling *him* something.

"I-I...I...uh. W-Well I kind of have a...g-girlfriend."

I laughed again at the moment of lightheartedness. "I know, I just saw you two. It was the grossest thing I've ever seen."

Suddenly, TT looked tight again.

Quickly, I said, "Kidding. I'm sorry, I didn't—"

He cut me off. "N-No, it's not you. I-It's just...I-I also..." But he trailed off at the end without finishing what he was trying to say, then added, "W-We...we've also sort of...sort of...k-kissed."

"On the lips!" I yelled so loud I was afraid the entire school might've heard.

But TT just laughed, nodding several times. His smile was one of a kind.

"Well! How was it?"

TT blushed. "I-It was crazy, Ph-Phoenix. I-I actually really, really loved it and would, for sure, do it again if she wanted. I-I had no idea girls' lips were so...so soft."

"Okay. Enough man. Too much of that. Please."

TT gave me a playful shove.

"Who is she?" I asked, having not recognized her.

"H-Her name's Angie. Sh-She's new to Darling, but she's really nice. Y-You'd like her, Ph-Phoenix. Sh-She's really smart too."

The way he talked about her made it seem like he did care,

proving what they had was real. It was both sweet and strange.

Doing my best to make sure he knew I meant it, I said to him, "I really want to meet her."

"Y-You will. A-And I'm taking her to the Snowball."

I looked at him and smiled. "That's awesome."

It got quiet again. There was a pain and misunderstanding between us that was making it extremely awkward. Words were becoming forced. I just needed to give him the letter, and hopefully, everything would be alright.

Sensing the tension, I added, "Listen, it all hasn't been for nothing."

"Wh-What do you mean?"

I took a deep breath. "I found something. Something that belonged to my dad. It's been something that I've been working on. And…well, that's also what I needed to talk to you about."

A heavy look of doubt came over him. TT waited another moment, giving me the option to either walk back what I'd just said or further explain.

"I-I think it's good that you've found something to…help. B-Believing in something isn't a bad thing," he said with some hesitation.

"Do you believe?" I asked him.

He sighed. "Ph-Phoenix. Y-You're my best friend, and I think it's good that you've found something that helps you make sense of all of this. B-But sometimes it just…i-it just is. N-Nothing is going to bring them back."

"That's not true," I said. But before he could respond, I handed him the letter.

"Wh-What's this?" he asked.

"Just read it."

"Ph-Phoenix…"

"They can come back. They can. TT, I am telling you. You just have to trust me."

TT looked like he was in shock.

"Read it and start to find out for yourself."

As his eyes left me and went to the pages, I took a long breath. This was it. I had no idea how he would react, but I knew it would change him, alter his ideas about more than just me or him. Perhaps everything.

I searched for something, anything, as he read. Waiting. But then, he said something so simple.

"Th-This is even her handwriting."

~

Before walking home, I stopped by the locker to grab the final letter. I was excited to finally be on the verge of completing what my dad had started, but with each passing step, the darkness crept back.

No matter how I battled forward or how many wrongs I made right, it couldn't change that all of this tragedy had taken place. Nothing could, and no matter how strong I had become, it was a crushing realization.

Thinking about everything, I just stopped. On the sidewalk beside the football fields, I leaned all of my weight against a chain-link fence.

I'd put so much of myself into delivering the light that it was now all I had. I'd become dependent on the hope and the healing that was intended for the recipients, not me. Reading the letters once myself only to give them away and be forced to move on alone. The high of delivering a letter, followed by the low of not receiving guidance of my own.

To think now, though, that I had proof—real proof—that heaven was real gave me a quick spark. I'd needed to just say what was on my mind, because now, at least, I had proof that someone was listening.

I sat down and asked for what I wanted. The conversation of it all initially made me laugh, until I started to get to what was important. That was when I decided it was best not to ask for anything that directly had to do with me, but the people around me. For them to understand what I now did, in whatever way was alright for them. I asked that some of their issues be explained. I wanted them to see the world can be a good place. Whether they received a letter or not, I wanted them to know that someone, somewhere, was looking out for them. That we are not alone.

When I opened the door to Metropolis that night, the lights were on in the kitchen. The smell of bread rolls hugged my nostrils. My mom was standing over the counter as she cut carrots and other vegetables, sporting a checkered red and white apron.

"How was your day, sweetie?" she said to me with such warmth it caught me off guard. Not once had she ever called me, "sweetie," and the only other time I'd ever seen her wearing that apron was Thanksgiving when I was thirteen.

"It was good," I responded with a smile.

"Well, today just must be our day then."

She went back to dicing up more food and then took a roasted chicken out of the oven. The crisp, brown skin looked delectable.

It had probably been weeks since I'd had a decent meal. My hand came up to my stomach. I'd lost weight.

"Have a seat, Noodle."

I pulled up a chair, and she brought me a plate exploding with food. I immediately dove into a bite, and she stopped me with her words.

"I have something to tell you," she said with excitement.

I looked up but didn't say anything immediately.

"I got a new job…and the starting pay is better than my old one!"

My arms shot up. "That's great!"

"Just out of the blue, I got a call today and took it. I don't even know. So, get used to this, because it's going to be chicken dinner for a while around here."

My mom was so happy that her energy effortlessly spilled onto me. I don't even know why I'd asked how, because it wasn't even necessary. Then, I said something that I hadn't said since Dad died.

"I love you."

She stopped. Looking up at me while reaching across the table, she placed her hand atop mine. "I love you."

In my room later—with the last remaining letter in my hands—a feeling of achievement grabbed hold of me. I had done it. I was going to complete my dad's true calling. But as I flipped open to page one hundred of my dad's book and read to whom it would be delivered, I cringed. I had no idea how I was going to explain myself this time. This delivery was going to be unlike any before. I wasn't ready.

This place and this person didn't need to see me. They needed to see my dad. He was the only one who could possibly explain everything that had happened. He was the only one who could deliver this final letter.

But maybe there was one other person, another who could potentially say what he couldn't because this person was there that night too.

This letter was going to be unlike any other before it. But it was going to be different not because of who it was going to, but because, this time, I decided that I wasn't going to deliver it alone. Maya was just going to have to trust me.

22

Dear Grandma G,

I hope you're reading this closely, because I'm finally ready to reveal exactly how I did my greatest trick. My grand finale. But promise to keep this between just me and you. I don't want Curly to know I stole it.

My whole life, I wanted to be a magician. All of my other friends in school said that they wanted to make beats or be pro, but I never really liked that sorta stuff. I was more interested in surprising people. Using my tricks to help make the world see.

But Mom would laugh. She would hardly ever let me practice my tricks, and if she did, she would just tell me that they weren't real.

Mom wasn't always all bad, though. It was weird. Sometimes, when she was really thirsty, she was also really nice. Instead of making fun of me, she would even ask me to show her some of my tricks. I remember how, when I could smell her favorite drink in the house, that meant she was going to laugh a lot that night.

Sometimes, though, that strong stuff would make her stomach sick, and then I would get to come and stay with you. I always loved being at your house the most.

When I came over, we would have so much fun. You would make your special homemade bacon cheese pizza and sugar cookies. We would watch TV all day, and you'd let me help you in your garden. But my favorite was when you would teach me new tricks from Curly's Magic Manual.

The tricks were always hard to learn at first, but you just told me to keep trying. You would tell me that the best magicians never give up. You encouraged me a lot. I really liked that.

Then, that very special night came. I ran to your house after school that Friday to spend the weekend with you, but when I walked through the front door, I couldn't smell any yummy treats. I burst into your room to see what was going on.

"Baby Apple," you said, "I got two of them."

My heart nearly jumped out of my chest. I leaped across your armchair and onto you. We laughed and screamed—two tickets to Curly's Magic Show.

The theater was a deep red, and a lot of the people dressed really fancy by wearing those funny shirts with the collars around their necks. Then, he flew onto the stage. It was like seeing a superhero. We watched Curly do trick after trick.

Toward the end of the show, he took out a white sheet and announced that, for his grand finale, he was going to make someone from the audience disappear.

He jumped down and started sprinting through the aisles. Searching for someone worthy of his magic touch.

We were trying so hard to get him to notice us that I didn't even realize I was holding my breath. But when he stopped and looked at me, I thought I was going to pass out.

"You," he said.

He showed me to my spot on stage and told me that all I had to do was hold my breath, close my eyes, and let it all sweep over me. That the magic would take me to a beach with the sand and asked that, as proof, I grab a handful of it to bring back. That was it.

Then, Curly started counting down. Once I felt the white sheet come over me, I held my breath, closed my eyes, and let it all sweep over me. Just like he said.

I looked up, and instead of seeing the crowd, I saw an incredible ocean. I felt the sand beneath my feet. Just like Curly asked, I reached down and grabbed a handful.

Just as quickly as I'd arrived, I was snapped back onto the stage. The crowd began to clap, and Curly asked me to open my palm. With his help, I spilled the sand onto the stage as proof.

It was so cool, Grandma. So, so cool.

It was late, but after the show, we were both in the mood for some of your homemade sugar cookies to celebrate. We stopped at the store on the way home to get the supplies.

After finding a bag of pure cane sugar, we hopped into line. I remember how we smiled as we talked more about the show. We got to the front of the line when you realized that you'd forgotten your purse in the car. You told me to wait there and that you'd be right back.

The first thing I remember after you left was a lot of yelling. It was coming from all directions. I thought someone was hurt, but then I saw the guys in masks. I watched them jump over the counter.

I dove to the side. I tried my best to hide. Everything was okay. Even though I was starting to get scared, I knew I was safe. I was trying to make sure they couldn't see me. I was just going to wait there until you got your purse.

But the yelling got louder. More time started to pass, and I couldn't see you anywhere I looked. I didn't feel safe anymore. I didn't know what to do. Then the idea came. I had a power that could save me.

With the strongest magic I knew, I did exactly what I was supposed to. I held my breath, closed my eyes, and let it all sweep over me. And it worked.

I could feel the sand at my feet again. When I looked out, I wasn't inside that store anymore, but in front of that incredible ocean. I'd done it; the magic had saved me.

There was no more screaming, no more yelling. It was all beautiful. My grand finale. My greatest trick yet.

I'm sorry that we never got to eat sugar cookies together that night, Grandma. Your words, your lessons, and your smile are still with me here at the beach each day. Now, I always feel the sand beneath my feet. And one day, I cannot wait to feel it with you.

I promise the magic is still real.

Love,

Aloanso

Late that night, as I crept out of my house, I realized that this was it. This would be my last time sneaking my dad's keys off the mantel and my last time cutting through the night. But inside the Ferry, the thought of going to Gloria's blue house made me feel sick. I'd so deeply ached for her from afar, but to have to come face to face with her was something I knew in my bones I couldn't possibly do alone. There was only one other person that knew about this pain. I needed the person my dad had once relied on. The one person that could help me finish what my dad had started was Marcus.

I turned off the radio and rolled down the windows. I'd hoped the night air could cool my nerves. Eventually, enough of a chill went through my shirt to adequately startle my system.

Turning onto Marcus's street, I saw Shay's and my old lamppost. It was one we used to meet at every summer before my fateful birthday. The grooves on the settled concrete and the shine of the light created a shadow around it. In a world where it seemed like everything had changed, it was oddly satisfying to see something that had remained the same.

As I continued to drive closer and closer, passing by residential home after home, the car felt like it slowed down on its own. The horrors of that day came back with vivid reality. But more than the lamppost, more than her street, and even more than Aloanso's letter, it was seeing her front door. Seeing it was like watching them speed off in their police cruiser again. It was like seeing her face again, Shay's young cheeks torn by tears.

With the Ferry in park, I took my time peeling myself out of the driver's seat. Step by step, my feet crawled up to the front door. I knocked twice and waited.

I looked around at all of the other houses. It was so late that it felt like they had to be empty.

I turned quickly as the door creaked open. Standing before me was not Marcus as I'd hoped, but Shay.

"Phoenix?" She rubbed her eyes. "What's wrong?"

She was in a pair of black pajamas with her blond hair tied up into a bun. Loose strands of hair pointed out in all directions.

I'd really wished that I'd thought more about how I was going to explain myself. I had nothing to say.

We just stood there in the doorway. It felt like, the longer I just looked at her, the more she'd started to understand.

"Come on," she finally said as she led me into the house. "My mom is going to hear us if we just stand outside like this. Get in here."

Shay led me into her room and quietly closed the door.

Looking around, I saw her desk beside her window. It was so neatly organized with small ornaments and mementos. A mess of pages was at the forefront of the display.

"Oh," she started, once my attention shifted. "Working on the ending. Originally it was a sad wrap-up, but I decided that I wanted to change it to a happier one."

"Why?"

She carried on with ease. "Real life is sad enough. I wanted to write something that leaves people feeling…well, I guess…feeling sort of hopeful."

The rest of her bedroom was a vibrant array of colors. The walls were decorated with stars, and the photos she did have adequately captured the nostalgia inside each memory. Everything had its place.

"Sorry," she said. "I really need to update my room. I've had the same wallpaper since I was eight."

Shay stacked the papers on her desk and put them into a neat pile. Swiftly, she undid her hair, letting it naturally bounce to her shoulders, and took a seat crisscross atop her bed.

"Most of the time, I can't believe real life," I began.

Shay patted on the spot in front of her on the bed. I took a seat across from her.

"I really used to believe that it was all sad, all of the time. So many sad things happen," I finished.

Shay looked past me for a moment, out beyond her window. We both went silent.

"So, you're here to tell me you hate it?" Shay asked with a playful frown.

"Hate what?"

"Phoenix!" Shay quietly sort of yelled back, lightly pushing me. "The first two chapters of my book!"

Quickly, I tried to explain. "No. No. Shay, I'm so sorry. I still haven't had the time to read it yet. But I promise I will soon. I promise."

Shay let a soft smile escape. "It's okay. You're just making me go crazy over here, that's all."

I smiled back and just looked at her. Everything about her in that instant seemed so interesting. I couldn't help it.

"What?" She smiled.

"Nothing," I said quickly.

"Well, what is it, then, that the Preponderant Phoenix Iver has requested my services for at one in the morning?"

I tried my best to contain my laughter. "Your dad. I need his help."

Shay shook her head. "Sorry. He's covering for someone. Something about them not having enough officers at the station at night."

I looked down and suddenly felt like leaving. I needed Marcus, and without him, there wasn't much reason to try and finish the book tonight.

"You know, Phoenix," Shay started while reaching for my hand, "we can be made again."

I wasn't sure what she meant, so I just looked back at her and waited.

"We aren't our parents. Their mistakes are not our own. We may agree that the world is sad, but when it is our turn, we will have the chance to make it whatever we want."

"How's that?"

She squeezed my hand in hers. "Old people made the world sad, but that doesn't mean we have to. We can be the fresh start if we want. We just have to believe we can."

I looked at her and was enraptured. Her optimism was infectious.

"It is up to you and me how we write it." She smiled.

She was right. As sad as all of this was, and appeared to be, it didn't mean that we couldn't at least try to do something about it. We certainly had every reason to just sit back and play the victim, but that's not how change happens. I wanted to change the world, but for as long as I'd known Shay, she had also always wanted to do the same exact thing. Then, it occurred to me. It was certainly not my intention to take this leap of faith, but I felt it in my heart. No matter the risk, it all suddenly became so simple.

Still looking at her, I started slowly, "Do you think there's anything too absurd…too absurd to believe?"

Shay gently crooked her neck, her eyes bright, and whispered, "Never. Not in infinity plus one years."

I turned and pulled the letter out of my back pocket. In my hands, it now felt heavy, powerful.

Shay then asked, "What was it again you said you needed my dad's help with?"

~

I handed the letter to her once we were in the car and explained everything as we drove. After she finished it, I told her about each of the letters before this and about all of the deliveries my dad had completed before me.

Shay hung on to each word. Her fixation was impossible to misinterpret.

I realized then that my hope in telling her had less to do with my needing her help and more to do with making sure she knew. After seeing the darkness weigh Shay down, I wanted to give her something to help restore her light.

"You've been doing this all along?" was the first thing she asked.

I thought about all the places I'd gone, the different people I'd met. But then I explained to her that this one was going to be unlike any before it. And somehow, she knew without having to ask why.

"It's a gift, you know," she said once I'd finished explaining everything.

"I know," I responded. "These letters...I cannot think of a better gift to give someone."

"No, not the letters," she began. "Your ability to deliver them."

I started driving slower as we got closer to the blue house. It was even more terrifying in person than in my memory. I could also tell that Shay was now just as afraid as I was.

Once we parked, Shay and I just sat inside the car. We were in no rush. I didn't want anything other than to be sitting beside her.

We watched the clock. It was Friday night, but we were about fifteen minutes early.

"That night...the night that our parents had the accident...it was him. It was Aloanso," I finally admitted.

I kept my eyes on the house the entire time, afraid that if I looked away, I might miss something.

"Your dad…he told me…he told me everything," I said to her.

Shay reached across the center console and put her hand over mine again.

Softly, her voice followed her touch. "It's just like you told me that night…that night outside the library. We may not ever understand why, but we have to be okay with that."

Just then, Gloria's automatic light flipped on, and she took her first step toward the garden.

Her mannerisms were deliberate and oddly ritualistic. As if we were watching her move through her morning routine, each movement appeared as though she'd done it thousands of times before. It was exactly the same as that first night I'd watched her with Marcus.

The small flower in her hands was set just a few inches to the side. The bush before her gave Gloria a sense of seclusion. Her gloves had partially aged. On her knees, and despite the cold of the night, she began digging.

I looked at Shay as she intently watched the old woman's every movement, her hand still over mine.

I couldn't resist it this time. I couldn't push it away. Seeing her there, now, the death and the destruction became not just a memory anymore, but the real thing. I was trapped again. It was happening.

I'm slowly pushing through the dark red and black colors that pass me by. As if I'm wading through some sort of black water, I keep going. I know I need to be somewhere.

Maya's red sign shines over me from the other side of the water. It's weighing me down like a creeping muck that's sucking me under. I won't let it win.

The bell above the door rang as I push through and walk inside. The aisles are full of all the others around me, and I can see them. They're all wearing the same clothes my dad used to, but looking down at myself, now, I am too.

As the shirt and tie protect me, I see that all of them, every one, are looking at me. Their heads nod in bows and their hands clap, but there is no noise. It's completely silent inside of Maya's. I walk to the front.

The flame of the candle burns before Aloanso's photo. The dates below flash before my eyes. It's all I can see. I fall to my knees.

I feel Maya's hand on my shoulder. Her grip is strong.

"It was always meant to be you and her that finished this, my child. We must forgive, but we must never forget. The mistakes of those who came before us aren't just mistakes, but important pieces of history. Yesterday. Today. Tomorrow. There is no difference between any of them, other than what is in our minds. Control your fear and you will become unstoppable."

I turn to look at Maya. Her hand then goes from my shoulder into my palm. This time, I squeeze it back.

"But we are most powerful when we work together."

I stop when I feel her. In Maya's with me is the touch. But not from Maya, a human one. It's willing me. It's telling me without saying anything.

I move back toward the front door. I know what's there. I know that I am afraid of it. I know that, one day, this place will crush me. I know that rain will soak me. I know that I won't be able to stand forever. I know that I will probably just be pushed back down into Maya's for the rest of my life, but I don't care. I have to push. Not for me. Not for me.

"Phoenix," I hear her say.

My eyes flew open. I was back in the car. I looked down to see Shay's hand still atop mine.

"Are you alright?" she asked.

"Yes," I began softly. "I'm ready."

We made sure to be quiet as we got out of the car and crossed the street. Coming up on the gate, I slid it open and took my first step in. Shay was right behind me.

Looking in, Gloria hardly flinched. She was laser-focused on her digging.

"Excuse me," I said softly.

Gloria didn't move.

Trying again, I asked, "Gloria? Excuse me?"

Still nothing.

I didn't want to startle her, but I wasn't sure how else to get her attention.

"Gloria," I said, this time with more strength behind my voice.

She shot up. From behind the bush, Gloria stared at us both.

Then, she came directly up to me, getting only inches away from my face.

"Baby Apple?" she said in disbelief.

Startled, I fumbled back. "No, I…uh—"

But Gloria cut me off. "What took you so long? I was waiting for you at the car? We were supposed to be having my sugar cookies?"

I looked back at Shay before Gloria added, "It's no bother. I suppose I can just start making some now. Were you able to get that cane sugar?"

I was freaked out. I hadn't the slightest idea what to say to her.

"Gloria, I…I'm not Aloanso," was the best I could think to say.

Still, she persisted, "The sugar, Baby Apple? Where is it? You're meaning to tell me you've been gone all this time, and you didn't get *any* sugar?"

I was completely out of ideas when the front door to the blue house opened. A middle-aged woman walked toward us.

"Mama, what's going on?" she asked.

Gloria turned back toward the woman and said, "It's Baby Apple, sweetie. He's home. Look. He finally came back home again. I told you he would. I told you."

The woman sighed as she looked at Shay and me. She grabbed hold of her mother gently. "Mama. That's not Aloanso. Aloanso passed away six years ago. He's not coming home anymore."

Gloria slowly looked into her daughters' green eyes and studied them with acute intensity.

"Remember?" the woman said.

Slowly, Gloria nodded, appearing as though she'd understood.

"We're sorry," Shay piped up.

The woman turned her attention toward Shay and me. "What are you two doing here sneaking up on an old lady like this? Do you know how late it is?"

Shay and I both searched for an answer but came up with nothing.

"Let's get you back in your garden. Here." The woman walked Gloria back to her flowers. It was only then I noticed that there was more dirt and stone than actual plants.

The woman then returned to ask us again, "So?"

Finally, I looked up at her and explained, "We came here to give your mother something."

The woman then sighed even more heavily than the first time. "Sorry to disappoint you both, but I'm not sure there's much of a point. She hasn't quite been herself since my son…"

I looked over at Gloria once more. She'd resumed gardening so effortlessly that it appeared as though we had never even interrupted her in the first place.

"Dementia," the woman explained.

Shay beside me deflated. What we'd hoped could help Gloria seemed now as though it served little to no purpose at all.

"I'm sorry about your son," I said to the woman.

"It was much harder on her than on me. I was…I wasn't much of a mother to him. But once we lost my Aloanso, I had to become *her* mother. Somebody had to, since he was gone. They were…they were best friends."

"I'm sure that your son is glad you're here…here with her," Shay said.

The woman smiled at us both. "I'm sorry my mom startled you both. I'm Michelle."

"Phoenix," I said and then looked toward Shay. "And this is Shay."

"Phoenix, Shay. Why don't you come inside? We can talk more."

It was dark out as Shay and I followed Michelle into the blue house. The night's stars and the city lights painted themselves beautifully across the glaucous sky, like a piece of fine art. I could only smile as I thought about my dad then, about what he would do and what he would say. Somehow, I knew he wasn't far away. Pretty nights were his favorite. Things as simple as the shine of the stars and the color of the sky. The powerful sensation that is stillness.

Inside, Shay and I took a seat, and the woman came and sat across from us.

"How does your mom garden like that…this time of year? Doesn't she get cold?" Shay asked Michelle.

Michelle paused for a moment before answering, "I'd hardly call it gardening, it's more like a form of meditation or medicine for her. After her diagnosis, her doctors explained to me that people with her condition can fixate on certain—sometimes random—things. But I think it's something that calms her deteriorating mind from all the things she's seen and dealt with in her life. You're both young, but as you grow older, you see a lot of things that are hard. And the plants are something I give her to bring outside on Fridays…I'm just trying to do what I can."

As Michelle looked at us, I thought about how much we'd all seen, and how sometimes the strangest things to others, make complete sense to us.

"Now, what was it that the two of you came to bring my mother?" Michelle asked matter-of-factly, as if we'd just returned after borrowing their can opener or bottle of ketchup.

Shay looked at me then, and I just continued to look around the blue house. Despite it being rundown on the outside, the inside was well kept. A true home feeling. All different signatures were atop stools and tables. Blankets slung over the sofa. It smelled like cleaning detergent and wool. My eyes became heavy.

I looked back toward Michelle. She looked stressed and exhausted. Her eyebrows were frayed, and her hair could've used a wash, but she was gorgeous otherwise. Sharp eyes and smile. A warmth even now, after it all. I thought about what she looked like then when she had Aloanso. How even though she wasn't ready to be a mother at the time, what his loss meant to her now. How little she probably talked about it. How pain is a brutal and gut-wrenching part of life, but how it is a miracle to even be a part of life. How much losing him changed her.

How much losing him changed me.

"Phoenix?" Michelle repeated.

Shay was looking at me still. I saw parts of her, then, that I'd never imagined I would again. Having her beside me now made it clear to me how much we could change. She was here, now, with me. Shay, the girl I'd spent so much time thinking of, was real. As real as the floor beneath my feet, the breath in my lungs, and the light in my hands.

"My dad," I began slowly, "*our* dads, were the police officers who cost your boy his life that night…my dad was the one who took your son."

Michelle tilted her head in a way that made her look as though she were questioning whether I was serious or not. But after another moment of silence, she could tell that I had no reason to lie to her otherwise. She knew it was real.

I didn't say anything further as Michelle continued to let it all sit. Then, she stood up and started pacing back and forth.

"Your dad…he took my son? And now…now…" But she stopped midsentence, unsure of where she was headed, until she picked up again with more frustration than before. "Where is he? Why isn't he the one who's here right now? You're both…you're both kids."

Shay put her hand over mine as I spoke. "My dad…he passed last year."

Michelle froze once more. Knowing then that we'd had more in common than when she'd initially met me and Shay. She sat back down.

"But we are here tonight to tell you that, when you die, that doesn't mean you are gone. My dad, Aloanso, and everyone else who's ever lived and died on this Earth, they will always be a part of all our lives. No matter whether you believe or not, they are here."

Michelle's hands slowly rose to her chin and face as she sat before us. Shay got up and went to her side. Without saying anything, they began to hug. The two of them held onto one another as if they'd known each other their whole lives.

I sat across from them and thought about how much pain Michelle had been through. How, even though I'd always thought I was alone in my personal loss, this was a loss I now shared with her.

How many others must have lost just like us too.

"I should have been a better mother," she cried as Shay still held her tightly. "I should have been there more for him. He deserved better than what he got."

Shay replied, "Trust me. He knew he was loved. I'm sure of it."

Michelle then powerfully looked at Shay. Like she knew, even before we'd told her, that heaven was real. That Aloanso was somewhere looking down on us now. As if, for a moment, Aloanso, in his own special way, that only his mother could see, told her.

"We're here to give you this," I said, walking toward Michelle and handing her the envelope. She took it gently from my hands.

Pain is in us all. But we bottle it up because we feel like we are alone in our pain. That's just how it is, I guess. We walk around all day and all night with this pain but try and find ways to use it. That's what my dad did; that's what I'm going to try to do too.

Shay remained by Michelle's side as she quietly read Aloanso's letter. After another moment, I decided to step outside and check on Gloria.

The stars and the night continued to shine. Gloria was still in the garden.

"Do you mind if I help?" I asked.

Gloria turned slightly toward me. "That would be lovely."

Carefully, I helped her tidy up where she'd been gardening.

Looking down, I saw the memorial she'd made for Aloanso. It had his full name carved into the stone and the same photo as the one of him at Maya's. Under Aloanso's name, it read, *Magician*.

"My grandson," she began. "He was the most talented boy."

As she carried on cleaning around the relic, I saw another memorial just beside the one for Aloanso. It was almost identical.

"Who's that for?" I pointed.

Gloria said, "This very nice man. I never knew his actual name, so I just called him Guardian Angel."

"That's so sweet," I said back.

Gloria carried on. "Yes, he was. After we lost my grandson, he started coming over to help me in my garden. He came every Friday night. He would tell me stories about his family, and I would teach him about flowers and gardening—he had a boy just like my Baby Apple—but then he just stopped showing up all of a sudden, without saying anything. For months, I had no idea why. Then, I was watching the TV one day and saw his photo on the news. They said he died in a shooting at a school."

She moved a flower away, and I saw the second grave. It was the same exact stone, but instead of having a name on it, like Aloanso's, it had a pair of wings.

"I like to think now that, instead of Guardian Angel keeping *me* company, he's spending all his time protecting my grandson."

I reached for the bare stone and felt it with my hand. It was beside a bed of all different types of flowers, although one, in particular, caught my attention. A flowering Colorado blue columbine was just beside where my fingers now were. The two were touching.

Gloria said, "I just wish that he and Aloanso could've known one another."

I turned to Gloria and finally replied, "I'm sure they are together now, in heaven."

Gloria smiled widely back at me. "Now, that would be like magic."

We then went back to cleaning up the garden in silence. Taking a few of the dead plants and replacing them with new ones.

23

I drove alongside the sun that morning. Shay gently slipped into a soft sleep in the passenger seat beside me. We'd been up the entire night. Her breathing was slow.

After I'd finished gardening outside with Gloria last night, Michelle put her to bed and made some coffee and breakfast for both Shay and me. We all ate together, and Michelle asked me all about the other letters and how amazing it must have been to meet everyone. We talked, ate, and laughed for hours.

But now, it was all over. Every one of them had gotten their love, their healing, their hope, and their rebirth.

On a trivial road into town, I looked out the window and caught sight of a man cutting the grass of a small football field. He was driving a personal-sized lawnmower as he sequenced his way up and down. Dew glistened on the blades.

It wasn't long before I was out in front of Maya's. It was now close to seven in the morning, and the sun had now begun to peek over the hill.

I parked in the shade so Shay could continue sleeping.

I walked through the doors into Maya's shop with my dad's notebook in my hands. Looking around, I quickly saw her but nobody else. Standing there, I watched her for a moment before saying anything—she was cleaning one of the windows with a rag.

"You've made an old lady proud, child," she said without taking her attention away from the window.

I took another step closer.

"How come you didn't wake your friend so you could introduce me?" she asked.

Caught off guard, I jumbled, "Maya...I...I just needed some help. I promise that we can trust her. I—"

But she quickly stopped me. At the sight of her smile, I suddenly knew it was alright. It was all going to be alright.

"I know why. And I'm glad you told her. You finally opened up and asked for some help. I guess I can make just that one exception. Sometimes it's okay to break the rules."

She stopped cleaning for a moment and threw the rag over her shoulder. "Your father. I know that he is so very proud of you, too, Phoenix. We all are. Thanks to you, Wings may peacefully rest, knowing that all of his work has been completed."

For some reason, I felt a frown come across my face. All of this loss—including my own—despite all of my hard work, still hadn't gone away. I wasn't sure what I'd been hoping for at the end of this journey, but this certainly wasn't it.

I'd delayed the mourning of my dad until now. The instant I'd learned about the book, I'd put off any sense of saying goodbye, but now I had no choice. Only now, I didn't have to say goodbye to just him anymore, but Maya, this shop, and all of the souls and faces I'd met while delivering mail from heaven.

I reached out and gave Maya my dad's book. "I don't want this to be over."

Softly accepting it from me, she responded, "You know, your father was a big fan of the Irish writer Samuel Beckett. I cannot remember a single day he would go without sharing one of his favorite Beckett lines with me." Maya stopped, then added more carefully, "Samuel Beckett wrote a novel called *The Unnamable* that your father invariably referenced. But my favorite line from the entire story comes in the end. Beckett wrote, 'It will be I, it will be the silence, where I am, I don't know, I'll never know, in the silence you don't know, you must go on, I can't go on, I'll go on.'"

She then placed her fingers under my chin and lifted me up as she finished explaining, "You've done it, Phoenix. You've completed your father's mission. Be proud. But now you, much like all the others you've met, must also go on."

Maya then took the rag off her shoulder and went back to cleaning the same window, as if nothing had changed at all. I stood there and watched her complete the task with careful patience—reversing her circular motions after every minute or so. In the store, I just stood there and watched her clean window after window. Maya carried on, continuing to act as though I wasn't standing right there beside her. She was just preparing her store for yet another day. Then, I reached for a rag just beside the counter and cleaned the window next to her. Maya looked at me and smiled as we began cleaning together. In the morning silence, she and I wiped clean all of the windows in the store—every single one.

"All done?" I asked.

"All done." Maya smiled. "Come, my child. I have something for you."

She led me to the vending machine and down the staircase into the main mailroom. As I walked beside her, I saw all of the other messengers buzzing around, preparing for their next adventure. Still following her, we walked into her office, and I took a seat.

Shuffling behind her desk, Maya came back up with a box wrapped with an orange bow. "For you."

Slowly I pulled the bow off and unwrapped the box. Inside was a CD. Our favorite CD. *Verities & Balderdash* by Harry Chapin.

"How did you…?" I started.

"The day you first came into my store. I've never seen anyone look at anything with such endearment."

Holding it in my hands reminded me of the beginning—of the time when I'd hardly known what was possible. What this store really was, and about how I looked at the world then, and how I looked at it now. I didn't even say anything before leaping across the table and giving Maya a massive hug.

"Thank you…for…for it all."

"You have a village now," she said with my arms around her.

I wasn't sure exactly how I was going to use all that I'd learned under Maya's tutelage, but I guess that's the whole point. You never know what's next. What you carry forward with you, though, are the tools—those may be recycled.

Looking back at Maya, I tried to remember as much of her office as I could. Taking a mental snapshot of the yellow legal papers, her books, and the simplicity. I wanted to know this room. I wanted to capture its strength.

"Thank you for helping my mom."

Maya said to me, "That was all your doing, my child. You understand now how we are all connected in life and in death. Instead of thinking just about yourself, you prayed for the well-being of another. But you never just prayed and did nothing. You acted on every prayer you sent forward. You always did the hard part. I just got to provide you with some help along the way, that's all."

I smiled as I tried to be strong while asking, "Will I still see you?"

Maya sat down again, pointing her hands to her office around her. "My child, please. I was with you long before we met that day in my store, and I will be long after that." Then, she stood up and added, "My store is always open."

Maya led me back to the vending machine, and I hugged her once more. I wasn't sure I ever wanted to let go. But just as I was about to say my final goodbye, the lights flickered off and back on. It was quick.

I couldn't be certain, but once the lights fully powered back on, it looked like Maya winked at me.

"Even though it's easy to see the bad through all the darkness, remember to see the good through all the light," she said with a smile, once the door was open.

Maya then turned and walked back down the staircase. I watched the vending machine door slowly close behind me until it hid everything down below once more, concealing it all as if it had never even been there in the first place.

Back at the car, I startled Shay awake while hopping back behind the wheel. I threw the CD into the back seat.

"Where are we?" She yawned.

I wasn't sure what exactly to say, because I wasn't really sure myself. But somehow, that felt alright. It felt like that was how it was supposed to be all along.

"Nowhere," I replied.

Shay just looked at me while rubbing her eyes awake. Not giving it a second thought. I was pretty sure she was still half asleep.

After dropping Shay off, I slid the Ferry into its normal spot and walked into Metropolis, where my mom was sitting there waiting for me. Her voice quickly followed.

"Phoenix Iver, did you just take the car without asking?" She sounded angry.

I was so startled that I didn't say anything back. I just stood in the doorway with the keys in my hand. I tucked them behind my back.

"Well, what were you doing?" she asked.

"I uhh… I was…studying," I said to her, hoping that she was at least in a good mood.

She stood up and walked toward me. "You can't just disappear like that, Phoenix. I need to know where you are. At all times. Do you understand?"

"I know, I'm sorry. It won't happen again, Mom."

Luckily, she seemed to have calmed down quite a bit.

Standing there before me, she exhaled hard. I understood her frustration with me after all that had happened. She had reason to be mad.

"Good to hear you were studying, though. I was afraid you'd been putting off your prepping for tomorrow. We haven't even talked about it at all," she said to me.

"Prepping?"

My mom laughed. "The State Bee, Phoenix. What? Did you think I'd forgotten?"

I nearly passed out. I hadn't studied a single card for the competition. I couldn't believe it. All this time, I'd completely forgotten about my studies, and I had no idea as to any of the words. I'd completely lost track of the State Bee.

"I…I gotta go," I said to my mom and flew into the Bird's Nest as quickly as possible.

I heard my mom call for me again, but I just slammed my door.

In a mad dash, I scrambled to find all the words for tomorrow's competition. I put around 350 of the hardest words I could find onto flashcards.

I had eighteen hours until the opening word was going to be announced. I planned on using every second.

~

My brain was mashed potatoes. The only sleep I'd gotten throughout my rapid studying was during the two-hour drive from Darling to Denver.

Once my mom and I arrived, she woke me up, and we quickly got into the check-in line.

Standing there, though, all of it was starting to feel like it had just been one long dream. The library, the book, Maya's, the blue house, the locker, the letters—it all felt like it couldn't have been real. To be back in the exact same line as last year felt oddly unfamiliar— as if the only thing that had changed was me.

Of no surprise to me, when we arrived at the front of the line, it was the same exact check-in lady as last year.

"Hello, again," my mom said to her.

Behind the counter, the lady took off her glasses as she said to us both, "Hello, Mrs. Iver. Welcome back. I hope that the last year has...been... Oh." She stopped once she looked at her clipboard. "I'm so sorry. I'd forgotten...that you guys are... That's my mistake."

"Thanks," was all I could think to say back.

The lady looked to my left, and before she could ask, I said, "Just my mom and me again."

The woman forced a smile and handed my mom a guest pass. "Good luck, Phoenix."

Walking down the hall, all of the other contestants started staring at me. They weren't even trying to be discrete. Although I'd started to become accustomed to the awkward looks.

Once to my spot at the end of the hall, my mom stopped me. "Listen, don't pay attention to any of them. They don't know how strong you are. You can do this, Noodle. You're ready."

She squeezed me tight. Suddenly, I felt like I had everyone I needed.

"Two rows up from the left side of the front?" I asked.

She smiled and rubbed my cheek with her thumb. "Always."

They called us to start walking onto the stage. I turned and started heading up the stairs to the auditorium when my mom called for me once more, "Phoenix!"

I turned to see her running back toward me. I hopped out of line and ran down the stairs to meet her.

She said simply, "Do it for him."

As I walked up and onto the stage, I moved into my seat carefully and quietly. I was as prepared as I could be, and there was nothing any worrying would do to help. I had to focus now on doing the best I could. That was all I could control.

The fear of being uncomfortable was something I'd have to push beyond. I had to stand tall with my chin up.

The loudspeaker came on, and we were all welcomed to the 2000 Colorado Annual State Spelling Bee. We stood up and were greeted by an even louder and more boisterous audience than last year.

When I heard her scream my name, I turned toward the direction of where my mom said she'd be. I smiled at how much the belief of one person could mean. As strong as a sixteen-year-old with a piece of lined paper.

The first student walked up shortly after, and we began the single-elimination tournament. One misstep and incorrect spelling of a single word, you're out. Sent home if one letter was out of place.

I swallowed hard as I heard the first word. I'd never even heard it before, and it was what they were leading with. It was only going to get harder from here.

The student began nervously. "S...M...A...R...A...D...E... A...N...E. Smaradeane."

The bell rang, followed by the loudspeaker flying in.

"That is incorrect. The correct spelling is S...M...A...R...A... G...D...I...N...E."

She was already out. Her full year of hard work was lost just like that. I felt so bad. If that were my first word, I would have been on my way back home seconds into the competition too.

Moving quickly, contestants fell one after the other. Every other kid who went up to the front had the bell ring. I had never seen that in any other bee before. The bell of defeat just continued to ring.

Finally, they called my name, and I slowly shuffled to the front of the stage and found the microphone. But it came to me that, ultimately, this was just spelling. These were just words, and nothing about this was life or death. Nobody's life was on the line, and there was nothing to get too worked up about. I decided to enjoy the moment for what it was. I was going to have fun.

"Welcome back, Phoenix Iver from Darling. Your first word this year is KNAIDEL."

Wait a second, I knew this one. I'd heard about this word years ago.

My breathing slowed, and I was in control. The idea and concentration came more easily than ever before. I was prepared for this moment in a way I hadn't thought possible given how little time I'd studied.

I closed my eyes and let it all slow down. The letters came.

"K...N...A...I...D...E...L. Knaidel."

I waited for the bell to sound. To signal my imminent defeat, but it didn't. Nothing happened until the speaker came on.

"Correct," the committee member announced. But before I could celebrate, a loud cheer erupted from my mom's section. The claps and yells were much louder than just one person. I turned to look and what I saw blew my mind. It wasn't just one person. It was an entire crowd—my people.

It was my mom, but it was also TT and his dad. It was Pounds and both of his parents. It was Ronnie's mom. It was Mrs. S and Christopher. It was Milan. It was Teresa. It was Gloria and her daughter, Michelle. It was Shay and Marcus. It was everyone, all of them. And they were totally going nuts.

I thought back to the moments when I'd sat with each of them— cried beside them. We'd mourned together and remembered together. My bond with all of them was so strong, but to see them now united was something stronger than love or support. I was blown away.

In that moment of pure elation, the only thing I could think to do was just point at them. All of them. Together, they all laughed and pointed back. It was my family. They made it. They all made it.

From my first letter to my last, I remembered watching the birds with Teresa, and I remembered sitting down to have a cheese omelet across from Milan. I remembered my first cup of coffee with Ronnie's mom, and I remembered gardening with Gloria. The most random assortment of people I could think of.

I'd now come to know each of these people so intimately and

so deeply. I really knew a side of them that was so private that, in turn, they knew me in that similar way. They were my friends, and I couldn't let them down. They needed this as much as I did.

With my new cheering section in full force, I flew through word after word and round after round. It was like the entire world was now behind me.

My confidence was now sky-high, so moving through the competition wasn't difficult. But one other student was able to easily keep up with me—James Jamson. In his same Superman cape as last year, Super Jimmy was back to defend his fourth straight Colorado state title.

As the herd began to thin, eventually it was just him and me for the crown. Again. I only had to beat one more person to win it all.

Super Jimmy was up first. He strutted up the mic.

"GUETAPENS."

Dang it, I knew this one, as well.

"G...U...E...T...A...P...E...N...S. Guetapens."

"Correct."

The audience cheered as he moved back to his seat as though this was just some waste of his time.

I was starting to get more nervous as I moved to the front toward the mic. He was better than me. He knew it, and I knew it. For him, this was just another steppingstone.

My eyes went down, and suddenly I just wanted to be home. I wanted to listen to my dad tell me a story about Greek mythology, tell me his favorite quote, or what he used to be like when he was my age. He always knew how to make everything alright. He could always explain what it all meant.

But then I felt the key around my neck with my fingertips. I looked in the direction of my team. I thought about what each of them had been through, the loved ones they'd lost hold of. Their support system. A pain that I shared, not only with each of them, but they with each other. We'd all fallen overboard—out into the middle of the open ocean—only to now be picked up and brought here. The last place that any of us thought we'd be, but here, nonetheless.

I continued to look at all of them, and them back at me. They were all brave enough to keep living, so I had to be too.

"MENAGE."

I was flushed with confusion. I'd never heard of such a word. But I slowly found comfort in this unknown. The strength to go deeper than talent or focus. Deeper than dreams or aspirations.

"Definition," I asked.

One of the judges looked right at me as she only said one word, "Family."

I closed my eyes as I let my heart do the talking, "M...E...N...A...G...E. Menage."

"Correct."

I clenched my fist and threw it down at my side as I headed back to my seat.

Back and forth, we continued with neither of us slowing down. He was better than I remembered, and I was impressed with each correct word he strung together. He was so fast it seemed like he hardly stopped to think.

Super Jimmy stepped up to the mic and looked back at me with supreme endurance, while I was beginning to feel as though I was fading. My lack of sleep the previous night was catching up with me; my adrenaline was running low.

"ALBUMEN."

He scoffed as he received the word before instantly beginning, "A...L...B...O...O...M...E...N. Albumen."

The judges looked at one another, and then the bell rang. A judge finally said, "Incorrect."

The crowd gasped, and Super Jimmy quickly tried to recant his blunder, profusely stating that he knew his mistake. But they wouldn't have it. The only way he could now stay alive was if I spelled the next word incorrectly, or else I was the new state champion.

On his way back to his seat, Super Jimmy whispered into my ear, "Try not to have another panic attack."

It made me stop right in place. I couldn't move. My nerves got stronger, and I started to feel like it might happen again. The same thing that had always happened, only this time, it wouldn't just be in front of my mom.

I snapped my eyes shut and again tried to slow it all down.

B...R...E...A...T...H...E

I could hear Mrs. S in my ear as I relaxed. I went to spell it one more time.

B...R...E...A...T...H...E

But, as I slowly arrived at the mic, the judges announced a word that made me believe in something so much bigger than just this spelling bee. It convinced me that all of it hadn't just been some dream.

That was when I knew that heaven is a real place. That Maya had told me the truth and that my dad really was a hero. That there were angels, and the greater good was out there, if you took the time to look hard enough. All of this suffering and struggle was all for a brighter tomorrow. That we didn't know when it would come, but if we kept forward, it would. We just had to believe.

"AILERONS," the judges announced.

A word that had defined all that I had worked for—represented everything. I could only smile as I asked for the definition. A definition I knew, but I figured I'd just ask for anyway.

"Wings," the judges said in unison.

I took a deep breath. It was all happening for me. It was all falling right into place.

"A...I...L...E...R...O...N...S. Ailerons."

"Correct."

My section, along with the entire theater, exploded in a cheer. I fell to the floor and started to cry. Instantly, my entire family flooded the stage and lifted me back to my feet, kind of like storming the court.

"Y-You did it, Ph-Phoenix!" TT said while pulling me into his shoulders.

"I'm so proud!" Shay said, joining TT in getting herself wrapped around us both.

"Well done, little hummingbird. Well done, indeed." Teresa smiled.

Then Michelle, standing beside Gloria, handed me a bouquet of sky blue flowers. "From our garden."

In their own personal way and own personal language, all of them said the same thing. All that I heard from all of them was, "I love you." So, that was what I said back to them—my family.

With everyone all around me, the judges joined us on the stage and presented me with the gold medal as the new Colorado State Champion. Then, we snapped a picture.

24

That following Monday, I didn't want to wear my gold medal to school, but my mom insisted on it. I'd also decided on walking to take in the day's uncharacteristically warm temperature.

Each step, with one foot in front of the other, brought a gradual sense of renewal. I'd walked these exact steps many times, but never like this. Today, my feet felt less heavy, my shoulder less tight, and my chin was lifted toward the sky. I was able to move through the world a little lighter.

As I entered Darling High, eyes were stuck to me. I hadn't the slightest clue as to why, but it was alarming. Although I'd dealt with odd gawking most of my life, this somehow felt different.

I quickly made a turn away from the quad, where I thankfully ran into TT.

"Ph-Phoenix! I-I need to show you something!" he blared, much too loud.

I wasn't really in the mood, but before I could even answer, TT grabbed hold of my arm and started pulling me along.

"It-It's right over here."

I initially didn't have much of a problem with his pulling, until I could see that we were headed straight for the library.

"No," I said to him, trying to slow us down. "TT, I'm not

going in there."

"T-Trust me. Y-You're gonna want to see this."

I sighed deeply and allowed him to continue dragging me along.

I hadn't been back inside of the library since. It stood for everything wrong. I wished they would just tear the thing down.

As TT pulled me, the sadness that the library had gone through and how emotional this past year had been exhausted me. How, in one instant, a place that had been home to free thought was now looked at as a pit of darkness. The final place classmates of mine would ever inhabit. The final place *he* would inhabit. A stain that I wasn't sure could ever be washed off.

I caught glimpses of some of the same books, desks, and windows. But when I looked at the books, I thought of body armor. When I looked at the desks, I thought shields. And when I looked at the windows, I thought of an escape. All of it had now shifted from items used for educational enrichment into life-saving beings—a far cry from their once-benign function.

The new librarian turned to look right at me; the whispers got louder. My head started to hurt. It was getting harder to think straight. My ears stung at the piercing sound of chatter all around. Eyes cut into my skin, so I snapped my eyelids shut. I wanted to leave and go back home. Something didn't feel right.

I could hear the cracks through the air again. The screams of children outside, fleeing for their lives, using some of their last breaths to call for help. I could feel the worn book pages wrapped around my skin—Shay's frightened voice in my ear. But, doing my absolute best, I tried. I tried to focus more on putting one foot in front of the other than thinking about that tragedy. A day that, no matter what, would forever follow all of us.

I decided to take each step after that, not because I couldn't remember every detail of that day, but, in fact, because I could. And I promised that, no matter how bad each of those details hurt to think about, I would never forget them.

TT's hand touched my shoulder, and I snapped around toward him.

"L-Look." He pointed at the wall.

It was a massive banner with a photo of me and my entire family that read, "Congratulations to our very own Phoenix Iver on winning the Colorado State Bee!"

As I turned to look, I realized then that I hadn't heard cracks from gunfire, but actual claps from hundreds of classmates—the hands of Darling students coming together.

I turned to look in every direction all around me, which was now booming with love as they cheered. Everybody was clapping and smiling, and it was the coolest thing ever. Coming together not to mourn but to do something that we weren't normally accustomed to doing together in Darling.

Later at lunch, TT was still having more fun with all of it than even I was. We were sitting around all his teammates, who he'd introduced me to. He was right. Surprisingly, they were all actually really cool guys. None of them were mean at all.

TT and his girlfriend, Angie, sat beside me as they shared a barbeque chicken pizza.

"Y-You're like a celebrity now!" TT started, and all I could give him in return was a laugh.

TT then pulled out a copy of the *Colorado Press* and read the headline for the thirtieth time today before shoving it in my face. "Y-You're literally on the front page! L-Look!"

Survivor Phoenix Iver Brings Colorado State Spelling Bee Title Back Home to Darling

Beneath the headline, I noticed that it was the same photo that the library had used.

Downplaying the situation, I said, "So are you!"

He took the paper back and was excited to realize that I was right. "Oh-Oh, I-I am too…w-we're both celebrities!"

I laughed along with Angie as we continued to enjoy our lunch.

"Are we going to see you at the Snowball Friday night?" Angie asked.

The dance hadn't even crossed my mind.

"No, I don't think so," I responded.

"Oh-Oh come on. Y-You would steal the show if you showed up!" TT said, still attempting to contain his jubilation. "J-Just think about it," he continued. "B-But, heya, Phoenix."

"What?"

He had pizza all over his face. "C-Could you sign my paper?"

We both laughed as we continued to joke our way through the remainder of lunch. Each time I let my mind wander, though, I would catch myself looking for her. Shay had just sat down a few tables away from us and appeared to be alone. She looked gorgeous. But as she ate her lunch, it surprised me to see someone so seemingly perfect without the attention of the entire world. I wanted so desperately to be beside her.

My gawking must have been obvious, as TT finally quipped, "G-Go talk to her already."

"Who?" I asked, acting as though I hadn't the slightest clue as to whom he was referring.

He just laughed as he and his girlfriend picked up their pizza and declared, "L-Let's go, w-we'll come with you."

Then, the three of us went over to Shay, who smiled as we approached.

"M-Mind if we join you?" TT asked.

"I would really like that," Shay responded as she made room for us to sit.

I took the seat next to Shay while TT and Angie sat across from us.

"I didn't know I'd be having lunch with a celebrity today," Shay jested.

Before I could appropriately respond, TT jumped in. "S-See! I-I tried to tell him the same thing, b-but he wouldn't listen!"

I shook my head before responding only to Shay. "Thank you for coming to the competition."

"I couldn't miss you win it." Shay smiled back.

How someone could look both striking and sweet was beyond me. Her soft curls bounced in such a way that made my whole body quiver. Her easy laugh quickly disarmed me. Plus, I'd been sitting close enough to notice she smelled really pretty too. It made me want to try to scoot as close as I could.

"S-So, Shay," TT began, "A-Angie, and I need to jet…b-but it was great seeing you!"

I scoffed. TT didn't need to go anywhere. I couldn't believe he was just going to abandon me.

With Shay and me alone, it suddenly got quiet between us. I was getting nervous fast. Suddenly, I had no idea what to say.

She put her hand on mine under the table. "I like this," she said.

Just as quickly as I was beginning to lose my cool, my breathing slowed with her presence. I was more than okay; I was comfortable.

"Me too," I responded.

We sat together and watched the other students race around us. For that moment, it was almost like Shay and I were in our own little biosphere. Everything around us was happening, and we could see it, but for the first time, maybe in my entire life, nothing happening out there could ruin how perfect this moment was.

I looked down, and her feet slowly inched their way toward mine. Our knees gently touched. She slowly but carefully leaned her head and let it fall right onto my shoulder.

"Are you still not going with anyone to the Snowball?" I asked as I sort of choked and sputtered. My heart was suddenly bursting out of my chest.

Shay sat up and looked at me. "Well, I'm not sure. I've sorta been waiting for this one boy to ask me and he hasn't yet."

I dropped a little bit more, my shoulders visibly drooped, and I fixed my glasses with my pointer finger as I responded, "Oh. I'm sorry…I didn't know that."

She got quiet. "It's okay."

"Pounds?" I asked, unsure of where things were with them. But she just put her head down and shook her head. It made me feel even worse.

"It's okay if you don't want to tell me. I understand," I said.

Shay must have been able to sense my anguish. "Don't worry. I'll tell you who it is, but it has to stay between you and me, okay?"

"Okay," I agreed, although I truly didn't care who it was. I just agreed to amuse her.

"We grew up together. He's super sweet, but kinda shy, so I've had to be patient. He's also super smart and…well…I've always been close with him, since we were really young."

"What's his name?" I asked. My interest had certainly been piqued, and I didn't mind at least trying to help her out.

"I don't know…it's silly, really," she began. "He's kind of a big deal now, so I've probably already blown it."

I stood up tall, knowing I needed to help her see how amazing she was. Clearly, her confidence had been lacking, but with all that I'd now learned, I could, at the very least, help her get out of this apparent funk.

"Shay, listen to me. You're the prettiest and coolest girl in the whole school. In the whole…world. You're also so nice and so smart. Any boy would be totally stupid not to ask you to the dance, and I can't imagine a person at this school who doesn't want to go with you."

I hadn't planned on saying all of that, and I was quickly embarrassed. Only when I could, I looked at her. Her cheeks had gone rosy.

But then, she started to say something. "So why won't you just ask me then?"

"What…what are you talking about?" I stumbled back, confused.

"Phoenix," she said.

"Yeah?"

"Phoenix," she repeated. "His name is Phoenix."

I looked back at her. She smiled, so I decided to smile too.

"But…he hasn't asked me yet, so we'll see."

I looked back at her and did my best to not sound like a complete dork. More or less, I was trying to act like one of those superheroes at the end of the movies.

~

"S-Suits! W-We need suits ASAP!" TT yelled at me after I'd told him the good news. I had to agree that we would go right after school, or else he wouldn't stop yelling.

We went back to Metropolis afterward to go over the plan when my mom walked through the door.

"H-Hello, M-Mrs. Iver," TT said as she walked in.

"Good to see you, TT," she responded.

I didn't even greet my mom before deciding to immediately begin my pleading.

"Mom, can I *please* borrow a hundred dollars to rent a suit?"

She looked aghast. "Suit? What on earth do you need a suit for?"

"Th-The Snowball. I-It's this Friday night. I-I'm taking my girlfriend, A-Angie," TT chimed in.

"And who are you going with?" my mom asked me.

I turned away as I was, for some reason, nervous to say her name out loud, like somehow, I still couldn't believe it.

"He-He's taking Shay," TT answered for me.

"Wow, look at you." She started while unpacking groceries. "I'm not surprised. Her father and I had a long talk about you two. I heard you snuck over there the other night."

I blushed as TT elbowed me for good measure. "Please, Mom…" I begged while looking down.

She sighed and then began shuffling around in her purse. TT looked back at me in excitement.

My mom reached out her hand with a small wad of cash in it. "Get her a nice corsage with that, too, Phoenix. Nothing cheap. That should be plenty. And be home before ten, I mean it."

I looked down and quickly counted the money she'd given me. It was two hundred dollars.

"I will! I promise!"

"C-Can we borrow the Ferry too?" TT quickly asked.

I elbowed him.

My mom just smiled. "Phoenix knows where I keep the keys. Be safe, boys, and home by ten, like I said."

"Thanks, Mom!" I yelled back.

TT and I had the keys and were instantly out of the house.

"Sh-She's so cool!" TT said to me as we hopped into the Ferry.

"Yeah," I began. "She isn't all that bad."

We pulled out onto the road and rolled to a stop at a red light. I looked over at TT and noticed the CD in the back seat.

Reaching for *Verities & Balderdash*, I popped it into the CD player just before the light turned green. Harry Chapin's voice singing the first song on the album, "Cat's in the Cradle," shortly followed.

TT started rhythmically bouncing his head to the music. "Wh-Who is this? I-I love this song!"

But I didn't say anything. I could only just smile.

"What kind of suits should we get?" I asked.

TT looked over at me as he said with a sinister smirk, "S-Something tight."

I laughed. "Two-Time Tommy in a tight suit. I like the sound of that."

"Th-Thanks for spelling that out for me, ch-champ."

There was a place just down the street, but we decided to go to the custom suit store on the other side of town. We were going to make a night of it.

25

To be free to just sing and dance, not many can say they've really had the chance to do that. We all have responsibilities, goals, and dreams, but tonight wasn't about any of that. I was just simply a lucky boy taking the perfect girl to the dance. Nothing more.

I was off to pick up Shay at her house so we could drive together. TT let me know that he and Angie would be waiting for us out in front of the gym once we arrived.

As I drove over to Shay's, the early evening sky gently welcomed me into nightfall. Once out front, I reached into the back seat for the flowers and corsage I'd bought and walked up to the front door.

"Phoenix! Well, look at you, kid. You look great!" Marcus said as he warmly welcomed me inside.

"Thank you, Officer Stexton," I said, adjusting my glasses.

Marcus called out toward the stairwell, "Shay, honey! He's here!"

Through her door, I could hear Shay's voice as she yelled back, "Just one more minute!"

"Sorry about that. You know…girls," Marcus jested.

Just then, Shay's mom, Brianna, walked in from the living room. Her deep brown eyes and serious face caught me by surprise. At the sight of her, I initially got extremely tense. She looked different than

I remembered.

"My, you've grown up quite a bit. You're starting to look just like him…" She trailed off at the end, and Marcus took her under his arm. "It's great to see you again," she finished.

I handed her the flowers. "Here. These are for you."

"So thoughtful, Phoenix. Thank you."

Taking the flowers, Shay's mom gently kissed them with the tip of her nose. I could smell them, too, from where I was standing. It was pretty nice.

"Come here, kid. I've got something for you," Marcus said, showing us into the garage.

Standing beside them, I watched Marcus make his way toward an old brown box. Peeling it open with his hands, he pulled out a bag. The bag jingled as he unzipped it.

In his fingers was some sort of a badge. Its glimmer was unmistakable. A glimmer I'd so long imagined seeing again.

"Your dad's." Marcus walked toward me. "It's just his nameplate, but I think he'd want you to have it. I've been hanging onto it for a long time."

I walked toward Marcus and ran my finger over the glistening silver, reading his name, *Officer Herman Iver*.

I stood beside both Shay's mom and Marcus in the silence of their garage, examining every detail. Thinking about all of the nights and all of the days this very nametag had been attached to my dad. How, for so long, he'd sacrificed so much. But, also, how that single night had shaped my entire life.

"I'm sorry…about all that's happened," Shay's mom began suddenly. "I can only imagine how hard all of these years have been."

I was surprised as I looked up at her. I really thought I had been the only one with my mind currently on that night of my birthday, but it appeared as though we all were.

Still standing beside Marcus, Brianna continued. "You should know now, Phoenix...even adults...we make terrible mistakes."

"We should have never put a distance between you and our family. It wasn't right. It wasn't...it wasn't what any of us wanted," Marcus added.

The way they both looked at me let me know how sorry they were, but also how much they were willing to move forward. Something that, no matter what, we all have to do eventually.

I took the nameplate in my hands and ran my fingers over it once more. "I'll always miss him. I think he's the greatest person I've ever met." I looked directly at them and smiled. "Thank you."

We walked back into the living room. Shay stood elegantly at the top of the stairs.

As my eyes walked toward her, I thought I was looking at royalty. A rose pink dress flowed, and sequined earrings danced beside her warm cheeks. It looked as though she was floating as she cascaded down the stairs. Her dress parted at the ankle and, at first I wasn't sure, but then I knew. I saw Shay's vintage pink Converse sneakers again.

"Phoenix, you are looking mighty handsome tonight."

"So are you. I mean, not handsome...I mean...pretty."

She laughed softly as she made it down to me. "This suit fits you well," she said as she fixed the collar on my shirt and adjusted my tie. She smiled. "You look very...classic."

I slipped the corsage around her wrist, and then I handed her my dad's nameplate. She just looked at me and smiled. Instead of the matching flower, she pinned his nameplate to my suit jacket. Her fingers stayed over it for an extra moment.

"A photo! I'll need one, of course. You two little lovebirds are delightful!" Shay's mom said while pulling out her camera.

"Mom!" Shay argued before succumbing to posing for the photo.

Shay slowly backed into me, and I gently wrapped my arms around her—doing my best to act like I wasn't in my own little paradise. As we stopped to take the shot, I caught a glimpse of a photo of my dad and Marcus together in uniform over Brianna's shoulder. They didn't look much older than Shay and I were right now.

I wished he could be here, could have seen all I had tried to do for him. I know that's not how it works, but I wanted him to see that everything was back to the way it used to be. But with her in my arms, I realized Shay had been right. We *could* be made again.

You only get so many chances, really, fewer than you always think. Never let go of those you care about because the opportunity to hold anyone is a blessing.

To hold means to be. To be means you can love. And if you can love, you have everything.

I attempted to focus less on the gravity of it all, though, and focus more on my hands over hers. The smell of her perfume. Her small smile that slowly seemed to be getting bigger.

~

In front of the gym, I saw a tall human in a white suit, white top hat, and peach cream vest. His date was in a matching peach cream dress. As Shay and I got closer, I could see that the figure was TT standing beside Angie.

"Oh no," I started.

"Oh yes," Shay added.

Once Shay and I were close enough to appropriately confirm their fashion ensemble, we couldn't help but shake our heads and laugh.

"I thought you guys went shopping together?" Shay said to both TT and me.

"Y-Yes, we did. Ph-Phoenix wussed out, th-though, and settled on a more conservative approach."

Shay shook her head as she looked at me. "I'll have to go shopping with you both next time, because I would love to see Phoenix in a pink suit."

"Me, too," Angie added.

We all stood around each other and laughed easily. There was something so simple about all of us out in front of the dance as we talked. I was so openly myself that I wanted the moment to continue to roll on forever.

Several other couples walked by as they entered the dance, and we said hello to most of them we knew. Then, Pounds walked up in a dark blue suit and tie beside someone who was dressed exactly the same.

"What's up, Phoenix?" he said as he came up to us.

"Hey, Paul." I gave him a fist bump.

"Congrats again on the spelling bee. That was really cool, man."

"Thank you for being there," I said to Pounds.

A brief moment passed before Pounds said to us, "This is uhhh…Alex."

"N-Nice to meet you, A-Alex. I-I'm TT, and this is my girlfriend, A-Angie. S-Say, I-I love your suits!" TT said, as usual, a little bit too loudly. We all started laughing together.

"Sorry about him," Angie said to them.

"It's alright. Thank you, TT. Nice to meet you guys," Alex said warmly.

"Well, see you guys inside," Pounds said, then he and Alex walked into the gym.

I looked over at Shay, and she dipped her shoulder slightly before leaning into me. She closed her eyes and rocked side to side.

"A-Alright, enough is enough, you two," TT joked, then asked, "Sh-Shall we?"

I looked down at Shay and asked, "Ready?"

"Ready," she said back with a smile.

Shay put her arm through mine, and we followed TT and Angie inside.

The gym was shining everywhere we looked. Sparkling faux snowflakes hung from the ceiling and powdered snow lined the pathway into the main area of the gym. I'd never been to a school dance before, but I was impressed. Everywhere you looked, a different ornate decoration hung from each corner of the building. And a strobe light flashed off and on as I watched TT and Angie in front of me. Like an old movie reel, they cut in and out.

Shay looked up at me, and with nothing holding her back at all, she smiled widely. Shay reached for my face and gently took off my glasses. Slowly, I watched her do the same with her own. She placed them both on a small table beside us.

"Dance with me," she said and before I knew it, we were twirling in the center of the dance floor—as carefree as you could possibly imagine. Spinning about like two ice skaters in the center of a wintry lake. Back and forth, we spun, and I couldn't imagine what we must have looked like, but I wasn't sure how much I cared. For that moment, it really was just us.

As we danced and danced, the night around us did its best to catch up, although it didn't stand much of a chance, really. We were having far too much fun for time to play its evil trick. Since I'd met Shay, time could never keep up with her. Now, it seemed, being in her presence meant I'd been included in her magic. Pausing just for us.

I looked over to see if I could find TT and Angie. I stopped, so did Shay, and her eyes followed mine. I searched, and then I saw them. They were kissing off to the side of the dance floor. Falling from two blobs of white and peach cream, becoming just one. I watched them with acute intrigue, and Shay's attention fell onto them as well.

I stopped watching another moment or two, and I looked at Shay and she at me. Her blue eyes. She slowly tucked a lock of her blond curls behind her ear.

"Well, come on then."

I was here, and she was here. Life, it seemed, was exactly what I was living.

~

The dance wound down all too quickly. TT and Angie left right after it was over, so Shay and I had to say our goodbyes at the gym. It appeared nobody had a better time than they did.

I didn't much want to go home, and I'd hoped Shay didn't either. So, as she and I walked out of the dance, I didn't mention anything of the sort. Instead of going back to the Ferry, Shay and I just kept walking, without any destination in mind. Her candid demeanor was soothing, and with each step we took, another layer of her true character was revealed. Listening to her, I was intrigued by everything Shay chose to say. We'd been walking for some time. The stars lit our path.

"Look at them all." She stopped and looked straight up.

I stopped beside her and did the same.

"I feel like, even though the stars are so bright, they still only take up a small part of the sky," she said.

I kept watching all of them spray their light as best they could. Several of them appeared so bright that it looked like, somehow, they were getting closer with each passing breath.

"No matter how bright they are, they can't possibly burn long enough to outlast the night," Shay finished.

She turned to look at me, although I was still so focused on the stars.

"It's the light vs. the dark," I finally said to her.

We continued walking along without much of a care in the world. Nothing else was on my mind but being right here.

Eventually, our feet ended up taking us all the way to Logan Park. It was so late that the park was entirely empty. The grass still.

"Let's walk around here," I said while taking hold of her hand.

The pond was mirror calm as it reflected the night's sky—each of the stars like lily pads at our feet.

She looked so beautiful in her dress. But as I felt her beside me, she didn't feel any different from that same little girl I'd grown up down the street from. I felt like that was still her. And as different as I felt from the little boy I once was, in probably more ways than I knew, I was the same in her eyes too—both out exploring again.

Maybe it was the park, or maybe it was the night, the stars, or even Shay, but my mind fell upon us as those kids again. A memory of sometime after my tenth birthday. Thinking of the day when it seemed like things might—after all that I'd seen—be alright.

~

Sitting beside my dad in the Ferry, I'd let my eyes drift out the window. They caught the trees, birds, and all sorts of different things. There weren't any clouds in the sky, though. The day was magnificently sunny.

"Aren't you going to ask where we're going?" my dad asked.

The question snapped me out of my trance, but I didn't care.

The days now were always so gray. Everything was weird and complicated all of the time. My mom never left the house, and my dad was never *in* the house. I just wished things could be the way they used to.

I kept my eyes trained out the window as my dad continued to drive. Staring into a cloudless sky, wondering if anything could be beyond or if everything was as it seemed. There were those birds, though, that were flying. Freely, they coasted through the sky. A group of them felt like they were following us.

My dad let out a long sigh beside me. Looking at him for the first time, I saw the droop in his shoulders. How his shirts he wore nowadays weren't as clean as they used to be. How the spark in his eyes wasn't what it used to be.

Just as he noticed me looking at him, he pulled the car to a stop and unbuckled his seatbelt.

"We're here."

I felt the warm breeze on my shins as I turned out of the car door.

We were at a park I'd never seen before, which meant we were a long way out of town. I'd only been this far away from home once, for a hockey tournament.

"What are we doing, Dad?" I asked with young fear.

But he bent down to my level and slid my light jacket off my shoulders.

"Don't you ever give up on those that you love. No matter what they do. Don't ever give up on them."

I could tell my dad was really serious, so I just looked at him and nodded. He smiled and kissed me on the top of my head.

"Phoenix!" someone yelled from off in the distance.

Turning then, I saw that, just before a long green slide and monkey bars was Shay. Bouncing toward me with her curly, bleached-blond-colored hair.

I took off and started running toward her. I was running as fast as I could.

She started to laugh as we got closer. I was close enough to see every part of her full smile.

"Phoenix!" she yelled a second time in between peals of laughter.

We ran right into each other and started hugging. We were both completely out of breath.

I never wanted to let go. Under the sun, we hung onto each other.

Shay finally looked at me and laughed. "Come on, they have a slide!"

She pulled me with her hand as we bolted toward the jungle gym. We kicked up all the woodchips beneath our toes. Up and down, for hours and hours, we went as fast as we could. I followed her every move as we played all afternoon, not stopping once.

As the sun began to go down, though, I was just getting off the slide when I saw Shay had stopped to wait for me. I hopped off and ran toward her.

"What's wrong?" I asked, afraid that something had happened.

Shay looked at me and slowly said, "My dad says I gotta go now."

Both our moods dropped. My head fell, too, as we stood before one another.

I was suddenly afraid again. What had at once been a glimpse into how good life *could* be, seemed over. A short moment in time that had already flared out. My shooting star, gone.

Shay went for one more hug as she pulled me in tight. I was all sweaty and gross, but I could tell she didn't care.

I had no idea what to say as she kept holding on. I was afraid— even more than before—to let her go.

"Will we see each other?" I said as I felt her chin starting to leave the crook of my shoulder.

Then, just before Shay ran back toward where Marcus was waiting in his car, she looked at me and smiled. It was her smile. It was Shay, the person who would forever be my person.

"We can do whatever we want."

~

"You still in there?" Shay poked at me, snapping me out of my daze.

"Yeah." I smiled. "I'm here."

We eventually settled at my dad's and my favorite overlook. It was the best place in all of Darling to look at the night.

"Now this," I said, "this is *my* favorite thinking spot."

Shay smiled as she slid to be beside me against the railing. "I still think about that story you told me here. The one about the elephant and the giraffe."

With Shay's elbow right beside me, my finger found and brushed over the scar on her arm.

She lifted her elbow to allow the rest of the scar to become visible.

"Every time I look at this, I think about how special you always made me feel…even then," Shay said.

I tried to contain my internal bubbling as Shay sunk deeper into my shoulder. It seemed, no matter how much time it had been, nothing had changed.

"I think I always knew I'd go to a dance with you someday after that," she finished.

We both softly laughed.

"I read the first two chapters of your book," I said with feigned trepidation.

Pausing for a while, Shay started to squirm more and more.

"*And*…!" Shay yelled, which made me burst out laughing.

I explained, "One day, I think people all over the world are going to read your book and know what really happened that day. But instead of them reading about it and being sad, they are going to be full of inspiration. They are going to want to change the world."

"You really liked it?! You did?" Shay could hardly control herself.

"I did." I smiled. "Shay, it was incredible. I can't wait to read the whole thing."

She hugged me as tight as she ever had.

"So, you have to finish the thing already," I quipped.

"I know, I know," she admitted. "I'm working on it day and night."

We went back to the stars as we continued to sit beside one another. The sky was wide open.

"It was hard to read it at first, because it reminded me so much of my dad. This was…was his favorite spot too. We used to come here all the time," I admitted.

Shay asked softly, "Are you thinking about him right now?"

"I think about him every day," I admitted, almost sounding embarrassed.

Even more slowly, Shay began, "After you fell out of that window…I…thought that was it. I thought I was gone. So, when I heard the first shot, I closed my eyes. I don't know…I don't know why, but I thought about where I would go once I was gone…what would I be? What would happen? But…but then I opened my eyes, and I was fine. I was alright. And when I turned to look toward the door of the library, Phoenix…I saw him. I saw him, and I promise you he wasn't in any pain. He looked at me and he smiled. I ran right to his side, and I told him that you were safe. I repeated it over and over and over and over. He…he saved my life. That terrible day was all one big disaster, but your dad was…he *is* a hero. The way he swooped in…his final breath…I was right beside him. I made sure of it."

Shay stopped and then added in a different tone, "So, when you think about him, make sure you remember that, too. Remember that he is a hero."

I couldn't help but think about Gloria, Aloanso, and my dad. I couldn't help but think about the night Aloanso was killed. I couldn't help but think about all those years and all those nights my dad had gone to visit Gloria in her garden. How, Gloria was probably mourning in that same garden right now. I couldn't help but think about my dad in that library on that very awful day. I thought about how death really is much harder on those we leave behind and how much I still missed him. I thought about how much of our time I'd taken for granted and how I would do anything to go on one more walk with him. How here, this park, had now become *my* medicine.

"I'm glad you said *is*," I finally responded.

She put her hand on my cheek. "Because your dad will always be an *is*. For the rest of our lives."

Shay leaned against me, and I held her. She shivered slightly, so I took off my suit jacket and wrapped it around her.

The cool night had fully settled. Now it was just us and the stars.

"Thank you for being my infinity plus one," she said.

I smiled easily. "Thank you for being my friend." Looking back up at the stars, I added, "They might not burn bright enough to outlast the night, but they are able to burn. They are able to burn so bright that, even from here, all of these miles away, and despite all of that dark between us, we can still see them."

Shay looked up at me, and we both continued to take it all in. It felt like there were millions of them all over—each of their possibilities and each of their lives. Over time, we were able to discover more and more. As if every few minutes a new one was born.

"Is that a shooting star?" Shay pointed.

I quickly looked in her direction. It was a bright light just ahead of us atop a hill that was dancing up and down. It certainly wasn't a shooting star, but I had no idea what it was.

"Let's go check it out," she said.

Arriving at the top of the hill, we stopped to catch our breath following the trek. We'd gotten closer to the light, but we still couldn't tell what it was. It was too dark to see much of anything. But after taking a few more steps closer, we were able to see that it wasn't a star at all. It was the old trashman's headlamp.

"Oh." Shay stopped once she was done huffing and puffing, but I kept walking toward him.

"Phoenix, we shouldn't be a bother. Leave him be."

I was now only a few feet away from him.

"Hey, King," I said into the dark.

He looked toward me—his voice raspy. "Phoenix. Nice to see you again."

I looked deeply at him. "It's too late for you to be out working so hard like this."

It was dark still, so I couldn't really tell, but it felt like he was smiling as he said, "Too much work to do. You should know that by now."

I couldn't help but look down for a moment. Thinking about all of them.

"Thank you...for talking to Maya. For helping me get my second chance."

But instead of answering, King put his bag down and asked, "Did everything come together for you?"

I turned to look back at Shay before answering. "More than I thought anything ever could."

"Good. That's good, son."

Just before me now, King reached into his garbage bag. "One final thing."

I looked back at Shay. The stars were painted just over her. She had her arms crossed, my jacket still wrapped around her shoulders. She shook her head. But despite the darkness, I could see a glimmer of her as that kid again.

King handed me an envelope. I didn't look down at it right away. I just continued looking at him. A moment passed without us breaking our knowing stare.

Down in my hands, I saw it was just a plain manila envelope—a plain manila envelope with the number one hundred on it. Carefully, I peeled it open.

But I knew. I knew right away. My name at the top was written in his handwriting. A handwriting that was the voice I'd always known.

Dear Reader,

You're not alone. I know it may feel like that at times, but one of my driving reasons for writing this very book, in your hands now, was to serve as a letter to you, illustrating this message. I wanted you to know that I am right here, with you. And now that you have completed my book and are reading this letter, I now humbly ask you to write your own.

Write to a parent. Write to a friend. Write to a coach. Write to a teacher. In a world inundated with texts, emails, and push notifications that are fleeting, a carefully crafted letter has the unique staying power nothing else does. Our words live on long after we do.

Your letter can be about anything, and it can be any length. The only thing I ask is for your letter to start with that simple—yet powerful—reminder that "You're not alone." None of us are.

My goal with this letter-writing campaign is that that every person who participates will empower someone else to write to their someone. Who then can write to their someone, and write to their someone, and write to their someone, and write to their someone. And it all starts with you.

To watch the magic of your words, among the many others, unfold, visit: www.darlingyourenotalone.com

My love always, JD Slajchert

According to the Center for Homeland Defense and Security at NPS, a school shooting incident is classified as each and every instance a gun is brandished, is fired, or a bullet hits school property for any reason, regardless of the number of victims, time of day, or day of the week. Since September 28, 1999, in the United States, in schools K–12, there have been a total of 1,308 school shooting incidents with a total of 360 fatalities. During that same period of time in the United Kingdom, there have been a total of 0 school shooting incidents with a total of 0 fatalities. According to CNN, the United States has had 57 times as many school shooting incidents as all of the other major industrialized nations combined. In 2018, the US averaged one school shooting incident a week. There were more school shooting incidents in the US in 2019 alone than in 1970, 1971, 1972, 1973, 1974, and 1975 combined. Because of the Coronavirus Pandemic, March of 2020 in the US was the first March without a school shooting incident since 2002.

May all 360 of these children never be forgotten.

AUTHOR INFORMATION

To contact me, visit my schedule for upcoming interviews or personal appearances, please visit my website and subscribe to my blog.

jdwritesbooks.com

You can also find me on:

Twitter: JD_Slajchert
Instagram: JD_Slajchert
Facebook: JD_Slajchert

Please do not hesitate to reach out or just say hello on social media. I would love to get to know all of my readers and personally hear from each of you.

Cheers.

ACKNOWLEDGMENTS

My goodness, everyone, this has been quite the odyssey. As I sit back at my desk to write this very note, I can only laugh, cry, smile, and cry again as I think about all of the impactful moments and wonderful individuals that led to this book's creation. There have been so many events and specific people that influenced this project. Each of these dreamers went above and beyond whatever was asked of them in order to bring this book to you today. The sacrifices—across the board—were significant. I've been blessed with the most spectacular team on the planet. Now, allow me to brag all about them.

Gun violence, unfortunately, has been a part of not just my writing but my real-life story. On the evening of May 23, 2014, the school year prior to my arrival as an undergraduate at UC Santa Barbara, six individuals were shot and killed by a disgruntled gunman who then took his own life. On November 7, 2018, a mass shooting occurred in Thousand Oaks, California, the town I was raised in, claiming the lives of thirteen souls just outside of the Borderline Bar and Grill. I myself didn't personally know anyone who was lost in either of these incidents, but I witnessed the lives of countless close friends of mine forever change because they did. Then, gun violence impacted my life in a very real way. I was close enough to one incident, in particular, that forever changed my life too.

On October 1, 2017, I was out to dinner in Santa Barbara, California, with one of my dearest friends, Karlie Mack, and her younger brother, Eric Mack, who I was meeting for the first time that night. Karlie invited me to join them for burgers—a proposition I, of course, couldn't in my right mind refuse. That night, as Karlie drove, I sat in the back seat while Eric joined her sister up front, when "Tiny Dancer" by Elton John came bursting through the speakers. Me, being a complete philistine, had never heard of such noise before. As you'd expect, if you knew what kind of lively soul Karlie is, she freaked out, and she and Eric turned up the song and, in a full duet, sang every word. In the back seat, I happily absorbed their entire performance. It was the most amazing thing. After sufficiently stuffing my face with In-N-Out, they dropped me off back at my place.

About an hour later, I got a phone call from Karlie, sobbing. A friend had informed her that both her parents had just been shot at the Route 91 Harvest Country Music Festival in Las Vegas, Nevada. As quickly as I could, I made my way back to Karlie and Eric. We stayed up all night together, waiting for news. We hardly let go of each other. But, thankfully, we learned that night that Karlie and Eric's mother, Lara, had been hit by a ricochet, and was not badly wounded, and that her husband, Karlie and Eric's father, Brian, had successful emergency surgery to remove the bullet that directly hit his abdomen. They would both go on to make full recoveries.

Ever since that night in 2017, I'd told myself I would write a story in honor of the victims lost and countless affected by senseless gun violence. After it so massively altered my view of the world, I knew I had to.

To Karlie, Eric, Lara, and Brian, thank you for always looking out for me during my time in college. Thank you for opening up and offering me your home. I've never forgotten your generosity, and I never will. One minute you are eating cheeseburgers and singing Elton John, the next, you are holding your friend, reassuring her that she is going to see her parents again. That night will never leave me, and it is the night that inspired me to write this very book.

Once pencil went to paper on this project, it was my little brothers, Wes and Clark, who kept me levelheaded and relaxed. As writer's block would strike, these two would pull me out of my hole to go and do some crazy hill sprints or pushups to failure. We would sprint the Malibu dunes, race each other in the pool, and even get some quick pickup basketball games in. Both of these dudes were more important to my process than they could ever fully understand. They helped me both stay focused and clear my head. They were with me every step of the way and always will be. Thank you for your ears at the many Blu Jams, lads. I love you both, along with my other brothers, Taylor Hange, Luca Simplicio, and Oliver Simplicio, endlessly.

As the book then began to take *some* shape, it was my trusted writing professor, Mashey Bernstein, who took the first collection of pages into his aficionado hands. Captain M, thank you for taking draft after draft after draft over the years with such care. Your notes and ideas always leave me so inspired to write. In more ways than not, I'm always writing to try and make you proud. We've come a long way, and I look forward to much more ahead. O, Captain, My Captain! I'll follow you anywhere.

No project of significant length is accomplished without the care and consideration that goes into the many late-night coffees, story shares, and snacks at Mel's Diner, and for that company, I have no one else to thank other than my "underground manager," the great Neil Koenigsberg. Now, Neil is someone who I was fortunate enough to meet as I moved along with this project, but it was our chance introduction that has blossomed into an incredible bond. He's an amazing reader, person, teammate, and friend. Neil, thank you for always looking out for me and for taking not just my stories to great heights, but my career as a whole. I'm humbled by your representation and honored to stand beside you. See you after your haircut this week.

To research for this project, I visited several locations where mass shootings have occurred. I felt the bullet holes that have since been painted over from the UC Santa Barbara shooting in Isla Vista, California. Just down the street from where I now live, I spent time around the now-former Borderline Bar and Grill. I read the notes and cards from loved ones placed beneath each of the thirteen hearts. No matter how hard it was to read them all, I always made it a point to do so each visit.

I also traveled back and forth to Denver, Colorado, on several occasions. On one of these trips, I also did, in fact, visit Littleton, Colorado, and more specifically, Columbine High School and the Columbine Memorial. It was one of the most grounding and moving experiences of my entire life. To see the place, feel the building, feel the library, and feel the memorial with my own bare hands is something that spoke to me in such a powerful way. With my two feet there, I felt the strength in the town. A very special thank you to all of the lovely staff, security, Uber drivers, and brave police officers, who were more than happy to answer all my questions. You are heroes, and it was an honor to meet you all. I hope this story means something special to each and every one of you directly and indirectly affected. Also, another thanks to the especially tall waiter at The Lake House Kitchen & Tavern just across the street from Columbine High

School. Despite the emotion in my visits, you always passed along a subtle strength that helped keep me going, probably more than you even realized. Thank you all for your kindness.

The artists of all artists, Nuno Moreira, you've done it again, my friend. I've never worked with a more consummate professional in my career. You are such a talent, and the cover is spectacular. It was incredible to sit beside you before a glass of wine and plate of cheese while rapping about cover concepts for this book in Lisbon, Portugal. I'll never forget you showing me around your part of the world—a real slice of heaven! Thank you for taking such precision and excellence into account when creating a home for my words. You are a true gem. And enjoy those extra bottles of Ginja. Perhaps save me one for next time if you can.

Now, on to my first editor, Alison Rolf. Alison, from the moment we met, I knew you were the woman for this job. Your sharp eye and knack for detail were apparent day one. But out of all the tools you so clearly proved you had in your toolbelt, it was your heart that I knew would be your biggest asset. You cared for this story as much as I did. You related to it in ways that even I couldn't. Your heart ached for all of these characters in a way that makes me smile, even now after our work together is complete and out in the world. And, as the superwoman you are, you edited this entire novel while bearing your first child! You really are amazing. I hope you are holding your lovely Atticus now, and I look forward to the day he will read this story we created together. I can already tell you how proud he is of his amazing mom. I cannot wait to meet him and Casey. Thank you for all of the tears. Now that you may finally enjoy a cocktail, champagne on me!

To the next woman who was directly responsible for taking this story across the finish line, my second editor, Christine Nielson, thank you. It is rare that you get to work with someone who you not only respect as a professional, but also quite enjoy as a friend. Thank you for coming in, adding a dash of magic, and helping me take this story home. No matter my crazy schedule while abroad, you always found time for me, and I'll forever be grateful for that. I'll always enjoy our phone calls on the go. It was spectacular to work with you again. Much obliged for helping this sunny, California writer.

To my final set of eyes on this project, the thorough and detailed Shannon Cave, thank you. I cannot possibly emphasize enough how much your critiques and suggestions helped guide me in my final days with this book. I enjoyed every moment of reading and executing your insightful notes. You helped me say goodbye to the project that had been my life for so long. You're amazing!

This special thank you goes to my dear friend Andrew Pickles. Several years ago, my friend and former college basketball teammate, Andrew, tracked down all of my closest friends and, for my birthday, had them all write me a handwritten note in a blank book. This massive birthday card nearly grew into a novel of its own with all different colors and font sizes. Andrew spent months collecting notes from people of all different parts of my life. What he gave me for my birthday that year was the single greatest gift I'd ever been given to date. But what he didn't realize at the time was that it would become my inspiration for the concept of mail from heaven. In many ways, Phoenix and Andrew have the same exact heart. When creating Phoenix's character, I imagined Andrew running around town collecting signatures from some people whom he'd never even met and thought to myself how amazing that must have been for him too. One letter at a time. I am so grateful for you, my brother, the book you gave me hasn't left my sight since. In fact, it's right beside me at this very moment.

Also, a special thank you to my business partner and co-manager, Matt Steinman. I've yet to find someone who can match your level of care and work ethic, and I'm so lucky to have you. Thank you for getting involved with this story from the beginning as one of the earliest readers and making all those phone calls on my behalf. You're the hardest working person I know.

To my Summer House Publishing family and, more specifically, Spencer Daniels, Ben Manhan, Clifton Powell, and Alex Varonos, and all the future writers to come, thank you for joining us on this ride. It means a great deal to me to be a part of this collection of Summer House scribblers. I look forward to even more great stories for us ahead. Keep writing, gentleman. Let's make impactful stories that change the world.

A massive thank you to my publicists, Anthony Turk and Steve Rohr. Thank you for believing in my work. The reason this very book is most likely in your hands right now is because of their undying passion for this project's success. When I first spoke to Anthony about potentially working together, I knew he was the man for the job when he completed almost half of the book that same day. Anthony, you saw the heart of this story instantly. And Steve, it was your sense of humor that roped me in. You make me laugh, man! Anthony and Steve, you each brought such originality and fresh life to this project, you believed in me more than anyone else I've ever worked with has, and you pushed me to get this deserving story out into the world. You're both an author's dream. Team *Darling, You're Not Alone* forever.

Also, another special thank you to not just Anthony and Steve, but everyone who worked on the publicity for *Darling* at both Turk

Entertainment Public Relations & Productions and Lexicon Public Relations. I owe everything to you all.

A special thank you to my early readers Allie Broome, Alex Gruszynski, David Mandell, Sean McHugh, Laura Slajchert, and Franco Simplicio. All your notes, ideas and thoughts were taken much more seriously than you could ever fully grasp.

To everyone at Body Logic Sports Therapy, and more specifically, Katie Baker, Taylor Kahanowich, and Calle Johnson, I adore each of you tremendously. Thank you for having my back.

To the true inspiration behind my favorite character in this novel, Herman Iver, my dad, thank you. Much like Herman, you've always been the light that shines in the darkness for me. I can remember many times when I was just a scared, lost, little guy, but it was always your soothing demeanor that calmed me down. From our car rides to even your mantras today, thank you so much for your stoic support. I couldn't have written this book without you, and I promise to always keep my store open. Even though you're obsessed with tuna sandwiches, I still love you.

Mom, I love you a ton. I cannot believe this book is finally in your hands, and I'm sorry it took me so long to finish it. I wanted to make sure it was perfect for you. I have you to thank for all the love and support that fueled me to finish this story. I can see you smiling now as you make it to this note, but, I guess, I just wanted to say that everything I write is always for you. Thank you for looking out for me. And to have this book released the year of your sixtieth was a dream come true. I hope it was the birthday present you'd hoped it could be.

Last, and certainly not least, my manager, Chris Varonos. He, more than anyone, understands how much this book was as much of his life as it was mine, so the following I wanted to write primarily for all of you.

Chris is the epitome of grit. He spends hours and hours on things from marketing strategies, complete rewrites of chapters, editing of speeches, or even more simply, wrangling my strange story concepts. If I'm involved in something, best believe Chris is right by my side. I look to him for counsel in the stressful moments of both career and friendship. I'd trust this man with anything, which should explain why it was him who even came up with the title of this very book. In one of the many Saturday morning meetings Chris and I had over the past several years, we argued back and forth on potential titles, when he struck lightning. It was a relief for us both. Chris never misses a call and never misses an opportunity to work. He bled for this story and these characters. His dedication and passion make me feel like the luckiest writer in the long history of writers. He deserves as much credit for this story as anybody. Chris, thank you for taking my scraps and always turning them into magic. With you by my side, I'm always prepared to take on the world.

To all of you mentioned by name, and also those of you not, thank you. I am here today, writing this very note because of all of you. Because, for some reason, all of you decided to stick around and share your worlds with me. I will be forever grateful for each and every one of the sacrifices you've all made. So again, from the bottom of my heart, thank you.

Now, I'm off to grab a cup of coffee and another slice of gluten-free cheese pizza to get started on the next one. Hopefully, I'll be seeing all of you again very soon.

Keep carrying the light.

JD

JD Slajchert is an American novelist, short story writer, and screenwriter who was born and raised in Southern California. He wrote his debut novel, *MoonFlower*, during his final two years as a student-athlete at the University of California, Santa Barbara. When tragedy struck and he lost his biggest fan, Luc Bodden, to sickle cell disease, he knew he needed to preserve Luc's spirit and honor his memory by writing his first book. Following his many trips to Mammoth Lakes, California, he became moved to write his first short story, "Joining the Choir Invisible." He credits much of his inspiration to many of the authors from the lauded Lost Generation and has aspirations of one day living in Paris. He is currently working on his third novel.

sh